For everyone who loves the misunderstood, morally gray character.
He's a psychotic murderer, but hey, he's hot.

PREFACE

This series is dark. It's **VERY** dark.

No one is a good guy.

Some characters may be **irredeemable**.

Please only read if you are comfortable with the following triggers. The books in the series will get progressively darker.

Trigger Warnings:

abuse, attempted rape, blood (gore), blood play, death, derogatory terms, death, drugs, guns, graphic violence, graphic sexual situations, depictions of torture, gaslighting, grooming, homophobia, incestuous situations, infertility, kidnapping, knife play, murder, mental illness, non-con/dubcon, substance abuse, mentions of suicide.

Chapter One

Noelle

"I'm sorry about the inconvenience, officer," my brother tries to reason with the men who'd arrested me, probably bribing them in exchange for letting me go.

I turn my gaze to the floor, digging the heel of my shoe into the dirty road and watching how a few ants surge out of the earth and scramble around my foot. I hum a quiet melody as I keep my eyes on them, ignoring my brother and the soon departing police cars.

"You really went and did it this time, Noelle," he says, exasperated, as he reaches my side. "For God's sake, you could have killed yourself. You don't even know how to drive!"

I raise my head to look at him, blinking. Once. Twice.

Then I resume my ant watching.

"Noelle!" He snaps, grabbing my hand and urging me to pay attention to him. "Goddamn it, this is not what I signed up for," he mumbles under his breath.

My fists clench by my side, my lips curling in annoyance.

Of course it's not what he signed up for. It never is.

"What do you want?" I finally ask, narrowing my eyes at him. My throat is sore as I say the words, my voice that harsh sound that I'll never get used to.

And it's all his fault.

"You promised mother you'd behave."

I shrug.

"Noelle, I can't help you if you don't help yourself."

"Who asked you?" I ask, my words bitter. "Go back to your wife and leave me alone. It's the least you can do." I grit my teeth, stopping myself from hurling all the insults crossing my mind.

"That's exactly the issue. I can't leave you alone," he sighs, leaning back and placing his hands in his pockets. "Mother can't deal with you anymore, and you can't be left to your own devices. Clearly," he mutters drily as his gaze moves past me to the car currently stuck in a ditch.

"I'm twenty-two. I'm an adult." My eyes flash at him in protest.

"You might be an adult, but your medical file says you need supervision."

It takes everything in me not to start screaming at him at the mention of the medical file. Of course he'd hold that over my head, as if he weren't the main culprit behind my condition.

"Whatever," I keep my tone in check. "Take me home."

I turn on my heel, going to the car he'd parked on the other side of the road.

"Noelle," he calls out, but I don't listen. I just continue walking, sliding into the passenger seat and waiting for him to take me home.

After all, there's nothing to be said between the two of us. Not that there ever was.

"Damn it," he curses as he settles into the driver's seat, buckling his seatbelt and resting his hands on top of the wheel.

"Some things need to change, Noelle. I can't gallivant around the city to get you out of every trouble you get yourself into."

"No one asked you," I simply reply, my gaze distant.

"So that's it. You want to go to jail?"

"At least in jail I'll be my own person," I shrug.

"Fucking hell," he groans. "You know you're not well. You know that, and you still pull stunts like this?" He shakes his head at me, his features filled with disappointment.

Once upon a time, I might have cared.

Not now.

Not after everything that's happened.

I shrug.

"And whose fault is that?" I throw the jibe at him, reveling on the inside at the way he blanches, his lips pursed, his entire countenance changed.

I know he feels guilty. And that's even worse. Because he'd known what he was doing to me, but he'd done it anyway. For his fucking selfish reasons.

Since I'd returned, he'd never even asked me what happened to me, because if he knew—if he really knew—then he wouldn't be able to still look me in the eye, or demand anything of me.

But that's just the thing. No one asked me. Everyone circles around the issue, knowing that something's wrong, but *not* wanting to know exactly what.

He doesn't reply as he clenches his hands over the wheel, steering the car on the road and doing his best not to explode on me. His body language tells me he's barely holding himself together and an instinctual sliver of fear goes through me at the thought he might snap—truly snap.

"I talked to our mother," he says as we enter the city. "We've decided that it's no longer a viable option for you to stay with her."

"What?" I whip my head around, surprised at his words.

"You can't blame her, can you? She's nearing her sixties, Noelle, and since you've come back you've given her heart attack after heart attack. She can't go on like this, wondering if the next time you act out you're going to turn up into a body bag—or worse, not at all."

"What's that supposed to mean?" I frown.

"You're coming to live with us in the city. You'll go to your therapy appointments and you will learn how to act like a fucking human being again."

"Why, so you can sell me again?" I ask drily.

He doesn't answer my taunt, although I note the way his body is teeming with unreleased tension.

"Why can't you just let me live? Why can't I have my own life?"

"Because you can't. Not only are you not mentally fit for that, but you know that someone of your standing can *never* have a normal life." He gives a dry laugh. "This might be the twenty-first century, and you might have more freedoms than a lot of women before you, but you're still a DeVille, Noelle. And *that* comes with dangers."

My lips stretch into a thin line as I turn to look at his profile. I know that he's right, and that hurts even more. Because every little thing I do to rebel—to feel I'm still my own person—does nothing more than prove to me that I wouldn't be able to survive even one second in the real world on my own.

"Then what am I supposed to do for the rest of my life? Wither away in loneliness?"

"Who said anything about loneliness? You'll have your family. And I can even arrange for you to meet with eligible bachelors..."

"Oh," I laugh ironically. "You do plan to sell me again."

"I didn't sell you," he answers through gritted teeth. "And I'm not going to sell you."

"Sure," I snort. "You just exchanged me."

"Noelle, this is for your own good. I'm sure you'll want a family of your own at some point, and I'm willing to work with you to achieve that."

"After I'm not crazy anymore, right? Because that's all I am now. Crazy, deranged. A lunatic."

"Don't call yourself that," he chides. "It's normal to be affected in a certain way after what you went through. And you'll move past it."

"By locking me up," I mutter.

"Noelle," he takes a deep breath. "You totaled the car. You were lucky you didn't get hurt. What about next time? Aren't you tired of these tantrums?"

"Tantrums?" I lean back, scandalized.

"I know you're doing this for attention, and maybe I should have intervened before. But I'm doing it now."

I scoff at him, anger simmering inside of me and threatening to rise to the surface the more he talks.

Attention?

He thinks I'm doing this for attention?

"You know nothing," I hiss at him. "You're just a sick control freak, trying to keep everyone around you on a tight leash."

"Maybe," he chuckles. "I might be a control freak. But you're moving in with me and Yuyu. That's already been decided. I've sent Alfredo to pick up your luggage from mother's house."

And so I realize that no matter what I say to him, he won't change his mind.

Everyone thinks I need constant supervision, but they don't realize that they are only stifling me, making me feel even more trapped. And after everything that happened...

We ride in silence until we reach his house. Stepping inside the brownstone, I'm suddenly struck by my childhood memories—admittedly the only certain and relatively pleasant memories in my life.

I look around the hallway, the pristine staircase in the middle, surrounded by a combination of black and white furniture and walls.

My brother had had everything redone after our father had died, and he'd transformed the entire place to suit his personality—clinical and detached. Laughter bubbles inside of me at that thought. Since when has he ever been anything but?

Everything is familiar yet foreign, just like the people residing here.

"Cisco?" A feminine voice asks before her figure emerges down the stairs.

She's small and dainty, wearing a sheer nightgown covered by a satin robe. Her hand rests atop her belly as she's cradling her bump.

"Yuyu," he calls out her name, his voice suddenly shifting to a gentler tone, his eyes softening as he looks at his wife.

Of course.

After all, isn't *she* the reason he'd given me up?

"And Noelle," her eyes widen when she sees me. "What a surprise to see you here."

"Yeah, she had a narrow encounter with the police today," my brother mentions, going to Yuyu's side to help her.

His hand immediately settles on the small of her back in an affectionate gesture that I've never seen directed towards anyone else—not even me, his own blood.

I school my features, not wanting to give away just how out of place I feel here.

"Really? Are you ok?" She turns her gaze towards me, her features drawn up in worry.

It would be so easy to hate her. But I can't. Not when I know that she's not a bad person *at all*. She'd been a victim of circumstances just like me.

My brother on the other hand... He's the one who orchestrated everything. He knew what he was doing and he just did not care.

"Where's my room?" I ask flippantly, not wanting to stay around for small talk. Yuyu might be a nice person, but I'm not about to sit here and pretend everything is ok when it's not.

"Do you want some hot chocolate? I was just about to make myself some and..."

"No, thank you." I answer curtly, earning myself a scowl from Cisco. "The room. I want to sleep," I tap my foot restlessly. At the moment, the only thing I want is to be alone, without any pitying glances or condescending voices.

Without having anyone tell me what I have to do.

"Greta," my brother yells for his housekeeper, his eyes watching me intently. "Please show my sister to her room," he instructs her when she appears from the back of the house. "The usual room," he nods at her.

As Greta leads me up the stairs, I can't help but glance back at Cisco and Yuyu, witnessing a rare tender moment for my brother as he leans in to brush his lips against her forehead, murmuring something against her skin. He places his hand on her bump, rubbing it and smiling at something Yuyu says.

That sight of happiness on my brother's face is foreign to me. Growing up, I'd barely seen him so much as crack a smile. He'd certainly never bothered with me, mostly keeping aloof and to his own business.

Later, when he'd taken the leadership mantle, our relationship had just become more and more strained, until he'd done the unforgivable—he'd sold his own family for a stranger.

I'd never thought him capable of doing anything to go against the interests of the family, but for Yuyu... He'd done the impossible. Sometimes I wish I could hate her as much as I hate him. After all, if it hadn't been for her, I wouldn't have suffered so much.

There's a light pressure in my chest as Greta unlocks the door to my room, inviting me inside and quickly getting me clean linens and towels.

When she finally leaves, I find myself enclosed between four walls, the darkness of the night providing a modicum of comfort.

Stripping my clothes, I take a tentative step inside the bathroom, heading for the shower. But as I tiptoe across the tiled floor, I can't help but turn my head, my gaze colliding with the wall-sized mirror at the other end of the bathroom.

A shiver of revulsion goes down my spine at the sight of my body—at the many scars that no one knows exist.

That no one wants to acknowledge exist.

From head to toe, my entire back is covered in scars, some white, some red, and all the shades in between.

I gulp down, pushing the feeling of déjà vu away. I remember how I'd gotten some of them. Others...not so much.

Shaking myself, I step inside the shower, finally letting out a relieved breath as the hot water touches my skin, the steam infiltrating my pores and offering long awaited relaxation.

If my mother is done with me, then maybe I *have* finally gone off the rails. God knows, I've certainly done everything that had crossed my mind in order to get a rise out of them. From shoplifting, to getting drunk, to stealing a car and driving without a license... But that's just the issue.

They don't understand.

They don't get it that I don't even know who I am anymore, or that I feel like a fucking prisoner in my own body and in my own home. They don't understand anything of what I had to endure all that time I was away.

They know what the doctors told them—a quick medical exam that identified everything that was wrong with me. But they don't know the root of it. They don't know that they sent me to the wolves and they chewed me up alive, spitting me out broken and damaged.

They don't know, and they *don't* want to know.

And *that* hurts the most.

Chapter Two

Rafaelo

I release a tired breath as I jump off the treadmill, grabbing a towel from a nearby table to wipe the sweat off my face and chest.

"One hour on the dot at full speed. I'm impressed," Carlos whistles as he strides in, his eyes on the digital clock. "Your body is recovering well," he comments, grabbing a bottle of water and flinging it to me.

"As well as possible, all things considered."

The path to recovery had been grim—still is. You don't get clean overnight, especially not after the drugs I'd been on. I've managed to recover my muscle mass but my stamina is still lagging behind.

"How's the craving? On a scale from one to ten?"

"Eleven," I state honestly. "A thousand?" I shrug when he gives me an odd look. "We both knew it wasn't going to be a smooth journey."

If anything, it's still bumpy. The only improvement has been that I've managed to increase the time between my doses. Now I don't need one daily—just every few days. Almost two years later, and I still haven't managed to relinquish the hold it has on me.

"I swear I don't know what they put in that shit. I've never seen drugs like that, and I've been surrounded by dope my entire life."

"It puts fentanyl to shame," I give him a strained smile.

And it does. If anything, it puts *most* drugs to shame.

Prevalent in restricted circles, it's mostly used in one particular industry—human slavery.

The drug inhibits free will, making one pliable to taking orders and ensuring that the self takes a back seat in favor of the *master's* desires. Not only does it turn one into a human puppet, but it also ensures an insane dependency, creating an everlasting bond between slave and master. You live to obey, or you die a wretched death trying to beat the cravings. Been there, done that and wouldn't recommend it.

Carlos' men had tried to identify the compounds of the drug in an effort to help me beat my addiction, but they'd only managed to discover that it's based on synthesized scopolamine in combination with a few other mysterious compounds.

Since we hadn't been able to replicate the exact formula of the drug, we'd had to look for alternatives to help me slowly wean myself off it. A cocktail of known and unknown drugs later, and we succeeded in replicating a weaker but more chaotic version of it. And *that* is the only thing that keeps me afloat.

"You think you can do it next week?" he asks grimly, and I nod.

"I'm ready." Or as ready as I'll ever be.

We'd compiled a schedule with fixed dates when I would considerably lower my dosage. All in an effort to eventually get clean. And next week will probably be the worst so far since we're limiting my dosage to only once a week. When the withdrawal will strike… I wouldn't want to be around myself.

"I told doc to be on standby and everyone is ready to help," Carlos adds.

"I'll be a nightmare, won't I?" I attempt a joke, though he doesn't laugh. But then, he never does. He's always a surly motherfucker, but he's the only one I trust. Without Carlos, I don't think I would have managed to get to where I am. He'd been the first person I'd reached out to, and by some stroke of luck—or rather common enemy—we'd both struck a reluctant partnership that had turned into a full blown friendship.

We'd quickly realized that we had more in common than we'd thought, including bone deep betrayals and family issues that would give any normal person the chills.

"We have an emergency meeting," he relays, his gaze distant.

"How bad is it?" I ask, knowing he wouldn't have personally come to get me if it wasn't urgent.

"Worse than we thought," he sighs. "We need to regroup."

I purse my lips at his pronouncement, quickly pulling a shirt over my head and following him to the conference room.

"Gentlemen," Carlos greets them as he takes his seat at the head of the table.

I pull a chair next to him, aware how I look dressed in shorts and a sweaty shirt. But the others don't seem to mind it too much. Not with how motley our entire crew is.

There are five people in the room, Carlos and me included. And it's the only circle of people that both of us really trust.

To the right, Anita has her elbows on the table, an eyebrow raised as she regards Carlos expectantly. In her late twenties, she has a permanent scowl etched on her features, making her appear grumpy and unapproachable. She's the most secretive of the bunch, and from what I'd gathered, she is on the run from the Venezuelan government. She's a dissident through and through, made even more valuable by her expertise in military grade weaponry—and the state secrets she'd smuggled with her.

She's definitely helped me get comfortable with all types of weapons.

For someone born and raised in the mob, you'd think I would already be a pro at it, but I'd tried to avoid getting involved in the unsavory part of the business as much as I could. Too bad, though. The more you want something, the less you have a chance of getting it. And I'd experienced that too many times.

Too. Damn. Many. Times.

My first wake-up call had been when I'd found myself locked in a cell, with a needle stuck in my arm, miles away from home and about to be put on an auction block.

No matter how much you want to stay neutral, in this life

there's no such thing as standing on the sidelines. You're either in, or you're out—in a body bag.

So I'd taken my lessons in stride, and in two short years I'd learned everything I should have learned in twenty—and more.

Anita had been a patient teacher as she'd dealt with my dimmed focus after a drug withdrawal, or my erratic self during a drug session. Yet I'd persevered, and in the short time we'd been acquainted she'd managed to get me in top shape with all types of weaponry.

Next to her, leaning back in his chair and with a straw in his mouth is Pancho—Panchito. Two years younger than me, he's a computer whizz on the run from a Colombian cartel. His prowess with coding and creating all types of software had ensured his reputation soared across the Americas, and with it, his name has drawn the attention of various bounty hunters. After all, he *had* hacked into government files and is in possession of the names of a lot of corrupt officials.

On the other side of the table is Thomas—our resident MMA fighter. A thirty something year old wall of muscle, he'd been involved in illegal fighting since he was a lad, first in South London and then across the pond, becoming a celebrated fighter in Boston—where he'd also met Carlos. For all his success, though, he'd angered some pretty important people when he'd refused to lose an important fight to appease a VIP guest. His family had been killed in retaliation, and he'd subsequently become a wanted man.

Everyone at this table is a fugitive—an outlaw—one way or another. What we all have in common is the bounties on our heads—a combined twenty million between the five of us.

But we also have a common goal—revenge. And together, we'd decided to help each other pay back those who'd hurt and betrayed us in spades.

"Is this meeting necessary? I was trying to fall asleep." Panchito sighs, massaging his temples. His eyes are completely bloodshot, and I have no doubt it's been a few days since he's last slept.

"*Ay, no te quejas, Panchito. Toma!*" She whips a small container, throwing it towards him. "Drink this after the meeting and you'll hit the pillow like a newborn," she winks at him.

He turns the container around, looking at it skeptically.

"It's just valerian, you dolt." She shakes her head at his suspicious gaze. "I'm not going to drug you and molest you in your sleep," she rolls her eyes dramatically.

"As if I need to be asleep for you to do that," he grumbles, but I note the hint of a smile on his features.

"Me?" she cries out in outrage. "Me?"

"I think he refers to your birthday when you got a *little* too handsy," I joke, immediately regretting my words when she turns her gaze towards me.

"I did no such thing."

"You did too," Panchito purses his lips in amusement. "You pinched my ass and told everyone, and I quote," he pauses, coughing to adjust his voice to sound like Anita. "*They don't make them like this anymore.*"

"You little shit," Anita jumps out of her seat, intent on tackling Panchito. Seeing the imminent danger, he ducks under the table.

Panchito might be a computer genius, but he's not a fighter. And Anita could very well end him if she wanted to.

I keep my chuckle to myself, though, not wanting to wake the raging beast any more than it already is. Their bickering is well known, and though they look like they can't stand each other ninety-nine percent of the time, they would still have each other's backs in a life and death situation.

But that's the beauty of this team—of *Fenix*, as Panchito had baptized it. For all our differences, there are far more things that bring us together than keep us apart. After all, we've all risen from the ashes to reclaim our positions.

"Can we focus on the meeting?" Thomas intervenes, placing his massive arms on the table with a thud and looking between Panchito and Anita. "I thought we agreed that you two would stop squabbling like two teenagers."

"Teenagers?" Both Panchito and Anita scoff at the same time before looking at each other and bursting into laughter.

"Thomas is right. Cut it out you two," Carlos finally intervenes, getting out of his chair and turning the projector on. "There's a reason I called you this early in the morning," he continues as he pulls some images on the screen.

"Panchito managed to get us some pretty damn rare footage," Carlos praises.

There are four pictures on the screen, all pixelated and blurry, suggesting they'd been captured from a low quality security camera.

But as I focus on making out the people in the picture, some features immediately jump out at me.

"That's..." I frown.

"Ortega," Carlos points towards the older man in the picture. "And a newcomer." He turns towards me, trying to gauge my expression.

"Why? How?" The questions tumble out of my mouth as I find it hard to believe what I'm seeing.

"I don't get it," Thomas mentions, squinting at the screen.

"That," I point to the younger man in the picture, "is my brother."

Everyone frowns in confusion.

"But why would your brother be in contact with Ortega?" Anita asks.

"Why indeed," Carlos muses.

Ortega is one of Carlos' biggest enemies. Once the leader of a small cartel, he'd joined forces with Carlos' father, Arturo Jimenez, in order to build an impressive network running all along the East Coast.

Jimenez had been a force to be reckoned with within the underground world, and he'd managed to build a far-reaching empire by swallowing smaller cartels and giving them a new purpose—total domination. It had worked wonderfully until he'd dropped dead some years ago. Since then, his empire had crumbled and all the sharks had started feeding on the smaller fish.

Ortega had been one such shark, quickly trying to gain the upper hand and keep as many people on his side as he could, in the process stealing what should have been Carlos' birthright.

But with everyone assuming Carlos had died, and with him mortally injured in that intermediary period, it had been easy for Ortega to take everything for himself.

Carlos had kept tabs on him for the last couple of years, tracking all his weaknesses in hope to intervene one day and get back what should have been his.

To see Ortega with my brother, though? That's one hell of a shock.

"When was this taken?"

"Two days ago in Philly. At the port."

"The port?" My eyebrows shoot up.

Carlos gives me an understanding nod.

"What's with the port?" The others ask.

"After he took the Guerra leadership, Michele got the family involved in some shady stuff," I explain. "Human trafficking and illegal organ harvesting."

I'd gotten a snapshot of what had gone down courtesy of some of my contacts in New York. There had been a big bust involving a lot of the crime families in the area, which had resulted in the end of the human trafficking ring.

"So you think he might be expanding this? With Ortega?"

"It would make sense why they would meet in Philly," I grunt. "From what I managed to uncover, Michele's side of the business was based exclusively in New York. He was involved with another Ukrainian guy, Meester. But he died a while back and the entire operation was squashed. It might have been too suspicious to have the meeting in NYC," I add thoughtfully.

"Did we have anything on Ortega and human trafficking?" Thomas frowns. "I thought he took over the drug part of Jimenez's business."

"He did." Carlos replies. "But I don't know if it was enough for him," he sighs as he pulls a map of the East Coast on the screen. All the routes are marked, and every territory is color coded to show who owns what.

"There are too many players in New York for Ortega to manage *anything*. He may have taken over the people who stayed behind after Jimenez died, but he would have still had to fight the other established players for supremacy," I say, leaning back in my seat and perusing the colored spots.

"The Italians have a monopoly over the city, while the Russians control the areas around," I start. "And with how things have shifted lately, they are all connected to one another. Agosti has claim on human trafficking, and the Russians from Brighton Beach control the drugs that come and go from the city. Lastra and Marchesi are tightly connected with both, so that leaves only two outsiders."

"DeVille and Guerra," Carlos adds as he pulls info on the two families on the screen.

"Exactly. And DeVille isn't known for openness. Although their business is thriving and they own most of the casinos in the area, they aren't known to interact with *anyone*. Now, Guerra..." My hands clench into fists. "My brother took power rather suddenly and I'm not sure what people think of it. He's unstable. Erratic. Everything a leader *shouldn't* be. But he's also the only remaining member of the main family."

"Except you." Thomas raises an eyebrow.

"Except me," I nod bitterly. "And that would also make him the perfect candidate for someone looking to expand into the city."

"Raf's right. The only way for Ortega to become relevant in NYC would be to get a strong ally. Someone who already has an *in* so to speak."

"And Michele is probably looking for outside backing, since no doubt everyone else has turned their backs to him."

"Your brother's a hottie," Anita whistles when his picture shows on the screen next to Ortega's.

With his dark hair, pale skin and eerily light eyes, he's always been considered quite the catch.

"He's also most likely a sociopath," I add drily.

"Of course," she shakes her head. "Why are the crazy ones always the hottest?" she sighs, and I catch an odd look on Panchito's face.

"Our return to the city might just need to be hastened." Carlos interrupts with a stern look. "We need to figure out what Michele and Ortega plan, and make sure it doesn't come to fruition. Because if they do join forces..."

"It's going to be that much harder for us to break them apart," I continue.

"Really?" Panchito drawls, looking between Carlos and me. "Have you two forgotten that *everyone* here has a bounty on their head? How do you think we're going to get into NYC undetected and stay there? *Alive*."

"I have an idea. Which is why I called you here." Carlos' eyes find mine as he holds my gaze. "We might need to find an *in* of our own."

"No," I put a hand up, groaning. I can already tell what he's thinking and a million reasons go through my head as to why it would be a bad idea. "DeVille would never agree to partner with me. I'm still a Guerra, remember?"

Theoretically it would be the best course of action, because if there's someone who hates Michele as much as I do, then it's DeVille. But there's also the small detail that DeVille hates *every* Guerra out there—me included.

Our families' enmity is legendary, and everyone knows we've never, and likely will *never* mix. For generations, both families have engaged in a war of attrition meant to weaken the other and their last stunt had ended with the ruination of my sister, Gianna.

I still remember that day, and more than twelve years have passed. DeVille had sent one of their men to infiltrate our family, posing as Gianna's bodyguard with the sole purpose of seducing her and broadcasting her shame to the world. And it had been very public, and very shameful, as he'd posted a video of them fucking for the entire world to see.

Since then, they'd been rather quiet, but still exercising a financial embargo over our family in certain business sectors.

"The enemy of my enemy is my friend," Carlos smirks. "I think it's worth a shot. With DeVille's protection we might be able to move undetected in the city while we gather more info and plan our next move."

"Unless they kill me first," I grumble.

"You can give them what they've always wanted," Carlos says, moving back to the table and taking a seat. "Complete annihilation of the Guerra family."

I narrow my eyes at him.

"It's worth a try," I eventually shrug.

The idea of finally paying Michele back for all my suffering sounds madly appealing. And with DeVille by my side I know his downfall would be infinitely sweeter.

A cruel smile pulls at my lips as I think about Michele and his eventual fall from grace.

Just wait for it, brother. You'll get your due.

And then we'll see who's the last one standing.

Chapter Three

Rafaelo

"You'll get out of here. I promise you."

The voice is so soft, so melodic it's tugging at my heartstrings.

Long ago memories start to surface, and like a movie playing before my eyes, I find myself unable to do anything but watch.

I don't know what she looks like, but I know her heart. I know her voice, and the words that come from her very soul.

I know *her*.

Lucero. Mi luz.

"Have you ever been in love?" I find myself asking her.

Looking around, I note I'm in a small cell. Three concrete walls, a metal grid and desolate coldness surround me. There's only gray —different shades of gray that only enhance the loneliness and desperation I feel clawing at my soul.

"Love?" she scoffs. "Love is for those who have a choice," she continues, a sadness underlying her tone. "It's not for people like us."

"What if it could be?" I ask. I barely recognize my own voice. It must be because it's been too long since I've spoken out loud.

It's only with her that I get to remember that I used to be a person—that I am a person. It's only with her that I remember I'm still alive.

But even that comes at a price, and the knowledge that we are to be forever separated by a wall, by circumstances and by fucking life doesn't help. If anything, it makes me even more desperate for more of her—more of anything I can get of her.

Even the sound of her rhythmic breath can soothe me, giving me a purpose to wake up in the morning and not succumb to this wretched state I find myself in.

"What are you asking, Raf?" Her breath hitches, a small sound but one that doesn't go unnoticed. Not when I'm attuned to every little vibration that comes from her direction.

And as I drag myself to the wall, leaning against the cold surface and placing my ear against that one barrier that keeps me away from her, I wait.

Inhale. Exhale.

Hidden by the howling of the wind as it makes rounds along the cell blocks, her breath is barely audible. Still, there's something inside of me that refuses to let anything interfere with the evidence of her presence.

Closing my eyes, I force myself to bottle my feelings, not wanting to alienate her with my strange desires. After all, who but a madman would have fallen in love in these grim circumstances?

Yet she is it for me. My one respite from perpetual pain. The only one who can calm my clamoring soul and stop my invisible wounds from bleeding.

"Before. Before you came here," I revise my question, holding my breath as I await her answer.

"No." The answer is curt and straight to the point, and a million feelings attack me at once. Relief, sadness, but more than anything a deep pleasure at knowing she's never given her heart to anyone before.

"Have you?" The question comes after a pause, as if she tried to fight with herself whether to ask it or not.

"No," I whisper.

Not until you. Not like this.

But I don't say that. I no longer say anything. I just rest my back against the wall, my eyes closed as I try to imagine her before me. Just a few meters away from each other, yet we're worlds apart.

Both prisoners, both subjugated and condemned to a life that no longer belongs to us.

Yet that doesn't stop me from taking comfort in her presence—the mere fact that she exists. She's the only thing that still keeps me going.

Sweat envelops my entire body and my muscles start spasming uncontrollably. I try to ground myself, but everything is too sudden.

Images flash before my eyes, incoherent words sounding in my ear before a deafening silence ensues.

"I love you," she whispers.

The memory is distorted, and I don't think I can trust it.

I can feel her. I can feel her in my arms—a mirage, but a welcome one, nonetheless.

My hands move up her body, tracing the curve of her waist before settling on her ribcage. She's naked, her bare skin on top of mine.

Her breath on my cheek, I inhale the freshness of her scent, the nearness that at one point had proved impossible.

"I love you, too," I murmur in her hair, slowly thrusting in and out of her—making love to her body *and* her soul. "*Luz. Mi luz,*" my voice becomes frantic as I feel her walls close around me, milking me until I find my release inside of her.

Her voice—that sweet, sweet voice I'd fallen in love with—sings in my ear as she reaches her own climax, her soft moan caressing my very being, marking me as forever hers.

I hold tightly on to her—to the illusion of her. But it doesn't last.

It never does.

The more I grasp at her form, the more she dissipates until she becomes nothing more than a phantasm haunting my mind.

"No, no, no," I keep chanting, my voice harsh and seemingly far away. But the more I struggle, the more I scream to the top of my lungs, the more I realize that I'm losing it—I'm losing her.

And as I open my eyes, the sunlight peering inside the room, small particles dancing through the air and greeting my tired gaze, I know she's already lost to me.

A lone tear makes its way down my cheek and I can't even brush it aside, my hands and feet tied to the bedpost in an attempt to keep me leashed.

I stare at the ceiling, replaying the scenes in my mind, a deep disappointment settling inside of me when I realize that she's gone. *She's truly gone.*

"Look who's awake," Carlos remarks as he enters the room. "I didn't think you'd ever come out of it."

"How long?" I croak, my throat dry, my voice hoarse.

"Almost twenty-four hours. It's getting worse, Raf," he notes grimly, coming to my side to untie my binds.

"It always gets worse before it gets better," I add drily. "I've made it this far, I'm not going to stop now."

"Doc was worried. He said he doesn't know if your body can take it for such prolonged periods of time."

Since my body has become used to a certain time between doses, every time we increase that interval, I go into withdrawal. This was no exception, and I know I will continue to feel sluggish for a few days to come as my body slowly starts accommodating to the new schedule. Still, doc might have a point. The more I delay my doses, the harder my body seems to take it. But quitting is out of the question.

"It will. It has to," I reply resolutely. "I know what I have to do, Carlos. And I'm not going to stop until Michele's dead and buried. I'm not going to stop until he feels on his own skin what he did to me—what he took from me," I take a deep breath. "I promised *her*," I whisper, looking away.

"I know you did, Raf. But if you're forcing your body like this…"

"I need to be at full capacity so I can beat him. I know him, Carlos. He might be an unstable son of a bitch, but he's not stupid," a bitter laugh escapes me. "He's anything *but* stupid. And to beat him, I'll need to be at my best."

"She wouldn't want this for you," he mentions as I get up to stretch my aching limbs.

I turn sharply, leveling him with my gaze.

"She made sure you got away to *live*, not waste your life..."

"No," I interrupt him. "This will be for her too. I need to know her death wasn't in vain. I need..." I take a deep breath, shaking my head. "I'll go take a shower," I mumble, not wanting to dwell on the subject anymore.

Carlos purses his lips as he looks at me, clearly disapproving.

Turning my back, I decide to ignore him and everyone I encounter on my way to my room.

And as I take off my sweaty shirt and pants, stepping inside the steaming shower, I allow the residual adrenaline to pour through me.

The pain, though, is as vivid as ever.

It's always the same cycle.

I go through a withdrawal episode where I hallucinate she's next to me, where I fucking feel her skin next to mine. Then there's the period of time following the episode when I have to live with the realization it was never real.

That she's gone and nothing will bring her back.

I steady myself against the shower stall, my breath coming in short spurts, my senses too fucking full of her.

Letting my head rest against the tiled wall, I pretend for a moment that she's on the other side. I pretend her voice talks to me, asking how my day's been. I pretend I hear her sing, that sweet fucking tone that could bring me to my knees.

And as I fist my hard length in my hand, stroking myself, all I can imagine is *her*. The tightness of her pussy as she would welcome me into her body. The way she'd be so snug around me, her walls clamping down on me with the power of her orgasm.

My eyes snap closed, my lips parting as I keep pumping, using my imagination of her to help me take the edge off,

"Fuck," I curse when I feel my balls draw up, a flash of light appearing before my eyes as I come in thick spurts.

My strength threatens to leave me, and I barely manage to scramble out of the bathroom, crashing face down on the bed.

Reaching under my pillow, I pull a small necklace from its safe place, lifting it in front of me as I watch the light hit the golden stone, the tiny gemstone shining brightly and bringing back painful memories from before—when it hadn't emitted any light in the pitch darkness of my cell.

"Why are you giving me this?" she'd asked, almost reverently as I removed the necklace from around my neck. "It's the only thing you still have from…"

From my old life.

"Do you know what stone this is?" I'd asked her, taking her hand and laying the necklace in her open palm.

One whispered *no*, her breath fanning over my cheek as I'd felt her close to my body—not seeing but feeling.

"Garnet. It symbolizes victory."

"Victory…" she'd repeated, her small hands cupping the stone and trying to make out its shape.

"There's also another meaning," I'd added sheepishly, my fingers brushing against her hair.

"Really?" The excitement in her voice had been evident. Just as evident as the sigh of pleasure she'd released when I'd fumbled to place the necklace around her neck.

"Eternal love," I'd whispered against her nape, letting my lips touch her skin, inhaling her essence and carefully storing that precious memory of her.

"Raf…"

"Shh. I want you to have it. When you feel that you can't bear it anymore, think of me. Just like I think of you."

That had been one of the few times I'd been able to touch her, feel her… In the darkness of my cell, with my eyes sealed shut, purple and swollen, she'd been there, worrying about me, *caring* for me. I can almost make out the contour of her form, but her expression is forever out of reach. Yet her features are eternally engrained in my mind even from the few times I'd seen her in daylight—her blonde hair and pale skin, the way her mouth curved up as she tried to help the other slaves.

Closing my eyes, I tighten my fist around the garnet necklace, the pain threatening to overtake me.

When the one year mark had passed, I thought I was doing better. But instead of healing, every day seems to be a battle with myself to stay on course—to finally pay my brother back for all the suffering he's caused me.

And for her.

I'd promised Lucero once that I wouldn't give up. That I'd escape and get revenge for what Michele had done to me. But I'd promised her many things.

I'd promised her I'd save her.

I'd promised her we'd find a way to be together.

I'd promised her forever.

But I failed her.

Even if it kills me, at least one of those promises I *will* keep. The only one I still can.

"You're not getting away this time, brother," I mutter to myself.

Time and time again I'd stepped aside, ignoring his psychotic tendencies and making excuses for him.

Until he put me on the auction block and killed everyone.

Sick laughter bubbles inside of me as I think back to my last interaction with Michele. How he'd looked into my eyes unflinching, giving me that twisted smile of his while he'd taken a drag from his cigarette. One moment we'd been talking, the next I'd awoken miles away from New York, not a person anymore—just cargo.

"Soon, brother. Soon."

Chapter Four

Noelle

"Your brother was worried, Noelle," Dr. Chadwick, my new therapist, mentions as she reclines in her chair. She's a very beautiful woman in her early thirties, her blonde hair flowing down her back, her big honey eyes hidden behind a pair of spectacles. Pushing her glasses up her nose, she looks me up and down in that typical manner of hers—as if she could reveal all my secrets at once.

Maybe she can. After all, it's her job to make me talk. But right now, the mention of my brother alone doesn't make me very inclined to accommodate her.

"Did he tell you to give me more pills? Maybe cure the crazy in me faster?" I grumble under my breath.

"Don't say that. Your brother is just worried for you. You missed six appointments before he brought you here today. What happened?"

I shrug.

"I went for ice cream instead."

I changed a number of therapists in the last year, and Dr. Chadwick is Cisco's latest attempt at making sure I *know* how crazy I am.

I cannot fault the woman though. For all my aloofness, she's been the epitome of calm and serenity for the past hour, trying to coax me into revealing all my secrets.

Too bad even *I* don't know them.

"Noelle," she sighs. "Your attitude is not helping. And I can't help you if you don't want to accept my help."

"I'm not sure anyone can help me, Dr. Chadwick. That ship sailed a long time ago."

"Don't talk like that. You're only twenty-two. You have your whole life ahead of you."

"Then why do I feel so old?" I whisper, raising my gaze to meet hers. "Why do I feel so much older than that?"

"Talk to me." Her expression is one of kindness, and I find it hard to be mean to her when she's been nothing but sweet to me.

"I don't know what to say. I really don't," I take a deep breath.

"Tell me about your husband," she urges and I freeze. "You never talk about him," she continues.

My chest feels heavy, my entire body racked by pain as memories assault me.

"I don't like to talk about him," I say softly, dropping my eyes to the floor.

"You were married at eighteen, right?" she probes, and I see that she won't be satisfied until she pries the information from my lips.

"Yes." I answer curtly.

Maybe it will help if I talk about it. Maybe pretending to be detached will actually help me detach myself from it—from my past.

"How was he?"

I blink, rooted to the spot as the images from my wedding—my cursed wedding—dance before my eyes.

"He wasn't a nice man," is all I say.

His face as he'd smirked at me resurfaces, his fingers fumbling with his belt while I'd backed away from him in fear.

Smack. Smack. Smack.

I squeeze my eyes shut as I try to push the memory away. Still, my skin cannot forget. My scars cannot disappear. The pain—that bone melting pain—is still fresh in my mind.

"Noelle?" Dr. Chadwick's voice jolts me back to reality.

"He wasn't a nice man," I repeat, adding more confidence to my voice.

She purses her lips, studying me.

"Why don't we switch this up a little," she proposes, shuffling some of the papers in her lap. "It says here that you have selective dissociative amnesia," her eyes meet mine as she waits for me to continue.

"Yes."

"What's the last thing you remember?"

I'm going to fucking kill you, bitch.

"I don't know, really. It was just a regular day, I guess," I reply, scratching my arm. "We were preparing for a party at the *hacienda*."

"I see," she says as she jots something down.

What? What do you see?

"Why do you think you suppressed your memories?" She asks.

"Isn't that your job to figure out?" I roll my eyes at her, but she just smiles.

"I'm curious to see why *you* think you blocked them out."

The question gives me pause. I've thought about that countless times, trying to figure out what could have been so terrible I'd simply erased those memories from my mind.

"Everyone died. *Everyone*."

I was the only survivor. One foot in the grave, but I was the only one who made it out alive that day.

"Right. In the fire," she nods. "Who died? Anyone you cared about?" She continues to probe, and somehow I find myself going along with her questions, the answers tumbling out of my mouth.

"Yes. My friend," I pause to wet my lips, my throat suddenly dry. A flash appears before my eyes, words echoing in my mind—all branding me a killer.

I squeeze my eyes shut, trying to block everything. Still, the whispers in my ears continue, haunting me and promising me the retribution I deserve.

"I killed her. I killed..." I shake my head, mumbling the same nonsense, almost on a loop. "I killed..."

My limbs start trembling, a shiver running down my back and making me huddle deeper into the couch.

"I killed her," I repeat, my eyes wide and unblinking as I see her face right before my eyes.

She'd been the only decent person in that house. The only one who'd taken pity on the stranger who barely spoke the language. She'd guided me and helped me learn and accommodate to the culture. Without her...what was already hell would have been much worse.

"What do you mean you killed her?" Dr. Chadwick frowns.

I shake my head aggressively, the memory just within reach, but so far away.

"I don't know... I don't remember. But I'm sure. I'm sure..."

An ominous feeling envelops me, and deep down I know something is wrong—that *I* am all wrong.

Maybe they are right and I *am* crazy.

Though I've denied it from the beginning, there's the unmistakable sensation that something is missing—that my memories, once restored, will uncover something monstrous inside of me.

"Don't strain yourself, Noelle. The memories will come with time."

With time... But do I want them to come?

It's already been two years, and the blank in my head still remains—memories from before *and* after my time at the hacienda blurry or simply absent.

I can only remember *him*, and his punishments. I can remember all the pain and suffering and I have to ask myself. Why hadn't my mind blocked that too? Because if whatever happened was more traumatic than what I remember... Then I'm not sure I *ever* want to remember.

"Why don't you tell me about your friend, then," she says, her notebook in front of her as she keeps jotting things down.

Almost absentmindedly, I take my shoes off as I bring my knees to my chest, folding myself into a small ball to preserve heat. Goosebumps erupt all over my body the more I think of the past.

"Noelle?"

"She was nice. She only spoke some English, but she always made an effort to help me. We taught each other," I smile at the memory. "She would help me with Spanish and I would help her with English."

"That sounds lovely," Dr. Chadwick smiles.

I return the smile tentatively.

"She had a lover who spoke only English. We'd spend our evenings trying to come up with flirty things for her to tell him," the memory is pleasant, and my lips curl up even further into a warm smile.

"Why do you think you killed her?" Dr. Chadwick asks, and I frown, the suddenness of the question taking me by surprise.

"I… I… I don't know," I keep shaking my head.

"Don't strain yourself."

"I don't remember, but I know," I mumble. "There's something inside of me that *knows* I killed her. God," I start breathing harshly, something tugging at my conscience. It feels like I could almost grasp it—that elusive memory.

"You can't know for sure if you don't remember, Noelle."

As if being struck by something, I stumble back in my seat, my arms around my body as I try to warm myself up. Tears soak my cheeks. My throat is clogged with emotion as I realize my intuition had been right all along.

"But I do…" I look her in the eyes. "She died because of me. Lucero died because of me."

"Noelle, you need to calm down," Dr. Chadwick tells me worriedly, rising up from her chair to come to my side.

"Don't… don't touch me," my voice is barely above a whisper as I shy away from her.

"I'm not going to hurt you. You're safe here," she coos, slowly reaching out for me with her hand.

"Shh, it's fine," she tugs me into a hug and I simply break down.

Sobs rack my body as I finally let go of all the bottled up pain.

Her hands trail down my back, her touch slowly bringing me back to the present and grounding me.

"I'm sorry," I sniffle when I feel I have a better grasp on myself.

"You have nothing to be sorry for, Noelle. But I'm going to be very honest with you," she leans back, regarding me with a serious expression on her face. "There's a lot of trauma in your past, a lot of it that you have never dealt with and it's causing you distress now. I can help you and guide you to understand it better. But I can only do that if *you* are willing to put in the work."

I nod at her.

"What if I can't take it? What if the memories are too bad? Too..."

"Is that what you want? To never remember? To never know what happened to your friend?"

I shake my head. I want to remember, but I also don't want to.

"I'm scared. The little snippets I *do* remember don't give me much hope for the rest. And I'm already hanging by a thread..." I trail off, taking a deep breath. "I don't know how to function anymore. I don't know how to be...me." I finally admit the crux of the issue.

"What do you mean?"

"I don't know who I am anymore. My entire identity was wrapped up in being a wife, and then...a widow. A broken widow. I know who people see me as, but I don't know who *I* am."

Dr. Chadwick purses her lips, removing her glasses and rubbing her eyes.

"We'll start small then," she eventually says. "What's something that you used to enjoy doing? Before you got married. Before everything."

I tilt my head as I look at her, trying to think of an answer.

"I used to play the piano," I admit, almost reluctantly. Because while I've been playing the piano ever since I was a little girl, I'd also been forced to do it at the *hacienda*. Sergio had enjoyed bragging about my skill, forcing me to perform in front of his guests, and *that* had never been pleasant.

"When was the last time you played?"

"Before... Before the fire."

"Why don't you start again? Would you like that?"

I think for a moment as I slowly nod my head.

"Good. Then that's your assignment until next time. Try to play something. Anything. And report back how that made you feel."

"That's it?" I ask as she gets up, heading back to her chair and placing her notepad on a table.

"Yes. That's it for today," her lips tug up. "You know, from what your brother told me, I expected you to be more difficult."

"And?" I ask, my own lips curling in response.

"I think there's still hope for you," she winks at me, before showing me out.

I don't know if there is hope for me, but I am willing to try. Contrary to what everyone seems to think of me, I do want to get out of this limbo and I do want to find myself again.

But it's not easy. And it certainly won't be a smooth journey.

I just wish I had someone by my side—someone to support me unconditionally.

Someone to love me.

The foolish thought creeps into my head and I still as I realize the direction of my thoughts.

When I was younger, I had dreams. Like any girl, I'd thought about meeting my prince charming and living happily ever after. But all those hopes were dashed when I was told I would marry an unknown man from Mexico.

All those hopes were dead and buried on my wedding night, with the blood I shed from deep wounds, now forever seared in my flesh.

I'd stopped thinking about love when I'd come face to face with my new reality.

And having seen what the world has to offer, I don't think there's such a thing as *unconditional love.* Not after I'd been traded like cattle by my own family. Not when *no one* had intervened even when I'd called one day, crying and scared that my husband was going to kill me.

No one had tried to help me.

It seems I'm bound to be forever on my own.

"WHERE IS SHE?"

The voice reaches the landing of the second floor, making me hurry down the stairs. My eyes widen in surprise as I see my two brothers, Thadeo and Amo, standing in the hallway.

"Noelle?" Amo is the first to spot me, his features softening as he opens his arms for me to jump into.

"Amo," I exclaim, taking refuge in his hug. "What are you guys doing here?" I ask on a breathless tone.

I haven't seen Amo in months. With him spending most of his time traveling the world and Thadeo living with his family on the other side of the country, it's hard to see my brothers often. But while Amo had dropped by every now and then, Thadeo had been the most elusive, and the last time I'd seen him in the flesh had been before my wedding. But I have an inkling why.

I push that thought out of my mind, enjoying seeing Amo again and looking forward to spending some time with him. He is the youngest man in the family and the closest one in age to me. Even so, he's still ten years older than me.

Maybe that's why I've never been close to any of my siblings, since by the time I was old enough to comprehend certain things, they were already forming their own families—at my expense.

Granted, that can't be said about Amo since he's had his own demons to grapple with over the years. He's the only one who's always been completely unattached, and I don't think he's ever had a stable relationship. I may not be privy to much, but from what I've gathered, he's been battling some type of addiction for over a decade.

"Noelle," Thadeo grunts from behind, and my lips press in a thin line.

Raising my gaze to meet his, I feel a small pang of pain in my chest as I realize that if Thadeo is here then so is *she*.

"Cisco didn't tell me *you* were coming," I lean back, placing some distance between us.

"We didn't know for sure either," Amo replies, giving Thadeo a look.

And just as I'm about to ask what this is all about, *her* voice rings out.

"Yuyu says dinner will be ready soon," she comes into view, stopping when she sees me. "Noelle, how good to see you," she exclaims, though I know her concern to be fake.

Like everything else.

"Camilla," I nod noncommittally at her.

There's a flurry of movement and conversation as we are led to the dining hall, everyone sharing various anecdotes from their lives and trying to add to the discussion so it's not as awkward as it already is.

I'm in the back, just watching everyone pretend they are having the greatest time, cracking a smile every now and then.

"You should eat more, Noelle. You need to stay strong," Yuyu comments, laying her hand gently on top of mine and giving me a small smile.

I turn to her, taking in her features. The way her black eyes seem to sparkle with warmth and genuine affection, it's even harder to muster a backhanded reply.

She'd been an orphan before Cisco had found her on the streets, taking her in and caring for her like he had never cared for anyone else. And when he'd finally married her, her lack of parentage as well as her Chinese heritage had caused an uproar in the family.

Cisco hadn't cared though. He'd never cared about anything but her.

"Thank you," I force myself to reply as she places some meat on my plate, urging me to eat more.

Cisco is watching our interactions like a hawk, probably making sure I'm not rude to her.

The others seem oblivious to the tension in the air—everyone but Camilla.

She's watching me covertly, her eyes the same shade as *his*—the monster who'd been my husband.

I know what she must be thinking. She's afraid I'm going to

speak out, that I'm going to tell Thadeo what his bitch of a wife did.

She barely touches her food as her gaze finds mine every now and then. It's only after dinner that she manages to catch me alone, taking me aside in one of the unoccupied rooms.

She's restless as she paces in front of me, her features stained with the fear of being discovered.

"I'm sorry," she finally says, and my eyes widen in surprise. Of all the things I thought she was going to say to me, that had *not* been it.

"You're sorry..." I repeat, slowly.

"I know what I did was unforgivable. But I was scared. I was scared that he would choose you and give me up," her lower lips trembles. "We weren't in a very good period in our marriage, and I knew that one word from you and he would have spurned me."

"Camilla," I take a deep breath, feeling a headache mounting.

"No, please. Let me say this. I've been living with that guilt for so long, I don't think I can do it anymore," she shakes her head. "I knew what Sergio was like, because he was like that with me, too. I'd lived it on my own skin, and yet I condemned you to the same fate. I..." She takes a deep breath, closing her eyes.

"You can tell your brother that I picked up the phone that day. You can tell him that I listened to you begging for help and I hung up on you. You can tell him everything. I can't take this anymore," she sniffles a sob. "What I did to you... it's unforgivable, and I'm sorry. I'm ready to face the consequences."

I can only stare at her wide eyed.

Camilla was supposed to be married to the heir of our family, but instead, she'd fallen in love with Thadeo—or, at least that's how the story goes. I may have been young, but I'd always seen a certain tension between them. Sergio, her brother, had taken it as an insult that Thadeo had sullied his *precious* sister, and he'd threatened an all-out war if reparations were not made. So they'd offered me—a bride for a bride.

Sergio had been thirty years older than me, but it hadn't mattered. None of it had mattered when Cisco had gotten his beloved Yuyu and Thadeo his cherished Camilla. I'd been but an afterthought.

But then again, I'd been so young when I'd been promised to Sergio—not yet a person. At least that's what I think my brothers told themselves as they pushed through with the deal.

On the day I turned eighteen I was given away to a monster. All so that my brothers could have their happily ever after.

I'd taken it. After all, I'd been raised to expect an arranged marriage. But even my suffering in silence had reached a boiling point when I'd thought Sergio was about to kill me—for good that time. So I'd made a call. The call that Camilla had answered, but pretended it never happened.

"If he had actually killed me," I start, looking her straight in the eye. "Would sorry have cut it?"

She blanches at my words, looking more distressed than I've ever seen her.

"I..."

"Call Thadeo here. Tell him yourself what you did. At least have the decency to take responsibility for your own mistakes."

She's trembling from head to toe, but eventually she gives me a jerky nod.

And as Thadeo comes into the room, his expression slowly morphing from one of disbelief to one of disappointment as he looks at his wife, I can't help but feel sorry for her.

But why should I when she made her own bed?

"God, Noelle. I'm so sorry," he rasps as he takes me into his arms, kissing the top of my head.

I lay still, taking his platitudes, but remaining unmoved by the display. The time has long passed for anyone to pity me or the situation *they* thrust me into.

"I'm fine," I reply, my tone even. My gaze flickers between the two of them, the tension thick as Thadeo can't even bring himself to look at Camilla. "I'll leave you two," I add briskly, quickly hurrying to my room.

There's no satisfaction at knowing the truth is out now. There's no satisfaction at knowing that my brother's marriage will most likely fall apart.

There's only numbness.

Heart-wrenching, bone-deep numbness.

Because sorry doesn't work when you're already dead. And while my body may be alive, my soul has long died a slow, torturous death.

Chapter Five
Rafaelo

Taking my sunglasses off, I glance around the bustling street. My nostrils flare as I inhale the characteristic New York smell—piss and gasoline.

Alas, I am home.

As I nod at Carlos, we both step towards the imposing brownstone located in the heart of Manhattan. Unlike the other families who prefer the upstate area, DeVille is the only one that has its main residence in the city.

One of the nicer areas on the Upper West Side, the brownstone is roomy enough to house the current don and his immediate family.

The moment we ring the bell, we're received by an elderly woman who looks askance between the two of us, her eyes stopping over Carlos' scar before quickly remembering herself and inviting us in the hallway.

"I'll let Signor DeVille know he has guests," she mentions in a disapproving tone.

"Ten dollars he's gonna try to kill us," Carlos adds suspiciously.

"Fifteen he might succeed," I mutter, scanning the surroundings. With how confined the space is, the chances of an ambush are high, especially since we are on *his* territory.

I might have only recently become versed in physical combat, but I'd spent the better part of my teenage years engaging in strategic multiplayer games from the confines of my room. Maybe not as outstanding as having an impressive body count by the time I'd turned eighteen—as is fitting for any mafioso's son—but it still gives me an edge over others. Considering how asocial I'd been—trying to seem as inoffensive as possible so as not to draw unwanted attention—I'd had enough time to excel at the theoretical side.

The moment I take in the layout of the house, I'm already mentally mapping all the places that could serve as spots for potential assailants. And as I see the slight reflection of silver glint in the sunlight, I tug Carlos to the side, the bullet whizzing right past my head.

"Damn," he mutters.

"Silencers," I smirk. "What else to expect when you live in the heart of the city," I joke just as I duck, more bullets flying towards us from another direction.

One nod to Carlos, and we split, each tackling one of the men.

Most of our training sessions had been together—as a team. We're both very well acquainted with each other's weaknesses and strengths and we'd striven to complement one another on the battlefield.

Given my lack of experience in the field, though, my strengths lie in my strategic orientation, speed and relative strength. My weaknesses, however, are my decreased stamina—a side effect of the drugs I'm on—and an inability to multitask when faced with several opponents at the same time. On the bright side, these are all things Carlos is an expert on, having trained as a fighter for most of his life.

Once we both have eyes on the shooters, it's only a matter of avoiding a direct hit and reaching them before they do any damage.

I keep my focus on the barrel of the gun hiding behind what I can only assume is a door leading to the basement. And as I duck once more, rolling on the ground before getting to the door, I orient my feet forward, using the strength in my lower body to kick against the door, making the shooter lose his balance.

A soft thud announces the fall of the person behind the door, and I quickly jump up, my hand on the handle as I open once, kicking the person again, before finally wrenching the door open to come face to face with a man currently fallen on his ass, his eyes wide as he looks at me, his gun a few steps away from him.

There's a second where we both stare at each other before we dash towards the weapon, making a run for it. According to my great teacher, Thomas, my speed is something I'd been blessed with genetically, only enhanced by rigorous training and his masterful tutelage. Case in point, the other man is barely halfway there by the time I wrap my hand around the gun, quickly pointing it towards him.

But I don't press the trigger. That would defeat the entire purpose, since we did not come here to wage war.

Instead, I keep the gun in one hand, using the other to offer to help the man up.

His brows are drawn up in confusion, but he doesn't refuse my help.

"No offense, it's not personal," I tell him as I lead him back to the main hallway, the barrel of the gun pointed towards his temple.

Carlos is already there, his own *prisoner* on the floor, the butt of the gun aimed towards his forehead.

"Nice," I wink at him as we round both men up.

"What now?" he asks, but before I can answer him, the sound of someone clapping becomes louder and louder before we see a man descending the stairs.

In his late thirties, Cisco DeVille has an olive complexion complemented by black hair and a pair of mismatched eyes—one brown, one green. Though there are no reports of his physical prowess or combat history, he has the physique of a fighter—one who works out on the regular.

"I trust you've had your warm up?" He casually inquires when he steps on to the landing, coming face to face with us.

He reaches with both hands as he cups the barrel of the guns, lowering them to the ground. "We won't be needing those," he smiles, giving a stern look to his men and waving them away.

I frown, a little taken aback by his response. He certainly hadn't reacted as I'd expected him to.

Bringing his gaze to mine, he takes a moment to survey me, those mismatched eyes seemingly seeing right through me.

"Rafaelo, isn't it?" His lips tug up, his eyes crinkling in feigned amusement. "Why don't we retire to my study? My wife is pregnant and she hates loud noises," he shakes his head, nodding towards the end of the hall and barely sparing a glance to us before moving forward.

"Hasn't anyone told you not to turn your back to your enemy?" Carlos grumbles, almost as thrown off as I am by DeVille's behavior.

He doesn't react to the taunt. He merely stops, a few steps away, his head turning slightly, only his profile visible.

"Is that what we are?" he asks in a knowing tone. "Enemies? Hmm," he hums, marching forward and disappearing around the corner.

I give Carlos a shrug, following suit. He groans behind me, and I know he's not the best when it comes to diplomacy, so I just motion for him to keep his mouth shut and let me do the talking.

The room DeVille had disappeared into is a spacious library with a conference table in the middle.

Seated at the end of the table, he only nods for us to sit down too, his eyes never leaving us as he's clearly assessing our weaknesses and strengths.

"Surprising to see you here," he smirks.

"Is it?" I raise an eyebrow.

I'd done my homework on the man.

Not only have our families been rivals for more than a century, but there's something to be said about the way a Guerra is taught to hate a DeVille since birth—and vice versa.

Still, in the past I hadn't given that much thought aside from the backhanded comments my father would make about them. After all, I'd been trying my hardest to stay out of the politics of the family, putting on a smile and trying to get overlooked as the useless son.

And it had worked for a while.

Until it hadn't.

But I can't dwell on that. Not when I have to bring my best arguments to the table to convince this man—admittedly our family's official nemesis—that we could both benefit from a partnership.

Cisco DeVille. Thirty-eight. Ruthless.

He took the reins of the family business when he was in his early twenties, his father too ill to continue overseeing things. And according to all reports, he's ruled with an iron fist ever since.

Some might say he's unyielding—too set in his ways. But his personal life shows that he does in fact make allowances—pretty big ones too.

He'd married his wife while his father had still been alive, and the outrage had been far-reaching. I remember my father commenting on the issue and hoping the conflict would cause a rift between father and son and thus change the line of succession. Because even then, two decades older than Cisco, my father had been afraid of him.

Certainly, after how the disaster with my sister had played out, he'd had every reason to. We'd plunged into such a deep financial turmoil, it had taken us years to regain a semblance of balance.

And it was all because of him.

He chuckles, reaching for a pack of cigarettes and placing one in his mouth.

"I have to admit, my wife and I were placing bets when you were going to reach out."

"And? Who won?" I ask, a smile on my lips.

"She did. She always does."

Carlos narrows his eyes at him.

"Now, I have to say I did not expect *that,*" he motions in the direction of Carlos, blowing out smoke as he sizes him up and down.

"Why is that?" I counter.

"You've grown, Rafaelo. Now you're making alliances," he

laughs, taking another drag of his cigarette. "That's why you're here, isn't it?"

"If you already know, then we can cut to the chase," I say and his eyes widen briefly.

"Please do."

"I think you're aware of the situation with my family," I start, watching for his facial cues.

"Indeed. Your brother's been rather..." he pauses, his lips pursing, "loud. He's certainly made sure everyone knew he was in charge of the family, the implication that he killed Benedicto out in the open for everyone with a brain cell to figure it out."

"He's never been able to help himself," the corner of my mouth pulls up. "He's always been an attention whore, but now it's more than that, isn't it?" I probe, knowing I hit a spot when Cisco sets his eyes on me.

"He's not only loud. He's looking for trouble. The kind of trouble no one would want."

"Go on."

"From what we've been able to gather, he's been looking to bring outside influences in the city."

"Is that so?" Cisco asks, raising an eyebrow, a cloud of smoke all around him.

I recognize what he's doing. He's trying to intimidate me, perhaps even making me cower under his intense stare.

But it won't work. After all, I've been through, I doubt anything would work at all.

When you experience the worst humanity has to offer—hell on earth, so to speak—there's little that fazes you anymore.

Cisco might be a smart man, and he might lead a powerful organization, but all that power means nothing for a man who has nothing to lose—just everything to gain.

"He's already in contact with Ortega, with whom I suppose you're familiar," I add, noticing a twitch in his jaw.

Since DeVille's money comes mainly from casinos, a lot of them scattered all across the East Coast, there's absolutely no way he hadn't butted heads with Ortega when he'd been under Jimenez.

In his heyday, Jimenez had been famous for his casinos and clubs that offered *everything*. He'd mixed every vice possible under one roof and he'd given everyone a run for their money with how he managed his businesses. The only advantage the Italians had over him had been New York, since that had been Jimenez-free for the longest time.

When he'd finally infiltrated the city... That had gotten everyone's attention.

And as his eyes flicked to Carlos, I know he's thinking the same thing.

"Ortega," he muses. "I thought he would have gotten the clue that he's not welcome in the city."

"He did. When he had no other recourse and was basically chased out of the city. Which is why he's looking for an *in*."

After Jimenez's empire had fallen apart, a power vacuum had been created, and people had fought to control any small bit of business they could get their hands on. It's not a secret that Ortega had been left with a big chunk of Jimenez's investments.

"So you're saying I should help you because Ortega will form an alliance with your brother, therefore threatening my own business?" He asks, languidly, almost as if the entire thing is one big joke. "What about big boy over there?" He motions to Carlos. "Why isn't he dealing with Ortega?"

"I'm in the process of doing that," Carlos grits out, and I can feel the tension radiating off him, the topic a sore spot, so I quickly intervene.

"It's not just the threat to your interests. I'm willing to add something else to the deal. If you're willing to work together, that is," I smile.

"Hmm," he drawls. "I'm listening."

"The end of Guerra. I *will* kill my brother. But I won't take his place. I'm willing to serve Guerra to you on a platter. What you do with what will be left of it, I don't care," I shrug, enjoying the look of surprise that crosses his face.

"You'd go as far as selling out your own family?" He leans back in his seat, his gaze on me as if he's finally taking me seriously.

"The family sold me out first. I have no loyalty to it. Just a thirst for revenge. Michele falls, and so does Guerra. That is my offer."

"Intriguing."

He narrows his eyes at us, popping another cigarette in his mouth and lighting it.

"What do you want?"

Of course he'd jump at the chance. Given the infamous Guerra-DeVille conflict, if he is the one to end Guerra, it will go down in the history books. It will also give his reputation an edge. All things that I'm noticing Cisco cares very much about.

"Protection, for a start. Michele put a bounty on my head. And in order to solve our little problem, I'll need to be able to move unencumbered around the city."

"Easy," he exclaims, waving his hand in front of us dismissively. "Now, tell me what *else* you had in mind," he smiles wolfishly at us.

Chapter Six
Rafaelo

"You still think this is a good idea?" Carlos asks as he paces around the room, checking for hidden cameras and mics.

We spent the entire afternoon in negotiations with Cisco, talking about strategies and what our goals are in the long term.

The interesting thing about DeVille is that he already knew I was going to reach out, just like he already knew he was going to accept my offer to join forces.

For once, I have to wonder what Cisco's goal is, too. There is certainly more to him than meets the eye, and he'd been entirely too ready to agree to all of my terms.

Of course, what I'm offering is invaluable, and he knows it. Still, I'm not going to trust him just yet—if ever.

In a sign of good faith, he invited us to stay in his home, where I would be protected from any direct attempts on my life—at least until word gets around the city that I am under DeVille protection.

Carlos, however, ever the skeptic, refused the offer to stay here in favor for an old, dilapidated warehouse in Brooklyn, where Anita, Panchito and Thomas had already relocated.

"It's the only viable idea. You know too well that we can't do anything on our own. We're outcasts," I sigh, unbuttoning my shirt.

"We need someone's backing to move around the city and *actually* have a chance against Michele and Ortega."

"I don't trust him." Carlos says quietly.

"I don't trust him either. But if staying here will strengthen our partnership, then I'll do it. There's no way he's going to try something in the house where he lives with his wife and family."

"I still don't trust him," he mutters. "What you're offering him might be appealing, but he also knows he's the only one who can help."

That he does. He asked me why I hadn't gone to any of the other families for help, bringing up my former engagement to Sisi as a reason to seek out Lastra.

The reason, however, is very simple.

Lastra doesn't have a stake in this. No one besides DeVille has a stake in this. And to get to Michele, I need someone equally as invested as me—which makes Cisco the only logical option.

"Then we'll have to make it so that I'm the only one who can help him too," I add thoughtfully.

Carlos grunts, but he doesn't seem convinced. Because of his own past, he's always suspicious of everyone's motives.

"I'll deal with DeVille," I continue, settling on the bed while Carlos takes out his kit. "You and the guys look into Ortega. As soon as either of us has something, we'll regroup and plan our next steps."

"Cisco was right in one respect. You've grown, Raf," he says quietly, lifting his eyes to meet mine.

"One has to when there's no other choice," I reply grimly.

"Not everyone goes through what you did and remains sane," he notes, his lips flattened into a thin line.

He's probably remembering the first time we met, when I unknowingly ran into his territory and all but died on his land.

I was skin and bone, on the brink of starvation and in the throes of drug withdrawal.

"Back then I had a purpose," I say, my gaze distant.

He knows how hard I pushed myself even when I was teetering on the edge, with one foot in the grave. And I only managed to pull myself together because I had something to look forward to.

Something that was taken from me.

"You still have one," he mentions, opening the small case and getting the syringe and the vial ready.

"No. It's different," I correct, turning my gaze towards him. "Before I had a purpose. Now I just have a goal."

He frowns at me, looking confused.

"Aren't they the same?"

A dry chuckle escapes me.

"No. They are fundamentally different," my mouth curls up slightly at the irony of the situation. "A purpose is a direction," I pause, the memories suffocating. "It's what defines you as a human being and keeps you going when things get tough. A purpose is never ending. A goal, on the other hand, is ephemeral. After you reach it... There's nothing else."

He narrows his eyes at me, and a cynical smile forms on my lips.

"*Nothing*," I repeat, laughter bubbling inside of me.

"You're young, Raf. I get that you had feelings for Lucero. I get that," he starts in that fatherly tone he uses to give me advice. "But you have all the time in the world to meet someone else. To fall in love again. Don't limit yourself."

"Would you be able to say the same if Izzy was dead?" I ask, raising a brow.

He doesn't answer, merely pursing his lips, his jaw twitching.

Izzy has always been a sore subject for Carlos. I don't have too many details on what happened between them, but there are those rare times when he gets shitfaced and stares at her picture for hours on end, though he'd never admit it while sober. Still, he's dedicated his life to her even when there are no chances of them ever getting back together. *Especially* not after he caused her to go blind.

"You know just as well as I do that this isn't *just* about loving someone. It's about finding that one person who completes you," I sigh. "Sometimes I wonder if I should be thankful that I at least found her," I look up, focusing on the play of shadows on the wall and remembering the small flicker of light in my cold cell, how every little beam of light would imbue me with optimism for the next day. But back then, I'd had her. The idea of her had helped me get through everything, and I'd like to believe that it had been the same for her.

"Is it better to feel the presence in order to know the meaning of absence? Or is the state of *not* knowing either the greatest blessing of all?" I muse out loud, my fingers absentmindedly reaching for my necklace. Remembering how bad my fits can get, I take it off, placing it safely under my pillow—far but near at the same time.

"I don't like this," he mutters.

It's not the first time he's expressed his disagreement with my outlook. After I'd escaped my captivity, Carlos had helped me strengthen my mind and body in order to get my Lucero back. Instead, all I'd found had been her incinerated body, the necklace clutched tightly in her hand.

Maybe it's a small satisfaction that even in death she'd prized it more than anything.

But after I'd been faced with the evidence of her death, I simply lost it.

I trained. I got better. I did everything to fortify my body and my mind—and I succeeded. But my purpose has shifted to *one* goal. Finish my brother off for all the suffering he'd caused me—and for that one promise I made her.

That was it.

"It's not for you to like," I look him in the eye, patting him on the shoulder. "Be thankful you're not in my position. Because there's only one thing that awaits me at the end—only one thing."

We stare at each other for a moment, and I know he grasps my meaning. But he's not arguing or even trying to dissuade me. Saying it out loud would manifest it into existence. And he still wants to pretend I can be saved.

He goes about his business of setting up my dose, strapping my arm and prepping my vein.

"You're sure you want to do this here? You know it can get bad sometimes," he changes the subject.

"You'll be down the hall," I joke, since he'd reluctantly agreed to stay *one* night to supervise me. "You know very well that if I miss the timing it'll be even worse."

Especially now that my body had gotten used to the more inter-spaced dosage. Until my next appointment when I'll lower the dosage again, I have to be pretty anal about the amounts and timings of the drug. Otherwise, all the work we'd done up to this point will have been for nothing.

"Just this time," he sighs, and I know it's costing him a lot to make that one allowance, since he hates sleeping in foreign places —I doubt he'll sleep much anyway.

He's right that I could have gone to Brooklyn to get through my drug session, but that would have meant opening myself up to Cisco's scrutiny, which would have undoubtedly led him to finding out about my drug issue. And the last thing I want is to start a partnership with my glaring weakness out in the open.

No, in order for this to work, I need to put on my strongest front. And if that means bearing this session in silence, then so be it.

Once the syringe is prepped, Carlos quickly administers it before handcuffing my wrist to the bedpost.

"How is it?" He raises an eyebrow as he takes a step back, assessing my state.

"Go," I nod for him to leave.

"If you need anything, I'm down the hall," he repeats before leaving the room.

I lean back on the bed, my vision already swimming.

You'd think I would have already gotten used to being high out of my mind with the amounts of drugs I've consumed over the years. But every single time it's different. Every time I have to prepare myself for the worst, knowing that these drugs can awaken parts of my subconscious I want to stay buried.

Closing my eyes, I pull against the restraint, happy to see it's holding nicely.

My body becomes boneless in the face of the many sensations prickling just under my skin. I take a deep breath, surrendering to the feelings. Because I've learned that the more I fight them, the worse it gets for me.

The blackness under my lids slowly shifts to a kaleidoscope—colors and shapes bursting through the surface and making certain parts of my body twitch in rebellion.

A spectator in my own body, I slowly feel myself slipping.

The worst thing, though, is that the memories never stray far from my mind. Almost like being seated in front of a gigantic screen, the flashes start appearing.

One second I'm in front of a black screen, the next I'm staring at a closed door, the light dimmed, the heat blistering as I force myself to breathe in and out.

A hand on my nape holds me down—it always holds me down. Bent over the desk as I am, I can only focus on the door, picturing my escape—that never forthcoming escape that always remains a forever out of reach dream. I take in the lines that go for miles, the slight bent shape of the wood, and the decaying color of the wallpaper.

A dump.

It's a dump that I feel in my very being—in the smells, the sights, the feels.

The pressure of the hand increases, and my cheek makes contact with a cold surface.

I wish I could fight it. I wish I could move enough to get out of his grasp. But I can't.

Collard, drugged, enslaved.

I am but I am not.

Not anymore.

The pain is transient too, and even as my focus switches to the shelves of books on the wall to the right, I find that I can't block everything out.

I certainly can't block the grunts, the hot breath on my neck or the sweat that seeps from his body into mine, staining me—staining my fucking soul.

And I can't block the pain either, no matter how brief, or everlasting. I can't stop feeling, because I'm *not* meant to not feel.

Because this man can *only* get off on my pain.

I know that just like I know that the drug he's given me makes me a stranger in my own body. Like someone switched on the autopilot and kicked me to the curb. Yet I'm still here, watching, feeling. I just don't own the remote control.

I blink.

Fingers tighten over my neck, wet strands of hair plastered on my cheek as I part my lips on a gasp, the feeling of being torn in two almost too intense.

"Good little slut," the voice grunts out.

And everything turns black.

One step in front of the other, and I find myself in the middle of a dark tunnel, my palms on the cold walls as I try to find my way out.

I stumble.

I fall.

Pain radiates from my knees, and everything spins with me, the black becoming white before changing once more to each color of the rainbow.

Suddenly, my hand is propped on a wall as my feet take me forward, my wrists sore and bruised.

But I can barely feel the pain. Not when an angelic sound reaches deep within me and beckons me closer. That succession of piano keys creates such a powerful tune that I feel my entire being tremble in the face of magnificence.

The sound becomes louder and louder, and I can only follow it, needing to get as close as possible.

There's a side of me that recognizes the melody, that recognizes the pain hidden behind each note. There's a side of me—deep inside of me—that emerges to the surface as seemingly all my suffering is transposed into note after note.

My body feels light, my feet gliding on the floor as if the sound is holding me prisoner, calling me to it, capturing me in a trance-like-lasso.

But then it stops.

A soft gasp permeates the air, and in my cloudy mind, I can barely make the shape behind the piano. There is someone, of that I am aware. Yet I'm unable to identify any human traits.

My ears prickle at the sound of someone's voice, but the words are foreign—barely intelligible.

The only thing I am aware of is that the pain flourishes again in my chest, and it's only because of the absence of music.

Desperation claws at me as I put one foot in front of the other until I'm standing next to the instrument, the little human seated on the bench peering at me with confusion.

I can make out as much, yet I can't tell if it's a he or she. I can only tell that they have the necessary means to put me out of my misery.

Somewhere deep within the recesses of my mind, I know I have the information to make sense of what is in front of me. And like pieces of puzzle, they are scrambled before me, giving me clues, yet not the whole picture.

Still, I don't care about the little human. I don't care who it is or what it's doing here. I only care about the power of its hands—those small hands that even now rest on the keys of the piano, their skin a deep tan opposite to pristine white.

Pure instinct alone drives me at this point, and as the little human tries to get up and bypass me, I immediately maneuver it back on the bench, sitting next to it. My palm makes contact with the back of its hands as I force them back on the keys.

But just like its language fails to register to me, language fails me, too. I know what I want to say, a strong desire blooming inside my chest as I wish for nothing more than to hear that divine sound again. Yet I can't verbalize it. I can't speak. I can only glare, imbuing my stare with all the meaning I can muster.

Through the haze that blinds me, I start seeing small flickers of light, and a little clarity returns to me as I focus on one spot, and one spot only—its eyes.

A deep, chocolate brown swirled with specks of green, its eyes are looking back at me, trying to understand the abstruse.

And so I move again, trying to steer its hands with my own as I push against one key, the sound taking me by surprise but filling me with unimaginable warmth.

It's maybe on the third or fourth attempt that the little human understands what I want, its fingers gliding over the smooth surface of the keyboard as notes start dancing before my eyes.

It's the same melody from before—that deeply saddening tune that seems to speak to my very soul.

There's something inside of me that recognizes this piece; something that recognizes that it means something to me—that at one time it might have meant the world.

My mind rebels as I keep probing for information, the sound awakening a piece of me that I'd long thought forgotten.

My eyes squeezed shut, I can't help but feel that something is missing, and my hand tightens over the little human's.

But as I open my eyes, it's to find those motley colored eyes looking at me with something akin to understanding. And as I keep squeezing its hand, it seems to get a clue into what plagues me.

Pushing my hand aside, its fingers nimbly glide over the surface of the keyboard, the melody resuming its glorious momentum. This time though, it's not alone. An almost quiet voice joins the piano before going into a full mezzo voice, the combination of the voice and words making me reel.

Dona eis requiem.

There's something achingly familiar as my mind hones in on the words, the delivery touching me deep in my soul.

Eyes closed, lips parted, I can only give myself to the melody as I search for its hidden meaning—for that part inside me that seems to awaken as the crescendo reaches its peak.

Without even realizing, I lean in, my nose buried in the crook of the little human's neck, deeply inhaling its fragrance.

In the absence of my vision, the other senses are leading me, steering me towards a place that I'd long gotten rid of—or so I thought.

Its scent only complements the way its fingers touch the keyboard—elegantly yet with tenacity. There's something rather addictive to be found in both. And in my drug-addled mind, it's like manna for a starved man.

How many times over the last years have I felt deprived of the power of my senses—of hearing and of touch, of scent and of sight. Because in my limbo, I'd only allowed the bare minimum.

This isn't the bare minimum.

It's so much more, and the richness of the sensations threatens to overwhelm me. Behind my lids, the other senses are turned into colors—warm yet striking colors. It's softness wrapped in a core of steel. It's sweetness, but with an edge.

My senses mingled together, I finally start to make better sense of the piece that's playing, its color becoming richer and richer, just as the scent of the little human is invading my nostrils and making my entire body quake with want. Of what, I don't know.

As I reach further, my fingers wrapping around silky strands of hair, the song ends on a harsh note, the little human out of my reach and stomping away out of the room.

It's instinct. Pure instinct. Because I don't think I can control my body, the rational side of me still relegated to the deep confines of my subconscious.

No, there's nothing logical about the way I move with uncharacteristic swiftness, rising to my feet and following the scent of the little human.

And as my need for it completes the crescendo the little human was just playing for me, I wrap my fingers around small arms, bringing an even smaller frame into me and burrowing my nose into its hair.

Sweet yet smokey.

There's something infinitely familiar yet achingly painful about the way it smells.

Its hands are pushing at my chest, trying to escape my hold. But the disparity in our sizes is too evident, the little thing barely reaching my chest as I push it against the wall, caging it further and bringing my nose down its neck.

Holding both arms over its head, I let my face nuzzle against the warm skin, the scent even stronger.

I wonder how it would taste...

The idea comes unbidden, but the result is immediate.

My lips open over the tawny skin, my tongue making contact with warm flesh and...

Jesus Christ!

Sweetness coats my tongue as I continue to lap over the bit of exposed skin, bringing my teeth into contact with it and nibbling gently. A sweetness just as potent as the cadence of that melody.

My ears are full of the sound of harsh breathing, the little human's pulse pounding like a drum.

And it's the culmination of everything.

Scent. Smell. Hearing. Touch.

And in the absence of sight, pure colors dance before my eyes. But this time, there's no warmth.

A bloody red swirls in circles, white spots forming intermittently but being drowned by the scarlet sea.

Everything is red.

Everything.

Until everything turns black.

And I fall.

Chapter Seven

Noelle

"So it's my fault now?" I turn to Amo in disbelief, and he has the decency to look embarrassed.

"I didn't say that."

"Really?" I cross my hands over my chest. "You just implied I was purposefully trying to split Thadeo and Camilla up."

"Noelle," he sighs, taking a bottle from the table and pouring himself a drink. "This is exactly your problem," he starts and I frown. "Everyone is always against you. You're the only one who can do no wrong."

My mouth opens and closes as I blink repeatedly. Did he just…

"So you agree with Cisco. You think I'm doing this for attention."

"Noelle…"

"Don't!" I put my hand up. "Stop before you say something you will regret, Amo. You are my brother, and I love you very much, but that's it."

His features draw up in confusion as he regards me, and my lip twitches in annoyance.

"We cannot choose our families. That much is true," I tell him, my chest feeling heavy with disappointment. "But we can choose who we have in our lives. And I find I'd rather lose some people along the way."

"You don't mean that."

"But I do," a sad smile plays on my lips. "You and everyone else are so quick to crucify me when you don't know the full story. Actually," a dry laugh escapes me, "you think I'm making it all up, don't you?"

"Cisco's been in contact with your therapist, Noelle. We know that you're not... well," he chooses his words carefully, not realizing that the more he talks the more he's breaking my heart.

"So Dr. Chadwick is breaking patient confidence now?" I counter.

He rolls his eyes at me. "Cisco is your legal guardian, Noelle and you're under his conservatorship. He has access to your health records."

"And he still doesn't believe me. And neither do you," I purse my lips, tears burning behind my eyes as I try my best to not show any weakness.

"It's not that," he says in an exasperated tone. "After what you've been through, it's normal to have some residual trauma. Hell, you were the only survivor there. But you need to let us help you, and it won't work if you're always on the defensive."

Shaking my head at him, I take a step back. And another. Until I turn on my heel, stomping out of the room and dashing up the stairs, Amo's voice calling out my name just a lingering echo in the wind.

Why?

Why does everyone think I am crazy? Why do they think I'm suffering from some type of PTSD when in fact there's only one answer to my behavior.

Anger.

I'm angry.

Angry at my family. Angry at the world. And angry at myself.

Maybe there is some buried trauma from everything I've lived. After all, I don't think anyone would escape intact from Sergio's loving hands.

But Cisco and Amo are trying to make me sound so unstable I can't even take care of myself. So unstable I can't be on my own.

A prisoner.

Laughter bubbles in my throat at the realization they will never let me live my own life.

I mean, here I am. Legally an adult. Once married, now widowed. And I still have no control over my own person.

Just because one useless piece of paper says I need a guardian to take care of me—a piece of paper I have no doubt Cisco paid money to manufacture.

And why? Because he's afraid I'll sully the family name with my behavior? That I'll tell everyone who will listen that they *all* sold their barely legal sister to a sadist and promptly forgot about her?

I've lived through hell to get here. And yet, I'm still a prisoner.

My hands balled into fists, I can no longer control the tears of frustration that pour down my cheeks, or the feeling of uselessness unfurling in my chest.

Anger.

Yes, anger is good.

And as my feet carry me to the attic, the place that houses my once beloved treasure—the place that *no one* visits anymore—I finally let everything inside of me loose.

Closing the door behind me, a scream makes it past my lips as I release all the frustration I'd bottled up inside.

A hoarse groan echoes in the bare room, my voice responding to me and mocking me with the evidence of what I'd become.

Why?

"Why? Why? WHY?" I yell at the top of my lungs, my throat constricting, my vocal cords straining and wrenching an involuntary gasp from me as I fall to my knees.

Tears fall uncontrollably down my cheeks as my eyes zone in on the forlorn piano in the middle of the room.

Once, it had been the center of my world. But it, too, had failed me.

I will my feet to move, taking a seat on the bench, my palms making contact with the cold and dusty surface of the piano.

Closing my eyes, I simply let myself enjoy the proximity.

Oh, but how I'd dreamed about this at one point. How the memory of my piano had kept me warm at night when despair threatened to overtake me.

My love for music had been my one refuge.

Until he'd taken that away from me too.

Lifting the lid, I take in the keys, the white stained with yellow from unuse.

One time. Just one more time.

Dr. Chadwick had urged me to try to play again, and I wish for nothing more, especially since from a young age, playing the piano had been a medium through which I'd expressed my feelings.

All had changed when I'd been coerced to perform, forced to witness the debauchery that would take place at the *hacienda*, and forced to entertain Sergio's reprehensible guests.

Bit by bit, even music had failed to rouse me—until I'd simply lost hope.

My fingers linger on the keys and although my mind rebels against it, my body yearns to play.

One second I'm just tracing the outline of the keys, the next my fingers press down, a low sound reverberating in the air.

I close my eyes, that one note filling me with so much warmth my soul weeps with joy.

"How could I do this to you?" I murmur softly, suddenly ashamed that I'd let it get out of shape, the sound rusty and out of tune.

Focusing on the matter at hand, I thrust all other thoughts out of my mind, my eyes only seeing one thing—the instrument before me.

Slowly, the sound begins to gain a familiar cadence, my eyes closing, my ears opening up as I simply let my fingers roam over the keys, producing a sweet melody that makes me yearn for oblivion.

And just as I start playing, I lose it. Everything I'd kept locked away—locked tightly inside of me—floods to the surface. Each note is imbued with every emotion I've ever felt—every tear I've ever shed.

I feel... liberated.

From Chopin's Etude No. 4 to Bach's Fugue in D minor, my fingers hit the keys with an intensity that makes me reel, the sound reflected back only inciting my anger further, the bass of the lower notes hitting my entire body as goosebumps appear all over my skin.

It's only when the anger starts abating that the melody shifts, and I find myself giving into sorrow, Mozart's Lacrimosa flowing from my fingertips.

Eyes squeezed shut, I continue playing, repeating the same melody all over as if I could not bear to part with it.

The slight eerie tune as well as the emotion it evokes in me make me unable to stop. It's as if all my pain is oozing from me and into the piano keys, my wounds bleeding in the air, my sorrows materializing before me.

As I drown myself in the succession of notes, I simply become one with the melody.

It's too late that I feel the presence of another person in the room, and my fingers suddenly still on the piano keys as my eyes take in the intruder.

He's leaning against the wall, his eyes closed. He's naked except for a pair of black pants that sits low on his hips, the contours of his muscles unmistakable. A lean frame hardened by muscle, the breadth of his shoulders is intimidating as his arms slowly flex, his biceps gaining contour even in the poorly lit room. Then there's his chest... My lips part on a barely audible whimper as my eyes widen at his pebbled abdomen, a sculpted v leading down...

I gulp down, heat enveloping my cheeks. Realizing the direction of my thoughts, I snap my eyes back to his face. It's then that I realize he's staring at me—he's been watching me ogle him all along.

Embarrassment burns at my cheeks, but it's a natural reaction, isn't it? It's not every day that I see someone so attractive, especially with how little freedom I'm allowed by Cisco.

Shaking myself from my musings, I'm about to question his presence in the attic. But just as I open my mouth to speak, he moves. Faster than anyone I've ever seen, one moment he's by the door, the next he's in front of me, the moonlight from the tiny window hitting his face and eliciting a loud gasp from my lips.

I blink rapidly, as if trying to dispel what can only be a mirage appeared before me. Because there's no way such a beautiful man exists. There are no other words to describe his visage. Angular features as if sculpted in marble, his golden skin is only complemented by the messy blonde locks curling around his forehead. Sharp jaw and high cheekbones, he's all male. Yet there's an ethereal beauty to him that's simply ineffable. For all his male harshness, there's also softness in his full lips, or the thick lashes that encase the most beautiful pair of eyes I've ever seen.

I'm simply rooted to the spot as I stare into his blue eyes, a shade so deep and clear it reminds me of the Mediterranean sea as it hits the shores of Sardinia. And as our gazes meet in a quiet staring contest, it's like I'm suddenly pulled back into another time—one that promises only happiness, the salty smell of the sea and the echo of seashells. My heart aches in my chest at something ineffable, the atmosphere heating just as my breathing grows harsher.

My eyes take in his imposing body and the many marks that mar his sculpted muscles. He's been hurt...badly. I don't know why that one piece of information makes me swallow painfully, as if biting down on shards of glass.

He cranes his neck, his pupils visibly growing in size.

"Who are you? And what are you doing here?" I barely find my voice to ask.

But he doesn't seem to hear me as he moves once more, this time coming around the piano, his hand caressing the instrument with innate reverence. I'm almost in his thrall as I watch his slow movements, their graceful quality belying his hulking size.

When he comes closer and closer to me—so close I can smell him, my nostrils flaring as I take in a masculine scent that is both threatening and alluring at the same time—it's finally enough to make me react.

I swiftly rise from the bench, moving to bypass him, trying to escape this maddening proximity. There's something inside of me that knows he is dangerous—to my body and to my senses. And one more minute in his presence could prove too perilous.

I don't get to take one step when his hand circles my wrist, his skin hot against mine, the touch scorching. My head whips up, my brows lifting up in a silent question mixed with confusion at his actions.

"What are you doing?" I ask, trying to escape his grip.

All efforts are in vain, though. Not when he seems to be over a foot taller than me and at least a hundred pounds heavier. If anything, my attempts seem to amuse him as the corner of his mouth quirks up, a slight arrogance seeping through.

He hasn't spoken so far. He hasn't said anything, yet the way he's looking at me seems to convey everything. There's an intensity in his gaze that leaves me reeling, and my knees feel weak under its scrutinizing pressure, ready to buckle at any moment.

But that doesn't happen. Not when he easily pushes me back towards the piano, maneuvering me so that I'm back on the bench, far on the right side as he takes a seat next to me.

The bench is barely big enough to seat both of us, and his hard thighs brush against mine, his naked torso so close to mine I feel a blush envelop my features.

"What do you think you're doing?" I repeat my question, and he suddenly turns to me, those beautiful blue eyes pinning me to the spot and making me lose myself in their depths.

God, but I don't think I've ever seen a more beautiful man. He's like an Adonis come to life, his golden skin and blonde locks only emphasizing his angelic—almost otherworldly—looks.

His lips part as if he's about to answer me, but no sound comes out. His brows furrow in confusion, his pupils noticeably contracting, the black a harsh contrast against the pure blue of his irises.

He looks frustrated as his mouth cannot form the words he

means to convey, and after a visible struggle, he decides to ditch verbal attempts in favor of non-verbal ones.

His hand is still on mine, and by some sort of sorcery, I don't think I want him to remove it. That sentiment is even more evident as he moves, the absence of sensation leaving me bereft in a way that tugs at both my conscience and senses, a foreign feeling of familiarity unfurling in my chest. My heart is already beating at the speed of a thousand beats per minute, my pulse out of control. Yet he doesn't notice.

He's focused on his own objective, and as he pulls away from me only to come back, grabbing both my hands and pushing them towards the keys of the piano, his intent is clear.

He wants me to keep on playing.

A frown on his perfect face, his hands cover mine, pushing at the keys. Surprise envelops his features when he hears the sound.

He keeps on pressing my fingers against the keys, trying to emulate the previous melody in a strange manner, his rendition sloppy but impressive nonetheless.

Somehow, I know I should leave. That I shouldn't spend another moment alone with this unknown man. But no matter how much I tell my body to move, it doesn't want to obey me. There's something oddly appealing about him, and while his gaze rests on the piano, his attention rapt on the instrument, mine is on him.

Who is he?

He must be an acquaintance of my brother's. Otherwise he wouldn't be here, freely moving about the house.

I've never been good with strangers, and perhaps my past with Sergio could explain my apprehension towards men and their potential intentions. Yet in this stranger's presence I don't feel threatened. Not in the least.

Not even as I feel the intensity rolling off him, the way his muscles flex and expand under my gaze. His nakedness should have distressed me—it should have terrified me. Instead, I find it distracting—in the most delicious type of way.

His grip tightens over my fingers as he prompts me once more to play for him. And without even thinking, I do.

I let my fingers glide over the keys once more, Lacrimosa taking shape as note after note resounds in the air, the sadness of the melody imbuing the atmosphere with a lugubrious feel.

The sound strikes a chord in him—I can tell. Eyes closed, he tilts his head back as if he's being transposed into the music itself. For a second, as I look at him *living* the melody, I feel an affinity to him. Something that goes beyond the rational.

He understands.

His entire body is attuned to the music and he sways to the chilling notes ever so slightly. While his hands are no longer pressing down on mine, his skin is still touching mine in a light caress—the lightest I've ever experienced.

There's something about him and the way his presence alone seems to feed my song, making me play as I've never played before —as if I were whole again.

But just as I feel we've reached some type of understanding, his body tenses. His hand finds mine, urging me to do something more.

I turn to him, confused. Still, he does not say a word. He's merely holding tight to my hand as he tries to convey something. I see his frustration mount at his inability to communicate verbally, and so I do something out of character—certainly something I haven't done in years.

I sing.

I know the words to the melody. I've sung them often in the past.

But since my voice had been damaged beyond repair, I'd been afraid to even try to sing—terrified I'd hate my new voice even more than I already did.

Tentatively at first, my voice follows the melody as the words fit themselves to the notes in a quiet harmony. There is a harshness I expected, but some musicality remains.

It doesn't take long for him to calm down, his eyes squeezed shut as he breathes in time with the breaks I take between the notes, almost as if he didn't want to cloud his hearing with his own breathing.

My chest tightens with an unfamiliar emotion as my voice follows the piano melody, my eyes fixed on his form—and the way he reacts to my music.

At this moment, we're one.

I'm one with the music. He's one with the music.

There's no space, no boundary. There's only feeling. Feeling wrapped in musicality. Musicality wrapped in decadence.

My blood pounds in my veins, and I feel a flush envelop my entire body.

And as I give myself to the sad sound, I feel him move closer, his nose trailing very close to the surface of my skin, inhaling.

I keep myself still, but I feel him everywhere.

He nuzzles my skin, moving upwards, one hand grasping on to my hair and bringing it to his nose.

This time, he's so close he could imprint himself on me.

Without even realizing, I jump up, my hands off the piano.

No one's been this close to me in…forever. And the prospect of him coming even closer frightens me, so I take the easiest route.

I run.

But I don't get far.

Not with his speed and the way his arms reach for me, bringing me to his embrace.

I stand no chance. I know that. It's even more clear as I find myself plastered against his hard body, my head only reaching the middle of his chest. He continues his exploration of my hair as he stoops down, bringing his face in the crook of my neck and inhaling deeply.

What's wrong with him?

I bring my hands between our bodies, my palms splayed on the hard planes of his chest as I push against him.

It's in vain.

It's all in vain. Especially as he backs me further into the wall, his hand grabbing both my wrists and pinning my arms above my head.

Dangerous. He's dangerous.

Yet as I look into his dazed expression, I can't muster any of my usual terror. If anything, I can't muster any fear at all. There's only a distant heat that seems to beckon me as he brings himself even closer to me.

So close, I can feel him everywhere, skin on top of skin, hardness against softness. A gasp escapes my lips as I come into contact with another part of him—equally as hard—and a slight tremor goes down my body.

"Please," I whisper. But he doesn't understand. No, he seems to have a single-minded goal as his lips make contact with the sensitive flesh just below my pulse point. The brush of his mouth against my skin is magical—made even more so by the warmth that accompanies it as he opens his lips, his tongue swiping over the throbbing vein in my neck.

My knees buckle and I whimper, his tongue and teeth teasing my skin in what can possibly be the sweetest torment I've ever known.

He groans against me, thrusting his hips towards me, his hardness making contact with my lower belly and startling me out of my reverie. The spell is immediately broken as sense returns and I see myself—at the mercy of a stranger, allowing him intimate acts befitting only a husband.

Before I can think it through, I bring my knee up, nailing him in the balls. With a pained groan, he releases his hold on me, and that's all I need to make a run for it, pushing him backwards as I dash out of the room and down the stairs, locking myself in my room.

I ignore the way my pulse throbs. I ignore the way something else throbs. I ignore the tingle he left on my skin and the searing mark on my soul.

I just hide in my room, going to sleep and wishing it's all a dream—a figment borne out of my faulty imagination.

It's just a dream. It's nothing but a dream.

Chapter Eight

Rafaelo

A cold jet of water hits my skin, my eyes immediately snapping open.

"What?" I croak, sputtering as more water enters my mouth.

"Wow, good on you to come back," Carlos mutters from behind.

Looking around me, I realize I'm in the shower stall, still clothed. Carlos is sitting in front of me, a devious smile on his face as he aims the jet of water at me.

"Stop it," I grit out, shielding my face.

He doesn't though.

Rolling my eyes at him, I simply raise an eyebrow, leaning back and letting him have his fun. Knowing Carlos, it won't take long before he gives up.

"Damn. It's not fun anymore," his shoulders slump as he turns off the shower.

"Thanks," I mumble drily as he throws a towel at me.

"Not even handcuffs will hold you, huh?" He asks as he raises the pair we'd used to cuff me to the bed with.

"I don't remember that," I narrow my eyes, noting the damage to the opening mechanism. "Did I do that?" I get up, drying myself to the best of my ability before going to take a look at the cuffs.

"No one else," he whistles.

"Wait," I say, frowning. "How long was I out?"

The issue with the experimental drug that Carlos' men had concocted is that sometimes it gives me long periods of blackouts. Even more unpredictable than the original drug I'd been on, more often than not it tends to screw with my head pretty badly.

"It's late afternoon already," he says as he opens my suitcase, dumping some of my clothes on the bed. "And DeVille is expecting us for dinner. I managed to make excuses for you in the morning," he gives me a half-smile, "but he won't believe you're jet-lagged forever."

The fact that Cisco is expecting me for dinner barely registers. Instead, all kind of question marks appear in my mind.

"If the cuffs are broken, then does that mean I left the room? Oh, God," I groan. "For fuck's sake, the one time I try to go under the radar and this happens."

"If you don't remember then I can't help you," Carlos shrugs. "I did find you passed out in the attic, though, so hopefully you didn't bump into anyone else."

"The attic?" I close my eyes, bringing my fingers to my temples and massaging them. "Damn it," I mutter.

"Don't fret," he says, turning and placing his hand on my shoulder. "I spent the morning with the family to make sure they didn't question your absence, and no one suspects a thing. Not even Cisco."

I nod thoughtfully at his comment, quickly drying myself and changing into clean clothes.

"You spent the morning with the family?" The corner of my mouth quirks up at the annoyance that crosses his face.

Carlos isn't a people's person, and I don't think he's ever been. Even with the team he has his grouchy days where he simply will not talk to anyone. So to hear that he's been around other people, strangers at that too, is a complete surprise.

"Well, someone had to," he grumbles.

"*Well*, then do tell," I elbow him playfully. "What were your impressions?" Despite his lack of desire to socialize, Carlos is awfully good at reading people. Probably the result of a lifetime of looking over his shoulder in fear someone might stab him at any point.

His lips spread in a thin line and he takes a moment before he answers.

"Cisco and his wife are solid. More than solid. She's his weakness. The youngest brother was present at breakfast. Pretty talkative. One might say *too* talkative. I got the impression something happened with the middle brother because he and his wife left in a hurry."

"Interesting," I note.

I'd scoured every source of information available on DeVille, but it hadn't been much. For all intents and purposes, they are an extremely private bunch.

"His sister was there too," Carlos continues, and my eyebrows shoot up.

"His sister?"

I know he has a sister, but I've never been able to get much info on her. Other than her name and age, everything else is a mystery.

"The relationship is strained between them. I'd say she doesn't have much affection for her family. At least not with the way she kept dissing everyone the moment she opened her mouth. For all her insults, though, both Cisco and his wife were quite easy on her, which suggests that they feel guilty about something."

"Now *that* is even more interesting."

"She's not that much younger than you. You could definitely use her as leverage."

"Maybe," I shrug. "I need to get a better read of the situation before we make a plan to deal with DeVille. For now," I pause as I think about the odd position of making friends with my family's mortal enemies, "I'll be on my best behavior and try to earn their trust. I need Cisco's full cooperation to do this, not just his *protection*."

"Then we better head downstairs," he nods to the door.

Once I look more presentable, we go to the dining room where most of the family is already present.

"There he is," Cisco exclaims, quickly making the introductions.

"Now, who would have thought we'd ever have a Guerra in our home? And at our very table?" He shakes his head, amused, his hand resting on top of his wife's.

His brother, Amo, is looking at me with a strange expression on his face.

"And the prodigal son is back in town," he mentions, the hint of a smirk on his lips.

"Wrong brother," I fire back. "The prodigal son never left," I say as I raise my glass in a mock salute.

"Then where were you? You disappeared years ago but no one could track you until recently."

"Amo," Cisco intervenes. "Rafaelo is our guest. I'm sure he'll tell us," he turns to me, giving me a wolfish smile, "eventually."

Amo doesn't seem very impressed with his brother's decree, but he ceases his line of questioning.

And as the dinner is served, I realize that someone is missing from the table—the little sister.

Carlos is aware of that too as he raises an eyebrow.

But just as Cisco's wife brings up the topic, the sound of steps stomping over the hard wood floor reverberates. Soon, a small figure appears in the doorway, stopping at the entrance.

A frown mars her features as she seems to scan the room, quickly identifying an empty chair and taking a seat at the table.

Everyone is staring at the late arrival—me included.

Long black hair that curls around her back, she has strong Italian features set against a tanned complexion, freckles scattered all over her cheeks. Big, hazel eyes framed by thick lashes move around the room, taking in each person until they land on me.

Her pouty lips part on a gasp as her gaze meets mine, her expression a mix of surprise and curiosity.

She's stunning. Quite possibly the most beautiful woman I've ever seen.

Her appearance causes a visceral reaction in my body. It's like my insides are on fire as I simply stare at her, the irony of the situation confounding me. Pure rage, unlike any other, courses through my veins as I clench my fists, trying to get a hold of myself.

A twitch in my jaw threatens to make my mask of cordiality fall, the distaste I feel for her close to the surface for everyone to see.

I'd never thought I'd be put in such a situation—of wanting to cause bodily harm to a woman. But the one in front of me is the *one* exception. She might be the most beautiful woman I've ever seen in my life. But she's also the most poisonous.

Because her beauty is not the only thing that draws my attention. It's also the fact that I know her.

Oh, but I know her very well.

"Noelle, you're late. Again," Cisco chides, but she barely pays attention to him. "I see you've spotted our guest. Rafaelo, meet my younger sister, Noelle," he turns to me, looking a little exasperated as he apologizes for her lack of manners.

"Noelle, please behave," he gives her a stern look.

"Rafaelo," she says my name, her voice harsh and husky—belying her soft appearance. A bitter taste erupts in my mouth at the sound, reminding me of old days—of moldy cells, daily beatings and disparaging insults.

It's funny how all my life I'd gotten used to being called a retard, wholly immersing myself in the persona and not minding the acidic comments thrown my way. After all, the only way to survive had been by keeping my head down.

And yet, when faced with the reality of the world, with words that truly hurt and strip humanity from your bones, I'd finally learned that not all pain is physical.

She tilts her head to the side, blatantly studying me. Her eyebrows arch in a quiet dare as she peruses my face, her eyes holding the intensity of a thousand suns.

Once, her gaze would have intimidated, speaking of horrifying punishments for even meeting her eyes.

Now... the corner of my mouth tugs up as I take advantage to do the same, my eyes pinning her to the spot as I try to convey to her everything I'm feeling—every bit of disdain that I bear her.

My mouth slowly curls up in a cruel smile.

Things are suddenly a thousand times more interesting. And maybe, this is all a sign.

Noelle DeVille—formerly Villanueva. My master's wife. A cruel fucking bitch.

Someone who should have *died* that night instead of my lovely Lucero. Someone who should fucking suffer for all she's done.

Anticipation simmers in my blood as I realize I'm being given a second chance to set things right. To make sure *la diabla* gets her due once and for all—and this time it won't be just an easy death. No, that ship has sailed. This time she's going to suffer for *every* little thing she's done.

A blush stains her features at my direct stare, and she promptly looks away, fidgeting with her hands.

Alas, this sudden shy persona she's trying to embody doesn't work with me. Not when I know what a calculating cold bitch she is. And certainly not when I know everything she'd done to Lucero over the years. Why, I'm pretty sure the bitch killed her with her own hands.

My fingers tighten over the cutlery, the knife bending slightly at the tip. Carlos notes the change in my demeanor, and he gives me a small tug, trying to get my attention.

But I can't do that. Not now. Not when the only person I've ever hated more than my brother and my master is sitting in front of me, daintily helping herself to her food while pretending she's never seen me before.

"Raf, what's wrong?" Carlos leans in to whisper, once again attempting to shake me out of my reverie. "Cut it out. You're being too obvious," he grits.

My lips twitch in displeasure as I force myself to look away from her, knowing now is not the time to start a conflict.

"Marvelous home, Cisco," I praise, ignoring Carlos' knowing gaze. "I think I'll have a splendid time here with you and your family," I continue, my eyes briefly sliding over Noelle's form. "Splendid indeed," I mutter under my breath.

Suddenly, I have not one, but *two* goals.

My brother will die.

And the bitch will pay.

For everything.

Chapter Nine

Noelle

It's not a dream.

I'm forced to acknowledge that fact over dinner, staring into that beautiful face across me and willing myself not to break into a sweat.

When I'd woken up this morning, I'd *almost* managed to convince myself it had all been just a dream—a rather intense and exciting dream but one, nonetheless.

Now?

I try to keep a straight face as I look at the man from last night. *Rafaelo.*

Cisco proceeds to do the introduction, adding a few other things as he goes on a long soliloquy. I don't really care, though.

Not as my whole attention is channeled on *him*.

I hadn't imagined it. He's just as beautiful as last night. The only difference is the lighting that makes his features stand out more, the blue of his eyes an even more compelling shade. His hair is swept back, giving him a harsher look. If the other night he'd looked a little boyish with his unruly locks, now he looks all man—threatening, intense…alluring.

The urge to squirm in my seat is strong, and it takes everything in me to meet his gaze head on. Especially as he looks at me with such animosity, I have to wonder if I hit him too hard last night. Because that's the only explanation why his gaze would be this chilling and unfeeling, pinning me to the spot with a promise of sweet retribution.

"Pleased to meet you," I nod, suddenly feeling under the microscope as he narrows his eyes at me.

He's holding a butter knife in his hand, his grip so tight the tip seems to be bending. And it's all while he's staring at me.

I blink rapidly, a little disconcerted by the hostility I see in his demeanor. But as my brother engages him in conversation, the man seated next to him, Carlos, tapping him on the shoulder, he finally wrenches his eyes from me.

I breathe out relieved, the pressure inside of me decreasing slightly.

Maybe I should apologize for hurting him.

But why should I when he was the one invading my personal space in the first place?

Armed with a new resolve, I tip my chin up, silently observing the conversation around the table and the way charm seems to ooze off Rafaelo when he's not glaring at me. There's a compelling quality to his voice as words flow from his mouth, a certain innate musicality to the way he pauses after certain words. His sentences are characterized by an odd fluidity, one that calls to my trained ear.

It's without realizing that I simply close my eyes, taking a deep breath and focusing on that lilt of his, my entire body covered in goosebumps at the raw yet gentle sound. There's a deep bass that reverberates in the room every time he speaks, and the hairs on my arms stand up.

Lips parted, I feel almost in a trance as I focus purely on the sounds and their nuances.

For a short while I'm transported to a different time and place, and everything seems to fade away as I feel at peace for the first time in forever. Like a lighthouse beckoning me to safety while the storm rages on, there is a comfort in the way his words are spoken with such assurance, pure confidence drips from them. There's...

"Noelle!"

My eyes snap open to see Cisco scowling at me with mild annoyance.

"Stop being rude when we have guests," he chides. "You can't just doze off at the table," he shakes his head at me, his fingers drumming on the hard wood of the table in that restless manner of his.

"I'm sure she didn't mean to," Yuyu intervenes, placing her palm on top of Cisco's hand, the gesture seemingly calming him.

"I was not falling asleep," I mumble under my breath, rolling my eyes at him.

"Don't," Yuyu repeats, and I sneak a glance at them to find Cisco on the verge of an apoplexy.

Of course. He thinks I'm embarrassing them.

Amo, too, is regarding me with disappointment in his gaze, probably sure I'm doing this on purpose.

Like everything I seem to do these days.

"I can't be so boring as to cause her to fall asleep now, can I?" Rafaelo interjects, his head turning with predatory precision as he fixes me with his gaze.

My eyelids flutter as a blush envelops my cheeks at his direct perusal, and I suddenly feel the urge to hide. I don't know what it is about the way he's always looking at me, but it messes with my senses.

"Of course not," I reply, mustering half a smile.

My brothers are still watching me intently, almost as if waiting for me to mess up.

"In fact," I force my lips to spread even wider across my face, "I can't wait to get to know Rafaelo more," I add, fake enthusiasm imbuing my tone.

"My sister is new to the city. She's been staying with my mother upstate before, so she's not quite used to city life." Cisco interjects, as if I'd said something so wrong he needed to make an excuse for me.

My hands are balled into fists under the table, and I barely hold back a biting reply, since all he's done since I've been here has been to remind me of my supposed inability of taking care of myself.

"Is that so?" Rafaelo asks, his voice a velvet caress to my ears. It takes everything in me not to close my eyes again, focusing solely on his deep rumble and its effect over my entire being.

God, but someone should record the man. I'd listen to *that* all day.

"I'll be venturing quite often in the city in the days to come. Your sister can accompany me if she'd like," his mouth curls up as he extends the invitation.

I frown, taken aback by his sudden suggestion. I'm even more surprised considering that the disdain in his eyes has not diminished one bit, yet he wants to spend time with me and show me around?

I'm about to protest, but then I remember my brother and I almost scoff out loud. Considering my current situation, there's no way Cisco would let me in the company of anyone else, lest I get into more trouble or I embarrass him and his name—the only things he cares about. He barely lets me out with bodyguards, afraid I'd outsmart them somehow and run wild in the city. There's absolutely no way he would let me go out with a stranger—a male stranger for that matter.

No matter the relationship between Cisco and Rafaelo, my brother isn't stupid. If anything, I'm sure he's already thinking I might involve Rafaelo in my next act of rebellion—which is not a completely far-fetched idea.

Except I don't think Rafaelo would be amenable to that.

Not with the way he's shooting daggers at me with his eyes at this very moment.

"What an idea!" My brother exclaims in good humor and I whip my head around to look at him, shock written all over my face. "I've been so busy these days that I haven't had time to indulge Noelle. Knowing she'd be safe in your company would save me a world of worry. You'd like that, wouldn't you, Noelle?" Cisco turns to me, his eyes holding a dangerous glint, almost as if he's willing me to say yes. "I know you've been eager to go out and visit the city."

A small pause ensues as I stare at him flabbergasted, but I quickly recover as I realize this might be my only chance to escape the prison of his home.

"Of course," I smile sweetly. "I'd love that, Rafaelo. Thank you."

He doesn't reply, and I swear I note a twitch in his jaw as if he's barely holding himself together.

The matter settled, the conversation continues to flow as Carlos intervenes, a calming influence over Rafaelo from what I can tell.

And as arrangements are further made, it doesn't escape me the way Rafaelo keeps sneaking glances at me. But they aren't longing glances, or even interested ones.

No. They are filled with deadly intensity and a promise of pain.

I try not to mind him, yet the more time passes, the harder it gets to ignore him. Especially as my entire body reacts at the mere sound of his voice.

After dinner is over, we are all in the foyer seeing Carlos off when he invites Cisco to tour his warehouse in Brooklyn, a look passing between them and implying it's more than just a warehouse.

"I'll let Amo go in my stead," my brother politely declines, his hand on the small of Yuyu's back as he leads her towards the staircase. "As you can see, my wife is pregnant. I can't afford to be away from her even for a second," he declares, his eyes filled with love as he looks at her.

For all my brother's flaws, I have to admit that his love for Yuyu is all-encompassing—and quite possibly his only saving grace. When I was younger, I admired their bond and wished I could find someone who would care for me the way Cisco cares for his wife. But as I grew up, I learned that their love was built on top of others' sacrifices—mine specifically.

Perhaps that was the day I became disillusioned with everything of an emotional nature. If my own blood was willing to trade me so easily, why would anyone *not* related to me ever put me first?

My disappointment has only deepened over time, until I've simply given up on the idea. Why would I ever need love? Why would I need someone else when I have myself?

No one is going to care about me *but* me.

"Wonderful," Rafaelo's mouth tugs up in a knowing smile. "Everything is in place for the next part of the plan as we've talked."

"Now you're making *me* curious," Amo chuckles. "Cisco's been telling me all about Fenix and how you guys came into being. But I'm really curious to see what you're packing."

"Raf here's been the mastermind of this particular plan," Carlos slaps Rafaelo's back affectionately. "You won't be disappointed."

Rafaelo—Raf. Somehow the nickname suits him, yet I feel a gnawing discomfort at using it when I haven't been given express leave to.

"If that's so, then I can see why Cisco would risk getting involved with you," Amo replies thoughtfully, his eyes skimming over Rafaelo's frame as if he doesn't quite know what to make of him. "But I guess I'll be the judge of that," he winks at Cisco, who's sporting a satisfied smile on his face.

In the back, I'm simply watching all the interactions and some things quickly become evident. Whoever Rafaelo and Carlos are, they are involved in the unsavory part of the family business. Not that I'd had much hope they wouldn't be.

But what's even more interesting is the fact that my brother has entered a partnership with them, each side providing something to the other.

The question is what…

Studying Rafaelo, he doesn't look like a criminal. Not that my brother looks like one either, but compared to some of the men who work under him, or even Carlos, there's a world of difference between them.

In spite of the evident strength in their physiques, Rafaelo and Cisco have an elegance to them, a fluidity that seems to be absent in Amo or Carlos.

I don't know why, but the more I listen to the exchange, and the more I catch Rafaelo's eyes skittering back to me in flashes of anger, the more curious I become about him.

"I want to go," I chime in, and suddenly all attention is on me.

"You?" Cisco frowns at me.

"You said he could show me around," I shrug, pointing towards Rafaelo.

His eyes darken at my mention, but he doesn't reply.

Cisco purses his lips, and I know he's about to refuse me—not that I had high hopes in the first place. But I find that anything I can do to rile him up is worth it.

"I'll watch over her," Amo suddenly says, coming to my side and swinging his arm over my shoulder in a familiar gesture. "I think some time away from home could help her see we're not her enemies," he continues, looking down at me with a strange expression on his face.

"Yes. Amo's right. You need to start trusting me, Cisco."

"You haven't done anything to *earn* that trust," he fires back.

"Let her," Yuyu turns to her husband. "Amo's right that she needs to see we mean her well, and you can't stifle her forever. Certainly, you can't hold her prisoner in this house," she says and Cisco opens his mouth to argue, but ultimately does not speak as Yuyu continues, "Even if it's for her own good."

"I'm not a fool, you know." I add, folding my arms over my chest. "I know you're talking about something illegal," I shrug as I see his eyes widening in surprise. "I'm not innocent of the dealings in our world, Cisco. I haven't been in a long time."

Growing up, I'd always had an inkling about what our family was involved in, and I'd catch some snippets here and there that would help me paint a pretty comprehensive picture. It was only after my marriage that I was exposed to every ugly facet of the underground world, and how vicious it could be.

Cisco might not want to admit it, but I ceased to be innocent the moment he gave me away to Sergio.

"Let her," Yuyu repeats, pleading with him with her eyes. "It's time you tried a different approach, dear. Trust goes both ways. You can't just expect her to sing to your tune every time." She leans into him, whispering something in his ear.

He blinks twice, almost surprised at whatever she says, but soon coughs a grunt in her direction.

"Fine. You can go," his tone belies his words. "But you better watch her like a hawk," he points at Amo.

"Of course," he rolls his eyes.

"I'm giving you a chance to prove to me that you're over your tantrums, Noelle. Don't make me regret this, because you won't like the repercussions," he threatens, and Yuyu is quick to slap his hand, shaking her head at him.

"I'm serious. Things need to change if I want some modicum of peace in this house. And Yuyu is right. Trust goes both ways. Prove to me you're a responsible adult—not one prone to hysterical outbursts—and we might discuss again your outside privileges and liberties."

A lightness forms inside my chest as hope slowly suffuses my being. This is it. The moment I'd been waiting for.

"*But,*" he continues, because he wouldn't be Cisco if he didn't have another hundred clauses to add. "Do *anything* that might endanger the business or besmirch the family name, and I'll make sure you're never on your own again."

Speaking of drastic solutions…

"Of course. I promise I'll behave," I quickly promise.

Cisco doesn't look appeased, but Yuyu eventually convinces him to go upstairs, leaving me with Amo, Carlos and Rafaelo.

It hasn't escaped my notice that Rafaelo has been attentively listening to the conversation, his eyes shrewdly moving between me and my brothers as he'd no doubt made his mind about our relationship.

Not that he's wrong.

But something tells me that handing him that type of information could prove dangerous.

Very dangerous indeed.

Chapter Ten

Noelle

"I'm serious, Noelle. Don't give Cisco any ideas to lock you away, because he will," Amo decides to give me one last warning as the car pulls into the parking lot, next to Carlos' car.

"And I told you I'll be on my best behavior," I sigh as I turn to him. "I know he's exasperated with me, so I won't push my luck."

Exasperated would be putting it mildly, though.

Since he'd moved me from our mother's house and into his own, I've been under constant surveillance—be it from my family or my guards. The only time I'm allowed to go out is when I have my therapy appointment, but even then I have an entire entourage that accompanies me to and from the location.

"Good," he nods at me, quickly parking and making to leave the car.

Opening the door, I jump down, my feet making contact with the pavement.

Taking a deep breath, I realize I've missed the fresh air of the night. Being cooped up in the house has definitely given me a new appreciation for freedom and for open spaces. And so I take full advantage of this as I bask in the light breeze of the evening. It takes me a while to realize everyone's already moved away.

Amo is ahead of me, and as I swiftly turn to follow, I bump into a hard chest. Reeling, I stumble back, almost losing my equilibrium.

And as I raise my eyes up, it's to be met with chilling blue ones.

He's standing still, his hands behind his back as he simply watches me, coldness emanating from every pore in his body. It's in the way he's perusing me with a glint of arrogance, his mouth slightly curled up in disgust.

I teeter on the heels of my feet, barely stabilizing myself as I put a hand on the car door, gripping it for support.

He doesn't move. He doesn't make any effort to help me, though it would be the polite thing to do. He's just staring at me with unnatural stillness, his muscled arms bulging even under the suit he's wearing.

I blink, disconcerted.

It's almost as if he's holding himself back from doing me bodily harm.

"Sorry," I mumble, the silence doing a number on me as he just keeps on staring.

He doesn't answer. He merely tilts his head, as if studying me.

"Why?" He finally replies, his gruff voice sending a shiver down my back. "Why are you sorry?" he continues, narrowing his eyes at me as he awaits my answer.

Frowning, I give him a look of confusion.

What's wrong with him?

"For bumping into you?" I ask tentatively, watching for any signs of amusement on his face.

"How sorry are you?" he inquires in a bored tone, an eyebrow raised as he regards me with condescension.

"What?" I croak.

"I asked," he says, taking one step towards me. It's pure instinct that has me backing away from him, retreating as he's advancing. He notices that too, a low smirk pulling at his lips. "How sorry are you?" He rolls his *r*'s in such a way his throaty vibrations resemble a purr.

"Uhm," I purse my lips, taken aback by the entire exchange.

"Very?" I answer and his lips stretch out in a full, languid smile as he takes another step forward.

My eyes on his, I feel lost in his gaze, a prickling sensation of familiarity gnawing at me. He notices it too, and it amuses him to have such an effect on me.

It's even worse, though, when he takes one more step, placing himself directly in front of me. Still holding eye contact, he grabs a strand of my hair, rolling it between two fingers. As if hypnotized, I feel frozen to the spot, unable to break eye contact.

"Noelle!" My brother's voice barely registers, but it manages to tug me out of the mental fog created by Rafaelo's presence.

Without tarrying longer, I mumble something as I bypass him, rushing towards my brother.

It's not before I hear him say three words. Three perplexing words.

"You will be."

Chills run down my back as I hurry to Amo's side, his voice replaying in my mind as I try to understand why he's behaving like that with me.

From the very beginning his attitude had run hot and cold, and now I'm adding creepy to the mix.

The entrance to the warehouse is on the other side of the lot, so I thread my hand through Amos' elbow as we walk the small distance.

"What do you know about Carlos and Rafaelo?" I ask him, since I know he, more than Cisco, would be willing to share some information.

"Why?" He frowns.

"Because we're visiting their place?" I roll my eyes at him.

He grumbles something under his breath, but proceeds to give me a short account about Carlos and his association with Jimenez, one of the biggest drug lords on the East Coast, and how he's come back to reclaim his father's legacy.

"Rafaelo, though, is a bit more complicated," he takes a deep breath. "He's a Guerra."

I still, my fingers clasped over his coat as I tug him towards me, seeking his face for confirmation this is a bad joke.

"You're not serious."

"Afraid so."

"But we don't mix with Guerra," I frown.

"Usually, I'd agree with you," he chuckles. "But things have changed. At least according to Cisco. Rafaelo's brother, Michele, is currently the head of the family. He dispatched their parents and did something to Rafaelo that I'm still unsure of," he mentions, nodding thoughtfully. "But as it stands, Rafaelo's enrolled Cisco's help to destroy Guerra once and for all."

"What if it's a trap? It could be," I suggest, since why would a Guerra help us destroy his own family?

"No," he smiles. "Not a trap. The brothers' enmity is pretty legendary, just like the DeVille-Guerra conflict. No, he's serious about this. And Cisco has his own reasons for agreeing."

"That's odd," I say, pursing my lips.

He tugs me forward, moving once more as we reach the entrance, Carlos and Rafaelo hot on our trail.

I feel them before I see them—specifically one of them.

There's something to be said about the way Rafaelo is always glaring at me, as if he couldn't stand the sight of me. Is it because I'm a DeVille? It must be so, otherwise I have no other explanation for his behavior.

Carlos punches in a code at the door, inviting us in once it's opened.

Typical in height of an industrial warehouse, the entire place had been redecorated and smartly divided into smaller chambers.

"There are two sides to the warehouse," Carlos notes, pointing to the far end corner where another room seems to start.

We walk inside, and I take a moment to wonder at the creativity behind the construction. A second floor had been built in, but only covering half of the space. And as I strain to see up, I realize those are the living quarters, each having a makeshift divider for sleeping spaces.

"There you are," a woman's voice resounds, and my attention shifts to the middle of the room.

There are desks everywhere and a big network of computers seems to have been installed, screens lighting up with different feeds. A man is on a reclining chair as he looks between each screen, a frown of confusion on his face.

Soon, though, he shakes himself, his attention on us as he stands up to greet Carlos and Rafaelo.

A thud from the back startles me, and I note yet another man dropping a pair of weights to the floor, his torso bare and covered in sweat. In fact, that entire part of the warehouse seems to have been converted into a gym, and I spot more sports equipment lying around.

As he comes forward, the woman, too, appears. Red hair that flows down her back, she's a very pretty woman in her late twenties. And as she runs straight towards Rafaelo and Carlos, I can't help the way my heart jumps in my chest, curiosity eating at me.

Especially as she stops in front of Rafaelo, leaning in to whisper something.

He nods at her, his hand covering hers in a gesture of assurance.

I blink rapidly, and before I know it, my mind goes in a thousand different directions at once.

Who is she? And what is she to him?

I don't know where these questions come from, especially since I haven't known the man for more than a day. Still, there's a discomfort in my chest as I watch their interactions.

His head tips up, his eyes making contact with mine over the top of the woman's head. He holds the contact for a few seconds, his gaze steely and full of hate before a slow smirk pulls at his lips. It's like he's daring me to stare at him, daring me to...

I shake my head, turning my attention to my brother and pretending to be immersed in the conversation he's having with Carlos.

It's been less than twenty four hours since I've met Rafaelo, but somehow he's managed to affect me more than anyone I've ever known—and I'm not sure it's a positive thing.

I can't deny that he's an attractive man, but it's more than that. There's something mysterious about him and his chilly blue eyes that won't let me be until I figure him out.

More than anything, I want an explanation for the other night and his subsequent behavior. What does he have against me?

Though he hasn't said the words, I can tell that something isn't quite right. It's in the way he's always looking at me as if he'd like nothing more than to wrap his fingers around my neck and slowly snuff the life out of me.

For someone with my history, that alone should make me run as far as I can from him. Instead, all I want is to get closer—figure him out.

I release a tired sigh, huddling closer to my brother as the newcomers start their introductions.

The one who'd just finished his exercises is Thomas, and he has an accent I can't quite place. The other man introduces himself as Pancho, explaining he's the resident computer geek.

The woman is the last to talk as she finally wrenches herself from Rafaelo's side.

"Anita. Nice to meet you," she nods cursorily to Amo and I.

"And the merchandise?" Amo asks, and I look up at him in confusion.

What merchandise?

"The other part of the warehouse," Carlos nods to the back. "Come on, I'll show you."

"Why don't you wait for us here, Noelle?" he suggests, the question his polite way of dictating that I *should* stay back.

"Sure," I shrug, rolling my eyes at him.

I know I'm already lucky enough I'd been allowed out of the house. I'm not going to push my luck by arguing further. Especially since Amo's tone doesn't seem to leave room for discussion. My guess is that they are hiding some type of drugs in the back and my brother doesn't want me to see that.

It's not as if I'm not familiar with the whole practice, since the entire *hacienda* had been a smokescreen for a drug factory where they'd synthesized some type of novel drug.

Everyone starts towards the back of the warehouse, and Anita stops for a second, assessing me with narrowed eyes.

"I'm fine on my own. You don't need to sit with me," I give her a tight smile.

She frowns, her eyebrow quirking up as she gives a dry laugh.

"I wasn't offering, *querida*," she says before turning with a huff and following the others.

Flustered, and a little embarrassed, I wait until everyone is out of sight before I let out a deep sigh.

When I hear the door separating the two sides of the warehouse close, I become a little daring as I go up the stairs to the second floor, curious about the living arrangements.

There are partition walls made of light wood dividing the sleeping places. And as I slowly walk around, I quietly inspect each, trying to guess which belongs to whom.

One of them is full of tangled wires, so I'm quick to assume it's the computer guy's space. The next has a more feminine touch, and I note a couple of make-up items strewn on the table next to the bed, immediately confirming it's Anita's.

I continue walking, and while the next room is pretty bare, the bed is unmade, suggesting someone had recently slept in it. Considering both Carlos and Raf had slept at Cisco's house, I can only guess it must be Thomas' room.

The next two rooms, though, are almost identical in their sparse decoration. I look around, curious for any clues that might give me an idea which one is Carlos' and which is Rafaelo's. Going inside the first one, I see there's a small luggage under the bed. Against my better judgment, I stoop down, curious to see what hides inside.

My fingers barely touch the zipper of the suitcase when I hear a voice behind me.

"Find anything interesting?"

I whip my head around, embarrassed to be caught red-handed.

Rafaelo is leaning against the balustrade, a smirk of satisfaction on his face as he dares me to defend myself. He's sporting a languid expression, his entire body language relaxed. But it's all an illusion as our eyes make contact and I note the undisguised distaste. He's watching me like a hawk, his easy going stance only a camouflage to put me at ease enough to make a mistake.

I jump up, kicking the luggage back under the bed with my foot. Smoothing my palms over my jeans, I decide to play his game and put on a smile to let him know he doesn't affect me.

Liar.

Of course he does. There's something about him that scares me —that terrifies me on a cellular level. And finding myself alone with him puts me firmly out of my comfort zone. Just like the other night, his proximity threatens to undo me.

"I'm going to find my brother," I mumble, making to pass by him.

"But your brother's not here, is he?" he quips, a sardonic smile on his face as he takes a step, firmly placing himself in front of me and blocking my path.

"Yeah, well, I'll go find him," I mutter, moving to the right. But he moves at the same time as I do, stepping forward and making me take a step back in return.

"What are you doing?" I frown when I see he's backing me further into the room.

"What does it seem like I'm doing?" He arches a brow in derision.

The back of my legs hit the frame of the bed, and I realize I have nowhere else to go. In an attempt to stabilize myself, I put my hands up, resting them on his chest as I also try to stop his advance.

He looks down at the spot I'm touching him, his mouth curling up in disgust. His eyes flash in anger at me for a moment before he's back to his state of cynical amusement.

"What's wrong with you?" I suddenly burst out, done with his cryptic behavior and the undeserved hatred I see in his eyes.

His brows arch up before he bursts into laughter. It's not for long, though. Before I can understand what he means, his hand is wrapped around both my wrists as he holds me captive against him.

A shiver goes down my body at the contact, and I can't help the sliver of fear that courses through me at his expression.

"Let me go," I whisper, willing my voice to not betray the apprehension I feel inside.

"I have to give it to you," he chuckles. "You're one hell of an actress," he says and I frown, looking at him in confusion.

What is he talking about?

"Ah, there it goes. That little pinch between your brows that always appears when you want to feign ignorance," he smirks just as his other hand comes up to touch my face, his fingers settling on my forehead as he traces the ridge of my brows.

"What's wrong with you? My brother will come up any minute, and I doubt your business," I pause, scrunching my nose, since I don't know the particularities of their association, "will go as smoothly if he sees you manhandling his sister," I state proudly, lifting my chin up and looking him square in the eye.

"What if I tell him," he starts, lowering his head until his mouth is next to my ear, the warmth of his breath a contrast to the coldness of his words, "that his sister is a little sadist that gets off on others' pain?"

My eyelids flutter rapidly, his words only confusing me further.

"Wait," I say, pushing against his hand, "I don't know what you're talking about. I think you're confusing me with someone else," I tell him sincerely, since that's the only explanation for his accusation.

"No," he simply states. "I'm not mistaking you for anyone else, Noelle DeVille. Or should I say..." he trails off, and I can feel his mouth pulling up in a sick smile, "Noelle Villanueva?"

My eyes widen, my heart threatening to burst out of my chest. That one word—Villanueva—makes me still. My limbs start shaking uncontrollably, and he can feel it too as his hold on my wrist tightens.

"How... How do you know that?" The words are barely above a whisper as I'm internally fighting for control, that one name rattling me to the core.

But it's impossible... Very few people are aware of my marriage to Sergio. My brother had kept everything under wraps, ashamed, no doubt, about selling his barely legal sister to a monster. So where could he have gotten the information from?

"Come on, you don't remember me?" he continues, his tone mocking as he wraps his fingers in my hair.

He's so close to me, I can smell the clean soap combined with his natural musk off his skin, the scent both titillating and intimidating at the same time. A mix of feelings unfurl in my lower belly, all verging on an unnatural anxiety as he continues to speak.

"I shouldn't have expected much from *his* wife. After all, you're both cut from the same cloth, aren't you?" He gives a sarcastic laugh.

"I don't know what you're talking about," I shake my head, leaning back to avoid making contact with his skin—leaning as far back as I can to get away from him.

"Drop the act," he hisses. "It's just the two of us now. You don't have to pretend anymore."

"I'm not acting. I swear," I continue to deny, but he doesn't seem satisfied.

No, the fingers currently lodged my hair curl around the base of my scalp, his hold strong and unyielding as he brings me closer to his face.

My lips open on a small yelp of pain, and as I come face to face with him, noting the coldness in his eyes, a chill goes down my back.

"Why did you survive? Why did you have to live when everyone else died?" he demands sharply, his words harsh and biting, and I can't help the shock written all over my face at his question.

How? How does he know that? How does he know about Sergio?

It's not unlikely that I might have met him before, since I do have big chunks of my memory missing. But to have been what he accuses me of? I've never in my life hurt *anyone*, so I can't understand what he's so mad about.

"How do you know about that?" My lower lip trembles as I force the words out, confusion simmering inside of me.

He doesn't answer. His upper lip twitches in distaste, his nostrils flaring as he stares at me.

"You might be alive now..." he gives me a mocking smile, "but don't count yourself lucky yet. I'll make sure you rue the day you survived that fire."

There's an ominous quality to his tone that makes the hairs on my body stand up. But no matter how scary he seems, the muscles in his arm bulging as he grips my hair even tighter, there's something inside of me that won't stay put. Especially when I don't even know what I've done to him to deserve this treatment.

"Why? What have I ever done to you?" I ask, my voice steady for the first time.

"What you did to me?" He repeats, his gaze murderous. Taking one of my hands, he unfurls the small fist I'd made, splaying my palm open wide and bringing my fingers to his forehead, forcing me to touch what feels like a bumpy scar.

"You're telling me you don't remember this either?"

I frown, moving my fingertips over his skin a little more before he suddenly wrenches my hand away.

"You don't remember when you threw a plate at me, splitting my head open? When I lay bleeding at your feet and you didn't even bat an eye. What did you say?" he pauses, looking at me expectantly. "The trash is staining your carpet."

My eyes widen, unable to believe *I* would have said something like that. But then I remember Sergio's parties, and the events where I'd had to behave myself befitting of my role as his wife.

That person, *la doña*, would have easily done something like that. And she has.

Because while my memory might be fuzzy for the months before the fire, I do remember some of my time at the *hacienda*. I'd been the worst version of myself, but I'd played my part. I'd been mean, cruel and untouchable.

But this also begs another question. What had *he* been doing at the *hacienda*? And how did he know Sergio?

His smile widens when he sees realization seep into my face. And just as I'm about to apologize and explain the extenuating circumstances, his features darken, his fingers gripping even tighter at my scalp.

"I wasn't the only victim of your…caring side."

"What do you mean?"

"Lucero." There's an odd intonation as he says the name, a certain warmth infusing each syllable and revealing a different side to him.

I'm pinned to the spot as I can only stare at him, Lucero's name an echo in my mind.

Her, I know. Her, I remember. And her…

I break eye contact as I look away, shame eating at me. Because from the bits I do remember of her…

"It should have been you who died in the fire, not Lucero," he grits out, so much malice in his tone.

I close my eyes, the pain raw again as I remember the last time I'd seen her.

"How…" I breathe in, trying to stifle a sob. "How did you know Lucero?"

The corners of his mouth curl up in a twisted smile.

"Why? Afraid I know all your deepest secrets? Those shameful things you want to stay buried? Tell me, do your brothers know what hides behind this innocent act you have going on? Do they know that their sister is a bitch and a murderer?"

I shake my head at him, unable to reply. My mind goes into overdrive as I simply shut down, the implications too much for my already feeble psyche.

"Yes, that's right," he continues, "I know you killed her," he accuses in a low voice, the bass reverberating and traveling all the way down my body in the form of a painful shock.

"No…"

"Why? Why did you do it? What the hell did she do to you to deserve being burned alive?"

"I didn't…" I stammer. I couldn't have. No, he's wrong about this.

"Yes, you did," he states with extreme certainty. "Was it not enough that you abused her for years? You had to sign her death warrant too," he snides.

"I didn't. I swear I didn't," I continue to deny. Because there's no way I would ever do that to another human being. Tears gather at the corner of my eyes, the pain in my scalp becoming more unbearable.

"You may fool others with your tears. But they won't work on me," he smirks.

"I didn't kill her," I repeat, but my words have no effect on him.

"Then," he says, bringing me closer to him as his mouth skims the sensitive skin of my ear, "why was the box of matches in your hand?"

"What... How...."

A thousand questions are going through my mind at his pronouncement. But before my mind can conjure up countless scenarios, he confirms my worst fears.

"You should have stayed dead, Noelle," he whispers, his voice so cold and suffocating, it has me gasping for breath. "I killed you once," he smirks when he sees my terrified expression. "It seems I may have to do it again."

Pure terror envelops me, my chest constricting as I have a hard time breathing. Somewhere in the deep recesses of my mind, I recognize his words to be true. My body recognizes his words to be true.

The threat of death hanging over my head, I simply react, thrashing wildly in his grasp and seeking to free myself in any way I can.

But he's strong. Too strong.

The only thing I manage is to ruffle him, make him even madder than before. I'm past caring about the consequences, though. And as I bring my head forward, nabbing him in the chin, I catch him off guard long enough to slip my wrists from his hold.

But as I push at him, hitting and punching to get him out of my way, my knuckles hit against something hard that scrapes the skin off the back of my hand.

I barely feel the pain, though. Not as the object finally comes into view, the small altercation moving it over his clothes.

The amber stone shines in contrast to his white shirt.

His words ring in my ear. Again and again.

Because suddenly his accusations aren't just *that*. They are so much more... They are based on truth.

The truth staring me right in the face.

"I know you," I whisper, almost dizzy from the realization. "You're... You're Lucero's lover." A pain hits me in the chest the moment I utter the words out loud, a quiet certainty washing over me as all the pieces seem to fall into place.

"Bingo," he intones in a singsong voice. "And now," he smiles, a pure predatory smile that speaks of unfathomable horrors. "Your worst nightmare."

Chapter Eleven

Michele

Eyes closed, lips parted, he drummed his fingers on the surface of the polished table, following the sound of the music as it beckoned sweet victory. It wouldn't be much longer now, and he could finally rest in peace knowing that the balance had been restored—that revenge had been served.

Chopin's Prelude in E minor bathed the room as he gave himself to the melody, satisfaction simmering inside of him just beneath the surface. It was bubbly and almost out of control, and the need to gloat was eating at him. But not yet. He wouldn't jeopardize his plans by celebrating too soon. Not when the pieces had fallen so perfectly in his lap.

The sudden staccato woke him from his reverie, and he turned his attention to the decanter on the table. Filling the glass to the brim, he gulped it down in one go, rising from his seat and putting his jacket on.

It was showtime.

He'd tarried long enough as he'd dreamed up all sorts of scenarios, the anticipation almost killing him.

But it wasn't because of her. It could never be because of her.

She was just a pawn in his albeit flawless game, and she'd be quickly dismissed once she'd outlive her purpose.

No, this was the allure of the hunt. The knowledge that after months of dancing attendance at her feet, of pretending to be anything less than the monster he was, he'd finally get his due.

The beginning of the end.

The fact that he'd get some pleasure from her rather delectable body was just a side benefit. But he knew that he would be getting more than just simple, corporeal pleasure. He would be getting the satisfaction of conquering that which had not yet been conquered—fact that was made more potent by the power he knew he had over her.

He could sway her mind as he wished. He could command her to do his absolute bidding and she would not falter. That rapt adoration that dripped from her eyes whenever she looked at him —*that* was his undoing. It made him feel powerful and it provided him with a drug so strong it inundated his senses in an astounding euphoria.

He hadn't banked on that when he'd first approached her. He hadn't even given her much thought, if he were honest with himself.

But once he'd introduced himself to her, once he'd insinuated himself in her life, he'd realized just how potent her brand of hero-worship was. Because in her eyes, he could do no wrong.

The misguided little chit. A smile probed at his lips at the thought. He'd given her the one thing she craved—attention—and she'd laid her heart at his feet, offering to do *anything* to keep him happy.

She'd turned, one might argue, into the perfect pet—cute, adoring, and loyal to a fault.

He'd whispered a compliment here, a nicety there, and she'd been putty in his hands, all sense leaving her.

She'd stopped worrying about their age difference, or about the secrecy he'd sworn her to, and she'd definitely stopped complaining about the degrading things he would often make her do. After all, she had one purpose—to please. And she was nothing if not obliging.

Opening the door to his '63 Benz convertible, he hopped into the driver seat, pulling a cigarette from a nearby compartment and popping it into his mouth. Turning the volume up on his stereo, he revved the engine, the car purring to life as he led it down the highway and towards his destination.

He drove by the school, ready to pull into the parking lot when he saw her.

She was sitting by the gate, hands in the pockets of her hoodie, her head down as she tried to ignore the passing stares of her classmates. From his vantage point, he could only see the profile. But that was enough to make all the blood pool low in his groin.

He might have an ulterior motive for doing this, but there would never be any hardship in using her.

High, sharp cheekbones that descended into an equally sharp jaw, her features looked like they had been sculpted in marble. Her dainty heart shaped face was only made more striking by pale skin and a pair of hazel eyes that spoke of hidden fire and unreleased passion. Wavy mahogany tresses flowed down her back, the color stark against her porcelain pallor and making her look even more like a real-life doll.

A doll he'd have the pleasure of breaking.

She didn't look happy. But then, she never did. He knew her life was miserable just like he knew he was the only thing that brought her joy—real joy. After all, he'd banked on that from the beginning.

With a history like hers, abandoned by everyone in her life and never given more than a second thought, he'd known she'd be an easy target.

And as he pulled into the parking lot, the sound of the engine drawing everyone's attention, he watched slyly as her features changed. A lightness descended upon her face, her lips pulling into a small smile, her eyes wide and luminous and damn it all to hell if it didn't make him even harder.

He knew that today was the day—the day he'd finally own her, and a low hum of anticipation escaped him as he watched her trudge her way towards him.

She still kept her head down, even though the happiness was evident on her features. And as she reached his car, he noted her flushed cheeks and dilated pupils and realized he wasn't the only one awaiting their time together.

"You're here," she said, almost breathless.

He merely let his brows arch in a quiet invitation and she immediately slid into the passenger seat, swinging the backpack off her shoulder and throwing it in the back seat.

"Wouldn't miss it for the world, pet," he gave her a wink, letting his palm rest on top of her head in a semi-affectionate gesture. After all, this was the only tender thing she'd ever get from him. But she didn't mind that.

She was so far gone she'd take any scraps of attention he'd give her. Proof being the giddiness written all over her face as he drove them off, heading to the hotel he'd booked for the afternoon.

"I'm so excited," she let out a tiny squeal as her eyes roamed around the busy streets, her head tipped upwards as she gave herself to the light breeze that brushed against her skin.

The more he watched her, the more his urgency increased, his cock already at full mast as his mind conjured up everything he would finally do to her.

But he was as perplexed as he was aroused.

In his experience, sex left him completely cold. As a curious teenager, he'd had a couple of failed attempts that had completely turned him off the act. His abhorrence for touch and need for total control made for a lethal combination and had ensured that everything was over long before it even began.

He'd always lived according to a few self-imposed guidelines that maintained his sanity—or what little of it he had left. His life might be a chaotic mindfuck, but there were a few things that even *he* depended on—an order that belied his disordered mind. And he'd never steered off course before.

Never.

He was about to break all of his rules for her—for his revenge.

Because he'd never wooed a woman before. He'd never had to gain a woman's trust, and he'd definitely *never* been gentle with one either—though his capacity for gentleness was questionable at best.

For all the effort he'd put into this entire scheme, he knew the satisfaction would be tenfold.

He desired her, a good start since that had never happened before. He was also able to bear her touch without the usual revulsion—another first.

But she also made him hot with the way she looked at him as he could do no wrong in her eyes. As if he were her very own superhero. That adoration he always found in her gaze did things to his ego. Dangerous things that could turn into addiction if he weren't careful.

"How was school, pet?" He asked, sparing her a glance. She was huddled in her seat—her usual position. She was a beautiful girl—woman, really—if it weren't for her lack of manners. Sometimes he was ashamed to be seen with her in public, her outbursts often giving him a headache. Good thing, though, that their relationship relied on secrecy and he didn't need to wine and dine her to get in her pants.

Still, he couldn't help his reaction to her. There was something incredibly wild—almost feral—about the way she carried herself, as if she'd scratch someone's eyes out if they offended her. It was all carefully subdued when she was with him, but he knew better. After all, he'd watched her for a long time before he made his first move. He knew her inside out.

"Good," she shrugged, "the usual."

She'd wanted to spread her wings into the real world, but it had bitten her in the ass when she'd realized just how different it was from her imagination. She'd had to come face to face with her own failings and the fact that she wasn't like the others. She had no experience socializing, no experience talking to anyone other than her family. She certainly had no experience talking to boys.

And they'd wanted to talk to her. Oh, they had, because who wouldn't when she looked like a wet dream? She had no idea of her own appeal though, and it had been infinitely easy to make sure she wouldn't either.

One word here, one there, and he'd managed to turn her into an outcast, ensuring that no boy would look twice in her direction, no girl wanting to befriend her. He'd made sure she was isolated, because only then he could swoop in and save the day.

It had worked.

It had worked wonderfully, and a smirk pulled at his lips as he watched the way she sighed as she thought about school—the place she'd so desired to attend, but had failed to live up to her expectations.

He'd been her first kiss. Her first everything. And today he would seal the deal too, making her his forever and bringing him one step closer to completing his plan.

"Did anyone upset you? Tell me, and I'll make them pay," he offered with a knowing smile.

"No, no," she returned the smile with a tentative one of her own. "Don't worry. I'm happy I'm with you now," she added.

"Are you, pet?" His hand trailed up her leg until he reached her upper thigh. She was wearing a pair of baggy jeans—another result of the rumors he'd created. He'd wanted her appeal hidden, and for his eyes only. And so he'd made it so she wouldn't have the courage to show her figure.

Only *he* knew how she looked like naked, how shapely her long legs were, or how smooth her skin was. Only *he*'d seen her like that, and only he ever would.

She felt the heat of his palm through the material of her jeans, and a blush enveloped her features. Especially as his hand slowly climbed up, reaching the junction of her thighs.

"You're finally going to be mine, aren't you?" He asked in a husky voice, and her cheeks heated at his question, color climbing up and staining the paleness of her skin in a deep shade of red.

She gave a jerky nod, almost ashamed.

Lifting his hand, he touched her jaw, letting his fingers trail over the work of art that were her features. Damn it all, but he could see himself keeping her. She wasn't just the perfect pet, but she was also the most beautiful sight he'd ever seen, and the thought of her serving him forever had never sounded more appealing.

He turned her so she could face him.

"Don't be ashamed, pet. This is what happens when two people love each other," he gave her the words he knew would sway her.

"You...you love me?" She asked in a tremulous voice, her gorgeous eyes turning a different shade as the sunlight hit them at an angle. By Hades, but she was stunning—and soon to be his.

Only his.

"Of course I do," he lied, letting his lips widen in a seductive smile. "I've loved you from the very beginning," he murmured.

His capacity for love was as nonexistent as his capacity for gentleness. In his world, there wasn't room for any. But women were romantic creatures, and they thrived off meaningless declarations, so it didn't hurt him in the least to give her the words he *knew* would prove her undoing.

She placed her hands in her lap, fidgeting. The corners of her mouth threatened to erupt in a full smile that she barely held in check—probably not wanting to come across as overly enthusiastic.

But he knew. He knew her so well, that every hesitant play of emotion he found on her face was a certainty for him.

"I love you too," she whispered in a small voice, her eyes dropping to the floor.

The monster inside him preened at the words, his ego doubling in size as he realized he had her exactly where he wanted.

Reaching the hotel, he gave the keys to a valet, helping his pet out of the car and leading her to their designated suite.

"Are you having second thoughts?" He asked as he swiped his card at the door, opening it wide and motioning her inside.

"No," she quickly shook her head. "Of course not. I'm just nervous," she said, lowering her head and tucking a strand of hair behind her ear.

That one gesture felt like the height of eroticism and he found himself yearning for her in a way he'd never done for another before.

"Take off your clothes," he issued the command, the urgency in his voice evident. His control was already slipping.

Putting some distance between the two of them, he regarded

her through hooded eyes. And as she started to remove her clothes slowly, hesitantly, so did he.

She took off her hoodie.

He took off his shirt.

She unbuttoned her pants and lowered the zipper.

So did he.

He mirrored her every movement, until she stood naked like the day she was born, her body bared and ready for him.

And he was too. His cock was straining against the plane of his stomach, hard and leaking, the tip already smeared with drops of pre-cum as the sight of her continued to arouse him to no end.

"On the bed," he ordered, and she obeyed.

Her lower lip was between her teeth as she bit on it in apprehension. Still, she did not disobey him. She laid herself on the bed, her entire body at his disposal.

He stalked towards her, his intent clear. But as he reached the end of the bed, he stopped, merely admiring.

She was such an exquisite creature, all creamy skin and sinuous curves, and as he gazed upon her lovely form, he fisted his length, giving it a good pump.

"You're all ready for me, aren't you, pet?" he asked in a smooth voice, and she quickly nodded, her eyes full of love as she turned them towards him.

"Good," he purred, slowly lowering himself on the bed and moving towards her.

He parted her legs, settling between them.

Then, in a gesture of unprecedented kindness, he bent his head and took her lips in a sensuous kiss, his tongue probing deep in her mouth and inviting her to a slow dance. He brought his hand to her nape, holding her to him as he took his time ravishing her mouth, the action making her slowly lose her inhibitions as he aroused her desire.

She brought her arms to his shoulders as a small moan escaped her lips, her breathing already labored as every stroke of his tongue made her lose herself even more in his embrace.

He continued to kiss her, sneaking a hand between her legs and probing her flesh—she was wet enough, he supposed.

He wasn't the type to bother with such niceties. After all, this was all for *him*, not for her. And as the thought crossed his mind, he realized he'd been nice enough to her—certainly more than he'd ever been to anyone else.

Fisting his cock, he aligned it to her entrance, pushing inside. He felt her snugness and the way her cunt gave way in the face of his advance, felt the tear as he ripped through her barrier in one smooth slide.

Her mouth opened on a scream, but it never reached his ears as he swallowed it, forcing her into a kiss as he pushed himself even deeper in her body. Every inch he pushed inside of her felt like he was closer to heaven than he'd ever been.

Her hands were pushing at his shoulders, her mouth moving wildly under his. But only when he was fully seated inside of her did he lean back to look at her.

Her eyes were damp, and tears were running down her cheeks, and hell if that didn't make him harder, his cock swelling inside her even more.

"It hurts," she whimpered, looking at him like a wounded puppy. He knew that a normal person would react to that. A normal person would stop and ask if she were alright.

But not him. Never him.

"You have to bear it, pet," he told her in that affectionate tone of his. "You have to bear it for me, right? You love me, don't you?" he murmured low, leaning down to lick the tears off her cheek.

She nodded, biting her lip as she peered at him through her wet lashes.

He held off a chuckle as he realized her tears turned him on even more, the sight of her puffy and tear-streaked like that doing things to his cock and intensifying his pleasure as he rocked against her.

Gods but she was tight. Tighter than he'd ever imagined, her walls milking his cock like her pussy had been made for him and him alone.

Lowering his hands to her hips, he held her to him as he retreated, his cock slipping out of her completely before he surged back, the friction making him see stars as he felt his pleasure mount.

"Ah," she yelped in pain, crying out louder and louder with every thrust that he had no other recourse than to bring his hand to her mouth, forcing her to shut up.

"It will be over soon," he told her, thrusting into her until he felt himself slip, a staggering pleasure hitting him as his orgasm neared.

His hand on her mouth, he tuned everything out as he kept on fucking her, ignoring her thrashing and her muted whimpers of pain.

He just continued to avail himself of her body until the moment came, and on a guttural cry he released himself inside of her.

"Fuck," he muttered as he collapsed on top of her, allowing himself five brief seconds of reprieve before he turned, rolling away from her.

His entire body was covered in sweat, his mind still foggy from his climax, and for a moment he had to wonder what it was about her that had given him so much pleasure. And it had been more than *just* pleasure, crossing into the all-encompassing realm of ecstasy that gave meaning to the French saying *la petite mort*.

Rising from the bed, he spared her a glance to find her huddled against the headboard of the bed and clutching a sheet to her chest. Her eyes were wildly assessing him, a pained expression enveloping her features as she sought to get as far away from him as she could.

He stilled, his mouth curling in disgust before he realized he could not afford her fear—or any other negative emotion from her. Not while his plan was still ongoing.

He let his gaze roam over her form, noting the blood on the sheets and staining the pale of her thighs.

With a low curse, he strained a smile as he turned his charm on her, rounding the bed and taking a seat next to her. Reaching out to touch her, he noted her slight flinch as she moved back, her eyes still full of fear.

"It won't hurt forever, pet," he forced out the words in a pleasant tone. "It's only the first time."

She blinked, more tears gathering at the corners of her eyes and spilling on to her flushed cheeks.

Goddamn, but the sight of her hurt like this was more potent than any drug, and before he could help himself, he leaned towards her, his tongue sneaking out to catch the falling tears.

"Now you're mine," he whispered against her cheek. "All mine," he drawled, primitive satisfaction brimming to the surface as well as an insidious gloating as he knew where this would all lead.

"I..." she stammered, and for the first time she looked as young as she was.

"I know you liked it," he didn't let her continue. "And it will only get better over time," he lied. "Because we love each other. And this is what people in love do."

She stared at him for a moment before slowly nodding her head.

Trailing his hand down her front, he reached between her legs, finding cum mixed with blood leaking out of her cunt. He twirled a finger at her entrance, his eyes on her face as she stifled a wince at his touch.

Good. She was learning.

He continued to play with their fluids, pushing two fingers inside of her and massaging her walls.

"This," he raised his fingers, showing her the white mixed with red. "This will stay between your legs at all times," he told her in a stern tone. "I want you to carry me around you wherever you go," he continued and her cheeks reddened as she dipped her chin in a quick nod. "If it leaks, you push it in," he said as he jammed his fingers inside her, pushing his cum back into her body. "But you must never, *never*, let any drop out. Understood?"

Her eyes were two big orbs as she looked at him bewildered, the words foreign to her ears. He knew he was going too far, but he didn't care. No, he didn't want to care. Not when she was his *pet*, and her only purpose was to serve for his pleasure. And it pleased him to have her marked like this—smelling of him and feeling him in her body long after he was gone.

"Yes," her whisper was barely audible, but it was enough to please him.

"Good," his lips pulled up in a twisted smile. Removing his fingers from her body once more, he brought them to her lips, urging her to open her mouth and suck them in. "Good girl," he praised when she did. "This is why I love you, pet," he added, and her features immediately lightened up. "You always listen to me."

She preened at his declaration and sucked his fingers clean. When she was done, he stepped back, an odd expression on his face as he took in her ravished appearance and the way she looked at him as if he could pluck the moon from the sky and give it to her. She was so taken with him, she quickly forgot all about her pain, and for once her obsequiousness struck a chord in him.

"Go clean yourself," he rasped harshly, turning so he could put his clothes back on.

He heard the rustle of sheets and the sound of the bathroom door closing, and only then did he let his true emotions reach the surface and infuse his features with an arrogant smirk.

Pulling a cigarette out of his pack, he lit it up, staring out the window as he inhaled deeply.

One step closer. He was one step closer.

And no one would stand in his way.

Chapter Twelve

Rafaelo

"I'm not sure Cisco will appreciate your absence, all things considered," Carlos notes as he comes from behind, his arms crossed over his chest as he is undoubtedly waiting to give me an earful.

"I'll be back to the house by dawn," I reply, continuing to punch the bag in an attempt to exercise all the anger out of me.

"And he will know you've been absent," he sighs. "Look, I wasn't on board with you staying with them in the first place, but since you committed to it..."

"If I'd gone over to the house," I interrupt him, stopping the reeling bag as I turn towards Carlos, "I would have killed her. I would have strangled her or worse, I would have cut her to pieces right in front of her brother. Is that what you want? Because I'm sure Cisco wouldn't appreciate *that*."

He rolls his eyes at me, taking a towel and handing it to me when I finish my set.

"I'm surprised the youngest one, Amo, didn't catch on to your murderous intent. If we'd come back even a moment later, I know you would have killed her."

Carlos, better than anyone, knows how much I *despise* Noelle and everything she stands for—my nightmares and the scars that still mar my body. To think that she's still alive…

"And I'm still not sure I won't," my lips twitch. "Even sitting across from her at the dinner table was pure torture, but to be in the same house as her and *not* kill her?" I shake my head, wiping the sweat off my face and taking a sip of water from a nearby bottle.

"Look," he starts again in a serious tone. "I know who she is to you and what she's done. I understand that. But we've already embarked on this. You need to put aside your loathing of her for a moment while we gain Cisco's confidence."

"I know. Trust me, I'm actively trying to suppress myself."

"Good. Just don't kill her yet. Who knows, we might find some other use for her down the line. But think about everything we planned—think about everything *you* planned," he points out and I nod.

"You're right. I need to get my head in the game. I've worked too hard to get here and I'm not going to let her take another thing from me. Her time will come. And while I can't kill her now… I'm sure I can find some ways to make her regret her existence," a smile pulls at my lips.

Maybe it had been fate that she hadn't died that night. Death would have been too easy for someone like her—an undeserved mercy. For the first time since seeing her, I'm starting to see the bright side in her survival. Now *I* can make her life a living hell. And damn if my chest doesn't buzz with excitement at the prospect.

"Good," Carlos chuckles. "Anything short of murder works. And now that we've gotten that out of the way…" he starts detailing what Pancho and Anita found while combing through the security footage—specifically that Ortega is loitering around New York.

"Bit of a coincidence, wouldn't you say?" I raise an eyebrow. "We just arrive and he's suddenly here as well?"

"Indeed. I'm going to look a bit more into that. You get your ass to Cisco's house and behave. We still need his influence and the protection of his name to move around. And your nightly expeditions aren't going to earn you any bonus points."

"You're right," I sigh, placing my hand on his shoulder in a friendly pat. "Wish me luck," I joke.

"Better not see you at a funeral next," he winks at me, "unless it's your brother's."

I give a low chuckle as I walk away, heading for the showers before cleaning up and heading back to Cisco's house.

I know I'm courting danger by the sole fact that I'm driving alone, at night, when I have a whopping seven figure price tag on my head.

Yet I needed that break.

I hadn't been kidding when I'd told Carlos I was close to fucking killing Noelle. Especially when she'd had the gall to look at me with that innocent look of hers that no doubt works with everyone else around her. She'd been so quick to deny everything and claim no knowledge of the situation, and *that* had enraged me even further. To add insult to the injury, she hadn't even remembered me, as if the times we'd crossed paths had been of such little importance to her that she'd promptly forgotten them.

But maybe they had been. After all, I'd been just a puny slave and she'd been the wife of the master. Still, the memory of her disdainful eyes as she'd thrown a plate at my head is still fresh in my mind. She might have forgotten all about it, but I haven't.

I can vividly picture the way she'd signaled one of her servants, whispering something in his ear and pointing towards me. It was a moment after that I'd been escorted—rather forcefully—out, because my lowly blood was staining the master's carpet.

That had been my first introduction to the infamous *la diabla* that everyone was talking about in hushed tones. And my opinion of her had only become worse over time, seeing her for the vicious little bitch she was, but also hearing from Lucero how badly Noelle treated her—her supposed friend.

My hands tighten on the steering wheel as pain hits me right in the chest at the thought of Lucero. But I can't go there. Not now when I'm one step closer to fulfilling everything I'd planned.

I'll honor my promise to Carlos and I won't kill Noelle—yet. But that doesn't mean I'm going to let her get away with everything she's done. Especially since I know for sure she had something to do with Lucero's death—with everyone's deaths.

By the time Carlos and I had reached the hacienda, it had been enveloped in flames, tens of charred bodies strewn around—people who had attempted to run out of the house while in flames. It had been something out of a horror movie, and I'm convinced that only someone with no soul could commit a massacre of that magnitude.

I reach the DeVille house before dawn. As I make my way up the stairs to my designated room, I hear the soft melody of a piano again.

Closing my eyes I take a deep breath, wondering if it's Cisco's wife that's playing, since I'd heard she was a lover of music.

Even so, the melody touches something within me, reminding me of those hopeless days I lay pitifully in my cell, not knowing if I was going to make it yet another day. In those times, music had somehow saved me. For all the death and gloom that accompanied my captivity, there had always been a sad yet sweet melody that had almost roused me against my will, making me fight for another day. Then, just like now, the taste had been bittersweet—a melody laced with pain, but underneath all the sadness there had been the hint of hope.

Realizing I'd been frozen on the spot in front of my door, I shake myself from my melancholic musings as I enter the room.

For the next few hours, until breakfast is served, I catalog every new piece of information we'd gleaned and I factor it into the equation. The only way to win this is to have every single basis covered, and that means minimizing our weaknesses while capitalizing on those of our enemies.

By the time I get to the breakfast table, everyone is already seated. Cisco and his wife are on one side, while Amo and Noelle on the other. From what I'd gathered, it's going to be this formation from now on. The middle brother and his wife have already left, while Cisco's eldest son is away at boarding school.

The moment I enter the room, though, all eyes are on me.

"Rough night?" Cisco raises a brow as he sips on his coffee, a knowing smile on his face.

I don't miss the way Amo hides a chuckle, Noelle blinking rapidly as she stares at me, quickly looking away the moment she's caught.

"You could say so," I grunt, taking a seat at the other end of the table, ensuring that I have an unperturbed view of Noelle.

She doesn't turn to me again, and I can tell she's forcing herself to pay attention to the food on her plate rather than meet my gaze. She's holding tightly onto the cutlery, her fingers almost white from the vicious grip.

A slow smile pulls at my lips as I realize our previous encounter must have rattled her.

"Amo's already given me an account of the warehouse, and I must say," Cisco notes, leaning forward, "I'm impressed."

"I told you I didn't come empty-handed," I reply, taking some toast and organizing my plate from the wide selection of cheeses and ham.

"I underestimated you, Rafaelo," he muses, his tone serious.

"Please, call me Raf. We're going to be associates from now on, no?" I ask suggestively, moving my gaze around the table before stopping at Noelle.

Her mouth is slightly open as she gapes at me—undoubtedly shocked I'm here to stay.

Stay and make her life a living hell.

Her reaction is only making me more excited about what's to come. Although I won't be able to kill her outright, who says I can't play with her a little? Give her a taste of the terror she'd so liked to spread to others in the past?

"*Raf*," Cisco chuckles. "I have a feeling we're going to be great friends, Raf."

"Ditto," I raise my water glass towards him, mimicking a toast.

The conversation flows, quickly straying from our particular business and into the mundane.

"Don't forget you have your therapy appointment today, Noelle," Cisco tells his sister in a stern tone.

"Of course," she mumbles, her eyes still on the plate.

Cisco doesn't seem satisfied with her reply, but then this appears to be the norm from what I'd observed. Everyone looks after Noelle as the youngest, but they also seem to think her a little out of control—a fact which might prove useful in the future.

I continue to study their interaction and I realize that although Cisco takes a fatherly tone towards her, hers is full of animosity, as if she's conversing with an enemy.

Interesting...

"You know what will happen if you skip once more," he chides, and his wife is quick to try to appease him—again, this seems to be the norm. Cisco will get mad at Noelle and Yuyu will serve as a buffer between the two, often trying to calm Cisco down.

"Right, you'll send me to the looney," she rolls her eyes at him.

"Noelle," Cisco's tone becomes more severe.

"I won't skip, I promise. Is that fine?" She turns to him, batting her lashes at him, practically baiting him to lose his temper.

I barely stifle a scoff as I realize Noelle is finally starting to show some of her real colors—the true colors of *la diabla.*

Her tone is enough to remind me of the nasty bitch I'd met at the *hacienda.*

"Raf," Cisco suddenly calls out, and my attention snaps to him. "Why don't you accompany Noelle to her appointment? I trust you will find something interesting along the way," his lip tugs up as he slowly raises the coffee mug to his mouth.

Yuyu regards her husband with warmth and what can only be described as pride, and that gives me pause.

Besides the odd nature of his request—not so strange since I did agree to offer my services should he need them—Yuyu's reaction doesn't suggest there might be a malicious hidden intent behind it.

I narrow my eyes at him, trying to gauge what he's after.

Noelle chooses that exact moment to burst out in a loud tirade.

"What the hell? Why? I already promised you, Cisco! You don't have to send *him* with me. I'm going to behave, ok? He doesn't have to come anywhere with me," she spares me a glance, and I could swear I see a shiver go down her back when her eyes meet mine.

Satisfaction blooms inside me at the thought that I scare her—oh, but this is just the beginning. And seeing her so outraged at the request, I can't help but bait her.

"It would be an honor, Cisco. I'll make sure your sister gets to the right destination," I dutifully accept.

Noelle turns to me, her eyes widening as she regards me.

"No," she shakes her head. "No. I'm not going anywhere with him!" She states staunchly, getting up and placing her hands on the table. "I'm not going *anywhere* near him," she continues.

"Noelle," Cisco massages his temples, almost out of patience. "Yesterday you were very thrilled to get to know him better. Now you don't want to be anywhere near him?" He asks, raising an eyebrow at her.

"That..." she stammers, looking between me and Cisco, "That..." she fakes a cough, no doubt realizing she's been caught in her own web. "That was yesterday. I've decided I don't like him," she raises her chin proudly.

"You don't like him?" Cisco drawls, narrowing his eyes.

"I'm sorry I rejected your advances, Noelle," I suddenly say, putting on my most stern look. "I didn't think you'd take it so badly, but you must realize it would be wrong of me to engage with the sister of the man I'm working with," I add with a slight shake of my head.

The entire table is quiet.

Noelle is frozen to the spot as she stares at me open mouthed. The tension is palpable in the room, and I can almost feel the slight tremble of her body. I regard her carefully, my eyes trailing over her face—that beautiful face wasted on someone like her—and to her neck, where there's the slightest indication of discomfiture in the way she swallows hard, a sheen of perspiration on her tawny skin. I zero in on a droplet of sweat, watching, almost transfixed as it trails its way from the hollow of her neck to the valley of her breasts...

Catching myself just in time, my gaze snaps back to her face.

"Why... I never..." she stumbles over her words, and the look on her face is priceless. A mix of anger, shock, annoyance and fear—it's all there for me to see and feast on. Why, her feelings of distress taste even better than my breakfast, feeding my need for destruction. There's nothing better than cornering her, getting her out of her comfort zone.

"I don't want things to become awkward between the two of us," I raise my napkin to dab at the corner of my lips, my back straight, my movements sharp and calculated. "I realize someone of your age is easily prone to infatuation, but I hope we can still be friends," I give her a small smile, as if I'm comforting her.

It takes everything in me to keep this game of pretense on—the smile on my face like acid on my tongue. But I don't waver.

This is just the beginning. If her own family thinks she's unstable, then why don't I turn it into reality?

"Noelle," Cisco sighs, while Yuyu gives her a worried look. "Is that why you were so adamant to go to the warehouse yesterday? To throw yourself at him?"

"I didn't..." she's still mumbling incoherently, as if she can't quite believe what's happening.

It seems I've shocked her poisonous tongue in place, and it's becoming harder and harder *not* to gloat at her distress.

"Now, Cisco," I interrupt, putting on the best act of my life. "Don't be too harsh on her. It's a totally normal thing to like someone if they are kind to you. Because that's what happened, isn't it, Noelle? You mistook my kindness for interest."

She's staring at me as if I've sprung a second head, a small frown marring her perfect skin as she blinks rapidly, her mouth opening and closing as she can't seem to find the words to argue back.

"Just because I refused your advances doesn't mean we can't continue on good terms. And to show you I'm not mad, I *will* accompany you to your therapist appointment," I lean back in my seat, plastering on a pleasant smile.

"Raf, you don't have to," Cisco sighs, looking between the two of us. "Maybe I was mistaken," he mumbles under his breath, but I'm quick to get a read of the situation, and my inner delight only increases as I file away another piece of information I might exploit later.

"Noelle..." Amo turns to his sister, "when did you have time? I turned my back maybe for a minute and you..." He bangs his hand on the table in frustration, making her jump up, her expression filled with apprehension.

"I didn't," she makes a poor attempt at defending herself. "I swear I didn't. He's lying," she points at me in a vicious tone. "You're lying! Just admit it! You're doing this for revenge, aren't you? Is this your little game of making me suffer?" she asks in an accusatory tone, but before I can intervene to stop her from mentioning something that might interfere with my plans, Cisco does it for me.

"Enough! For God's sake, Noelle! Revenge? Now I've heard it all. Why would he want revenge on you?" He shakes his head in disappointment. "I'll have a few words with your therapist about your delusions. This has gone on for too long. Hear that, revenge," he scoffs at her.

"But...but..." she tries to argue, incensed.

"No buts, Noelle. In fact, please apologize to our guest," he motions towards me.

"What? Of course not. It's not my fault!"

"Noelle," Cisco calls her name in an exasperated tone, and she notices too because she shrinks a little in her seat. "Apologize before I take away more of your privileges. Is that what you want? No access to your phone? Or to your laptop? Or maybe no more outings, either."

"You can't do that," she whispers, her eyes wide as she seems to barely stop herself from bursting into tears.

"I am your legal guardian in case you've forgotten. So yes, I can," he gives her a stern look.

She pouts, her expression defiant. For a moment I'm sure she's going to refuse, but then she turns towards me, her eyes shooting daggers at me as she says the words.

"I'm sorry," she mumbles in a low voice.

"I don't think I heard you," I say as I lean in, waiting for her to repeat the words. I heard her very well the first time, but considering how the words burn on her tongue, I can't pass on the opportunity of seeing her catch fire—this time for good. "Can you repeat that?" A smile pulls at my lips as I note the flames that spread to her eyes. She's looking at me as if she'd like nothing better than to kill me on the spot, and that's exactly the type of reaction I want from her.

I want her uncomfortable.

"I'm sorry," she repeats, louder but still on a mumble, looking completely dejected as she settles back in her seat. Her gaze is set on mine as she stares at me for a few more seconds, the intensity in her eyes promising retribution at some point in time.

Before she turns away, though, I feel compelled to bait her, and I mouth a low *bring it on* to her.

"It's ok. I won't hold it against you," I immediately add playfully, trying to lighten the mood at the table and distract the others from our little hidden exchange. "I'm not opposed to getting to know each other a little better, but insta-love isn't really my thing," I add jokingly, and everyone but her bursts into laughter.

I, too, pretend to be amused by the situation, but while my lips are tugged up in a perpetual smile, it doesn't reach my eyes.

My nostrils flare slightly, but everyone seems to be oblivious to our dynamic. In fact, my little lie seems to be received as an inherent truth, and it gives me even more ammunition against Noelle. Because now I know even her family won't help her.

I doubt anyone will.

The little bitch turns to me, her expression that of a feral cat that wants to jump on that which she considers a danger. Ah, but her mask is slipping. Seeing as the atmosphere at the table is decidedly not in her favor, she refrains from jumping at *me*.

I continue with my act, feigning amusement at her tantrums, though both Cisco and Amo keep making excuses for her behavior.

The meal goes on and I note Yuyu leaning towards Noelle as they engage in a heated conversation.

The corner of my mouth twitches in amusement as I realize I

can truly end her. No matter what lies I tell, no one will believe her. And it's all I need to know to address Cisco in a pleasant voice.

"Cisco," I start, taking a sip of my water and making my body language seem natural. "Since we're in the same industry, so to speak," I give him a smile, which he returns, "I was wondering about your take on a certain thing."

"Do tell," he nods at me.

"What would *you* do if someone killed your loved one?" He raises an eyebrow, but I just keep going. "How would you punish them?"

"Anyone in particular we're thinking about?"

"I'm sure you can guess," I give a vague reply, letting my gaze roam around the table to find a wide eyed Noelle staring at me with none of the aggression from earlier, just fear—palpable, sweet fear.

"That is a very complex question," Cisco chuckles, turning to his wife.

"You asked the right person," Yuyu purses her lips to stifle a laugh. "He's been known to try a thing or two before."

Amo settles back in his chair, shaking his head—clearly aware of Yuyu's implication.

"Total annihilation," Cisco states, his expression suddenly serious. "And I don't mean death, though that may work in extreme cases. But killing someone..." he pauses, taking Yuyu's hand in his and bringing it to his lips for a kiss, "would never be enough. No, my method is total annihilation of the heart and soul. Take everything from them until nothing remains but the shell. Afterwards, you can choose whether to kill them or not, but I find that death in that case would be a mercy."

"Interesting," I tip my head up, my eyes on him, though I'm still focused on Noelle from the periphery of my gaze, watching the play of emotions on her face and how she's becoming increasingly fidgety.

"You kill the inside and the outside quickly follows. Identify what they value the most, and attack that at full force."

"Like what you did with Guerra years ago," I observe.

Cisco pauses, but the amusement never leaves his face.

"Exactly what I did to Guerra," he smirks.

He'd identified my father's weakness—his obsession with his social standing and a need to get richer and richer—and he'd struck, using my sister Gianna to make our family the laughing-stock of the entire Upper East Side. I'd been in my early teens then, but I still remember the scandal, and the fact that my sister had disappeared soon after.

"Brilliant," I praise, showing there's no bad blood. Since I'd found out from some sources that my sister was living happily with her husband and children *outside* the famiglia, then there's nothing to begrudge. "I might borrow your tactic."

"Please do," he smiles wolfishly, "but remember it's always a war of attrition—never a blitzkrieg. The more you draw it out, the more they suffer."

"Indeed," I drawl, and just at that moment, Noelle jumps out of her seat, excusing herself to go change for her therapy appointment.

Chapter Thirteen

Rafaelo

As I wait for Noelle to meet me at the car, I can't help but think back to Cisco's actions and innuendoes and suspect he might have another plan afoot. Otherwise, why invite me to accompany his sister when I am, for lack of a better word, a ticking bomb? With the bounty over my head, even having the protection entourage on which he'd insisted, could prove dangerous. Why risk the safety of his sister like that?

Although the entire thing raises some question marks, I'm not about to pass up a great opportunity. After all, it's not that easy to find myself alone with Noelle. Certainly, it won't be now that she knows my intentions and considering the fear in her eyes.

Leaning against the car, I spare a glance to the other black car waiting behind—our protection detail for the day.

I have to wonder if the news that I'm back and under DeVille protection has reached Michele's ears. A small chuckle escapes me as I imagine just how he'd react—breaking something, no doubt.

But my mirth is quickly dispelled as the object of my disdain makes her appearance. She's wearing a black blouse that's fitted to her torso and a pair of high-waisted black jeans, both of which emphasize the contours of her curves. Catching the direction of my errant thoughts, I curse myself as I step aside, motioning for her to get in first.

Her upper lip twitches in displeasure at the sight of me. And as she gets inside the car, she slams the door closed after her, locking it. Catching a glimpse of a cheeky smile, I know this journey won't be easy.

Shaking my head, I quickly round the car, snatching the other door open before she has time to lock it too.

A scowl on her face as she sees me get in, she moves as far away from me as possible.

Taking a deep breath, I calm myself until the car starts moving, our entourage following close behind. When we're a safe distance away from the house, I simply roll up the partition and mute the speakers so the driver can't hear us.

"What... What are you doing?" She eyes me warily, crowding herself in that one corner as she fidgets with her hands in her lap.

The tinted windows make it so that the entire interior of the car is swathed in darkness, even though the sun is shining outside. Her face is bathed in shadows, but even so, I can make out the chiseled contours of her features, her small nose tipped upwards and the sharpness of her cheeks. Her mouth, slightly parted as her labored breath makes it through her lips, is small and dainty—like the rest of her.

She looks the epitome of innocence, all of it crowned by her eyes. Sometimes brown, sometimes green, depending how the light hits them, her eyes are round and big, speaking of naïveté and kindness—the exact opposite of her personality. She is the poster child for the old adage that appearances deceive, and my hands ball into fists the more I stare at her.

I'm mad at her for simply existing, but I'm also mad at myself. For noticing her. For noticing more than I *ever* should.

"Isn't it obvious? I'm giving us some privacy," I give her a wide smile as I settle comfortably in my seat opposite hers, raising an eyebrow as I dare her to do something about it.

"Oh, is this the first step in your torture? What were you and my brother calling it," she purses her lips, "total annihilation of the heart?"

"Bingo," I snap my fingers at her in a mock salute.

"Well," she forces a smile, bending forward. A beam of light hits her face, highlighting that beauty that I'd learned to abhor. "Too bad," she whispers in a low voice, "you chose someone who has nothing to lose, nor a heart to annihilate," she adds confidently.

"Is that so?" I parry. There's still quite the distance between us, but I can feel her presence filling the entire space. Her smell, in particular, floods my nostrils the moment she shifts in her seat. A mix of magnolia and bergamot, it leaves a sweet yet spicy taste behind as I feel her flavor on my tongue.

A sliver of annoyance spears through me, my body tense as I barely hold myself back from causing her bodily harm.

Barely.

"Everyone has something to lose, Noelle."

I speak from personal experience. I may not value anything currently, but my pending revenge *is* something I would not like to be taken away from me—after all, it's the only thing keeping me going. "It's just a matter of hitting the right spot," I mention and she blinks, frowning. "And you..." I trail off, enjoying unsettling her, "you do have something to lose." I smirk.

She looks at me intently before scoffing, bringing her arms over her chest in a way that emphasizes the swell of her breasts, beckoning my eyes to focus there instead on the matter at hand.

I quickly catch myself, my eyes narrowing as I realize what she's trying to do.

"Really? Let me guess. The fact that my brother thinks I may have a thing for you?" She smiles. "Why would you even go for that? Out of ideas, golden boy?"

I raise an eyebrow at her.

"Golden boy?" I ask, amused, before my expression turns serious.

In one second I have her by the throat as I lean into her, my voice caressing her earlobe. "That," I start with a dry chuckle, noting the shiver that goes down her body. She's holding herself still, but I can tell she's *not* unaffected. "Is just the beginning. By the time I'm done with you, no one is going to believe a word from your mouth."

"What..." she brings her hands up, her palms pushing at my shoulders.

"But it's not as if it wasn't true, now, was it?" I ask in an arrogant tone. "I see how you look at me," I purr seductively.

"What are you talking about?" She tries to protest, struggling in my hold.

Turning her head to the side, I grip her jaw as I stare into her eyes, our faces millimeters apart. I'm so close, her scent is even stronger as it settles on my tongue, the taste of her counterfeit sweetness nauseating.

"You like what you see, don't you? I don't disgust you now. You'd fuck me now that I'm not a slave anymore, wouldn't you?" I ask in a sinister tone, my fingers tightening over her delicate skin.

Ah, but it would be so easy to break it. Just a little more force and...

"I don't know what you're talking about," her voice quivers. "You're insane," she whispers, trying to turn away so she wouldn't meet my eyes anymore.

"Look at me!" I command. "You don't get to lie to me, Noelle. Not when I can see the truth reflected in your eyes. The lust, the desire," I chuckle, "the fact that you're horrified about it..." I trail off and her eyes flicker in reaction. "But most of all I see the guilt. The way you flinch when I talk about the past."

She moves her head from side to side, slowly shaking her head, her big eyes widening with fear.

"No," she whispers, and her husky voice full of fear does things to my self-control. It makes me want to put it on repeat, make her forever repent for what she's done.

"Come on, admit it," I laugh derisively. "Here, I'll even let you cop a feel," I say as I grab her wrist, bringing her palm to my chest. "I'm not trash staining your carpet now, am I?" I smirk as I take in her expression. Because she might deny it all she wants, but behind all the fear and disgust, there *is* desire.

"I don't know what you're talking about," she continues with her feeble pretense, still seeking to look away from me.

"You do," I snort. "What, now that I'm not just meat and bones waiting to wither away I'm suddenly a human being? A man?" I taunt her, getting even closer to her and succeeding in making her squirm. "Say it, Noelle," I brush my mouth across her jaw and her skin reacts immediately, goosebumps appearing all over. "Say it. Say what a fucking hypocrite you are!"

"Let me go," she tries to push me, but I easily subdue her. "Let me go!" She yells.

One minute she's struggling to move past me, the next I have her sprawled on the seat, my hand on her throat as I loom over her.

A maniacal smile erupts on my face as I see her wild eyes and the way terror seeps into them as she realizes there's no way out.

Her arms are flailing by the side as she hits and scratches, trying to get out of my hold.

"Yes," I purr, her attempts only increasing my enjoyment of the moment, "fight me. Fight me, Noelle, because even *I* feel sorry destroying someone as pathetic as you. So show me all that fight you have in you," I laugh at her.

She stops, going completely still as she turns her eyes to me, blinking.

"Kill me," she suddenly says, completely serious. "Kill me then. If my existence offends you so much, then kill me. But that's not going to bring Lucero back."

My hands tighten instinctively at the mention of Lucero's name and her breath catches in her throat as I apply more pressure.

"Don't you dare say her name!"

"Why? Didn't you say I killed her?" she grits out, her voice harsh.

"You..." my nostrils flare in anger at her gall.

My thumb brushes against her pulse point, and I feel the raging storm inside her body. For all the bravado on her face, it's all a pretense.

"Tell me why and I might just do it," I lie. Because even if she tells me, I won't go easy on her.

Her brother was right that death is a way out. No, the punishment should be life—hell on earth. The only type of suffering someone like her deserves.

She shakes her head, trying to move out of my hold.

"I can't."

"Why?" A sick smile pulls at my lips. "Afraid I'd find out how depraved you are, *sweetheart?*" Her eyes flash at the mock endearment. "Well, newsflash. Nothing about you surprises me."

A twitch in her eye alerts me that I hit a sore spot.

"Fuck. You!" she enunciates right before she spits at me, her saliva hitting my right cheek.

"Right," I chuckle, "you wish." Holding on to her with one hand, I wipe my cheek with the back of my other hand.

Her lips purse in aggression and her feral look from before is back. She sure has a lot of fight in her for someone who was just asking me to kill her moments ago.

"Why? Why can't you tell me?" I ask, deciding to play her game.

"You wouldn't believe me anyway, so go ahead and kill me," she simply says, raising her chin a notch to imbue some arrogance into her words—of course, only fitting of *la diabla*.

"Tell me anyway," I indulge her, curious what she'd cook up.

Those big eyes stare at me as she seems to search for her words, opening her mouth and closing it several times before she says something that has *me* pinned to the spot.

"I don't remember."

I blink at her, waiting for the joke to come. But she doesn't seem amused.

"I don't remember anything from the fire," she repeats, and fuck me...she's serious.

One second I'm staring at her, the next laughter bubbles in my throat, and I can't help myself as I simply fall back, holding to my midriff as I let amusement overtake me.

She quickly gets up, taking advantage of my distraction and dragging herself to the other end of the seat.

"You're slipping, *Raf,*" she snickers. "What will you tell my brother when he sees the marks on my neck?" She presses her fingers lightly to her neck, massaging the skin I abused.

Even in the poor lighting of the car I can see that I've likely left some prints on her, but the prospect only makes me more delighted.

I shrug, completely at ease as I settle comfortably in my seat.

"Really, Noelle?" I shake my head at her. "I thought you were smarter than that."

There's a pause as she frowns at me, clearly not understanding my innuendo.

"I'm sure your brother will understand that you might be into some kinky shit," I smirk. "Especially with all that crazy buried inside of you."

Her face falls in outrage at my words and she scurries even further, her back hitting the door.

"You're insane," she mutters, her eyes unblinking.

"I'm not. Not really. Certainly not like you."

"I'm not crazy."

"Uhum," I mockingly agree. "If you say so."

"I'm not," she says more vehemently. "And I didn't kill Lucero either."

"I thought you didn't remember?" I raise an eyebrow.

"That..." her brows pinch together in a frown. "I don't. But I'm sure I didn't kill her. I couldn't have. Not when she was my friend."

"Do you abuse all your friends?" I retort, watching her blench. The more she talks the more disgusted I become by the lies she's spewing and how she's trying to cover her tracks.

"I've never abused Lucero," she whispers, but there's guilt both in her eyes and in her voice, her tone slightly lower than before, and a bitter flavor coats my tongue at the sound.

"Liar."

"I'm telling the truth," she cries out.

"Liar," I continue, slowly advancing towards her.

There's nowhere to run anymore, so when I grab her arm, bringing her close to me and pinning her to my body, she can only attempt to fight me but without succeeding.

"You're such a liar, Noelle," the corner of my lip tugs up in a derisive smile. "Such a little liar." I muse out loud, her fiery eyes shooting daggers at me as she tries to stare me down. It's all quite entertaining, really.

A slip of a girl who cannot even escape my grasp, but who thinks her aggressive glare will deter me.

"I'm telling the truth," she replies, her tone confident this time. "Better yet, ask my therapist. She'll gladly tell you I have amnesia," she quips in satisfaction.

"Hmm," I murmur, leaning even closer and noting the way her body reacts to mine in spite of her fear—in spite of everything. A tremor goes down her spine, and I feel her boneless in my arms—entirely at my mercy.

"You're really devious, Noelle. Well played," I praise her. "You might have everyone else fooled, but I'm on to you." I tell her just as the car draws to a halt.

She wastes no time in pushing me off her and unlocking the door, rushing out of the car and into the building.

Chapter Fourteen
Rafaelo

I don't follow her, allowing her a brief reprieve while she undoubtedly plays the victim to her therapist. Instead, I occupy my time by going over the footage Panchito had managed to get of Michele. It's not much, but at least it's something.

My relationship with Michele had changed after we'd gone through puberty. We stopped being on good terms, both of us coping with the expectations placed on us differently. At the same time, we'd both put on masks for the world, so while I do know him, I don't—not really.

From the recent reports I'd gotten, it seems that Michele had been hiding more than his personality—but also an affinity for numbers.

When I'd realized he'd taken over the family business, I'd thought that he was going to run it into the ground within the year. To my eternal surprise, he hadn't.

If anything, he'd turned things around in such a way Benedicto could have only hoped to do.

He'd revived old businesses and invested smartly, all resulting in an increase in the family's net worth and marking his ventures as competitive and advantageous to the outside world—the reason Ortega's been trying to do business with him in the first place.

I have to wonder if this is all him, or if he was just wise enough to hire smart people for the job. Regardless, the more I find out about Michele, the more I realize I don't know my brother at all.

Starting the footage, it's to see him walk out of a building with an arrogant stride, his sunglasses perched up his nose as he looks right and left. There's an entire entourage of people behind him, following closely. And as he raises his head in the direction of the camera, lowering his glasses and narrowing his eyes at the lens, he goes into a tirade. His men are quick to react, one of them raising a weapon and shooting the camera.

Interesting.

The rest of the video feeds tell a similar story—they'd all captured him unaware after which he'd promptly gotten rid of the camera. And going by the few other details I have on him, it's safe to say his paranoia knows no bounds.

He doesn't like to be seen in public, or be captured by cameras. He rarely attends events, even though his presence is required at all times. If anything, the only time he seems to get out is during the night, with a few road cameras capturing his car on the freeway.

In the past, Michele had been nothing if not ostentatious, so to see him shying away from public appearances and taking so much care *not* to be spotted is intriguing.

I mark down some observations, but as I realize I'd been too immersed in my work, I quickly check the time, noting Noelle is running late.

Cisco's words ring in my ears and I can't help but think she might have tried to run away—apparently it wouldn't be the first time.

A scowl on my face, I instruct the driver to wait for us while I head directly to the therapist's office.

The elevator pings as I arrive at the right floor, and as I get out, it's to see Noelle in the hallway, chatting with another woman.

Narrowing my eyes at her, I take a step forward. But as the other woman turns, I freeze, feeling myself rooted to the spot.

She gives Noelle a smile as she brushes her hand down her arm in a comforting gesture. A slow smile appears on Noelle's face, her expression unguarded for the first time. But as she turns her head in my direction, her soft features become harsh as she glares at me. A nod at the woman by her side and she starts in my direction.

I'm not entirely concerned by her, though. Not when someone I hadn't seen in years is right in front of me.

"Wait for me at the car, Noelle," I bark the order, my voice leaving no room for discussion as her eyes widen. "Now."

I don't wait for her protest as I put one foot in front of another until I'm standing in front of the other woman.

She turns, finally noticing me.

Her lips part in surprise, her honey colored eyes sparkling with warmth as she gazes at me.

One moment we're both staring at one another, the next she runs towards me, jumping in my arms.

"Raf," she whispers as she wraps her arms around me in a tight hug.

"God, Gianna," I mutter in disbelief. "This was the last place I would have thought to see you."

"Well," she says sheepishly as she steps back, looking me up and down. "I might have had some words with Cisco."

It dawns on me why he'd suggested I accompany Noelle to her therapy appointment.

"Cisco?" I ask in disbelief, since he'd been the main culprit behind her fall from grace all those years ago.

"It's a long story," she mentions, quickly going over how she'd married her bodyguard, Cisco's uncle, and had reconnected with the family a while back because her husband had been worried about Noelle.

"We agreed I could try to talk to her since none of her previous therapists managed to break her out of her shell," she says grimly as she gives me a short account of what she'd been up to in the years that have passed and that she'd become a trained therapist.

The more she talks about Noelle and her problems, I can't help myself but ask.

"Is it true she has amnesia then?"

"Raf... You might be my brother, but she's my patient," she gives me a sad smile. "I can't tell you that."

"Just a yes or no," I insist, needing some type of confirmation.

"Her condition is delicate," she replies cryptically. "Be kind to her, will you? Some of the things she's been through..." she shakes her head.

"Are you sure she's not faking it?"

Her eyes widen at my question.

"No, she's not faking anything, Raf." She purses her lips for a moment. "I'm sorry I can't tell you more, but I will say this. Don't judge a person until you've walked a mile in their shoes. There's more to her than meets the surface. But then, you're familiar with that type of defense mechanism, aren't you?"

My cheeks heat and feeling a little chastised, I drop the topic. I focus instead on her and what she's been up to. She tells me about her family, showing me pictures of her daughters.

"They look like you," I note affectionately, her girls having inherited her beauty.

"You should come visit sometimes," she adds, her voice full of warmth.

"Maybe," I reply vaguely. Given the dangerous situation I currently find myself in, I don't think it would be the safest course of action to bring them into this mess.

We make some more small talk before she tells me she has to go since her husband is waiting for her. And as I lead her outside of the building, she gives me one more hug before we part ways. But not before she adds something.

"Be careful with Michele, Raf. He's... He's not well."

"I know. Trust me, I know. I'll see you around," I tell her, kissing both her cheeks.

As I get back in the car, Noelle is looking at me with distaste in her eyes. Huddled at the far end of the car seat, she's trying to put as much distance between us—again.

"Don't worry," I wave my hand flippantly. "I won't bite—this time." I wink at her before turning and ignoring her as I try to absorb what just happened, and the fact that I saw my sister for the first time in over twelve years.

"Why? Don't tell me you're too tired," she snaps, and I regard her with raised brows, surprised at the vehemence in her voice.

"Too tired?" I repeat, a little confused.

"That was quite the quickie, golden boy," she crosses her arms over her chest.

"Quickie?"

"She's married, you know," she shakes her head at me, disgust written all over her face.

It takes me a moment until it finally dawns on me what she's talking about, confusion leaving way to amusement at her reaction.

"Why? Jealous?" I taunt, and her eyes flash aggressively at me. "Maybe I have a thing for married women," I shrug as I continue to bait her, enjoying the way she's getting so riled up over nothing.

"You..." she grits her teeth. "I like her. If she cancels on me because of you, I'll kill you myself," she threatens, though I'm not sure how she means to be taken seriously when she's five feet at best and a hundred pounds soaking wet.

Even now, as she points at me with her finger, her stance that of a warrior, I can only stifle my laughter for so long.

"Interesting," I muse, and she blinks repeatedly at my words.

"What?" She snickers.

"Just a few hours ago you were ready to become my victim," I smirk as I come closer to her, all thoughts of Gianna and our encounter firmly out of my mind. "But now you're willing to commit murder for your therapist? My, my, Noelle," I whistle.

When I'm just a breath away from her she stiffens, her eyes shining with a new resolve as she tries to stare at me unflinchingly.

"You can't have her," she repeats, fake confidence imbuing her harsh voice.

"I can't?" I drawl, my amusement increasing by the second.

"No. You can't. So find another married woman, or whatever. Just not my therapist," she continues with the fake bravado, and there's something to be said about the way she's ready to die one moment, and appear so strong the next.

Bringing the back of my hand to her cheek, I brush it ever so slightly against her skin. Her breath hitches, her eyes growing in size as she meets my eyes.

"You'll learn, Noelle, that the more you tell me I can't..." I trail off, a slow smile spreading on my face, "the more I want to do it," I tell her on a whisper before I'm off her.

I move back to my seat, continuing to ignore her as I see about my business, but failing as the corner of my eye keeps straying to her and her awestruck expression. I certainly try to ignore the way she grumbles under her breath, her insults a melody to my ears.

Total annihilation of the heart...

Noelle claims to have no heart, yet that remains to be seen.

Crushed.

I sneak a glance at her, the mere fact of her being alive and well offending me.

Yes, she will be crushed.

And I have just the way to do it.

It's when we reach the house, however, that I realize Noelle isn't the simpleton I'd thought her to be.

When Cisco greets us, raising an eyebrow at his sister as he awaits the report, she can barely hide her smug expression as she starts talking.

"I think therapy is good for me," she mentions, giving me an inscrutable look.

"Is that so?" Cisco asks, unconvinced.

"It is," she nods thoughtfully, "it helped me realize that my infatuation with Raf was extremely shallow," she shakes her head ruefully. "I mean, why would I like him just because of his good looks, right?"

"Right..." Cisco repeats slowly, confused, his eyes skittering from me to her.

"I admit I was taken aback by how handsome he is," she continues, pursing her lips when she sees a smile erupt on my face.

"And?" Cisco asks impatiently.

"But he's so boring, Cisco," she cries out and my eyes widen in surprise.

"He's boring?" His eyes meet mine as he tries hard not to burst into laughter.

"He's like a grandpa in the body of a young man. Not my definition of fun," she sighs dramatically. "He doesn't have social media," she points at me in disappointment, "doesn't watch any current TV shows, and *only* reads some weird and boring books. He might as well be playing chess with the geezers in the park."

"Noelle..."

"That's why you sent him with me, didn't you? So I could see how boring he was," she purses her lips in understanding. "I get it. You wanted me to experience it on my own skin."

Cisco is speechless as he turns to me.

"Boring, is he now," he drawls, amused.

I just shrug, not deigning a reply. Not when little miss crazy is gloating at me, her lip twitching in satisfaction.

Instead, I merely play her game, taking a few steps towards her and grabbing her hand. Spreading her palm open, I place a key in the center.

"I don't think I'll need this if I'm so boring then," I add right before I move past her and her scandalized expression, giving a nod to Cisco and going upstairs to my own room.

I can barely hold off a chuckle as I hear Noelle trying to find excuses as to why the key to her room had ended up in my possession.

I have to give her credit at least for her attempt at countering my attack.

Not enough though.

She'll need more than that to beat me at my own game.

Chapter Fifteen

Michele

Bringing the whiskey glass to his lips, he watched the people walking up and down the road, their bodies tiny dots from where he was standing.

Since he'd taken over the family business, he'd found that he did not want to remain in the house that served as a reminder of his failure—the very definition of his nightmare. As soon as he'd had full control over the Guerra assets, he'd started a crusade of eradicating everything that reminded him of the past—of his childhood and of his teenage years when he'd been little else than a stain on the carpet for everyone to step on.

A slow smirk pulled at his lips as he remembered how they had all reacted when they'd suddenly found themselves on their knees and swearing allegiance to *him*. And he'd made that one ceremony even more memorable by having each man previously under his father's command crawl to him to kiss the ring that designated him their de facto ruler.

He'd taken a knife and plunged it deep in the core of the organization, cleaning it and getting rid of everyone who'd had something against him.

Once he'd felt satisfied with the results, he'd rewarded himself, tearing down the Guerra house and moving into a penthouse in one of the most exclusive areas of the city.

That was why his routine of watching people from his lofty place —those ant-like figures down below—brought him so much satisfaction. It was the physical evidence of everything he'd accomplished in such a short time. Of everything that should have been his from the beginning.

His fingers tightened over the glass as foreign thoughts intruded in his mind. A few years had already passed since he'd gotten rid of those who'd mocked and scorned him. Yet why didn't he feel completely at peace?

Why was there still a gnawing feeling within him? One that clawed deep at his conscience and urged him to do more—hunt more, kill more, destroy more?

He reckoned it was a side effect of finding out his dear brother had returned home. He'd heard the rumors a long time ago. Rafaelo was currently affiliated with an unknown cartel that went by the name of Fenix.

But it was more than that. It was the fact that he'd *dared* to come back and challenge him. Because his mere presence in New York was a challenge in itself.

When he'd gotten word of Rafaelo's new friends, and the fact that he'd made his new home somewhere on the border between Mexico and New Mexico, he'd been pissed. Royally pissed. After all, he'd gone to great lengths to ensure that his brother never saw the light of the day again.

And he'd been ready to let go.

If only Rafaelo had stayed put.

After the anger at his failed plan had subsided, he'd been smart in ensuring that while alive, Rafaelo would never be a danger to him—by putting a bounty on his head.

Every assassin on the East Coast had been notified of the price on Rafaelo Guerra's head, and Michele had been satisfied in knowing that no one would ever dare to face such danger.

It seems he'd misjudged his brother.

He pursed his lips, a small frown marring his perfect features.

Truth was, he'd made all his calculations on the meek persona Rafaelo had projected to the world, and that had been *his* mistake.

He'd known, for years, that there was more to his brother than met the eyes, his sudden speech impairment rather fortuitous considering the circumstances of the time. But while he'd suspected Rafaelo wasn't who he portrayed himself to be, he'd never thought he would be *this* shrewd. Foolish might be a better word for it, since only fools knowingly head straight for the guillotine.

He had to admit to himself that while the threat of the bounty was hanging over Rafaelo's head, and with him tucked away to God knows where but away from him, Michele hadn't planned on further retaliation. Which, he suspected now, had been a critical miscalculation.

Because had he eradicated the problem from the root, he would not be dealing with this right now. He would be able to enjoy everything he'd so hard toiled to achieve and get on with his *other* plans.

Allowing himself a minute to get his anger under control, he started plotting again. He might have taken mercy on Rafaelo once before. But now that he was on *his* territory, he was going to have to play by *his* rules.

And Michele wasn't known for playing fair. Far from it. He was known for chaos and disorder, his mercurial moods legendary among his men. And given his reputation…one thing was for sure.

This war would *not* be fair.

The corner of his lip curled up in anticipation, the smell of blood already flooding his nostrils, his brother's screams singing in his ears.

This time he'd make sure that Rafaelo *never* saw the light of the day again. And after he was done with his brother, he could continue his other order business—the remaining *pièce de resistance.*

Downing the remnants of his drink, he flexed his arm, throwing the glass at the wall-high window, shattering it to pieces. The whiskey glass fell to the ground below, the sound of a car alarm going off as it signaled it had gotten hit.

Almost entranced, he watched the hole in the window and how it increased in size, fractures appearing around the rim, the entire glass becoming a liability. One kick, just one kick, and the entire thing would fall.

He was *almost* inclined to see it through, but before he could take one more step, the door to his office opened, one of his men striding inside.

"There's someone to see you, sir."

He turned, one side of the face bathed in shadows while the other was suffused with sunlight.

"Who?" He asked, almost whimsically.

"Your sister, sir," the man gulped down, looking anywhere but directly at Michele.

Since he'd taken over the family, rumors had abounded about his personality and his explosive temper. More than a few men had experienced on their own skin what it meant to get on his bad side, and since then everyone took to handling Michele with kid gloves —always careful not to incite his ire.

And as the man's eyes skittered to the hole in the window, he was suddenly even more afraid he'd popped in at the wrong time.

"Show her in," Michele shrugged, turning from the window and coming around his table just as his sister, Gianna, appeared in the doorway.

"To what do I owe this pleasure?" he drawled, taking out two more glasses from his drawer and filling them with whiskey.

Gianna narrowed her eyes at him, regarding him as skeptically as he'd come to expect of her.

She'd left the family more than a decade ago, and she was the only one he'd never blamed for his descent in Tartarus. On the other hand, she'd also *not* been there to save him from it.

He couldn't fault her for leaving, though. Not when their illustrious father planned to sell her to a vile man more than twice her age. That she'd fallen in love with someone else along the way had been rather fortuitous.

She'd been the only one to see him as a human, not as a monster, and for that she'd always have his loyalty. In fact, it could be argued that she was the only person towards whom he'd ever acted in a selfless manner.

Alas, that was a lifetime ago, and many, *many* things had changed since then.

Not least of all *him*.

After he'd dispatched their father, Benedicto, and step mother, Cosima, he'd reached out to Gianna, extending her an invitation to return to her rightful place. She hadn't wanted to do that, and he'd respected her decision.

That hadn't stopped her, however, from continuing her communication with him.

And he knew why, too.

She could see the instability in him that sought to be released—the fact that he was a ticking bomb. She noticed something wrong with him and sought to correct it, thinking her degree in psychology made her an expert on *his* psyche.

And he'd let her. He'd even indulged her, every now and then, because in his mind, she was the only link to normality he still had. The only remnant of his old life—one where he'd been happy, albeit briefly.

"What did the poor window do to you?" She shook her head as she stepped deeper into the room, placing her bag on a chair as she quietly assessed him.

"Here," he handed her a glass, swirling around the amber liquid in his own as he waited for her to get to the point.

He knew *exactly* why she was here. The only reason she'd come to *his* home.

They stood in silence for a moment, each taking a sip of their glass, their eyes meeting in a small confrontation.

"Raf is back," she finally said, and he barely stopped a smile from overtaking his features.

He'd been right.

"So?" He raised an eyebrow.

"I want to ask you to leave him alone."

Gianna strengthened her back as she looked him straight in the eye. She was one of the few people who didn't cower in front of him, even though it was only a front. He knew that inside, she was terrified.

He could see the slightly erratic pulse at the base of her throat. She wasn't fooling anyone with her bravado, though he could admire the attempt.

"Why?" He simply asked, leaning back against his desk and assuming a relaxed stance.

"Because he's your brother, Michele. I know Benedicto and Cosima deserved what they got, but Raf?" She shook her head. "What did he ever do to you?"

He stared at her in silence for a second before he burst into laughter.

"What he did to me?" He laughed, turning so only his profile was visible to her.

That one question had the power to destroy his carefully curated calm.

What did he do, indeed?

"You forget, Gianna," he started, walking towards the broken window and tracing the fractured glass with his fingers, the sharp edge cutting into his skin and drawing blood, "that he's not my brother. Not really."

"Michele," she tried to protest, but he shushed her, turning and raising his bloody hand towards her.

"He's not my blood, is he?" He continued, his nostrils flaring at the thought.

"You grew up together..."

"So?" He tilted his head as he looked at her. Really looked at her.

His sister's beauty hadn't waned over the years. If anything, it was even more striking, her face the definition of symmetrical perfection. It was something they had both inherited from their mother, but whereas Gianna had also inherited her blonde hair from her father—like Rafaelo—he hadn't. He'd inherited *his* father's black hair. And *that* was the root of all evil.

He turned sharply, advancing towards her and noting the slight twitch in her eye—she *was* afraid.

Lifting his fingers to his mouth, he licked the blood, all the while never breaking eye contact.

"You should go, *sister,*" he said, his tone crisp and clear. "You won't find here what you're looking for. My problem with Rafaelo does not concern you."

She blinked, her body stiff. He recognized the inner battle within her as she tried to keep her ground and not show any fear.

"No. I'm sure we can talk about this like adults, Michele. I know about the bounty on his head… Please call it off."

"Fine," he answered, watching her expression closely. One small pause and immediate relief infused her features. The corners of his mouth tugged up in a sick smile as he leaned down, breathing down her neck. "I'll kill him with my own hands this time. To make sure he's *truly* dead," he spoke in a chilling voice.

"Michele… This isn't you."

"That's where you're wrong, Gianna. This is me. This is the only part of me that's left," he told her, his expression changing to one of disgust as he took a step back, shaking his head at her. "You left. You got your happily ever after. You don't get a say in what happens now when you weren't there."

Guilt marred her exquisite features as she looked away in shame.

"You know I couldn't stay. And you…" she trailed off, swallowing hard. "I wanted to take you with me. You know I did."

"I know. And I would have," he admitted ruefully. "But both of us would have never made it." He turned away, lest she see the truth in his eyes. "You got out. So stay out. It's not your business anymore."

"What could Raf have done to you that's so bad…" her voice was full of anguish as she took a step towards him, her hand on his shoulder in a gentle touch.

But even that soft caress elicited a shudder out of him, something so deep and ugly it threatened to make him ill.

He caught her hand in his gloved one, holding tightly as he looked into her eyes.

In another time, maybe he could have felt something for the affection he gazed into her eyes.

In another time…

Now, he only knew chaos—mind-numbing chaos that threatened to erupt out of him and ripple through his surroundings.

"You want to know what your precious brother did to me?" His mouth curled in a twisted smile as he pushed her, crowding her with his body and relishing the way her face finally gave way to fear, her entire body trembling under his.

"He made me half the monster I am today," he said when her back hit the wall. Stooping down, he brought his mouth to her ear, whispering all the crude details of what had happened—why Raf was not just guilty by default. He'd been tried and judged, and his sentence had been chosen carefully—oh, so carefully.

Her eyes widened in shock, before she bent forward, retching and emptying the contents of her stomach.

That's when he let go. He stepped back, slowly getting the anger rolling off him under control.

"I'm sorry," she whispered. "I'm so very sorry, Michele."

He was already far away. Both physically and mentally.

Shrugging his glove off, he slid his hand through the broken glass, trying to feel the pain as shards of glass became embedded in his flesh. Her platitudes were just like the pressure of the glass—there, but ultimately immaterial, for they couldn't break through his armor anymore.

He was quiet for a moment, and as he heard the door open, his sister almost on her way out, he finally spoke.

"So you see, Gianna, I cannot help you. His fate is sealed, and that of anyone who will try to help him."

Chapter Sixteen
Michele

Long after Gianna had left, he was still rooted to the spot, barely in control of himself as the memories threatened to explode in his mind.

He wanted to believe he'd gotten better over the years at controlling them, but there were times, like this, when any mention of the past brought them to the surface.

He should have known better than to believe that his sister would be on his side. After all, when had *anyone* been on his side? He'd always been in the wrong, even when he'd been in the right, and the memories were *killing* him.

Why was everyone *always* against him?

He paced the entire length of his study, his thoughts an erratic mass of threats, accusations and what ifs. Because now that his sister knew Rafaelo was back in the city…

Would she help him? Would she go to him and warn him that Michele was planning something against him?

Of course she would.

His lip pulled up in distaste.

She'd sell him out like everyone before her. And he could bet it would be under some type of misguided guilt, thinking she could bring the brothers back together.

His ire increased the more he imagined the two of them, laughing together and mocking Michele for his little plans of revenge.

Stopping, he balled his hands into fists, feeling his control slipping.

The sound of their laughter was in his ears, their derisive comments and their mocking insults. Just like those kids when he'd been young, who'd shunned and scorned him for being different. Just like his *father* and stepmother, who'd accused him of being a monster just for the mere fact that he'd been born.

But maybe that was the issue. Why had he been born in the first place? His whore of a mother should have kept her legs closed for once and he wouldn't be having so many problems.

A monster they'd branded him, a monster they'd created.

And after too long of hearing the same insult spewed all over again, he'd transformed its bite into a praise, faithfully *earning* that moniker.

Because he was a monster. He might have been one since birth—though debatable—but he'd certainly become one of his own making. And everyone had felt the wrath of the monster they'd created.

Everyone.

The laughter became louder, and he started hearing Cosima's insults in a loop. He brought his hands to his ears, trying to block the sound. But it wasn't enough. It wasn never enough.

"They hate me," he started uttering, almost incoherently. "Everyone hates me. Everyone wants to end me," he shook his head, sweat clinging to his skin. His field of vision was becoming blurry, his emotions explosive and barely held in check.

Poof.

He grabbed the decanter, throwing it out the window. He repeated the motion with each of the glasses he owned, until barely a few shards of glass remained of the window, the chilly air swinging inside and brushing against his wet skin.

And in a bout of spent adrenaline, he fell to his knees.

Staring into empty space, it took him moments to get himself together—to get his mind out of the gutter it was currently visiting and pull it back up to the safety of *this* reality. Because he'd succeeded. Everyone who'd bullied him was dead. Everyone who'd mocked him was dead.

Everyone *but* Rafaelo.

But he would follow.

Then he would complete his last revenge, and he would reign like he was always meant to—a king among corpses.

Pulling out his phone, he scrolled through his feed, a strange need growing inside of him.

And there she was.

He stopped at the photo. It was clear she'd taken it by herself, the angle telling. She tried to plaster a smile on her face, but even that was forced.

In all their time together, he hadn't known her to smile too often, the gesture almost foreign.

In that, they were equally matched for he could not remember the last time he'd smiled of joy—had he ever?

He studied the contours of her face, marveling at her coloring and the way her eyes seemed to sparkle even in the darkest of corners.

For a toy, she'd certainly fulfilled her purpose, her mere presence offering him the calm of knowing he owned her—she was his and his alone.

He'd never had anything that belonged solely to him. Growing up, Rafaelo had received everything while he'd been forgotten, or purposefully ignored.

He'd never had a toy. He'd never had a possession that belonged just to him.

Not until her.

Perhaps that was why he'd become so obsessed with her presence, though she was just a means to an end. For the first time in his life, he had something. And with the way she was always gazing up at him as if he could pluck the moon from the sky and gift it to her, he didn't think he wanted to give her up.

But give her up he must…at some point. Not now. Certainly not now. Not when his plan was going so smoothly.

He'd successfully implanted himself in her life so deeply, he knew that if he ordered her to die with him tomorrow she would.

He paused, the idea having some merit. He was sure her brother would grieve her loss. Still, eventually he would recover, and he didn't want that. He wanted his revenge to be something that would hit deep and take root, create such a wound never to be healed again.

Through her, he'd gained inside access to her household. Now it was only a matter of figuring out when to hit where it hurt.

But until then, he'd just enjoy her and her unspoiled innocence. Because even that would not last much longer. Not in his caring hands.

He continued to study her profile, looking at every picture in part, though he'd already seen them multiple times in the past.

Research. This was all research. Because he needed to maintain his cover, and most of all, he needed to keep her in his thrall—his obedient little pet. And that meant knowing all of her patterns and everything that made her *her*.

He was nothing if not meticulous when it came to his vengeance. And having planned it for years, he'd ensured he'd taken every step towards establishing a connection with her.

His finger stilled on the screen as he noted a new notification of a picture she'd been tagged in. His brows furrowed, he clicked on it, only to be met with the last thing he would have expected.

There she was, his little pet, standing awkwardly next to another man who *dared* to lay a finger on his property.

There was no time to think. No time to control his actions. He just saw red in front of his eyes. Because his little toy was *his* and his alone. And anyone who tried to steal it…

Abruptly, he stood up. It took him less than a second to dial up his men—the ones who should have been watching her and ensure nothing of that nature ever happened.

And as they promised to promptly report for duty, they soon

made their way to his office, their heads bent low as they entered the room.

"Care to tell me what this is?" he asked in a low voice, passing the phone to one of the men.

He'd chosen them specifically for the job for their unassuming looks. One was tall and gangly, resembling a postman, while the other was bigger and on the heavier side. They looked quite the pair together too, almost reminiscent of the Laurel and Hardy comedy duo.

"That..." the taller one, Kappa, muttered as he sneaked a glance to his partner.

"It must have happened during our lunch break," the other blabbered, his eyes wide as saucers.

"Lunch break?" Michele repeated, pacing around before stopping in front of them. "Lunch break? You took a *fucking* lunch break while she was still out? While she was letting another fucking man touch her shoulder?" His voice boomed, a twitch in his jaw denoting his mounting anger that would soon reach a critical point.

The men had the decency to look ashamed of having been caught slacking on the job, but it wasn't enough.

Michele took a moment to take them in, ugly jealousy forming inside of him and seeking to be let loose.

He hadn't trained his pet just so another man could avail himself to her charms. He hadn't spent so much time courting her just for an insignificant little boy to swoop in and steal her from him.

No, his toy was *his*. And she would soon get her due, too, for having let another touch her.

But first, he needed to deal with the losers that were under his employ. If they couldn't be counted on to skip lunch when his most important asset was out and about, exposed to countless dangers—and God forbid, temptations—then they didn't deserve to live.

They didn't deserve to draw another breath.

He regarded them through the red haze that covered his eyes, their punishment suddenly clear as a smile pulled at his lips.

Without breaking eye contact, he called his right-hand man, Andreas, instructing him to bring a few soldiers with him.

The two men cowered in fear, no doubt knowing what awaited them. Still, they didn't beg for their lives, or seek to run away. They'd known what they were signing up for from the beginning.

Michele could respect the fact that they'd decided to go to their death with dignity, and that thought kept him from going all out. After all, there was quite an impressive collection of weapons displayed on his wall.

He pictured himself taking one of the long swords, cutting them to pieces. It might be satisfying to assuage the thirst for blood that one picture awakened in him. It was, however, not what he needed to ensure that *everyone* realized he wasn't joking around when he assigned jobs.

He'd taken such care in selecting the perfect men to watch over his pet, yet it hadn't worked out.

Andreas strode in, a couple of men in black suits following behind him.

Michele gave him brief instructions, after which he stepped back, lighting a cigarette and watching the ensuing spectacle.

The men in black were already taking hold of the two men, dragging them towards the window.

It was the thirtieth floor, so Michele imagined it would be quite the fall to reach the ground. And with his window already broken, leaving way for his men to hold the two failures over the edge, it was only a matter of giving the signal now.

They were being held tightly right on the edge, the danger of falling making them scream at the top of their lungs in fear.

Michele shook his head. And he'd thought they'd die with dignity.

He'd always thought made men knew what they signed up for when they entered a life of crime. He thought they realized what it meant to work under *him*. He'd made everything clear when he'd killed people left and right, cleansing the famiglia from the inside out. When they'd sworn allegiance to him they'd known he wasn't lenient towards failure, and he was certainly *not* forgiving. If anything, his disposition bordered on the unnaturally maniac and vengeful. Certainly, with his tough beginnings in his position, he had a reputation to uphold.

If you slipped, you died.

It was as simple as that.

"Andreas," Michele spoke, his voice steady for the first time since he'd seen the photo. "Start a timer. I want to know who crashes first," he said, nodding to the two men teetering on the edge.

Andreas grunted, and at Michele's signal, the two men were flung down at the same time. Andreas' hand was on the timer, and soft sounds signaled the crash.

"Leo was first, but only by a millisecond," he reported back.

"Good. Make it public that fatties crash faster to the ground. And if anyone thinks to neglect their positions again, they can explain it to me with their brains scattered on the pavement."

"The police will be here soon," Andreas continued, looking down at the mess down on the ground.

"I trust you'll handle it," he paused, looking around the room. "Get a cleaning crew in here too. And do replace the glass. Something more durable next time," Michele spared him one last look before he took his coat, breezing past the door and heading to his car.

There was just one more matter that needed his urgent attention.

His pet.

He knew she was at home, under the watchful eyes of her family, and the thought of defiling her right in the house of his worst enemy vastly improved his mood.

He drove at full speed out of the city, parking his car at a nearby motel and heading to her house on foot—the only way to avoid the tight security of the place.

It wasn't the first time he'd come to her in her own house, and he'd taken fully advantage of each time he'd managed to successfully infiltrate it, planting bugs and other surveillance devices that were constantly feeding him information on his foe.

And soon his revenge would be done.

Michele might be unusually reckless on a daily basis, but his planning was meticulous and well thought out, probably borne out of his inherent paranoia and a need to control every aspect of his life.

When he reached the house, he used the feed from some of the cameras he'd installed to guide him towards her room, carefully avoiding the guards stationed outside and inside the house.

Only when he opened the door to her room to find her at her computer, her knees to her chest as she was watching a video, did he finally breathe relieved.

It wasn't because he'd been worried about her. No, it would never be that. It was a relief that spoke of the continuation of his plans, because as long as he removed every temptation from her side, she'd be his and his alone. And *then* he could complete his revenge.

That's what he continued to tell himself, though the sight of her in a long, oversized shirt did things to his body, waking him from the slumber he usually found himself in.

At the sound of the door clicking in place, she turned, gasping as she took in his appearance.

He knew he looked good and that she liked what she saw, which only increased the size of his ego as he saw the clear signs of arousal in her eyes.

She stood up, her long legs bare. Her shirt barely reached her ass, and he noted a blush staining her features as she tugged on the hem, trying to cover herself.

"What are you doing here?" she asked in a breathless voice, not daring to meet his eyes.

She was shy. He knew that. She was even shyer in his presence, a fact which he enjoyed tremendously because it spoke of how much he affected her.

"We need to talk," he snarled. Tugging on his leather gloves, he let them fall as he strode towards her.

She whipped her head up, her eyes widening in worry as she regarded him, her teeth slightly grazing her bottom lip. She looked like a fucking temptress and he found himself growing harder by the second. He liked the look of fear on her—it fed his inner demons in a way nothing else could.

"What...what happened?" She stammered ever so slightly, backing away from him.

In two steps he was in front of her, his hand on her jaw as he gripped tightly, forcing her to look him in the eye.

"I saw the picture," was all he said and her eyes immediately widened with awareness.

"It wasn't...it wasn't what it looked like. They were just making fun of me," she whispered, looking down.

"Making fun of you?" He asked skeptically.

She nodded, her lips trembling.

"Tell me," he commanded her, and she did.

She recounted how she was known as the loner at her school. That some of the girls had wanted to make fun of her by having someone pay attention to her and then humiliating her in front of the entire school.

"What did they say?" He asked, a sudden tick in his jaw at the mental image she was painting.

"That I was pathetic and that no guy would ever be *truly* interested in me," she sighed.

The more she talked, the more he understood what it had all been about, and for a moment he felt a sliver of guilt make its way into his chest at the fact that *he* had been the one to turn her into an outsider at her school. But he shoved it away. He didn't do guilt, just like he didn't do *any* type of emotions—except for anger. Anger was always good.

"Don't mind them, pet. You know you have me," he cooed in that sweet voice of his, a stark contrast to the tone he'd used when he'd first walked through the door. But seeing that his pet was only the victim of a malicious prank, he couldn't exactly find fault with her.

He smiled at himself. He was nothing if not magnanimous. And his mood improved considerably the more he heard her talk about the bullying that went on at her school, and how now, more than ever, *he* was her safe space.

It was what he'd wanted from the beginning.

And because his anger was slowly melting away, he decided he wasn't going to be too tough on those kids either. He was going to be *just*—though that didn't exclude murder. He'd have to think about that in more depth later.

Now? He was in the same room as his pet. Hard. It was only fitting that she'd make it up to him for the upset she'd caused him at thinking she'd allow another to touch her.

"I'm glad to hear that, pet," he told her affectionately, brushing his hand over her soft hair. "Because you'd never do something to hurt me, now, would you? You'd never let another man who is *not* me touch you, would you?"

"Of course not," she immediately replied, her voice spry, not the dulled one she'd used to recount the incident from school.

Like a flower in spring, she bloomed under his touch, and the more he murmured sweet things to her, the more she purred her approval, almost nestling into him in her desire to get closer to him.

But he couldn't allow that. Not when he found most human touch repugnant. He supposed his pet was the only one whose touch had a little more sweetness than bite, but even that was too much for him.

He gave her a strained smile, slowly disentangling her from him.

"Why don't you show me you're only mine, pet?" He asked, his hands on her shoulders as he pushed her down, her knees hitting the floor.

She peered up at him through her lashes, confusion simmering in those lovely eyes of hers.

He didn't give her the chance to protest—not that she ever would. His hands went to his belt, quickly unbuckling it and taking his rigid erection out, he thrust it into her face.

"Open your mouth," he instructed, his thumb parting her lips as he guided the head of his cock between her lips.

Eyes wide, she did as she was told, opening her mouth wide to take him inside.

He watched through hooded eyes as she started working on his cock, her hands stroking his shaft while her sweet mouth was sucking on the head, her tongue playing with the underside like she knew he liked.

He didn't think he was going to ever tire of this sight—of her on her knees, absolutely at his mercy.

He had never let another this close to him, touching him so intimately. But with her—with her sweet natured submission—he knew there was nothing to worry about. She would do just as he told her, and she'd never push the boundaries.

She was just…perfect.

A sigh escaped his lips as she took him deeper in her mouth, and he placed his hands on her head, guiding her movements. His fingers lodged into her scalp, he tugged at her hair until he was the one controlling her movements, using her mouth as his very own fuck hole—thrusting in and out as he sought his pleasure.

"Relax your throat, pet," he groaned as he hit the back of her throat, the warm heaven of her mouth making him shudder from an onslaught of pleasure.

Holding tight, he started thrusting aggressively into her hole, feeling every inch of that wet cave, but more than anything, enjoying having her at his mercy.

Tears were gathered at the corners of her eyes, spit dripping down her chin, yet she held on. She made not one sound of protest as she received his entire length—gagging loudly but still not trying to get away.

He closed his eyes, reveling in those sounds of distress that escaped her, the way he knew he could choke her to death with his dick and she wouldn't protest.

"Fuck," he cursed out as he felt himself near completion, his balls tightening before he released his hot seed into her waiting mouth.

He held her tightly, her lips near the base of his shaft as he shot his cum straight down her throat. Only when the last tremors had subsided did he let go, hearing a deep intake of breath as his pet struggled for air.

"Good girl," he praised, patting her on her head. He quickly tucked himself in his pants, his eyes still on her small form on the floor.

She looked so tiny, so helpless. It would be so easy to kill her...

Sometimes, visions of her lifeless body plagued his mind, and he didn't know whether it was his subconscious telling him he should kill her sooner rather than later, or just his ever-at-work mind trying to prevent that in order to complete his plans for revenge.

She brought her hand to her mouth, wiping the remnants of saliva and cum from her lips, her eyes big and innocent as she gazed up at him.

Fuck, but he could feel himself growing hard again. It was always her eyes. The way she looked at him as if he was her everything—as if he could take on the world for her, and win.

He'd never reacted to a woman like that in his life—to anyone. Before, even getting an erection had been out of question. The only way he'd ever gotten hard had been by mentally willing himself to do it, a fuck you to the world and what it had taken from him.

But with her? His body had stirred from the beginning, her innocence calling to him in a peculiar manner, making him want to preserve it and defile it at the same time. Even now, as he stared at her, the decision was still pending.

He'd defiled her alright. He'd made her his whore, and he wasn't ashamed of that—because she was only his. Despite the things he'd made her do, despite the humiliations he'd put her through, there was still a glaring, almost intoxicating innocence to her that had nothing to do with her physical purity.

It was all in her eyes—in that trusting way she gazed upon him. For all her anger at the world and her abandonment issues, there was a purity to her soul that couldn't be erased by anything—not even by his debasing touch.

He was perplexed. He was amazed. *He was pissed.*

He alternated between yearning for that purity of hers and

wishing he could destroy it once and for all, step on it—step on her—until there was nothing else left of her.

Nothing.

His lip twitched the more he studied her, an ugly desire to see her battered and bleeding rearing its head.

"Do you love me, pet?" He asked, stooping down on his haunches, finally on eye level with her.

She gave a tentative nod, blinking as she gazed at him in confusion.

"You'd do anything to make me happy, wouldn't you?" He continued, his fingers on her jaw as he stroked her soft skin.

Another nod.

His smile widened.

"Good," he purred, removing a knife from his jacket.

Her eyes widened when she saw the blade, and she instinctively moved back. He didn't let her retreat, though, his hand still holding tightly on to her jaw.

"Shh," he murmured, placing the blade at her throat and tracing it down her skin. He could see her pulse hammer against the column of her throat, her terror unmistakable.

He inhaled deeply, the scent of her fear so alluring and oh, so arousing.

"I need to put my claim on you, love," he cooed, bringing his face close to hers and nuzzling her cheek. "What better way to show you're taken than by having me with you at all times?" he whispered in her ear, his hot breath fanning on her skin and melting some of her apprehensions away.

"What do you mean?" She asked in a small voice.

"You'll see. Don't you trust me?"

"Of course," she replied right away, confirming the fact that for all her fear, she'd never turn away from him—*never*.

A twisted smile pulled at his lips, the satisfaction he felt at knowing he owned her even more potent than his orgasm.

"Good," he rumbled, leaning back and taking her hand.

Before she could realize what he was trying to do, he ran the blade in the middle of her palm, the sharp edge cutting deep into her skin. Blood immediately started pouring out, and he was quick to remove the other items from his jacket—something he'd bought *just* for her.

"What..." she trailed off as her eyes zeroed in on the small vials.

He popped off the cap on one, bringing it under her palm and filling half of it with her blood. He repeated the action with the second bottle, before he finally let go of her hand.

She grabbed it to her chest, holding it up and staring at the blood still pouring from the wound, her lashes coated with unshed tears.

"Look at me," he commanded, and she did—she was nothing if not obedient.

He raised the knife, bringing it against his own palm as he cut across it, red liquid reaching the surface as the blade ripped through his skin.

Her eyes were fixed on his new wound, watching his every move as he took the vials and poured his own blood into them, filling them to the brim before popping the lid back on.

She blinked in confusion, and before she knew it, he reached for her once more, his palm on top of hers, blood on top of blood.

"We're one now, pet. Don't you see it?" He asked in a sultry voice, urging her to look at the place where their blood mingled. He pressed his palm against hers, smearing his blood against her own.

"Yes," she answered softly, a look of wonder on her face.

"And this," he waved the vials. "You're going to carry this with you *everywhere*. Is that clear?"

She nodded vigorously, finally understanding the complexity of what he'd done, her eyes already greedily eating up the vial and the prospect of having his very essence with her at all times.

"You'll..." she trailed off, wetting her lips as she gained the courage to ask the question. "You'll wear mine too?"

"It's ours," he corrected. "It's our mixed blood. This way you have me, and I have you," he gave her one of his charming smiles, watching in satisfaction as she practically purred when he placed the vial on a makeshift necklace, tying it around her neck. She was on the verge of swooning when he did the same with his own.

When they were done, without even thinking, he brought her hand to his mouth, swirling his tongue across her cut, licking what remained of her blood and marveling at the metallic yet slightly sweet taste of her.

That ugly part of him that wanted to see her destroyed was momentarily appeased—the blood a temporary offering.

And as he watched the vial of blood against her pearly white skin, he couldn't help the way pride swelled in his chest that now she'd be carrying him around everywhere.

He was, quite possibly, even more enamored of his own vial. Because it was proof that he owned his toy and that she was his—and only his.

Anyone who'd see it hanging around his neck would recognize the mark of ownership.

He knew to her it must seem the height of romanticism to wear their combined blood around his neck, but her mind was too simplistic to understand the bigger picture—the fact that this was proof of his impending vengeance.

Proof of his success.

He smiled to himself as he held her half-heartedly, allowing her some of his body heat while still keeping a distance for his own comfort.

Soon.

Soon, both her and her family would pay for what they did.

Very soon.

But first, he needed to deal with his brother.

"YES," the clipped tone of an older man answered the call at the first ring.

"I have an assignment for you. Chase Fenix out of the city and I'll sign the contract," Michele said, his fingers tracing the new window gracing his office.

There was a brief pause on the other end.

"You have a deal."

He'd been contacted multiple times by the same man seeking to expand his business in New York and wanting to make Michele, and therefore Guerra, his partner. On the streets, he was known as simply Ortega. He'd taken over a failing drug empire and was about to rehabilitate it by going into other business ventures. With Michele's financial expertise, as well as his severed ties to all the other big players in New York, he'd thought Guerra would be the best partner.

They'd met a few times to discuss terms and division of power once they'd unite forces, but Michele had been reluctant because he hadn't trusted the man.

He'd heard the rumors from Ortega's time under Jimenez, and he knew he wasn't the most loyal subject. And in Michele's mind, once a traitor, always a traitor.

But given Rafaelo's affiliation with Fenix, and subsequently to Carlos Jimenez, he needed someone who *knew* how to work in that particular area. He needed someone who could defeat Carlos and leave the way clear for Michele to get to his brother.

A smile pulled at his lips as he saw all the potential scenarios playing before his eyes.

He wasn't the person Rafaelo thought him to be. No, far from it. Just like Rafaelo hadn't been the person he'd portrayed himself to be.

They'd both played their roles. His brother's had been driven by his insurmountable guilt, while his own had been a role given by *his* sire—playing the rogue, prodigal son and showing a careless face to the world.

Behind closed doors, they'd schemed and schemed, until all plans had reached their pinnacles as he'd killed Benedicto and Cosima and exiled Raf, finally taking the power for his own as it should have always been and paving the way for the ultimate destruction.

Too bad his sire had not been there to see it—his death an

unforeseen bump on the road. Still, he wouldn't let that stop him from accomplishing what they'd both so painstakingly planned.

Soon, his brother would cease to be a problem, his sire's assassin would pay, and the architect of his greatest misfortune would perish.

The balance would finally be restored, with everyone getting their due.

Plopping himself on his chair, he leaned back, lighting a cigarette and staring at the cloud of smoke forming in front of him.

Ah, but victory would be sweet indeed.

Chapter Seventeen

Rafaelo

"I received all the documents from your IT guy," Cisco says as he guides me to his study after dinner.

"I trust they were satisfactory?"

"Indeed," he gives me a wolfish grin as he motions me to sit down across from him. "I must say I'm rather impressed with what you've managed, Raf. In such a short time too," he praises quietly.

"I had the motivation," I grunt.

"Even so, it couldn't have been easy to wipe out a cartel and steal their merchandise. Especially when it comes to such heavy cargo."

"*Because* it was heavy cargo we had to cover our tracks, since if we'd let anyone live, they would have undoubtedly come after us."

"Why weapons?" He suddenly asks.

Amo must have given him a full report of everything we'd stored in the warehouse, and by the looks of it, Cisco seems intrigued.

"Why not weapons?" I retort with a hidden smile. "You remember Jimenez's ventures and where his monopoly lay."

"In human trafficking," Cisco promptly replies.

"Yes, and no. Human trafficking was what he was most known for, but he'd been dabbling in the illegal weapons trade for quite some time before he died. In fact, besides the drug business, *that* was what Ortega claimed when the empire fell. But he didn't have enough backing to stay in NYC."

Cisco's lips pull up in a sinister smile.

"I see what you're doing. Smart," he mentions and I smirk.

"It's one of the best ways to ensure that he *won't* have a place here. A market analysis will tell you that weapons are usually sold by one, maybe two suppliers. It's a very cutthroat industry and relies heavily on trust. Drugs, on the other hand, can be dealt by anyone. There will always be people who buy drugs, but there is only a select group of people who buy weapons."

"I'm even more impressed, Raf. You are correct that the weapons trade is more...eclectic so to say. And by having an established competition, you'll ensure that Ortega will have a hard time to infiltrate the market. Not impossible though," he challenges.

"I know. Which is where *you* come in," I nod at him. "With your support and vote of confidence, we should be taken more seriously on the black market. And given that there hasn't been a proper supplier in New York since Jimenez, I'd say people will be hungry for it."

"I have to give it to you. You've thought this out in detail, and I admire that. Say you've locked Ortega out from the weapon's trade. What about the rest?"

"I won't have to interfere with the drugs, since the Russians have stakes in that and will most likely intervene. My worry is the human trafficking element. I've gathered some data about what Michele has been doing, but it's not much. He's been very secretive about his investments after the illegal organ trade ring was busted."

"I'm guessing that's why he's been so loud in other areas. So people wouldn't suspect how he *truly* gets his money."

"Yes. The more I study my brother the more I realize I don't really know him. And at this point, information is really the most valuable asset."

"He doesn't go out much," Cisco notes. "The few times he showed on the map was because he *wanted* to create a riot—almost as if he wanted to make people aware of him."

"Exactly. I think he wants to be taken seriously because he realizes people talk, and my father's death couldn't have been an accident. There are still those who question his legitimacy."

"The other families have stopped interacting with Guerra since your brother took over, and it's well known no one likes him. I may not go out much either," he jokes, "but I do know of one incident when your brother first took over. There was a banquet organized by Agosti and Michele showed up. Everyone snubbed him," Cisco chuckles. "I think that was quite the hit to his ego."

"I bet," I laugh. "He knows he isn't welcomed anywhere. And from some sources, it seems he's become extremely paranoid about who he lets by his side."

"And yet he's letting Ortega?" Cisco raises a brow.

"Not without a good reason," I add drily. "After all, I am connected to Carlos. The enemy of my enemy is my friend and all that," I wave my hand.

"Good. Now that you've put all this together, what's next?"

"Carlos will take Ortega on, since their conflict is personal, and I'll draw Michele out somehow."

"Easier said than done if he's as paranoid as you say. And you'll still have to be careful with your movements. No doubt Michele must have heard of your arrival by now, as well as the fact that you're under my protection. I don't think he will dare do something in the open, but it's better to be cautious."

I grunt.

"If he becomes desperate, though," I add grimly, "he can strike at any point."

"Then we'd better take him out first," Cisco smiles. "And I might have an idea," he mentions.

"I'm all ears."

"I think it's time for DeVille to take back its place in the public eye. That should send a message that we're not afraid of a kid. And by supporting you... Well, let's just say things should get interesting."

My lips tug up at his unexpected offer. It had crossed my mind, but with DeVille's notorious stance against socializing with the other families, I hadn't thought it a viable option.

"Why, Cisco, don't tell me you mean to go all out?" I joke.

"Why not?" He retorts on a dare.

We sketch out a few plans and it seems that Cisco's given this some serious thought, especially when he suggests organizing a banquet and inviting all the families—all but Guerra.

Since Michele craves acceptance so much, it would be fitting to see him become a pariah in the city.

After a while, Cisco gets up, heading to his alcohol cabinet and taking out a bottle of scotch and two glasses.

"I hope my sister didn't give you too much trouble," he changes the subject and pushes a glass in front of me.

"No. If anything, she was the model of decorum. I think she took your warning to heart," I chuckle, and he raises his eyebrows in surprise.

"That's...unusual," he gives a tight smile, taking a swig from his glass. "She wasn't always like this, you know," he sighs, his gaze distant.

"What happened? If I may ask," I probe carefully, a little too curious to see what he can tell me about her.

He purses his lips, taking another drag from his cigarette.

"She's the youngest in the family. Sixteen years younger than me. I have to admit that I haven't always been... What's the word," he pauses, his expression serious, "affectionate towards her."

"Sixteen is a big age gap. It's understandable."

"I made my fair share of mistakes, that I admit. And her marriage to that man is one of my deepest regrets." He shakes his head ruefully, but he doesn't offer more details on that subject. "You might have heard that she was in a fire," he continues. "She was found very late, more dead than alive. We had her airlifted to the closest hospital, and the chances of her making it were very slim. But she made it," he breathes out, and I can see the relief on his face.

Well, too bad for me that she *did* live.

"That sounds awful," I offer a platitude, and he merely nods.

"She had extensive burns and her throat was badly damaged from a crushed larynx and smoke inhalation. But that was just the physical..." he trails off.

Leaning back in my seat, I listen as he continues, the information invaluable as I plan my next moves.

"The mental," he shakes his head, regret flooding his features. "We had her committed for a couple of months. She had bad seizures and was under the impression that people were out to kill her. She even harmed a nurse in one of her episodes, and that was when we realized she wasn't well. We've been keeping her under surveillance since."

My, my, but if that is true... I control my expression carefully, not wanting the internal glee to reflect on the outside, or that the fact that Noelle's suffering makes my insides heat up with pleasure.

It seems there is karma out there, and my excitement mounts as I think about balancing the scales even more and making her rue the day she survived.

"She mentioned something about amnesia?" I ask carefully, my eyes on his face as I try to gauge his expression.

"Yes. Her doctors called it selective dissociative amnesia. There are huge gaps in her memory. Mostly from the time in Mexico. But there are also things she forgot from before. She doesn't remember much from the months she was committed either, and the doctors haven't been able to find the cause. Mostly because she won't take her treatment seriously," he sighs. "You've seen how adamant she is about defying me. She's changed countless therapists and has missed most of her sessions by engaging in God knows what shenanigans. And it's all in an effort to get a rise out of me."

"She does seem to have quite the rebellious streak," I offer with a smile.

"A rebellious streak?" He scoffs. "If only. Since she was discharged from the hospital, she's been getting into all types of troubles. Stealing cars, partying with fake IDs," his brows pinch together in a frown, "she even got arrested on prostitution charges," he groans.

My eyes widen.

"Prostitution charges?" I repeat, unable to picture Noelle in such a scenario. For all her faults, that was the last thing I would have thought she'd do.

"She says it was a mistake, but she was taken at the station with a few other women who claimed she was asking them for tips of the trade. It's one of the reasons why I'm her legal guardian, since she can't be trusted on her own."

"But are you sure this isn't just her way of rebelling? She doesn't seem mentally ill to me." I narrow my eyes at him, still unable to believe Noelle would be taken in for prostitution, especially since for all her malice, there's a proud dignity to her that is objectively alluring.

"Her diagnosis says otherwise. And her latest stunt was the last drop. Either she goes to therapy and gets an exemption certificate on her own, or she'll forever have to answer to me," he states resolutely, downing his glass.

I don't comment further, mostly because I can see it's a sore subject for Cisco. At the same time, I have to wonder about the purpose of him offering up this information when he is the epitome of someone who is minute about details. Although that may make it easy to gauge him, it also complicates things since he probably has an agenda of his own.

"If you're so worried about her being on her own, then why haven't you found another husband for her?" I ask curiously.

It's been almost two years since the fire, and anyone in Cisco's position would have cut his losses and simply moved on to a better venture. After all, women are currency in the famiglia, and with how isolated DeVille is, it's one of the most valuable commodities they have to make alliances with—a reusable resource.

"She wasn't well enough in the beginning. Now..." he trails off, his voice distant. "I've been considering it for a while," he mentions thoughtfully. "I'll have to screen potential candidates."

An insane idea forms inside my mind—so insane I can't believe where it came from. But before I can think it through, though, I open my mouth and speak.

"Give her to me."

Surprise fills his features, and he tilts his face, regarding me carefully.

"You?

"We've already ascertained that she's not against me," I lie. "And I'd like to think I'm a decent prospect—all things considered." I shrug as I lean back.

"Why?" He narrows his eyes.

"I think we might get along with time. There's definitely something there, and I wouldn't be opposed to exploring it further—should you allow that."

I word my sentence wisely, since I know that Cisco's weighing everything I say.

"Hmm. She does like you," he muses. "But what about the issues I just told you?" He raises a brow. "She won't be easy to deal with."

Laughter bubbles in my throat at his words, and if I didn't know any better I could have sworn Cisco had been trying to *sell* his sister to me earlier—by making me pity her.

"I told you she doesn't seem mentally ill to me. Misguided? Maybe. Rebellious? For sure. Rather than treat her as if she were crazy, I think she just needs someone to give her the attention she craves." I cringe internally at the bullshit I'm spewing, but Cisco nods appreciatively, seemingly mulling over my words.

"You might have a point. Yuyu and I certainly haven't been able to give her what she needs," he sighs.

There's a pause where neither of us speaks, and it's clear he's deliberating. Especially as he suddenly stands up, filling his glass with alcohol again.

"I'll think about it," he finally says. "I'll convene with my wife and I'll give you an answer soon. We do, after all, want what's best for Noelle."

"I can promise you I'd never mistreat her," I state solemnly.

No, I'd just commit her to an asylum and give her *exactly* what she fears the most. I might have been here only for a few days, but I'd observed enough to realize Noelle's rebelliousness comes from a need to assert her independence. She resents her family for keeping her on such a tight leash, and her stunts are both a way to piss them off, and pretend she's *not* reliant on them.

I don't think for a moment that there's something wrong with her—mentally or physically. If anything, her amnesia might be her way of trying to avoid responsibility for her actions. And *that* makes me even more incensed. She doesn't get to just forget and move on. No, she doesn't get to be happy, period.

The idea of marriage is admittedly crazy, but it's also the easiest way to get close to her without anyone suspecting a thing. I'd earn her trust and that of her family, before I'd make it so that she has a sudden relapse and is in need of proper asylum care.

The plan taking root in my mind, I'm getting increasingly certain this is the perfect way to deal with her.

"I know that, Raf. I've heard enough about you to know you're a good man. One that's been given a shitty hand, but a good man, nonetheless. And I think that's exactly what Noelle needs."

"I'm also not one to allow her to run wild. If you give your sister to me, I can promise to take care of her to the best of my ability," I say, looking him straight in the eyes.

Oh, I'll take care of her all right—by having her locked away.

"We'll see," is all he replies, but I can tell he's positively considering the offer.

And given some of his previous actions, I rather think he's had the idea in mind before it had even occurred to me.

We continue to talk about our upcoming plans, and I can see that for all his feigned reticence, the deal is almost done.

Ah, my little liar, but the future has interesting things in store for you.

After more planning and a little too much scotch, I finally head back to my room. As I go up the stairs, though, the piano echoes down the hall. The sound of the melody makes me stop in my tracks as I allow myself to enjoy the sweetness of it as it seeps into my skin.

Without even thinking, my legs lead me back to the attic—the source of that divine sound. And as I put one foot in front of the other, I reach the door that leads to the attic, pushing it open and basking in the crisp sound that emanates from the piano.

It's too late, though, that I realize whose hands are creating those sounds.

Her gasp of surprise is enough to wake me of my reverie, my eyebrows furrowing in dismay as I stare at *her*.

Huddled behind the piano, she's looking at me wide-eyed, the beam of light coming from the window illuminating her features and giving her an ethereal look. Her bronzed skin glints in the moonlight, her eyes two dark orbs—like two bottomless pits of eternal damnation.

My lips twitch in displeasure, anger simmering inside of me as I start noticing other things. Like the curve of her neck or the sheer nightgown she's wearing, the outline of her body evident and infuriatingly distracting. Then there's the slow movement of her lips as her mouth opens and closes on a silent question...

So caught I am by the sight in front of me that even I can't form any words. For a moment, neither of us says anything. Our eyes are locked as we simply stare at each other.

Me in anger, her in surprise.

When I note her blink as her fingers moving slightly over the keyboard, a red haze covers my eyes as I realize she'd been the owner of the melody all along.

My reality shatters, my expectations destroyed.

How could I have liked *her* music? How could it have touched me in such a deep way when all I feel for her is anger and contempt?

My enjoyment of it is now forever tainted with the image of her behind the piano searing itself in my mind.

"What are you doing here?" She speaks first, her husky voice hitting me like a bullet to the chest.

Why? Why did it have to be *her*?

My hands balled into fists, I take a step forward. And another. And another. Until I'm by her side, my hand on her wrist as I grab it abruptly, forcefully tugging her to her feet and in front of me.

"What do you think you're doing?" I grit out, the melody still a haunting echo in my mind, the soothing sound now gaining a cacophonous quality to it.

And yet, my brain doesn't want to forget it. It doesn't want to erase it from deep within, no matter how much I'd like it to.

"Playing the piano, if that wasn't obvious." She rolls her eyes at me, trying to wrestle her wrist from my hold.

"That melody. Why that melody?" I ask in a punctured tone.

I refuse to believe it had been her then, too. I refuse to believe that her melody had been the one that had given me warmth on a cold night when I'd felt my mind slipping from me in the desolation of my cell.

I simply refuse to believe it had been her hands that had given me *any* type of peace.

"I don't have to answer you. Please leave," she says quietly, raising her chin and looking me in the eye in defiance.

"Answer me," I demand, my voice chilling.

"No. I said leave," she repeats.

I tighten my hold, bringing her even closer to me and waiting for fear to slowly appear in her eyes. But it doesn't.

"Not until you answer me, Noelle."

"Or what? What are you going to tell my brother this time?" she scoffs. "That I lured you to the attic with my music so that I could seduce you?" She laughs softly. "Or maybe," she raises an eyebrow. "You'll go one step further and take my dress off. Then you could say I was blatantly throwing myself at you."

"You have quite the imagination," I chuckle at her words. "Is that what you want, Noelle?" I inquire in a smooth voice as I push her further into the room. "You want me to strip you? Take off your dress so I can see what?" I ask snidely. "Your scars? Your ugliness?"

She visibly flinches at my words, looking as if I'd struck her.

"What... How..." she stammers, shaking her head.

"Do you think I'd be attracted to that? Do you think you'd be able to seduce me with *that*?" I continue on a derisive chuckle, noting the shudder that goes through her and realizing I've hit the mark.

"Let's see," I say as I push her until her back hits the wall, her body reeling. I take advantage of her disorientation to trail my hand down the bodice of her dress, grabbing on to the silky material and tugging it down.

Her arm goes to her chest, trying to cover herself while she renews her struggles to get out of my hold.

"Come on, show me. Show me how you're going to seduce me with that body of yours," I taunt her, pulling down with enough force that the material gives way, the sound of a tear rippling in the room.

She gasps, her mouth wide open as she stares at me in shock.

The tear is small, but it reveals the area from her neck to her cleavage—an entire expanse of unblemished skin.

Her tight hold against her chest only serves to emphasize the swell of her breasts more, the sight so tantalizing it gives me pause.

"You're vile," she spits out, thrashing in my hold. "Let me go," she speaks through gritted teeth, her eyes flashing angrily at me.

"Yes, I'm vile." I smirk, enjoying her discomfort. "I'm so vile, Noelle, you're going to rue the day you met me."

Without waiting for her reply, I maneuver her around, twirling her until her front is flush against the wall, her back to me.

Yes, it's better if I eliminate all temptation, focusing on *her* humiliation instead.

"Let me go," she breathes out, squirming under me.

"Why? It was your idea, wasn't it?" I drawl, the sound of her pulse combined with her errant breath the only noise in the room. "Now you've made me curious," I chuckle. "Show me those scars, Noelle. Show me that outer ugliness that reflects the inside."

A whimper escapes her as she stops struggling. I pull harshly on her gown, the material tears once more and falls to her waist. Finally, I'm met by what I was searching for. Stripes of pink reddish skin cover her upper back, the gnarly scars just as ugly as I'd imagined.

Yes, there is karma. And it's slowly catching up with her.

"Is this it?" I ask in a brusque tone, my fingers tracing the bumpy skin. Goosebumps erupt all over her skin as I touch her, a sob penetrating the air.

"Stop," she pleads in a small voice.

"What was that?"

"Stop, please," she sniffles, her body trembling under my touch.

Dropping her hand, I step back, watching as she crumbles to the floor, her chest heaving with every labored breath.

"Come on," I tell her. "Seduce me," I taunt, crossing my arms over my chest and watching her closely.

She whips her head up, her eyes angrily glaring at me. Tears coat her lashes while some make their way down her cheeks. One hand on the ground, she's using the other to hold on to her bodice. Sprawled on the floor like that, she looks almost enticing—almost.

"I'm waiting," I raise an eyebrow, quietly daring her.

Her nostrils flare as she stares at me, her arms trembling slightly.

Just when I think she's going to give up and beg me to leave her alone, she surprises me by slowly getting up. Still holding to the material of her dress, she takes a wobbly step in front of me.

I lean back, waiting to see her next move—a part of me hoping she'll actually try to seduce me.

Her eyes never leave mine as she stops in front of me. Before I can register what she means to do, her palm connects with my cheek.

The slap resounds in the quiet room, and I'm too stunned to do anything but watch her.

"You're vile," she repeats, her small hand balled into a fist that she brings against my chest in a light punch. She keeps hitting, the rage bottled within her seemingly having reached the surface.

The corner of my mouth tugs up as I let her continue for a few seconds, simply watching her wildly seek to harm me, though her fists are nothing more than a light caress against my skin.

"I'm disappointed, Noelle," I tsk at her as I grab her fist, stopping its advance. "Is vile the only word you know? I'm sure you can come up with something better," I smirk at her.

Her lips tremble in frustration at my amused expression, and without thinking, she raises her other hand, aiming to hit me again.

I catch it, gathering both her wrists in my hand, her fragility always managing to astound me—how something so delicate could hide so much malice.

"Let go," she utters angrily, her expression filled with animosity.

Well, well, it seems my little liar has a backbone after all.

And...

Lacking support, the material of her gown falls, pooling around her waist, her smooth, heavy breasts naked as she continues to thrash against me, each movement making the round globes bounce against her ribcage.

I can't help the way my eyes are drawn to the expanse of perfect skin that peeks out, her breasts beautifully formed and begging for attention as her nipples pebble right under my gaze.

Fuck...

Her mouth is parted in shock as she looks down at her semi-naked body, and then back to me.

As much as I'd like to, it's impossible to wrench my gaze away from her. I swallow hard, my body feeling uncomfortably tight under the confines of my clothes. My breath comes out in short spurts, beads of sweat accumulating on my forehead.

"Are you done staring?" Her voice snaps me out of my reverie, the vehemence behind her tone catching me by surprise—again.

Given her state of dishabille, I would have thought she'd get shy, maybe cry some more. Certainly *not* behaving like this.

"No. As a matter of fact, I'm not. Why don't you turn a little? I didn't catch the profile."

"You're an asshole," she mutters aggressively, pushing against my hold.

"Wow," I drawl. "Good job, little liar. You just discovered a new word," I say just as I release her.

She reels back, but she catches herself quickly. Instead of covering herself up, though, she pushes her chin up, giving me a defiant stare and turning to show me her profile.

"Like what you see?" she asks on a mocking tone. "Oh," her

voice goes up a notch, her hand flying to her mouth as she feigns a shocked expression. "It seems that you do." There's a smug smile on her face as she points to the bulge in my pants and the visible outline of my erection.

My jaw clenches, my physical reaction to her a blasphemy, my own body betraying me in the worst manner.

"It's just a pair of tits, *sweetheart*," I snarl. "Don't flatter yourself, you're nothing special."

"Just a pair of tits?" she repeats, amused. "Sure, *sweetheart*." A derisive smile tugs at her lips. "A pair of tits that doesn't leave you unaffected, it seems," she shrugs, her tits bouncing again with each move and drawing my attention to them once more, my eyes fixed to her pink nipples.

She clears her throat, tapping her foot as she looks at me with a raised brow, making no effort to cover herself. In fact, she's proudly standing there, daring me to keep looking.

My lips twitch in displeasure, and with a low curse, I turn on my heel, storming out of the attic and slamming the door in my wake.

"Fuck!" I curse out loud as I reach my room.

"Fuck. Fuck. Fuck!"

Chapter Eighteen

Noelle

I continue stare at the closed door of the attic. My body won't stop shaking, my breath coming in short spurts as I try to find a modicum of control over my trembling limbs.

Am I to never have a moment of peace?

My hand shoots out as I grab the edge of the piano bench to stabilize myself, my knees wobbly.

"Dear God, what just happened?" I whisper to myself, my eyes fixed on the door he'd just closed.

I blink back tears as I try to get myself under control, but my body doesn't seem to want to obey me. Not when so many feelings are mixed inside of me—so many contradicting feelings that leave me reeling.

From the moment he'd cornered me in the warehouse, I haven't known a moment of peace, his accusations ringing loud and clear in my head, his proximity both a blessing and a curse.

While my own memory was failing me, there were some snippets—images—that told me his words were *not* untrue.

For God's sake, but could it actually be true? Did I have something to do with Lucero's death? With everyone's deaths? The past is too blurry for me to attempt to answer that question. But what I do remember from *before* the fire makes me doubt my own self.

Raf isn't wrong.

He's far from wrong.

I may not remember *him* specifically, but I know how I'd had to act to please Sergio and his sick cronies. I'd buried my own self deep inside of me and I'd put on a show for everyone to see that I wasn't some weak, meek girl. That I was the mistress of the house, worthy of her husband's cruelty and infamy.

And those moments in time had torn at my humanity.

The *hacienda* had been hell on earth for many people, its vast terrain south of the U.S. border making it the perfect spot to develop new, experimental drugs to push on the market. But there's never just the manufacturing stage—there's also the testing one.

And from what I'd gathered from Raf...he must have been one of the test subjects.

A sob catches in my throat at the thought.

Memories of skinny bodies draped in rags, of people who weren't people anymore assault me. And worst of all? I'd treated them as the dregs of society too, because it would have *never* been fitting of the mistress to show any inkling of emotion or empathy—that would have been perceived as weakness.

Raf's claim that I had thrown a plate at his head? Likely true, since it had not been the first time I'd done that. And yet... Knowing everything I'd done back then, I still can't bring myself to believe I would have harmed Lucero.

She'd been my friend, my confidante. The only one who'd made that place more bearable.

Could I have been so ruthless as to show no mercy even to my only friend?

Because if that's the case... Then I deserve his hate. I deserve his contempt. And I deserve so, so much more.

I breathe in and out as images flash before my eyes, seeing myself at the *hacienda* making my skin crawl at the stranger I'd been.

It's not often that I think back, or more specifically, I *don't want* to think back.

That past is filled with so much pain, I fear I'd drown if I were to let myself go. It's also the reason why I don't want to remember the rest. Because if what I do know now is bad...

I shake myself, clutching the material of my torn dress to my chest. Coldness seeps into my skin as my thoughts stray to Rafaelo. The man with the golden beauty who'd made me forget myself for a moment—before everything had come crashing down.

Why is it that the first man to elicit such a strong reaction from me is also the most forbidden? The one who hates me, thinking I'd been the architect of his misfortune and that of the death of his lover? Why is it that the thought of him being intimate with Lucero pains me, an insidious envy forming inside of me? That the mere idea of him loving her burns a hole in my soul?

It must be his intensity, wishful thinking taking root inside of me as I imagine what it would be like to be the object of his affection.

He's staunch. Loyal. Dependable.

If what I've come to know of him is any indication, he's the ride or die type of person, going to any lengths to protect those he cares about.

Even with his spiteful words and those hateful eyes directed at me, I can recognize the qualities of the man that lay underneath. Lucero had been incredibly lucky to have his devotion—even for a short amount of time.

He's...the personification of everything I've ever dreamed of but never got—as exemplified by the fact that I'm currently the target of his disdain. And seeing how strongly he feels about that...I have no doubt he will not stop until he truly sees me destroyed.

Absentmindedly, I bring my hand over my chest, tracing the contours of my breasts as I picture his reaction to me. He hadn't been unaffected, and the knowledge fills me with something akin to anticipation—for what, I don't know.

I could tell that my behavior had shocked him. The fact that I hadn't cowered in front of him when he'd had me at my most vulnerable—at my most bare—had surprised him.

What he doesn't know, though, is that it had surprised me too.

It's been close to two years since the fire, yet *no one* has seen my scars. No one has seen my naked body—even if partially.

It had been a source of embarrassment and I'd been too self-conscious about it to even strip in front of a woman. Save for the nurses who'd taken care of me when I'd been incapacitated, there had been no one else.

Until him.

And yet, I hadn't reacted as I thought I would. I hadn't run away, crying in mortification.

I'd been humiliated, yes. But I'd also been determined to *not* show him my weakness. And as I stood proudly in front of him, unbothered whether he was staring at my breasts or not, I'd felt a different sort of rush go through me.

Adrenaline. Pleasure. Delight.

It had felt like the beginning of an addiction. Seeing the shift in his gaze, the alternation between hate and lust had done something to me.

Something that had made me act bold—bolder than I've ever been.

While I'd reveled in his reaction to me, I'd also had to admit something else.

I wasn't that unbothered, either.

A sigh escapes my lips as I realize the conundrum I find myself in.

After what I'd endured at my husband's *loving* hands, I'd never thought I would ever stand a man's touch—no matter how neutral. I'd never imagined I would gaze upon one with desire either...

But the truth is that for all the hate I see in his eyes, Raf doesn't scare me. Not in the way Sergio did. No, he scares me in a way that makes my insides tingle, a low hum taking root in my lower belly as my entire body quakes with a need to feel his closeness.

And *that* is the issue.

Because I shouldn't feel like this. Not when he wants to see me destroyed—or worse, dead. Not when he loves another. And certainly *not* when he's bent on unleashing a pandemonium into my already chaotic life.

He's forbidden in a way that would only end with my ruin.

But maybe that adds to the appeal.

I shouldn't yearn for his attention, knowing it will be negative. I shouldn't crave his touch, though it will be bruising. I should definitely *not* want him to want me. *That* would prove to be the beginning of the end.

It takes everything in me to admit that there is something about Rafaelo that draws me in—despite all the warning signs.

Maybe it's what he represents, an avenging angel ready to wreak havoc on those who wronged him and his loved ones—the avenging angel that I'd wished for but that had never come for me.

Maybe it's his physicality, that raw masculinity that emanates from him and awakens a side of me that had been dormant—a side that I'm both scared and ashamed of.

Not unlike the first time I'd seen him in the piano room, his physical appearance causes an uncomfortable awareness inside of me. It goes beyond his Adonis-like looks and his deep, rough voice that even now makes my skin tingle at the echo of his rumble. No, there's something that seems to vibrate at a cellular level whenever he's in my proximity, the hairs on my body standing up to attention at the intensity he exudes.

Or, maybe, it's his principles. Because for all his godly looks, he is more like Atlas—shouldering the weight of the world and trudging his way towards his goals.

He's everything I used to hope for.

That gives me pause, because I can recognize my own glaring weakness. For all the animosity and apprehension I feel towards him, that glimmer of desire—both for the physical and for the emotional—could prove my undoing.

And knowing *that,* I need to be more careful around him.

It's all foreign territory, and a sliver of fear goes through me as I try to think how to proceed further.

One thing is for sure, though. I may be already guilty in his mind, but until I know for sure if what he says is true or not, I will not bow to him.

I may have my own guilt that sometimes threatens to overwhelm me. But I also have my anger at the injustices done against me, at the pain I'd endured and the tears I'd shed.

Until I see evidence that I did, indeed, have something to do with Lucero's death, I won't let him walk all over me.

A new sense of purpose washes over me as I realize that now, more than ever, I must hold my ground. After all, I only have myself left, and as such, I must learn to put myself first. And I might have just the way to deal with Raf.

A smile pulls at my lips at the thought, anticipation humming in my veins.

It's a dangerous game. Very dangerous indeed. Because I will be playing with fire. And last time I did, I didn't get out unscathed.

"YOU WANT TO DO WHAT?" Cisco raises an eyebrow as he leans back in his seat. I plaster a light smile on my face, schooling my features so he doesn't call me on my bullshit. But if Rafaelo's managed to instill the seed in him, then I might as well take advantage.

"I don't have that many clothes. I was thinking Raf—Rafaelo," I catch myself, suggesting a familiarity between us, "could accompany me."

My brother narrows his eyes at me, and for a moment he doesn't speak.

The urge to squirm under his perusal is overwhelming, especially as he pulls a cigarette from his pack, lighting it up and watching me with the intensity of a hawk.

"Why?" he asks unexpectedly.

"I..." I stammer, looking down and trying to make myself blush. "There aren't that many opportunities to get to know each other better in the house," I mumble.

"So you admit you *do* want to get to know him better," he says, and I give him a brisk nod.

"Is that allowed?" I ask sarcastically, even though I know that Cisco is fine with me being around Rafaelo—more than fine actually.

He shrugs, still studying me as he takes a deep drag of his cigarette.

"Raf might be a Guerra, but he's different," he starts, his differently colored eyes glinting dangerously in the low lit room.

"Is he?" I barely resist the urge to roll my eyes at him.

"He is important for my future plans, so you'd better give up any ideas of using him to get a rise out of me, Noelle. But if you're serious about him, then I approve," he states blankly.

I blink, a little surprised by his easy acquiescence. After all, my brother's never been very enthusiastic about letting me hang out with men outside the family unattended.

"Does that mean I'm allowed to go with him?"

"You are. But don't stay out too long," he nods, giving me one last look before dismissing me.

Satisfied with the outcome of the conversation, I quickly go upstairs to change, knowing my brother will probably inform Rafaelo himself.

I'd spent the better part of the night trying to come up with a plan to beat Raf at his own game. Having seen his unexpected reaction to my naked skin, as well as his obvious loathing of it, I'd realized it would be quite easy to rile him up.

I'll just have to taunt him with what he clearly detests.

Choosing my clothes carefully, I decide to forgo a bra, putting on a sheer blouse and layering it with a black crop top. For the bottoms, I put on short skirt—a little *too* short for my liking. But I'm sure *someone* will appreciate it.

Styling my hair and applying some light make-up, I head downstairs to find a disgruntled Rafaelo waiting for me. A scowl mars his features as he taps his foot impatiently.

And as he raises his gaze to see me descending the stairs, his scowl only deepens, his jaw clenched as he peruses my form. His eyes linger a little too long on my almost bare midriff before they slowly dip lower, to my legs. His Adam's apple bobs up and down as he swallows hard, and a shiver of anticipation goes down my back.

He's definitely not indifferent.

He catches himself in time, though, swiftly looking away, his lips twitching in displeasure as a grimace overtakes his features. And as my eyes meet his in a momentary stare down, it's to see him turn on his heel, a low curse under his breath.

He's already on his way to the car as I hurry after him.

"I can see why you'd need new clothes," he mutters as he takes a seat on the bench opposite me, looking out the window and trying to ignore me.

"What's that supposed to mean?"

He turns slightly, the corners of his mouth turned downwards as his eyes briefly skim my body.

"Did your clothes shrink?"

"I don't know what you're talking about," I feign a huff as I lean back in my seat, crossing my arms over my chest. Placing them strategically right under my boobs, I watch expectantly his expression, satisfied to see his eyes drawn to my chest.

"Of course you wouldn't," he mumbles, his eyes narrowed at me in distaste. "Why did you want me to accompany you anyway?" He raises an eyebrow. "Don't tell me last night left you wanting more?" he asks in a smug tone, and the way he looks at me immediately changes.

No longer the unguarded reaction from before, he's now pinning me with a lascivious stare, no doubt wanting to get a rise out of me and scare me like the night before.

Too bad for him that I've already planned for that—and more.

"What if it did?" I inquire in a smooth tone, enjoying the way it throws him off.

I bend forward, placing my elbow on my knee, my hand under my jaw as I look at him.

"You're good at making empty promises, *Raf*. But you're not very good at delivering them," I give a low chuckle.

"Is that what you think?" He scoffs, amused. "That I'm not good at delivering my promises?"

"So far, I haven't seen anything but empty words. Or is it that you can't?" A smile tugs at my lips. "Not with you needing my brother's support."

His hands clench into fists and I can see I've hit a sore spot. His eyes are on me, those startling blue eyes that seem even lighter when the sunlight hits them. Pinning me down with his stare, he's trying to intimidate me with his intensity.

Before I lose my courage, I lean back, straightening my back and arching my spine, thrusting my breasts forward.

Raising my arms, I take a hair tie and I proceed to tie my hair in a ponytail. But as I bring my hands up, twisting my hair in the air, I feel my crop top rise up.

The material slowly moves up over my breasts, and through my sheer blouse, I know Raf is getting an eyeful. Enough that it gets a reaction out of him, the size of his pupils growing under my very gaze.

"Cover yourself," he snaps, confirming my suspicion.

"What?" I ask innocently, my arms still in the air. I roll my shoulders, ensuring the material of my top bunches up even further over my breasts.

"Cover. Yourself." He bites out the words, his jaw clenched as he looks at me as if he'd like nothing more than murder me on the spot.

"Why?" I feign ignorance. "I have a blouse underneath," I shrug, the motion making my tits bounce.

He notices too, his cheeks turning a deep shade of red before he forces himself to look away, turning his head to stare out the window. His fists are still clenched in his lap, and I know he's fighting for control.

"I didn't realize you were such a prude, Raf," I chuckle. "Is this what it takes to defeat you? A little side boob?" I bring my hand to my mouth as I give a low laugh.

One moment I'm laughing, the next I'm flush against his chest, his hand wrapped around my throat as he looks me dead in the eye.

There's no amusement in his gaze. Nothing but chilling coldness, and for a moment I fear I may have misjudged him.

His hold is tight enough to hold me in place, but not enough to hinder my breathing.

CHAPTER NINETEEN

NOELLE

"What..." the words tumble out of my mouth as a twisted grin appears on his face.

"So that's what you've been up to," he says, his mouth curling up in derision. "This cheap trick might work on other men, but you chose the wrong target."

"I don't think so," I reply confidently, willing myself not to panic, even though I find myself caught in his web. "I think I chose the perfect target," I drawl, shifting around so I'm sitting closer to his lap.

His hand tightens over my neck instinctively, his expression almost pained.

"A little thirsty, Noelle, aren't you?" he mocks. "Let me guess," he pauses, chuckling as he sets his cold eyes on me. "No one will fuck the crazy in you?"

My lips draw into a thin line, the jibe hitting the mark. I may be impervious to a lot of things, but being called crazy on a regular basis has a way of screwing with someone.

"I'm not crazy," I whisper.

"Still a little liar," he retorts, bringing me closer until his face is inches away from mine. "You might flaunt your body, and you might throw yourself at me," he pauses, his breath on my lips a tantalizing caress. "But you're the last woman I'd *ever* fuck," he resolutely states.

My heart drums in my chest, my pulse through the roof as I can only stare into his crystal clear eyes—a shade so painfully beautiful it's making my insides clench with longing. And as much as I'd like to remain unmoved in the face of his insults, I can't.

"Now who's the liar?" I fire back, trying to mask the hurt—anything to hide the way his words affect me. Going on the offensive might be the only way to keep myself in check. "You want me," I say, dropping my voice a notch and doing my best at sounding seductive—though I'm clueless at best at what I'm doing. "You want me and you hate yourself for wanting me."

"I don't," he grits out, his jaw clenched. His fingers, too, tighten over my skin, and a gasp escapes my lips at the sudden pressure.

"You do," I counter, a need to taunt him growing inside of me. "Why don't you give in?" I ask softly, bringing my hand to his face and cupping his cheek. He jerks at my touch, but he doesn't move away, his steely eyes still on me. "Who knows, I might please you better than Lucero," I whisper as I lean forward, our lips mere inches away from each other.

I don't know where this is all coming from. I'm being more forward than I've been in my entire life.

He holds himself still, but as he hears Lucero's name, his entire body becomes stiff, a terrifying frostiness entering his eyes.

"Do *not*," he starts, so much aggression emanating from that deep voice of his that I find it hard not to tremble in his grasp, "say her name. You're not fit to utter her name."

With that, he thrusts me away from him, flinging me backwards. My back hits the seat, a sliver of pain flaring at the brusque movement.

It should be enough to make me stop. It should be enough to make me realize that I'm way over my head, dealing with a dangerous man on the verge of snapping.

But there's something inside of me—something I don't quite understand and I *don't* want to understand. Because it's irrational just like the way he makes me feel.

Hate. Resentment. Abhorrence.

Arousal.

He despises me. That much is clear. And I should return the feeling—if only for the way he's treated me until now.

But why can't I? Why does the mere thought of him and Lucero cause me so much pain, making me act so unlike myself?

My usual self-preservation is long gone as I proceed to bait him, throwing all rational thinking out the window.

There's a twitch in his cheek as he still looks at me with murder in his eyes.

But his animosity only serves to spur me further. I lean back, slowly parting my legs. My skirt is bunched up around my ass and I know that any slight movement gives him a peek at my underwear.

He's doing his best to look me in the eye, but I can feel the tension radiating off him.

We spend long, drawn-out moments in a battle of wills.

Me, slowly spreading my legs even more. Him, trying his best to resist looking.

The tension is thick, and I can hear his breathing—harsh and barely controlled. His muscles are tightly coiled as if he's only just keeping himself from jumping on me—to kill me or fuck me, I don't know.

"You're playing with fire, Noelle," he grits his teeth as he addresses me.

"Am I?" I tilt my head to the side. My hands on my knees, I slowly trail my fingers up my inner thighs.

He's forcing himself to keep his eyes on my face, but the moment my hands near the junction of my thighs, he loses that battle with himself. His gaze snaps to my underwear, and I know I have him where I want him.

He swallows, unable to wrench his eyes from that particular spot. And to tease him even further, I lean back, arching my spine and bringing my pelvis closer to the edge of the seat.

There's a dangerous glint to his eyes as his pupils contract, his stare so intense I feel it in my core.

But just like he's currently captivated by my spread thighs, I'm not indifferent, either. Oh, I'm anything but indifferent as I feel a gush of wetness pour out of me, my folds slick with uncomfortable arousal.

"I *am* playing with fire. Hot, liquid fire," I rasp, my voice husky.

My lids flutter closed as I shift in my seat, seeking to alleviate the growing discomfort in my lower belly.

One moment I feel the slight friction of the leather seat against my aching core, the next I'm on my back, with Raf between my open legs, his knee close to that area that begs for relief.

A thunderous expression on his face, he wraps both hands around my neck, squeezing tight.

"I should kill you," he grits out. "I should fucking kill you."

I blink, trying to dispel the arousal clouding my mind.

"You should," I answer readily, bringing my hands up and covering his, urging him to tighten his grip. "So why don't you?"

He breathes harshly, his nostrils flaring in evident anger.

Yet that's not the only evident thing as my eyes dip to his pants. He'd worn a pair of dress pants, the hardness molding to the material unmistakable.

He doesn't reply, a wild look on his face as he takes me in, studying every inch of my skin.

"Are you so hungry for cock you'd open your legs for anyone?" he sneers at me, his face twisted in a malicious scowl. "Even someone who despises you?"

Of course he'd think the worst of me. It's not like I would have expected any less of him—and in a way he *is* right. The person I'd been at the *hacienda* had been my worst version. Sometimes I'm not even sure if that had been me. I'd felt like a spectator in my own body watching as events unfolded before me.

But I can't let that rattle me.

"Hmm," I drawl seductively, lifting my arms and trailing my hands down his torso. Stone hard muscle meets my touch and I'm reminded how beautifully built he is and the fact that he *could* kill me if he wanted. He could snap me in two. "I hear hate sex is the best," I continue, knowing I'm getting to him.

As my hands hover over the band of his pants, I stop, my eyes on his as I watch the swift play of emotions flashing over his face.

He's so tense, and growing tenser still. I can tell he's holding himself back, and for once I'd like him to unleash everything he has on me.

Wreck me.

"You hear?" His voice sends a shiver down my back. "I'm surprised it's not from experience. After all, someone with your track record..." his mouth pulls up in a devious smile. "I guess you prefer to be paid for it," he jibes.

"What are you talking about?" I frown.

"I've heard about your other hobby—prostitution was it?" He smirks. "Is that another kink of yours? Being paid for sex?"

My eyes flash at him in surprise. I guess Cisco had gone all out in telling him *everything* about me.

"So what if it is? You're one to talk?" I raise an eyebrow at him, trying to look unbothered. I know there's no point in explaining it had all been a misunderstanding. That I'd simply gone to a club and had started chatting up some girls in the bathroom when the cops had raided the place. But he would never believe that. After all, only lies can come out of my mouth.

"Me?" He scoffs.

"Seeing how you always go for my throat, I'd say you're the kinky one," I taunt. "What is it, does that make you feel in control? Does it make you feel strong and manly?" I quip.

His eyes widen, and something akin to regret crosses his features. But before I can identify the emotion, it's gone, the cold mask back in place.

"Oh it does," his mouth curls up in a cruel smile as he leans down, his face close to mine. There's no trace of warmth in his features—only hatred. Pure, unadulterated hatred.

And though I'd grown used to being the object of his animosity, somehow seeing it so blatantly—so up close—makes something inside of me break.

"Because like this," he starts, his breath caressing my cheek, "I can control whether you live or die..." he trails off, one hand moving up my neck as he cups my jaw and pins it in place. "I could fuck you too," he smirks. "But that would be giving you what you want. You think I didn't realize your game?" He laughs derisively.

I twist in his hold, suddenly uncomfortable at being bared before him like this.

"I see you've taken your seduction assignment seriously. Too bad you don't do it for me, Noelle," he grits out.

"I don't do it for you?" I give a dry laugh. "Keep telling yourself that, golden boy. One day you might believe it," I wink at him, bringing one hand over the bulge in his pants.

He freezes, his expression murderous.

"You're the last woman I'd ever fuck," he states angrily.

"Sure, you've already said that before," I laugh. "Is that for my benefit or yours? Because from where I'm sitting it doesn't look like that," I bat my lashes at him as I cup him through his pants.

His eyes widen in surprise. Mine would too if I didn't force myself to stay in character. I've never in my life been this forward, but I guess he does bring the worst in me.

"Impressive," I start on a confident note, but it only ends on a wheeze as I feel his hand tightening over my neck, my breathing limited. With his other hand, he quickly grabs my arms, pinning them above my head so I can't touch him. The situation is achingly familiar, and I blink rapidly to dissipate the fog that's seeking to lay siege over my mind.

"You're really testing my patience, Noelle," he grunts, his features tense.

A bump in the road and our position shifts as he's propelled forward. He's still holding on to me, but his pelvis is now in alignment with mine and...

We both stare at each other in shock, a low gasp escaping my lips as I feel his hardness right against my core.

His lips part in disbelief and he looks at me as if he's never seen me before. The pressure against my clit is too much, and I can't help it as I rock my hips against him, seeking some relief.

He doesn't pull away. Not immediately. He doesn't move as he continues to look at me through hooded eyes, the desire unmistakable beneath all that disdain.

But as the car pulls to a stop, he's off me, hissing at me to put myself together before he gets out of the car, disappearing from sight.

Chapter Twenty

Noelle

"Aren't you done?" he asks as I spot yet another store I want to check out.

"No. And you promised Cisco you'd accompany me everywhere," I stick out my tongue at him, dragging him with me towards the store.

After the car ride, he's been brooding all day while keeping a small distance from me. And as I'd taken him from store to store to try clothes on, he'd tried to stay aloof and not engage in conversation with me.

A smile pulls at my lips as I realize that my plan might be working after all. He obviously feels lust for me, no matter how much he'd like to pretend it's not true. His body language doesn't lie. He's almost constantly trying to adjust his erection in my presence. A blush envelops my cheeks at the thought, because I've been watching him—specifically that part of him—a little too closely.

But there's also his gaze that seems to become captivated by every bit of bare skin I show—fact that only imbues me with more confidence for my next step.

We go inside the store, and after picking a few items I motion him towards the changing rooms, asking him to wait outside.

Every time I change into an albeit sexy outfit, I exit the

changing room and I ask for his feedback. Every time, though, he gives me a half-assed ok as he looks sideways, barely glancing at me.

"Rafaelo!" I call him out when I see he's looking behind me instead of *at* me.

"Didn't you get enough clothes? Let's pay and go home already," he rolls his eyes at me, but still avoids my gaze.

"You're really boorish, you know," I shake my head at him, crossing my arms over my chest.

I'd specifically gone for a latex dress that molds to my body in hopes of getting a reaction. Well...maybe I should cut my losses since this doesn't seem to work particularly well.

"And you look like a stripper," he snaps, finally glancing at me. "Where the hell would you even wear that?" He asks, incensed.

Getting up, he comes closer to me, his nostrils flared as he peruses my body.

"Go change and let's go. You're not getting that," he states resolutely, all but shoving me inside the changing room.

"I am," I counter. "I happen to like it."

"You like looking like a stripper?" He raises a brow, his voice low and dangerous.

His deep tone never fails to send a shiver down my back, his timbre making my entire body erupt in goosebumps.

"What if I do? They get paid for it, you know?" I retort cheekily, pushing him out before closing the door to the changing room and taking the dress off.

I take a little more time to calm myself before I get out, noting that Raf's in a sour mood as he taps his foot restlessly, looking at me as if he'd like nothing more than to commit murder.

Pushing my chin up, I pass by him, ignoring his silent tantrum and going to the till to pay.

He doesn't say anything as he follows closely. But the moment we are out of the store, he snatches the bag from my hand, pivoting on his heel and heading straight for the trash can.

His intention registers a little late.

"No," I run after him, making it just in time to see my bag of clothes hit the bottom of the bin. "What's wrong with you?" I snap at him, my hands balled into fists.

Bending, I don't care if he gets a full view of my ass as I try to retrieve my shopping bag.

A masculine groan alerts me to the fact that he *is* in fact getting a full view of my ass, and for a moment I have to wonder if he's staring at it. Without even thinking, I wiggle my hips, making sure he gets a full show. Grabbing the edge of the bag, I remain bent over the bin.

Some whistles resound from around me, and I belatedly realize that it's not just Raf who's getting the show.

Damn!

I quickly get myself together, taking the bag and turning to see a Raf on the brink of an apoplexy. The veins in his neck are prominent, pulsing right under my gaze as he stares at me with anger in his eyes.

Another man stops a few feet away from me, his eyes on my ass as he continues to whistle lasciviously and leer at me. Raf surprises me as he turns swiftly, grabbing the man by the throat. A head shorter than Raf, it looks like child play as he leans in to whisper something in his ear. The man blanches, nodding repeatedly before Raf finally releases him, urging him to run—which he does.

"What did you say to him?" I frown, but he doesn't even hear me.

Coming closer, I can see he is *pissed*. His steps are measured, his body wound so tightly I'm surprised he didn't put the man in the hospital with all the aggression that's rolling off him.

"Aren't you ashamed to behave like this?" he grits out.

"Like what?" I shrug, making to move past him.

"Like a fucking whore," he spits out, his eyes narrowed at me in distaste as he catches my arm, holding me in place.

"What...?" My mouth drops open as I stare at him.

"First, you try to entice me to fuck you, and now, you're showing your ass to *anyone* who walks by?"

"You didn't want it. Others may. Not my fault you have bad taste," I smile sweetly at him.

His grip tightens on my upper arm as he jerks me towards him.

Tipping my head up, I find him gazing at me with an indecipherable look on his face. There's a twitch in his cheek as he purses his lips, seemingly trying to control himself.

"Don't force my hand, Noelle," he says in a strained tone.

"Or what? You're going to kill me? Oh, wait. You can't," I chuckle. "You can't do anything, can you?" I flutter my lashes at him as I'm daring him to do something.

"What I can do," he enunciates each word carefully, his eyes never leaving mine, "is paint your ass red so you never try something like that again."

I frown, not understanding what he means. But I don't dwell on that, changing the subject slightly so he doesn't realize I didn't get his jibe.

"You're on the losing side, Raf. You should just admit it," I wink at him before I push at him, my foot making contact with his shin.

Taken by surprise, his hold becomes slack enough for me to take flight.

"You can't catch me," I giggle as I make a funny face at him before I start running.

For a moment, I don't think he's going to follow. But a loud curse later, and I hear the footsteps behind me.

I dash into the first store I see, which coincidentally happens to be a lingerie one. Without even thinking, I grab some pieces off a rack and I turn to the changing rooms, locking myself in one.

The entire area is luxurious, and I'm impressed to find myself in quite possibly the most beautiful changing room I've ever seen.

There's a velvet bench that takes up the entirety of the wall, a table by the side and mirrors on all sides of the room.

Leaning against one wall, I sigh in relief.

But it's only a few moments later that I hear Raf's disgruntled tone as he calls my name.

"Noelle! Get out and come here," he yells as he comes charging towards the changing rooms.

Biting my lip, I try to think of something quick. The first idea that comes to mind, though, is so wild, I can't help but giggle to myself as I quickly shed my clothes and put on the lace bodysuit I'd brought with me.

The bra is a little tight and my boobs are almost spilling out of their confines. Lace flows down, molded to my body, the bodysuit making me really look like a stripper.

Before I lose my courage though, I wrench the door open. Raf is pacing in front of the changing rooms, a deep scowl on his face.

And as he sees what I'm wearing, he stops in his tracks, his eyes widening as he lets them roam greedily over my form.

"Like what you see?" I wiggle my eyebrows suggestively, leaning against the door in a seductive stance.

He doesn't answer me, not that I expected a reply from him.

Just to rile him further, since I know he is *not* indifferent, I proceed to move around slightly, emphasizing the curve of my spine as it leads to my ass, thrusting it towards him and pushing my breasts against the changing room's door.

A mix of emotions plays on his face—from anger, to annoyance, to desire and back to anger, he's an open book.

Except he isn't.

Not when, shaking his head, he mutters something under his breath before he strides determinedly towards me, pushing me inside the changing room and locking the door behind him.

"What…What are you doing?"

"You're such a brat, Noelle," he says, his eyes dipping to the swell of my breasts.

Suddenly, I have the urge to cover myself, feeling a little out of my depth. Maybe I've taken this too far? I've been playing the game all along thinking he'd *never* cross the line.

But as he continues to crowd me, pushing his body into mine, I realize I may have miscalculated a few things.

"You're not allowed in here," I say in a small voice, my eyes moving wildly about the room as I map escape routes.

And just as I utter the words, a knock sounds at the door, a sales assistant's voice peeking through.

"Excuse me, these are single use only. *And* females only."

Relief floods my features at her words and I nod to Raf to exit, folding my arms over my chest and waiting for him to leave.

His eyes narrowed at me, he takes a step back, opening the door just enough to address the sales assistant.

"You will turn around and you will forget you saw us here," he barks in a stern voice.

I can see the woman through the small space, and her expression immediately changes as she takes Raf in.

"Of course," I mutter under my breath. Who wouldn't find him attractive when he looks like a human Adonis.

"Are we clear?" He asks as he slips her a hundred dollars.

She nods her head, speechless, and Raf quickly locks the door again.

"That... You can't do that," my voice breaks slightly, and a shiver goes down my back at seeing that no one will help me now.

"Well, it seems like I can," he says in an arrogant tone.

Moving around the spacious room, he looks intently at me, his hand at his collar as he loosens his tie before he takes it off.

My eyes are drawn to his hands—those strong, big hands and the prominent veins that protrude with every flex. Wrapping the tie around his knuckles, he circles around me, almost like a predator circling his prey.

For the first time, I'm afraid.

Countless scenarios are going through my mind as my gaze hones in on the tie, before I whip my eyes back to his.

He's going to kill me—strangle me. That's it.

His expression is humorless as he comes closer. I try to dash towards the door, but he simply blocks my way, backing me against the wall and placing his arm above my head, caging me in.

"Uhm," I start, still looking around for an exit route. "I'm sorry?" I offer a fake apology.

"You're sorry," he smirks.

The change is unmistakable. Whereas before he'd been fully in control of himself—striving to keep a mask of civility in place—now he let loose.

I can feel it in the energy swirling around us, the air that seems to grow hotter by the second, just like his hot breath fans my face as he leans in, an arrogant smile on his lips.

"Not so brave, are you now?"

"Uhm," I mumble incoherently. "I think we should go. We've been gone too long," I give a nervous laugh.

"Not yet," he stops me from leaving. "I've decided to take you up on your offer. After all, when will I experience hate sex again," he laughs derisively, but it doesn't reach his eyes.

My entire body is trembling at this point, even though I'm trying to put on a strong front.

"Well," I wet my lips, willing myself to calm down. "The offer expired," I push against his chest.

"Did it?" he drawls derisively.

I raise my gaze to his and I almost get lost in those stormy blue eyes of his.

"I think the offer was never on the table, was it, little liar?" he asks as he drags his fingers down the column of my neck in the lightest caress.

Chapter Twenty-One

Noelle

"Bad, bad girl," his smooth voice does something to my senses, making me both breathless and a nervous wreck at the same time. "You're such a bad little tease, you leave me no choice but to correct your behavior," he continues, the corner of his mouth lifting up in a satisfied smile as he leans down, his breath caressing my earlobe.

"Wh-what do you mean?" I stammer.

"It's time you learned what happens when you invite danger but aren't quite ready to face the consequences."

My legs are wobbly, my knees almost buckling at the mere touch of his skin on mine. My breath catches in my throat, and I can only stare at him in awe, my entire being betraying me.

"We should talk," I blurt out—anything to ensure this doesn't go further.

"About what?" He gives me a crooked smile. "All the ways I'll fuck you?" he intones and I pale. "I think I'll start right here, against the wall. What do you say about that?" His voice is teasing, but there's still a hint of danger.

"I..." I trail off, feeling completely out of my comfort zone. "I think we should sit. I have a fear of heights, you see," I give him a feeble smile, belatedly realizing the idiocy that came out of my mouth.

"A fear of heights?" he repeats, amused, and before I know it, his hands grab my waist, lifting me in the air and settling me against the wall. My legs fall open of their own accord, and he steps between them, his hardness making contact with my center and making me gasp, my eyes widening at the fact that this *might* be happening.

This can't be happening.

But as soon as that thought surfaces in my head, it flies out the window at the smallest contact with his erection, my mouth opening on a silent moan.

"Are you scared now?" he inquires in a mocking tone, and my eyes snap open—*when had they closed?*

"Yes?"

"Good. You should be scared," he chuckles. "Because it would be so easy, little liar," he continues, trailing his hand down my neck and to the valley of my breasts. He doesn't stop, however, as he goes even lower, to the place that holds the seams of the bodysuit. "I'd open your suit," he drawls in a wicked voice, his fingers snapping the mechanism open. Air whooshes in my private area, meeting my wetness and making me whimper in a small protest.

I gulp down, my eyes seeking his and pleading with him to let me go as my mouth fails to verbalize my objection.

"I'd impale you on my cock in one swift thrust, making you yell in pain. Because I wouldn't care if you were wet, or ready to take me. Although," he chuckles, "you would be, wouldn't you? You're too much of a cock slut not to be dripping. Am I right, Noelle?"

I can't speak. His words ring in my ears, but I can only shake my head at him, unable to reply to his taunts.

He's not touching me there either. And it would be so easy for him to confirm just how wet I am. A sob catches in my throat at the realization. Because I'd been trying to make him slip, but *I* am the one who slipped.

"I'd fuck you so hard you wouldn't be able to sit down for days. You certainly wouldn't be able to flash your ass to anyone, because they'd see. They would *all* see. The marks on your flesh. The prints of my palms..."

The more he speaks, the more I feel myself slipping, his words a mix of intoxicating lust and a devastating promise of retribution.

"Stop," I finally manage to utter.

"What was that, little liar?"

"Stop, please."

"Why? Didn't you want me to fuck you? Well, congratulations. You're getting fucked. But it's on *my* terms. And that means you don't speak. You don't make a sound. You take it all like the bad little tease you are and you let me use you like my obedient slut. How is that, huh?" He wraps his lips around my earlobe and tugging it in a small bite.

"Raf..."

"How does that sound, Noelle? Will you let me use you? Work my hate on your body until you can't walk anymore? Until you're so thoroughly fucked you won't ever think about enticing another man? You'd like that, wouldn't you?" he continues in a perverse voice, and a shiver goes through my body.

"N—no," I whisper.

"You don't sound very certain," he chuckles. "I'll even make you a deal. I'll pay you for every service rendered, since you seem to prefer it that way."

"I'm not your whore," I force myself to say, my voice tremulous.

"Then whose whore are you?" He leans back, raising an eyebrow at me. His finger is in my hair as he twirls a strand around it.

His emotionless eyes are watching me intently—predatorily. He knows he got me backed into a corner and he's enjoying my discomfiture.

"No one's," I answer confidently, pushing my chin up and meeting his gaze head on.

He looks at me for a second, his expression serious, before he bursts into laughter.

"You could have fooled me," he laughs, and before I know it, he's off me, dropping me to the ground and taking a step back, watching me as I fall to the floor.

I'm breathing hard, my pulse out of control. Still, something inside of me doesn't want to accept that I've lost.

He's staring at me expectantly as I pull myself up, turning my gaze towards him.

"You'll pay for this," I sneer at him, making to leave the room—regardless of my state of undress.

"Not so fast, little liar. It's *you* who still has to pay," he smirks at me, bringing the tie up and playing with it in front of me.

"No," I shake my head. "We're done here," I state before turning.

But I don't manage to take another step before he has us both on the velvet bench. He maneuvers me around in such a way that I'm lying face down on his lap, his erection nestled against my lower belly.

"Wha—what?" I barely have time to ask the question as he wraps the tie around my hands, quickly securing them above my head.

"You need a lesson, Noelle. And it seems that words don't work with you," he tells me, and before I can question what he means, his palm makes contact with my ass.

Startled, I yelp in pain, jerking out of his lap and trying to move my immobilized hands.

"I told you," he pauses, and another palm connects with my ass cheeks, the sting bringing tears to my eyes. "I'd paint your ass red."

"Stop," I croak just as he spanks me again, but this time his hand lingers over my battered bottom, slowly moving up and down.

"Does it hurt?" His tone is brisk.

I nod. "Yes."

"Good. It's supposed to hurt," he states before he slaps my ass again, this time harder.

I'm pretty sure my ass cheeks are already a stringent red, and as he continues to spank me, each time taking a break as he slowly caresses my flesh, I realize I truly misjudged him.

"It's supposed to show you that every action has a reaction," he speaks again, just as he spreads his palm over the swell of my ass, moving lower until he dips his fingers between my legs.

"Well, well. I didn't actually think it would be true," he chuckles derisively. "But you *are* dripping."

Mortification burns at my cheeks, and as the *lesson* comes to an end, I have to admit to myself that for all my confidence in dealing with Raf, I'd been wrong about him.

So very wrong.

It's a few days later that I get to experience the full extent of Raf's cruelty when everything backfires against me. All along I'd been trying to make him snap, and now I fear I've pushed him too far.

"I don't understand where you're taking me," I tell him as he more or less shoves me in the car, barking some instructions to the driver.

"You don't have to understand," he raises a brow as he leans back, making himself comfortable in his seat. "You should thank me instead. I'm merely giving you what you want."

"What are you talking about?' I frown.

"Hmm," he smiles, a dangerous smile that doesn't reach his eyes.

He scans my figure, his mouth curling up in satisfaction at what he sees.

My brows shoot up in question and I fold my arms over my chest. I'm wearing a black mid-thigh dress, and its bodice, while tight, covers every inch of skin.

His perusal unnerves me, especially as I don't think there's anything in particular that he can see.

We spend the entire journey in silence, and I have a hard time grasping what he's trying to do. I know it must be some sort of punishment, or humiliation, since from him I can't expect anything better.

After all, he's already embarrassed me in front of my family, making me seem like a besotted fool who can't tell right from wrong. And so far all my attempts to rectify that have backfired.

I would have thought that if I turned the tables on him and

acted as he expected me to, I would have had an advantage. Instead, he's only managed to repeatedly disarm me, and show me that for all my bravado, I'm all talk and no action.

It is the truth, though, isn't it?

I'd tried to entice him with my body thinking it would embarrass him, but I'd ended up being the humiliated one.

What did I expect when I had no experience to back up my words? I'd put on a seductive front to fluster him and make him flounder. He's a man after all, and as we've proved, one that isn't immune to me—or at least my body. I'd based my behavior and actions on things I'd read on the internet and seen in movies, and for a while the femme fatale persona I'd assumed had given me a freedom unlike any other. But it had also backfired on me, putting me on the spot and showing me exactly what happens when I'm backed into a corner with my own weapons turned on me.

My cheeks heat as I remember the way my body had reacted to his nearness and to his obscene words.

I should have been scandalized, yet instead, I'd been turned on.

I'm a mess.

He turns me into a mess.

Out of everyone in the world, why is it that I have to react like this to him? Why is he the only one who's *ever* awoken these types of feelings in me?

My thoughts are interrupted as the car draws to a stop. I peer out the window in an effort to gauge what he has in plan, but all the buildings are nondescript.

Taking hold of my arm, he pulls me out of the car and towards one building.

"Does my brother know where you're taking me?" I ask, suddenly concerned. He *could* kill me, and no one would be wiser.

"He doesn't need to," Rafaelo smirks. "He trusts me with you," he chuckles, as if it were the most absurd thing. And it is, because my brother may have very well signed my death warrant.

There is a long hallway as he all but drags me towards a pair of double doors at the end of the corridor.

Opening the door, I find myself in a dark room, a kaleidoscope of colors on the wall, the only source of light—but even that is dim at best.

There's a chair in the middle, and by the side I see five men lined up, all with a number tag on their shirts.

"What...?" I turn to Rafaelo, alarm written all over my features.

"Since I'm not going to take you up on your offer, I thought these men would," he smiles.

"What do you mean?" The words are softly spoken as I refuse to believe what he means to do.

"What do I mean, Noelle?" He takes a step towards me, his thumb under my chin as he tips it up. "Since you're such a horny little bitch, I thought I'd give you a present. Of course. The best thing about presents is the element of surprise," he grits right as he brings me to him, my back to his front as he keeps me flush against his body.

"Look and memorize their faces," he whispers in my ear. "Any one of them could be your lover for the night. Isn't that what you wanted? Why you threw yourself at me?" His chilling voice makes me shudder, terror engulfing me as I realize he's not joking.

"No, no," I shake my head.

"Yes, yes," he mocks, and out of nowhere, he places a blindfold over my eyes, the material obstructing my view and making me blind to the world.

"You think you're such a seductress, well..." he trails off, amusement infusing every words. "Seduce away," he laughs.

Panic overtakes me and I start flailing my arms around in an effort to get away from him and get rid of the blindfold.

But I don't get to do anything as he has my wrists secure, a handcuff clicking into place.

"Let the game begin," he chuckles. "And don't worry. I'll be here to give them instructions," he says as he throws me over his shoulder. I keep struggling, but it's in vain as he places me on the chair I'd seen in the middle of the room.

And before I can think to stand up and run, he has my feet bound too, ensuring I have no freedom of movement.

"Rafaelo, please no. Please don't," I beg him, the desperation in my voice clear. "Anything but this, please."

"Tsk, tsk, Noelle," his tongue clicks with the sound. "Not so brave now, are you?" his laugh becomes more and more distant as I realize he's moved away from me.

"Too late, little liar," he says from afar, and my anxiety skyrockets.

Suddenly, music starts blasting in the room, the sound masking any other noise around and making sure I don't know what's going on around me.

And then there's his voice. In the speakers.

"Number 1. It's your turn."

My eyes widen behind my blindfold, my heart drumming in my chest. The music is so loud I can't hear anything—not steps on the floor indicating movement, nor breathing next to me, a sign that someone is near.

I'm completely in the dark.

But that's what he wanted, didn't he?

He wanted my terror. He wanted to push me beyond mere fear.

The absence of all my senses is already messing with me, and when I feel a hand touch me, I jump up, startled.

But the hand is not deterred. If anything, it becomes even more insistent as it glides all over my body.

I scream.

Or I think I do.

I can't even hear myself above the deafening sound of the music. My throat vibrates, but my ears don't pick up anything.

The pressure of the hands increases as they settle over my breasts, prodding, pinching and poking.

"Please, stop," I utter the useless words, tears burning at the back of my eyes.

But my cry for help is in vain.

The hands continue to assault my body, and I feel them everywhere.

My neck.

My breasts.

And lower.

"Number 2. Let's spice things up a little," Rafaelo's voice blares through the speakers, and I have a small reprieve from the roving hands—enough to draw breath again.

But that is short lived as I find myself out of the chair and laid on the floor on my stomach.

I struggle against my bounds, though I know it to be useless, all the while, Rafaelo's chuckle reverberates through the room, the sound of his derisive laugh the only thing making it past the barrier of sound.

My dress is pushed up my ass, and that's when my true terror begins.

The cold air hits my skin, goosebumps appearing all over. And it's then that I feel them again—foreign hands that roam all over my flesh.

My cries become more urgent, all in hopes he will be able to hear me and stop this madness—stop it before it goes too far.

But that's not his goal.

No, his goal is to humiliate me and strip me of any bit of human decency I have left. Isn't that what he said? That he would make me rue the day I ever crossed his path?

On the sidelines, Rafaelo encourages the man to continue, become bolder.

And he does.

Gripping my panties to the side, he rips them from my body, my most intimate place exposed in the most degrading way possible.

"No, no," I keep shaking my head, hoping this isn't true. That it's just a bad dream. That it's not actually happening to me.

"Number 3. Your turn."

I gasp, breathing deeply as I try to focus on this moment of reprieve. My hands are bound behind my back, but I don't let that stop me. Not as I keep bashing my wrists against the cuffs, thinking that broken bones are preferrable to being raped.

I push and I pull, everything in an attempt to get myself free of them.

And though my flesh bruises and my joints twist, I realize it's all in vain.

Especially as a cold touch sears itself into my skin, fingers trailing lower down my ass before dipping between my legs.

A strangled sound escapes me, but it's muffled by all the noise around.

Though I scream and scream, nothing works.

A finger probes between my legs, gliding over my folds before pushing inside.

My body freezes, my throat clogged with revulsion.

"Please no," the silent plea escapes my lips, but there's no one to hear it—much less listen to it.

I buck against the person, trying to push the hand away. But one firm grip on my hip and he has me in place, playing with me to his heart's content.

My breath is coming in short spurts, my anxiety already at its peak point as I realize everything I do is useless. Whether I want or not I *will* be raped.

And Rafaelo is undoubtedly gloating by the sides, watching me get assaulted by the random men he hired.

Sobs rack my body, a low tremor engulfing me and making me shake uncontrollably.

"Number 4. Let's take this to the next level," his voice resounds, full of amusement.

This time, however, not even the break between the switches is enough to help me calm down. Instead, I'm hyperventilating because I know what's coming. I know what the next level is, and my mind is already dying on me as it tries to make me block everything out.

But how can I, when the next time I'm touched it's to feel something hard against my ass.

My mouth opens, but this time nothing will come out.

He straddles me, his erection between my ass cheeks and that's when I know I'm fighting a losing battle.

It's only a matter of time now.

And as he separates my cheeks, gliding the hard length between them before positioning the head at my entrance, I squeeze my eyes shut.

"I want to die," I whisper to myself, a prayer to a void that won't talk back.

"Stop." Raf's voice booms. "I have a deal for you, Noelle. Number 4 can continue. Or," he pauses, and the anticipation is killing me—already willing to do anything to escape this.

My blindfold is already soaked from my tears, my throat sore and painful.

"Submit to me," he continues. "Crawl to me and beg me to spare you and I will," his malefic laugh echoes above the music.

He doesn't let me ponder his offer as he adds. "Lift your hands if you agree. You have three seconds."

One humiliation or the other. In the end, I'm not walking away unscathed.

But there is *no* choice as I immediately lift my hands up.

And just like that, the man is off me.

My cuffs give way as I move my hands and I realize my feet have been freed too.

Scrambling to put myself together, I pull my dress over my legs, quickly removing my blindfold.

I blink.

The sudden change makes it hard for my eyes to accommodate to the new light. But as I blink some clarity into my eyes, it's to see there's no one else in the room but me and Raf.

There are no men.

Not one soul.

He's sitting on the chair, his legs apart, his hands on his knees as he stares at me intently.

One hand turns, palm up, as two fingers beckon me to him.

He wants me to crawl.

I swallow hard, every cell in my body rebelling at the thought.

But the threat is still looming over my head, and if there's one thing I've learned in my twenty-two years of life it's that you should know when to pick your battles.

And *this* is already a lost one.

Positioning myself on my knees, I drag myself towards him.

His eyes narrow at me as he looks at me with an air of condescension. There's no doubt that he wanted me to crawl on my hands *and* knees, not *just* like this. This one small act of rebellion is the only way I can still keep a piece of myself, and so I am *not* willing to compromise.

Moving towards him, I lay at his feet when I reach him, waiting for his decree. It's when I'm by his side that I notice something. His pants are unbuckled, his zipper lowered, and I note the hard outline of his cock.

My gaze whips back to his, the question written all over my face.

He merely smirks, placing his two fingers under my jaw and bringing me closer. Using his other hand, he produces a small remote. And as he clicks on one button, his voice resounds in the speakers.

"Number 1. It's your turn."

My eyes widen as I realize what he'd done. Everything had been pre-recorded.

But why?

"You're mine to torture," he says cruelly. "Mine to torment," his mouth tugs up in a twisted smile. "And now mine to own," he chuckles.

"You're a bastard," I spit at him, trying to wrench myself from his grasp.

"And you're caught, little liar. This was just to show you you're at my mercy."

He lowers his face to mine.

"I can end you anywhere. *Anytime,*" he rasps against my lips. "So think twice before you try your wiles on me, Noelle. Because next time," his nostrils flare. "It might not end with this."

He flings me away from him, and I fall to my ass. I stare at him unblinking, somehow unable to react.

Adrenaline keeps pumping in my veins, the scare from before still strong in my mind.

He rises from his chair, heading to the door as he barks at me to put myself together. My gaze follows his retreating back, and I don't know what prompts me to inquire, but somehow my mind needs the confirmation.

"Was there ever…another man in here?" I ask, my voice groggy, my throat hurting with every syllable I utter.

He stops, only his profile visible as he half-turns.

"No," the harsh sound echoes in the room. "I told you, Noelle. Only *I* get to hurt you," he grits out before he's gone.

Chapter Twenty-Two
Noelle

My pulse drums in my ears as I startle from yet another nightmare. It's been weeks since the dark room incident yet I still haven't managed to move on. The fear of being violated in that manner is hard to overcome, and to an extent, it still lives within me. Then there's Rafaelo's cruel laughter—that ominous sound that follows me everywhere.

He set out to destroy me, and I fear he's well on the path to do so. Especially as he seems to have honed in on my weaknesses. In the beginning, I didn't want to believe he would be capable of something this terrible. Yet the more I get to know him the more I realize that the love that fuels his thirst for revenge is all encompassing.

The love for *Lucero*. I'm ashamed to admit that pains me more than anything.

I've been struggling with my feelings for him from the start. They are too out of control, fear and longing mixing together in a lethal combination. Add jealousy in the mix and I feel lost—truly, truly lost.

As I get out of my bed, I go about my morning ablutions, deciding to take breakfast in my room—yet again.

My initial plan of taunting Rafaelo clearly backfired—

immensely. If anything, I'm always the one who ends up on the losing side, no matter how much I try to keep my chin up and ignore his jibes. After the dark room, our interactions have only gotten worse, his words growing crueler with each passing day.

Before, I may have tried to defend myself and tell him that I'm not who he thinks I am, but he's too set in his ways. In his mind, I've already been tried and convicted. If my own family doesn't believe me...why would he, a stranger?

The more he insults me, the more I should learn to hate him, and the more he mentions Lucero, the more I should just bury my emotions.

But it doesn't work like that. Not when my heart skips a beat every time he's in the vicinity. Not when every waking moment my thoughts are filled with him. And certainly not when his voice is the only thing that can give my day some sense of normalcy.

Am I...getting used to being bullied? Is that it?

I've tackled this particular issue with my therapist and she'd suggested it might be a manifestation of my guilt and the fact that he does, in fact, embody the characteristics of my ideal man. It's just that those particular traits of his that I admire are *never* aimed at me.

And as we've gone on to unravel my subconscious, it has become clear that I am vulnerable when it comes to Rafaelo, and as such it is best if I avoid him.

Easier said than done when Cisco had taken that one request to heart, ensuring Raf accompanied me *everywhere* when I went out. I haven't had a moment of quiet. Every single interaction we have is filled with so much tension that often leaves me emotionally exhausted.

"Are you sure you're fine, Noelle? It's not like you to miss breakfast," Yuyu mentions from the doorway, but I simply burrow deeper in my blankets.

"I think it's the change of seasons," I fake a cough. "It must be messing with my body."

"I see," she nods, worried. "I'll have Greta bring you the food here then."

"Thank you," I give her a small smile.

And as she leaves, I finally breathe out in relief.

It's the third day in a row that I've asked to eat in my room. I can't blame Yuyu for being suspicious, but neither do I want to see Rafaelo. I've done my best to keep out of his way, but it's definitely *not* easy when we live in the same house and we bump into each other at every turn.

It's only when he's away with business that I get some breathing room—but *that* never lasts. In fact, I've even stopped playing the piano when he is around the house. Every time I'd start playing it, he'd show up, and without even speaking, he would plop himself in front of the piano, watching me intently as I'd play.

The only saving grace is that he disappears somewhere for a couple of days a week, which is when I can allow myself to relax a little. Even that, however, is short lived, because visions of him with someone else constantly plague me. I'm always left wondering who he's meeting and what he's doing. And *that* is not great for my peace of mind.

Although our situation had gotten increasingly worse, I have to admit I'd learned to gain a new respect for the man after I'd heard some of the things he's been through.

I'm not ashamed to admit I've been eavesdropping every now and then—after all, it's better to have as much information on your enemy as possible. And everything I'd learned so far has been quite enlightening. Like his enmity with his brother, or the fact that he's currently a wanted man in New York.

It had quickly become obvious why he needs Cisco's support, and why he's taken residence in our house—for his own protection.

And *that* gives me pause. Because if it hadn't been for my brother...

I'm positive he *would* have killed me.

A shudder goes through my body at the thought but I try to push it out of my mind.

As promised, Greta brings me a tray of food, and I quickly dive in. A little too hungry and focused entirely on the food, it takes me a while to realize I'm no longer alone in the room.

"What are you doing here?" I snap, placing the tray on the nightstand and raising my blanket to my chin.

"My, my," he drawls, coming inside my room and closing the door. He leisurely walks around, an arrogant smirk on his face. "I didn't think you'd give up so quickly, little liar."

"What are you talking about?"

"You think I haven't realized you've been avoiding me?" He makes a tsk sound at me before he stops right at the end of my bed, his eyes on me as he's thoroughly assessing me.

"Get out," I demand, pointing towards the door. "You're not allowed in my room," I try to imbue my voice with confidence.

"Really?" he chuckles. "Do you think I'll pounce on you?" he asks as he rounds the bed, coming to my side and sitting on the edge of the bed.

I quickly scramble away from him, but his hand shoots out, his fingers wrapped around my arm as he brings me flush against him. I blink rapidly, my body terrified of the nearness while my soul continuously weeps at the hatred I see reflected in his eyes.

When will this stop?

"I thought it's only fair to come and inform you myself of a new development," his mouth quirks up.

"New development?" I frown.

His fingers burn a hole in my arm, his touch both poisonous and revitalizing.

"You're getting married," he states squarely, his eyes emotionless as he stares at me intently.

"Married?" I squeak, my eyes widening in shock.

Now, *that*, is the last thing I would have ever expected, and I can't help the way my jaw becomes slack, my mouth opening and closing but no sounds coming out.

Marriage?

Another marriage?

Sick laughter bubbles inside of me as I realize Cisco is selling me again. What did I expect, really?

By all intents and purposes, I am young and still useful to the family. It doesn't really matter that I'm damaged beyond repair. I can still pull a pretty price.

"I didn't think you'd be this happy," he notes as he watches me burst out in laughter.

"Happy?" I repeat. "*Happy*?" I shake my head at him, the laughter soon turning into sobs, tears coating my lashes. "Is that why you're here? To gloat at my misfortune?" I ask, flinging his hand from me and getting out of bed. "Then congratulations. You've won," I breathe out, pacing the room as panic threatens to overwhelm me.

He doesn't reply, merely leaning back and watching me closely. The bastard must be preening inside.

That's when another thought arises.

"You had something to do with it, didn't you?" I stop, pointing my finger at him accusatorily.

"What if I did?" He smirks, plopping himself on my bed, and resting his head against the headboard.

"You..." I seethe.

Of all the things he could have done to me, I would have never expected this. But he's not an idiot. He must have heard all about my first disastrous marriage and had likely realized my weakness...

Damn! He's been biding his time all along, hasn't he? Pretending he couldn't actually harm me because he needed my brother while planning *this*—the ultimate hit.

"You do need a man to keep you in check," he raises an eyebrow at me, making himself at home on my bed. "Someone to keep you on a *very* tight leash," he chuckles.

"So this was your plan all along? Convince my brother I need another husband so what? So you could make sure I'll be miserable for the rest of my life?"

Words simply fail me as I stare at him and at the culmination of his so called vengeance. Because there's *nothing* worse than being married off—again.

And as his smile continues to grow, I realize that it *had* been his plan all along.

"Well done, Raf. Well done," I praise sarcastically, attempting to put on a strong front though my soul is slowly withering inside of me.

"Thank you," he replies cheekily. "I'm rather proud of it myself," he drawls, his eyes glinting dangerously as he looks at me.

"Who is it, then? Who did you decide would make the *best* husband?"

Countless scenarios play before my eyes, and I know that the options are limited. Another aging man? Maybe another sadist, since the first one wasn't bad enough. And if Raf had been the architect of this particular plan...then I expect someone disturbed enough to make my life a living hell.

"Wouldn't you want to know?" The corner of his mouth pulls up as he jumps up from the bed, prowling towards me.

Backing away, I can't help the way my body starts trembling at his advance. As soon as my back hits the wall, though, he's on me, caging me in and looking down at me with those cold eyes of his that have the power to bring winter into my heart.

"Let go," I whisper, looking away.

I don't know how much longer I can keep my bravado up. Not with the news I just received, and certainly not with his intoxicating presence demanding a piece of my soul.

"Aren't you curious?" He smirks down at me. "I can tell you. After all, I chose him myself," he brags, and a newfound terror envelops me at his confirmation.

"What is he, a wife beater? A rapist?" I ask in a hopeless tone.

"Do you want him to be?"

"What..." I shake my head at him, trying to push at his shoulders. "You're sick," I mutter, tears threatening to make their way down my cheeks. "When will you leave me alone?" I cry out. "I told you Lucero was my friend. I told you I would have never..." my voice wanes as I choke on a sob. "Haven't I suffered enough? Why..."

"You haven't, little liar," he says in a smooth voice, his thumb coming under my jaw and tipping me up so I'm looking at him. "You haven't suffered *at all* yet. But I'll make sure to remedy that. I told you I'll make you rue the day we met, and I aim to keep my promise."

"How many times do I have to tell you I didn't do what you're accusing me of? You think I was happy at the *hacienda?* You think I was fine being Sergio's wife?" My voice goes up a notch, all the frustration inside of me coming to the surface. "You have no idea what I went through," I tell him, banging my fist to his chest. "You have no idea what it was like living there, yet you judge me for what? For *one* glimpse into my life?"

"Ah, little liar," he chuckles. "Don't tell me you're the victim now?"

"And if I am?" I counter. "You knew Sergio. You knew what type of man he was—how awful and violent he was. Did you think he was any better than his wife?"

For the first time there's a flicker of emotion in his eyes. But as soon as it appears it's gone.

"Is that what you're going to go with now? That you were somehow a victim in the entire thing?" he gives a dry laugh. "Your brother warned me, you know. He told me you have this idea that everyone is against you—that everyone is out to harm you."

I shake my head, unable to believe what I'm hearing.

How many times have I tried to explain what had happened to me only to be met with disapproving and unyielding stares? How many times had I been told my perception must have been altered by my trauma? How many times have I been branded crazy just for speaking out?

Why is it so hard to believe that a man would raise his hand against his wife? That he would beat her again and again until there's barely anything left of her—until she might still draw breath, but her soul is long dead?

"You're all the same," I whisper, a feeling of loneliness unlike any I've ever felt taking root deep inside of me. "You only accept as truth that which serves your purpose. Never more, never less."

"Fine. If you were a victim, then explain to me what *I* saw, how you'd delight in making everyone miserable. Tell me why Lucero would tell me all the awful things you'd do to her and the people around you; how you would exploit and punish every slave that dared to look your way. Tell me why everyone called you *la diabla*." He raises a brow at my bewildered expression.

"Explain to me how *that* makes you a victim," he demands with a sick smile on his face.

I'm speechless as I turn my tear-streaked eyes to look at him. Because I have no answer for that. I don't remember any of that...

"You can't, can you?" He snides.

"I don't remember," I say, my voice barely above a whisper.

"How convenient," he tsks at me, his fingers coming up to brush the tears from my face. "Just like your tears. Too bad they don't work on me, Noelle. Not when I know what you're *really* like."

"But you don't," I retort in a small protest. "Not really. You only know what you've heard of me."

"Don't forget I have first-hand experience with your wonderful temper, too," he sneers at me, his hand closing over my jaw in a painful grip. "Say, *hypothetically*, that you didn't kill Lucero with your own hands. But you certainly had everything to do with the bruises on her skin. The way she could barely talk sometimes because her entire body would be too swollen from your lovely punishments," he says ironically.

"I didn't..."

"Save the excuses for someone who'll believe you, little liar. But make no mistake, from now on..." he trails off, his mouth spreading into a twisted smile. "I'll make sure you get what you deserve."

He's off me, taking a step back and assessing me with disinterest in his gaze—as if I were a no one. And *that* somehow makes my heart bleed. The fact that I'm little more than dirt on his shoe.

A whimper escapes me as he makes to leave, and before I know it, I launch myself after him, grabbing his arm and stopping him.

"Who?" My entire body is trembling at this point, my breath ragged. "Who is he?" I ask, dreading the answer.

His eyes darken, and in a satisfied tone, he utters the words that end me.

"Me. Who else?"

Chapter Twenty-Three

Rafaelo

It's her voice that I hear first—that sweet voice that soothed and consoled me when everything came crashing down.

The voice that had made me fall in love with her.

My feet move, my body drawn to the sound that has the ultimate power over me.

I walk and walk, lulled by the security I find in her soft and melodious tone.

Until I stop.

I see her in the distance. Her body half turned to me, she's gazing at me with confusion in her eyes. Her features are swathed in darkness and I can barely make out what she looks like.

But I know her.

I know her heart, and I can see deep into her soul. That's all that matters. Her looks are inconsequential as I know that her inner beauty shines so brightly it has the power to feed me like nothing else—revitalize me when I'm halfway to the grave and infuse power in my limbs when my strength leaves me.

A smile plays at her lips as she spots me, and she turns —slowly.

I don't even think as I start into a sprint, running to her, needing to have the physical confirmation that she is with me and this isn't a mirage.

My body makes contact with hers. Skin against skin as a jolt travels through my body at the divine feeling of being so close to her. As I wrap my arms around her form, feeling her warmth, a content sigh escapes me.

This is it.

This is heaven.

The scene soon shifts, and before I can blink, I find myself on a bed, naked and looming over her bare skin. My lips skim over the surface of her smooth stomach, laying soft kisses as I trail my way down. Her small whimpers of encouragement are everything I need to make sure I'm doing everything right.

I dig my fingers into the plush skin of her hips, feeling her soft flesh molding to my digits. Holding tightly onto her, I let my tongue peek out as I lick my initial into her skin, searing my possession of her.

"You're mine," I whisper among peppered kisses, the need to own her growing to an unfulfilled crescendo—make her mine in a way that no one would dare contest.

"Yes," her breathy voice goes straight to my cock as she urges me lower, her fingers in my hair as she guides me to her core.

Getting hold of her panties, I tug them down, easily slipping them off her legs.

It's only when I have her bared before me, her musky scent invading my nostrils, that I have to wonder how I've lived so far, my entire life flashing before my eyes and showing me my bleak existence before her.

I lay a chaste kiss to the top of her mound before going lower, parting her lips with my tongue for the first taste of her.

"Fuck," a low groan escapes me. "Fucking hell," I curse as I dive in, lapping at her like a madman.

Her sounds are my guide as I learn her pleasure, the goal of her climax spurring me forward to give it my best.

It's only when she comes with my name on her tongue while

mine is still filled with the flavor of *her* that I go up for air, gliding up her body and reaching for a kiss.

"Raf," she whispers as she turns her eyes on me—those hazel eyes that have no equal in this world.

Her features are brought into focus, a bright new clarity entering my mind as I peruse every inch of her.

"Noelle," her name is wrenched from my lips as I stare into her more than perfect face—that work of art that's become right at home haunting my dreams and making me slowly die with unreleased tension.

She has a dreamy look on her face, her entire skin glistening with sweat from the exertion, her beauty only enhanced by the look of pure ecstasy on her face. She's glowing from her pleasure, her eyes hooded as she gazes at me, her fingers threaded through my hair as she caresses me gently.

"Come to me," she urges and I'm helpless to deny her.

I'm helpless to do anything but lean in, my lips on hers in a culmination of loss.

Wounding her arms around my neck, she draws me in an intoxicating embrace, my dick sliding against her wet pussy lips, her moans swallowed by my mouth as I tease her. Her warmth engulfs me, her arousal dripping and coating my entire shaft as she arches her back, shifting her hips to position me at her entrance.

There's only sensation at this point—pure, unadulterated sensation. I feel her everywhere, my mouth devouring her whole...

As if reaching for air, I gasp, my eyes snapping open as the previous vision dispels from my mind. Panting, I stare at the ceiling as I squirm against the heavy chains that hold me to my bed, relief pouring out of me at the fact that it had been just a dream.

I haven't dishonored Lucero. I haven't tainted her memory by touching *her*.

I shouldn't want her. I shouldn't want to do anything with her. Yet the more I fight this attraction, the more potent it becomes.

We desire what is forbidden to us.

There are no truer words, as evidenced by my current dilemma.

I fail to grasp this maddening dichotomy—the way my body yearns for her, while my mind abhors her. But no journey is entirely smooth, and it seems my own road to vengeance will be pebbled with temptation.

I've survived worse though, and if my time in captivity has taught me anything, it's that there's an infinite quality to human will. One that is only discovered through sheer hardship.

Yet the allure of her proximity grows more day by day, only augmented by the fact that she would probably welcome me into her body, her pussy drenched for me to mercilessly shove my cock inside of her in a brutal assault.

Because I wouldn't be gentle with her.

Despite the soft nature of my wet dream—much as it makes my lips purse in frustration—I know I would be anything but gentle with her.

I'd take her hard and fast, if only to exorcize her from my mind and my body and the fact that she's become close to an elusive obsession.

I grit my teeth as anger slowly seeps in.

Why does my dick have to fucking burst at the thought of her?

The fact that I've never had such a visceral reaction to another woman only makes my anger mount, leaving me even more frustrated as my cock strains against the plane of my stomach, so fucking hard and nearly ready to pop.

And as my thoughts continue to stray to her plump lips, visions of her on her knees and choking on my cock invading my mind, I can't help the small tremors that overtake me, my entire body spasming as I thrash against my holds, my dick twitching as spurts of cum land on my stomach.

Fuck!

"Fuck, fuck, fuck," I curse out loud as I manage to free myself from my chains.

Even the euphoria of my orgasm is not enough to chase the clouds that settle over me. Maybe I would be able to thrust this out of my mind if this had been an isolated incident borne out of my drug induced state. But even my clear mind has trouble keeping her out of it.

She's become a restless phantasm in my head. Thoughts of her plague me every waking moment of the day, my skin prickling with anticipation to see her.

In the beginning I'd told myself it was purely my need to gloat at her misery. But that had soon shifted. And it seems that my dick can't take a fucking clue when it comes to her.

Sure, I'm still relishing her misery, but with a raging erection every time she's in the vicinity.

In a sudden moment of clarity, I'm forced to accept that her plan to seduce me might have worked—at least on my body. She flaunts herself in front of me so often, showing enough skin to make me intrigued, but barely enough to keep me guessing.

My jaw clenches as I realize I may have fallen into her trap.

Oh, she's good. I'll give her that. She's an experienced seductress and her mix of sophistication and contrived innocence had certainly hooked me, making me desire that duality in her while making me question myself and my initial motives for hating her. Her strategy is nothing short of impressive—advance and retreat, coming across as hot and cold until she sinks her claws into me.

And sunk them she has.

The anger becomes even more potent as I realize I'm likely not the first man she's used those wiles of hers on. After all, she must have perfected her seduction technique somehow. And *that* awakens something scary inside of me.

"Damn it all to hell," I mutter as cold water from the shower pours down on me—all in an attempt to squash this uncharacteristic and insane thirst I feel for her.

In a moment of weakness, I'm left to wonder if I should maybe just give in—fuck her once and get her out of my system. At least then I won't be so curious about her flavor, the feel of her pussy wrapped around me, or the taste of her full submission as I fuck the brat out of her. Maybe that could work.

But I know I would ultimately never forgive myself for being so weak as to fall prey to her charms. And that annoys me even more.

Because I'll be damned if I do and I'll be damned if I don't.

"You're scowling," Carlos notes hours later. Freshly showered and dressed, the hallucination has continued to bother me throughout the day, the simulated realism of it only making me yearn for the real thing more.

And *that* is a problem.

I can't act on this irrational desire. To do so would be a betrayal to myself, and most of all a betrayal to Lucero.

How could I contemplate touching the person who'd made her life miserable with the same gentleness I should have touched *her*? How could I even fathom engaging in the act of ultimate intimacy with someone so contemptible? With someone for whom I only feel distaste—raw anger that consumes me from the inside and threatens to erupt to the surface.

Already, I feel myself getting increasingly unsettled at the thought of Noelle, so I attempt to shove it out of my mind.

"It's nothing," I mumble under my breath, not in the mood to broach the subject with Carlos.

"I don't think it is," he tsks at me, leaning back and watching me closely. "You've been with DeVille for almost two months now. Granted, we've made some progress with the weapons and the market has welcomed us with open arms. But other than that?" He shakes his head. "You're supposed to focus on your brother, not get married."

"He's been MIA for weeks. If anything, I'd say he's scared," I chuckle. "He must have heard I've joined hands with DeVille and is expecting the worst," I deflect.

"That doesn't explain why you've become so fixated on that girl. I get that you want to get revenge for what happened at the *hacienda*, but is this really the right way? Marrying her?" He scoffs at me.

"Carlos is right. It's a bit too drastic, wouldn't you say?" Anita chimes in, carrying a bowl of cereal with her.

"Not you too," I groan.

It's not the first time that Carlos has questioned me on my plans with Noelle. Now to have Anita too...

"I have it all under control," I roll my eyes at her.

"I don't think you do," Carlos shoots back, openly challenging me. "Ever since you've met her, you've virtually put your plan with Michele on a black-burn."

"That's not true," I protest.

"Yes it is. You're practically obsessed with the girl. Every time I see you, it's always the same thing. *That damned, Noelle. I'll make her regret the day she was born,"* Anita jokes as she repeats my words from before. *"That little liar, I'll show her cruel,"* she laughs. "Seriously, Raf, you haven't talked about anything else *but* her."

"Well, it's an ongoing plan," I mumble, peeved at being put on the spot.

"No. The ongoing plan is to end your brother and Ortega. And in the process get rid of the bounties on our heads," Carlos adds drily.

"This was an add-on."

I should have expected they wouldn't understand what this means to me—the chance to pay her back for everything.

Maybe I *am* a little obsessed, but that's only because she's the only remaining link to the past that I have. One that I need to firmly exorcize from my life—and to a satisfying degree—before I can move on.

Yes, Michele is my primary focus. But Noelle's sudden reappearance in my life has been nothing short of fortuitous. I'm not about to throw away the chance of a lifetime.

"An add-on that took over your whole focus."

"It's only until I become her legal guardian," I bring my fingers to my temples, massaging them. "After that, I'll make sure she's committed, and she won't bother us again."

"Uhum, if you say so," Anita chuckles, and Carlos shakes his head at me.

"Are you sure it's not something…more?" he asks tentatively.

"Something more?" I frown.

"That this *revenge* you have going on isn't just an excuse."

"I don't know what you're talking about."

"She's a very beautiful woman, Raf," Carlos notes, and that one sentence has me curling my hands into fists. My gaze cold, I narrow my eyes at him.

"I didn't realize you were checking her out," I add sarcastically.

"And *thaaat* is my cue to remove myself from this situation," Anita declares in a sing-song voice. "I feel bad for you," she turns to me before leaving, giving me a pitiful look. "Poor, poor thing," she shakes her head, the corners of her mouth quirking up.

Watching her retreating figure, I blink in confusion.

Carlos, too, is sporting an amused look on his face, and it seems that everyone is in on a hidden joke. *Anyone but me.*

"What was that all about?" I frown.

"Raf," Carlos starts in that fatherly tone of his. "The fact that you don't understand is the issue." A smile pulls at his lips. "Fine," he nods as he pats me on the back. "Go ahead with your revenge and marry the girl. I'm sure the plan will work wonderfully."

"It will," I reply with conviction. "I'll own her and I'll be able to do whatever I want with her."

His features twitch with amusement.

"Indeed," he chuckles.

He's about to say something else when Panchito bursts through the room, a tablet in his hand and a broad smile on his face.

"I got it!" He yells enthusiastically.

"You got what?"

"Michele. I managed to find some traces of him." He says and my focus shifts immediately.

"Go on," I nod at him.

"He's been smart about covering his traces. I don't know if he goes out much besides this but..."

"Get to the point, Panchito," I tell him impatiently.

"These were taken at a few private recitals over the last month. I came across one by coincidence, and I couldn't help but notice this," he points to a figure in the back corner.

He's dressed in a black tux, a glass of champagne in his hand as he's gazing attentively at the stage. His face is a little blurry given that he's in the back of the room.

"Since you gave me a profile of Michele, I thought I'd try some underground art auctions or musical events, since," he pauses, turning to me, "you mentioned he showed some artistic inclination in his youth."

"He did," I nod. "He was always in his own world, often drawing or listening to recordings of classical concerts. Our father never approved of either, since he deemed them unmanly," I purse my lips, since that rule had applied to me too.

I refrain from mentioning that his interest in classical music may have started because of my mother. Since young, she would always play for me, the act giving her joy. But she'd never let Michele take part in our little tete-a-tete. In my mother's words, he'd been an interloper. He would, however, find ways to listen to her play. Although curiosity had been piqued in the beginning because he'd been banned from it, it had later turned into a full-on hobby.

But that had been a lifetime ago and during a period where I'd felt something akin to pity for Michele. After all, he had been ostracized by his own family. Still, nothing excuses what he turned into.

"I didn't know for sure if this is him, but I ran some simulations and everything from stature to body language matches. I'm pretty positive it was him."

"Good job," I say appreciatively, my eyes still on the picture.

"This was last month. But this," he swipes his finger on the screen, "is from last week," he pulls up another picture.

This one is more clear, and I can see my brother's features better. He hasn't changed—not much anyway. There's still a glaring emptiness in his eyes, as if he's truly soulless.

"So he's been attending private events," Carlos notes. "It's not much, but it's something."

"No," my lips pull up in a twisted smile. "It's everything, because I have an inkling of a plan," I say as I start explaining my idea.

Who said I couldn't shoot two birds with one stone?

"I'M NOT sure what you want me to say, Raf," Cisco raises a brow as he leans in his chair. "Your plan is sound, and I appreciate all the details you've outlined," he slaps the document I'd brought on the table. "But this is my sister we're talking about."

"And this is my brother," I counter. "We've been tracking his movements for a long time already, and you've seen how rare his public appearances are. For Fuck's sake, he has a body double that he sends out to distract people."

"Indeed, your brother has a strange case of paranoia. I won't deny that. But what if my sister gets hurt?"

I don't for one second think that Cisco truly cares about his sister getting hurt. After all, if he did, he wouldn't have given her to me.

No, this isn't about that.

He wants to ascertain my intentions and to play the devil's advocate.

"She won't. I'll personally see that she won't," I give him my charming smile.

"Then I'll trust you on this," he smirks. "Especially with how thorough you've been," he whistles. "I must say that I'm impressed."

"The proper channels have already been informed, and I've set an alias for her and a fake biography. Anyone looking her up on the internet would find only vague information that's bound to make Michele even more interested."

"You're sure he'll bite?" Cisco inquires. "It's just that your brother doesn't come across as...a man of culture. A psychotic mess of paranoia and misplaced grandiosity, yes. But a cultured man?" He shakes his head.

"He's always been passionate about the beaux arts. But he was never allowed to show an interest when my parents lived. Even now, as you can see, everything he does is covertly. My IT guy also managed to trace some art transactions to him. It's not something he advertises, which suggests it means a lot to him."

"Your brother would be an interesting man," Cisco notes, "if not for being the enemy."

"You know, there was a time I felt sorry for him. I know what he had to go through and why he is the way he is."

Cisco looks at me expectantly, but I don't expand on that.

"There was a time I thought he could be saved. But not anymore. He made his choices. And now I make mine."

"Indeed," he nods, lighting a cigarette. "Besides, you're infinitely easier to work with," he gives me a wolfish smile, implying that in the scheme of things, he wouldn't really care which side he'd be on —mine or Michele's. But only one of us is willing to give him what he wants, and *that* is the deciding factor.

Most of the time I don't know whether to admire Cisco or revile him for the way he does business. One thing is for sure, though. He's not someone you'd want as your enemy.

"Then it's settled. I'll have Panchito set everything up digitally. I will only need your help in finding a venue and inviting other influential people to throw Michele off our scent."

"Don't worry. I'll do that. Now on how to convince Noelle..."

We spend the entire afternoon planning, and as we discuss the various ways in which we'd get Noelle to agree to the plan, I can't help but feel a *tiny* sliver of guilt.

I'd sketched out the plan in a moment of anger and I'd been more than convinced that this would be the way to get rid of both thorns in my side.

But is it truly right?

Subjecting Noelle to my brother might just be the worst type of punishment I could ever think for her.

As the hour grows late, I realize I can't sleep, these thoughts plaguing me, doubts entering my mind when I should be nothing but secure in my goal.

So my feet take me to her room, surreptitiously opening the door to find her fast asleep.

Propping myself on a nearby chair, I bring my hand to my chin as I simply study her.

She looks so innocent in her sleep, huddled between those silky sheets. Her hair is draped over her bare shoulders, her nightgown a light piece of fabric that doesn't leave much to the imagination.

But as much as I look at her, trying to decipher my lingering obsession with her, I can't.

Carlos was right.

Regardless of my grudge against her for her role in my misfortunes at the *hacienda*, I should have never reacted this strongly to her. After all, she's just one of *many* on my list of tormentors.

Yet something is different.

Instead of focusing on my brother, who's been the bane of my existence for so long, I've funneled all my attention into *her*. Someone who, in the grand scheme of things, isn't even that important.

Yet it's someone I can't seem to stop thinking about.

Why am I obsessing over her day and night?

The decision to kill her should be a simple one, my mission notwithstanding. Yet the thought of her *dying*, of her lips turning purple and her face losing its vitality unnerves me. Something inside of me is stopping me from fully hating her and I cannot comprehend what.

I have the facts. I *know* what I witnessed and endured just as I know what Lucero told me. At the same time, things don't add up.

I may have known her only for a brief period of time, but she doesn't come across as a conniving bitch. If anything, there's an artless innocence about her, a vulnerability that makes me ache with want.

She makes me want to hug her and gut her at the same time, and that's my conundrum.

Is she that good of an actress?

She moves, her sheet sliding down her abdomen, her tits in full view through the flimsy material of her gown. Full and a size too big for her small frame, they are enough to lead a saint to sin. Certainly enough for me to fantasize about them.

At once, a wave of lust hits me as my eyes zero in on her erect nipples, the pink of her areola such a delectable shade, made for licking, sucking and biting.

A silent groan escapes me as I feel all the blood rush to my cock at the thought of her tits in my mouth, and my tongue on her flesh as I bring her to the edge only to leave her unfulfilled—the only thing the little tease deserves.

I swallow hard, the taste of her on my tongue palpable.

Sweet. She'd taste so sweet. Of that I have no doubt.

It doesn't matter that she's a facetious bitch.

At this moment, all that matters is how my mind perceives her. I'm like a drunk man as I let my eyes feast on her, drinking her in until my imagination can get to work and fill in the gaps.

A throaty sound escapes her and I palm my cock through my pants, that one sound my undoing.

Fuck.

It's madness. There's no other way to describe my addled brain. Because no one in their right mind would lust so hard after the person they're supposed to hate—that they *hate.*

But I can't stop myself.

I'm like a fucking slave to my baser instincts.

All my life I've seen men be led around by their cocks and I'd taken pride in being different—in leading a life of moderation.

But when I look at her, there's no moderation, just pure hedonistic abandon as I want nothing more than to sink into her warm depths.

My errant hand lowers the zipper of my pants and I take my cock out, stroking myself from base to tip at the sight of her luscious body and the wonders it contains. Her sweet pussy calls to me, and as I close my eyes, her scent and taste threaten to drive me crazy.

Because I've tasted her.

I tasted her when she had no idea. Dipping my finger in her tight pussy and not getting a taste would have been blasphemy. In the cover of darkness, taking advantage of her unawareness, I'd put that finger in my mouth and I'd sucked it clean.

Even now the memory threatens to make me fall apart—both from the pleasure of it and the pain. I'd lost control of myself. I'd lost all traces of rationality as I'd given in to the animal within me.

The animal that wants to devour her.

Not too long ago I'd had my cock positioned right at her hole, her heat beckoning and hypnotizing me. I have to admit that wrenching myself away from her had been the hardest thing I'd ever done.

The animal in me would have taken her.

And that's what shocks me the most.

I don't feel like myself anymore. She put a fucking spell on me that I can't seem to escape.

She's fidgety in her sleep, but the more she moves, the more she graces me with a full view of her exposed flesh.

I'm so fucking hard I'm almost bursting, and it won't take much more for me to come. My fist works my length as I continue to use her for my most obscene fantasies.

Ah, but the things I would do to her…

She turns on her side, her face towards me as her mouth opens on a low whimper.

My mind is immediately at work, conjuring images of her on her knees, those full lips of hers wrapped around my cock as she sucks me like the born seductress she is.

Fuck but she would obliterate me. Of that, I have no doubt.

The thought of her warm, wet mouth is enough to make me leak, and a few more strokes later I'm coming in thick spurts, the power of the orgasm making me see stars.

Everything is short lived. As the euphoria wears off, I'm left with a bitter taste in my mouth and a strong sense of revulsion.

With a silent curse, I stand up, tucking myself in my pants and condemning myself for my weakness.

I shouldn't want her. I shouldn't want *anyone*.

Not after Lucero.

Yet Noelle possesses something that no other woman I met before or after Lucero ever did.

The ability to shake me to my core.

Lucero had been my spiritual comfort, the other half of my soul, but there had always been a physical barrier between us.

With Noelle, there's none. She's flesh and blood. She's there for me to touch and feel.

For me to be tempted.

Maybe if my relationship with Lucero had been *more* or occurred in different circumstances, I wouldn't react so strongly to Noelle.

Maybe.

As I spare her one last glance before I leave the room, it's to see her eyes wide open, staring at me unflinchingly.

I let my lips curl into an unaffected smirk, giving her a mock salute before leaving the room.

Chapter Twenty-Four

Rafaelo

"Noelle still isn't here," Cisco mutters as he glances at his watch, tapping his foot impatiently.

Yuyu is by his side as she snakes her arm around his waist, laying her head on his shoulder.

"Don't fret, she'll be here soon," she tells him gently.

"I can go check on her," I immediately volunteer.

"I'm not sure..." Cisco starts but is interrupted by his wife who urges me to go on.

"Please do," she nods at me before turning to her husband and chiding him for being too strict with Noelle. "They are to be married after all," I hear her murmur as I head to Noelle's room.

After everyone had been made aware of our upcoming nuptials, Cisco had suggested we went to dinner to celebrate the engagement. Everyone had been in agreement—everyone but Noelle, that is. And seeing how vehement she'd been about it, I can only assume she's trying to pull something off to remove herself from the situation.

Too bad for her that any problem she'll cause will only irritate her brother. Yuyu is seven months pregnant, and the tiniest inconvenience when it comes to her has him blow up.

Reaching the third floor, I don't even knock as I push open the door, ready to catch the little liar in flagrante delicto.

As I take a step inside the room, I am met by an unusual sight.

She's sitting at her vanity.

Still garbed in a silky white robe, she's gazing melancholically in the mirror. Her hair is swept to the side as she trails a finger down the column of her neck.

So lost she is in her own world that she doesn't realize she's no longer alone in the room.

Like feathers, her fingers glide softly over her soft skin, the gesture unusually sensual.

I stop, my feet firmly planted in the middle of the room as I can only stare at the vision before me.

Her tongue peeks out to wet her lips, lingering over her upper lip. Her eyes snap closed as a small sigh escapes her lips.

I swallow. Hard.

I can't help the way my eyes are drawn to the expanse of skin available for my perusal. And as I continue watching her, I note that my breathing is now emulating hers.

She inhales. I inhale.

She exhales. I exhale.

There's only silence besides our joint breaths, the sound of a heart hammering in a chest almost deafening—not mine, it could never be mine.

Her fingers move, tracing the corded muscles of her neck, down to her clavicle.

Without even realizing, my feet carry me forward until I'm behind her, the mirror reflecting every single gesture she makes.

The tips of her fingers rest on the swell of her breasts, emphasized even more by the low cut gown she's wearing.

My eyes dip to the tantalizing sight, following her fingers as they continue to move gracefully down her front.

I feel my own pulse building to a painful crescendo as I continue to lose myself in visions of velvet skin and soft caresses.

"Done shamelessly staring?" she asks impudently, her eyes wide open. She's gazing at me through the mirror, a brow raised as she waits for me to reply.

My mouth opens and closes in an unspoken answer, words failing me as I become aware of my own mindless state. So caught off guard I'd been by her words that I can only stare at her flabbergasted.

The shock quickly wears off, however, soon to be replaced with anger.

Pure, insidious anger as I realize how mesmerized I'd been by the barest hint of skin—by *her* skin.

Mentally cursing myself, I quickly get myself together, strengthening my back and throwing her a cold look.

"I was waiting for you to find *your* shame," I retort on a snort. "Where are your clothes? You should have been downstairs five minutes ago."

Slowly, she turns. Crossing her arms over her chest, it's to bring her tits forward, her generous swell becoming more prominent and making my eyes inadvertently drop to them.

"Eyes here," she says sarcastically, bringing two fingers to her eyes.

"Not my fault you're advertising the goods," I comment, trying to switch focus from my errant gaze and the fact that once more, my body seems bent on betraying me. "Get dressed," I say flippantly, looking around and spotting a dress laid out on the bed.

"No," she replies defiantly, rising up and planting herself in front of me. "I'm not getting dressed, and I'm not going anywhere with you."

My lips quirk up at her little show of rebellion.

"Really?" I drawl, leaning back and watching her as she starts with her tirade.

"I'm not marrying you so I don't see why I would go to a dinner that celebrates a nonexistent engagement."

"You should tell that to your brother," I shrug, turning on my heel. "I wonder how *he* will react to that."

"He'll understand when I tell him just *who* he's allowed into his house," she pushes her chin up, her voice steady despite the small tremors going down her body.

An eyebrow raised, I look at her amused.

"And *who* is that?" I chuckle, wanting to see what she's trying to accomplish with this feeble attempt of hers.

She blinks twice, no doubt trying to come up with something clever.

"I'll tell him you only want to marry me for revenge," she declares smugly.

"Go ahead," I shrug, her eyes flashing when she notes my indifference. "Why haven't you told him until now?"

"I... I..." she stammers.

"Let me tell you why you haven't told him, and why you *won't* tell him," the corner of my mouth pulls up as I take a step towards her.

She backs away, but she doesn't get to move fast enough before I'm in front of her, looming over her and noting the way her bravado is just that—fake courage to disguise the way her entire body is shaking, even her lips trembling as her eyes continue to flash at me with animosity.

"You know I'll just dispute it, and it will be my word against yours," I add smoothly as I bring one finger to her jaw, slowly trailing it downwards.

She swallows, but her eyes never leave mine.

"Who do you think he'll believe? The sister with the mental problems?" I ask with a knowing smile, "or his valuable business partner?"

She doesn't answer, no doubt realizing the truth of my words. After all, she's not dumb.

She could have gone to Cisco to tell him the truth of our acquaintance from the very beginning, but she knows it will ultimately be her word against mine. And everyone knows the value of her word.

"He'll believe me," she grits, valiantly pushing her chin up in a show of contrived bravery.

"Hmm," I murmur as I lean in, my mouth close to her ear.

She stiffens at my nearness, but she doesn't move.

"Will he?" I muse, brushing my lips against her earlobe. The reaction is immediate as I feel her sudden intake of breath, her palms splayed on my chest yet not pushing me away. "Or will he just ignore you because he has something to gain from this marriage?"

"You..."

"The deal is sealed, Noelle. You'd better get used to it. Now move your ass to the bed and put the goddamn dress on. We're late," I tell her sternly before moving away.

I don't leave the room, though. I merely situate myself at the far end corner, leaning against the wall and watching her closely.

Her small hands balled into fists, she seethes at me for exactly one minute before she demands I turn around so she can dress.

"You had time to dress when I wasn't here. Now," I all but dare her, "you'll have to do it with me here. Don't tell me I intimidate you," I smirk at her.

Incensed, she mutters something under her breath before she starts slipping her straps off her shoulders.

With her back to me, she keeps her robe on her shoulders as she slides the gown off her body, quickly grabbing the black cocktail dress and putting it on.

I watch amused as she struggles to dress, her attempts clumsy as she tries her best to avoid showing me her naked body. As if it wasn't just a while ago that she'd tried to entice me with it.

I hold off a laugh as I realize this must be another one of her tricks—this time she's simply playing the shy maiden.

When the dress covers her breasts, she finally drops the robe so she can slip the straps over her arms, all the while trying to preserve her *modesty*.

"You might as well help," she calls out in a flippant tone, presenting me with her back and pointing to the half done zipper.

"Come here," I command her, my voice harsher than intended.

As my eyes feast on her form—especially the way her dress flatters her curves—I can't help but become increasingly annoyed with myself.

She does as told, placing herself in front of me, waiting.

And as I bring my hand up, my fingers on the zipper, my thumb makes contact with her bare skin. The effect is immediate as goosebumps appear all over, her breath a harsh sound that seems to clog the air.

I step closer, her scent invading my nostrils as I feel the tension in her shoulders—the way she's not unaffected by my proximity. One more step, and her enchanting backside would make direct contact with the raging erection I'm currently fighting to control.

Slowly pulling up the zipper, I let the back of my palm linger over her beckoning skin—the gesture half for me and half for her. The allure is simply too strong to resist. And for someone with plenty of experience with addiction... I'd say I'm heading on a path of no return.

Her breath hitches at the contact, and my cock jerks in my pants at her throaty sound, arousal building inside of me at the mere thought of being this close to her.

Infuriating. Maddening. Intoxicating.

All words I'd use to describe her effect on me. How is it possible to want to throttle her and fuck her at the same time? The paradox never fails to mystify me.

Fuck, but I'd been hard from the moment I'd gotten a peek at her naked throat, that one image enough to sear itself on my retina.

Once more, I'm faced with the unnatural way my body reacts to her. I may rationalize it as a purely physical reaction, but I find it hard to grasp the dichotomy—how can my body crave her when my mind loathes the very idea of her?

Even more appalling is the realization that Carlos had been right. Since I'd gotten my first glimpse of Noelle, my quest for my brother had taken a backseat. I'd become completely obsessed with making *her* pay, that I hadn't stopped to assess how this one fixation was interfering with my other plans.

I'd come to New York with the express goal of getting rid of the pest that is my brother once and for all. Instead, all I've managed so far has been getting distracted by a slip of a woman who seems bent on ruining every shred of self-control I have remaining.

Fuck. Me.

This needs to stop. I need to get a fucking grip on myself.

"You know," I start in a smooth tone, needing to rile her up and dispel this cozy atmosphere, "once I'm your husband I'll be sliding this *down*."

As if burned, she jumps out of my arms, her expression feral as she turns those fiery eyes towards me.

"Only if you're into necrophilia," she scoffs at me, putting some distance between us. "Since I'd sooner be dead than let you touch me," she hisses.

Ah, the familiar dynamic is back, and while my cock is still hard as granite in my pants, I can relax a little since the odds of any accidental and uncharacteristic touching have finally decreased.

"What's so bad about necrophilia?" I shoot back. "It takes the body a few hours to cool down. I'm sure I could get some use out of you before then," I shrug, moving towards the door.

From the corner of my eye I note the scandalized look that takes over her face.

A few low curses, and she eventually follows me out.

As we make our way to the restaurant, Cisco barely stops himself from chastising Noelle for her lack of punctuality.

I try to ignore the way she looks in that cocktail dress, or how I'm not the only one to notice as we walk into the restaurant.

Heads turn, appreciative male gazes shooting her way but she seems oblivious to the attention. Certainly more so than me as I barely hold myself from calling those men out for looking at what's *not* theirs.

We're led to a four person table, Cisco and Yuyu sitting on one side while Noelle and I are on the other. All the while though, Noelle is sporting a disgruntled look on her face, and Cisco is quick to call her out for it.

"I hope you're not going to start acting out again," Cisco turns his chilly eyes to his sister. "You need to grow up, Noelle. And the behavior you just displayed isn't that of an adult—but of a child."

"You expect me to be an adult when I'm not even in control of my own damn self?" she gives a dry laugh. "Pick a lane, brother. Either I'm a child in need of a guardian, or I'm an adult."

"Noelle," he grits his teeth.

"Let's not turn this joyous occasion into a fight," Yuyu intervenes, placing a hand on Cisco's shoulder and shooting Noelle a warning glance.

"Joyous?" Noelle laughs derisively. "Joyous for whom? Maybe for you," she nods at Cisco. "Because you're getting paid to get rid of me."

Closing my eyes, I take a deep breath, trying to calm down. Why is it that she's always trying to pick a fight with someone?

"We had a small fight," I interject, my hand suddenly on Noelle's thigh as I squeeze her flesh in a warning to shut up. "She doesn't like that there's an exchange, so to speak."

Cisco is quiet for a moment as he looks between the two of us.

"Right," he grunts. "Noelle never liked that aspect of our life. But it's a good starting point if you want to be an adult—with all the privileges included," he shoots her a glance. "Nothing is *ever* free."

"Including humans," Noelle mutters under her breath.

"Yes. Including humans," I add darkly, my own past flashing behind my eyes. "In fact," I drawl in a charming voice, all for the benefit of the audience cataloging our every interaction at this table, "I'd say you cost me a pretty penny," I murmur, satisfaction rolling off me as I note the blush that creeps up her cheeks.

She tips her jaw down, almost embarrassed.

"How much?" She asks in a low voice.

"How much, Cisco?" I laugh. "Just a few castles down in Sicily, isn't that right?" I add jokingly.

Her head whips around, her eyes widening as she looks at me.

"I see..." she replies, her voice unusually soft for someone who'd been bent on starting the third world war not a few minutes ago.

"Alas, enough of that," Cisco waves his hand in the air. "We're not talking about finances at the dinner table."

"Indeed. Tonight we celebrate," my lips curl into a twisted smile.

"To the much anticipated union of our families," I propose a toast as I raise my glass in the air.

Everyone does the same—including Yuyu who is drinking orange juice and a reluctant Noelle who's shooting me daggers with her eyes.

"I have to say, I can't wait until I have this pretty lady as my wife. The entire restaurant is already looking at me with envy." I add as I wrap my arm around Noelle's shoulders, tugging her closer in an attempt to appear like a *loving* couple.

I have to grit my teeth as I bring her to my side, but as her body molds to mine, I find that there's little hardship in the pretense.

Startled, she gives a small yelp, jumping up and almost landing in my lap.

"You two look so good together," Yuyu gushes as she takes her phone out, urging us to stay still for a picture.

Noelle isn't one to do as she's told, evidenced by the way she keeps moving around, accidentally brushing her hand over my crotch.

"Stop squirming," I whisper in her hair as we pose for the picture. "Or you won't like the result," I tell her as I fit my palm to the back of her hand, keeping it still on my thigh. Just a little higher and she would reach dangerous territory.

Chapter Twenty-Five

Rafaelo

She raises her head to look at me, her mouth opening as she's about to say something, only to close it as she blinks, her eyes moving over my face before focusing on my lips. Her pupils contract, her tongue sneaking out to wet her lips.

Fuck!

A low groan escapes me at the blatant invitation I see in her eyes. And I'm not the only one who sees her reaction, Cisco coughing awkwardly in his fist, while Yuyu looks away in embarrassment.

It takes her a moment to get her bearings together, shaking herself. Flushing a pretty pink, she redirects her attention to her glass.

The dinner continues and she quietly picks at her food, every now and then looking up at me with an inscrutable expression on her face.

"I'm curious, Raf," Cisco starts as he directs his mismatched eyes to me, his gaze chilling and meant to intimidate. "What drew you to my sister?" He raises a brow. "You're a worldly man." He chuckles, the double entendre not escaping me since he's been dying to know where I'd been in the years I've been absent, "While my sister is decidedly *not*."

Noelle, too, turns sharply at his words, looking at me with a mix of curiosity.

I guess everyone has a different definition of *worldly*.

"Noelle is a beautiful woman, Cisco. It's normal for men to be drawn to her," Yuyu comments, giving Noelle a sweet smile.

"Yes, but she's also willful, stubborn, and can drive even a saint to madness," Cisco mutters drily, giving Noelle a reprimanding look.

Her eyes widen at him, but she keeps her mouth shut, for once forgoing an insolent reply. The more I observe her, though, the more I realize that it's not for lack of want, but because the words *hurt* her. A look akin to pain flashes across her face and a low tension unfolds in my chest.

"It was her music that drew me to her," I interrupt, my voice steady as I cut over Cisco. "I happened to hear her play the piano, and it was such a wonderful melody that I couldn't help but linger outside the attic." I turn to her. "She was so immersed, her fingers gliding so gracefully over the keyboard that I couldn't help but be mesmerized."

She blinks, tilting her head as she looks at me in confusion.

"Her music," Cisco repeats, his tone skeptical.

"It's been so long since she played," Yuyu sighs. "I was so happy when I heard the piano again, right Cisco?" He grunts a noncommittal answer, but Yuyu isn't deterred as she continues, warmth and pride radiating from her voice. "Did she tell you she won quite a few competitions? Some of them were very prestigious."

While Cisco has always come across as cold and unyielding, Yuyu is the opposite. And her affection for Noelle is clear as she's always trying to take her side, her regard for her similar to that of a mother. But considering the fact that she'd watched her grow, it's not entirely unusual she should feel this way about her.

"No," I reply, my eyes on Noelle. Meeting my gaze for a second, she quickly looks away. "She hasn't mentioned that."

"Oh my," Yuyu gives a soft gasp. "Noelle! How could you not tell him that?" She chides, almost scandalized, before starting to recount in great detail how Noelle had started playing the piano at the age of four, immediately showing promise and being branded a prodigy by her teachers.

"She was only fourteen when she had her first big concert," Yuyu says enthusiastically, but Noelle doesn't share the sentiment as she lowers her head, fidgeting with her hands in her lap.

"Really?" I drawl, my voice going down a dangerous octave.

"She was praised for her distinctive style. Her teachers described it as brisk and innovative. She would take pieces and mash them together to give them a new, buoyant flavor," Yuyu continues to prattle. "She used to combine antithetic pieces and the result was very well received, isn't that right, love?" She turns to her husband, a bright smile on her face. Cisco attempts to return it, his not as authentic as his features are clearly strained.

"Is that so?" I frown, taking in the new information. "I don't think I've heard that from her yet. The only pieces she's played so far have been *very* gloomy. For a while I wondered if she only knows how to play funeral pieces," I joke, but no one laughs.

Everything comes to a standstill as Yuyu and Cisco share a worried look.

"Her style must have changed. Right, Noelle?" Cisco's stern voice cuts through the air.

Noelle has been silent until now, looking entirely too uncomfortable as Yuyu related her achievements—as if it wasn't something to be proud of.

Certainly, I'd noted from the first that there was something special about the way she plays. Even though the pieces she plays *always* have the same morose tone, it's impossible not to feel the emotion emanating from every note.

It hadn't been a lie that her skill had mesmerized me at first. Then it had simply angered me. Because I'd realized that I had heard her play before.

Many, many times.

Few things had helped me cope with my captivity, and even fewer things had helped me keep my spirits up when everything had seemed hopeless. Alone in my cold and damp cell, darkness and silence my only company, I'd been starved for *any* type of interaction.

And before Lucero had invited some semblance of light in my life, I'd had music.

A lone melody that seemed to echo in the deep of the night, the notes weeping as they propagated through those empty places filled with tragedy. The screeching sadness of the melody had woken something inside of me.

In the beginning, I'd thought it was a dirge meant to lead me on my last journey—a funeral march meant to signal the end of my life.

But the sound had persisted. And I hadn't died.

Long nights of writhing in pain with only the power of those sad notes to hold me awake and keep me from succumbing to my death, and I'd recognized that behind the desolate melody, there was also something else.

While the primary melodic line had a pessimistic quality to it, there were times where optimism prevailed. Like the downcast sky clearing after a storm, it was a sign that there is light at the end of the tunnel.

Even in my drugged up state, I'd clung to that, holding on to that hope.

It had been *her* music. Of that I am certain. And that only makes me more incensed that she'd been the source of my comfort in those dark nights.

"Right," Noelle mutters at her brother. "My music imitates reality," she starts, her gaze sharp as she gives Cisco an accusatory look. "When I was younger I could still see the beauty of life. Now..." she gives a dry laugh. "Not so much."

"You're being impertinent," Cisco chides.

"I'm being realistic," she shrugs. "Why should I play about something I don't believe in?"

"You don't believe in happiness?" I throw the question, narrowing my eyes at her.

She turns, her face emotionless.

"No," she answers promptly.

"But you believe in death?" I continue to probe. "Since your pieces are *only* about death."

"No," she shakes her head. "It's not because I believe in death. Though I don't think anyone would contest the existence of it," she gives a low chuckle, coldness seeping into her raspy voice. "Death is inevitable. I merely play to pave the way for it," she says cryptically, but I understand the subtext.

She's inviting death.

Our eyes meet, our gazes holding fast as a low undercurrent passes between us. For what seems like an eternity, I can only stare at her, a grim understanding uniting us.

But the moment is soon over as a waiter comes by, bringing our food, the sound of a plate touching the table startling me out of my reverie.

"Have you tackled *that* particular issue with your therapist?" I ask in a mocking tone, trying to regain some semblance of control.

A sad smile painted on her face, she turns to face the table.

"Yes, and she thinks I'm rather hopeless. It seems you paid a *pretty penny* for a defective product," she snides.

"Hmm, I wonder," I muse out loud. "I prefer broken things, myself," I let my lips widen in a charming smile. "After all, it's easier to mold them to a desired result."

There's a twitch in her jaw at my words.

"Is that so?" She raises a brow. "In my experience, one usually tires of fixing a broken product. And there's only one recourse for such things—you get rid of them," she says in a punctured tone.

"I rather think you're right," I chuckle. "But why miss on the fun of playing with the parts? Moving them around, replacing them..." I pause, sensing the tension radiating from her. "Making the product even more broken than before?" I ask rhetorically.

She doesn't answer, though I can tell she knows *exactly* what I mean.

"Why do I think we're no longer talking about music?" Yuyu intervenes.

Planting on my best smile, I interject.

"Oh, it *is* about music. After all, her music is beautifully broken.

I think that's what attracts people to it, isn't it? The raw emotion that imbues the musicality of each note."

"Wonderfully put," Yuyu praises. "That's similar to what one of her teachers said. He wanted to sign her to a label," she smiles ruefully.

"Impressive," my brows arch in surprise—or, better put, admiration. "Why didn't she do it?" I ask carelessly and silence greets me.

Eyes wide, Yuyu opens her mouth to reply, but one glance at Noelle and she stops.

Cisco, too, grits his teeth, looking almost embarrassed.

"Because I got married," Noelle eventually answers.

"Noelle..." Yuyu reaches across the table to grab her hand in an act of small comfort. Her face is contorted in pain as she gazes at her sister-in-law and I realize that the gesture would not be well received. More than anything, I see the way Noelle is itching for a fight, her entire countenance poised for conflict.

And knowing how Cisco reacts if anything were to disturb Yuyu...

My eyes quickly scan the room, a plan taking shape in my mind.

"I want to hear," I suddenly say, grabbing Noelle's hand and tugging her to her feet. "I want to hear what would have prompted your teacher to sign you to a label," I tell her rather forcefully, leading her towards the end of the restaurant where a piano is situated.

I don't wait for the others to reply as I push her on the piano bench, more or less putting her in the spotlight as everyone turns to watch her closely.

"What do you think you're doing?" she hisses at me through a fake smile as she gazes at the crowd observing our interactions.

"I'm saving you from more conflict with your brother. You know how he will react if you offend your sister-in-law."

"Of course," she mutters dryly. "And we would *never* want to do that."

"Exactly." I place my hands on her shoulders, holding her in place. "Now be a good girl and put on a show for everyone to see—including your family. We wouldn't want your brother to think we're not getting along, now, would we?" I murmur softly in her ear.

"Anyone with two good eyes would have noticed we aren't exactly...cordial," she says, a strained smile on her face.

"My, my, Noelle. You're rather clueless, aren't you?"

She stiffens at my words.

"What *you* see and what *they* see are two different things," I chuckle, my breath fanning her cheek as I nod in their direction. "They sense the tension between us, but not the murderous kind." I move closer, my lips skimming her soft skin. "Even now," I whisper, feeling her shiver under my touch. "They see our interactions. The way you tremble when I put my hands on you..."

And to show her, I gently move my hands down her shoulders, eliciting a small gasp from her lips.

"They hear your soft whimpers and the way your breath hitches in my proximity," I continue. "And they see the way I look at you."

"What... What do you mean?" She asks, her voice barely above a whisper.

"Like I can't wait to get you alone," I smirk against her skin. "Like my hands are itching to close around your neck, feel your pulse beneath my fingertips..."

The reaction is immediate, her breath erratic as she tries *very* hard to keep herself still.

"They see the way you arouse me," I pause as she opens her mouth on a throaty gasp.

Moving my hands back up, it's to circle them around her neck, gently massaging her flesh. "But they don't know that my dick gets hard *only* at the thought of snapping this lovely neck. That which they perceive as desire is merely my need to have you at my mercy."

Her entire body is quaking, her lids opening and closing as she fights for control. Her lips part as she's about to reply, but I quickly shush her.

"No. Don't speak," I command her. "Play for me, little liar. Play for me and show me how much you hate me."

And with that, I'm off her, backing away while holding her gaze captive.

For a moment I don't think she's going to do it. Not with the way she's looking at me, her expression a delicious mix of fear and desire.

But as I resume my seat at the table, a note echoes in the restaurant.

Everything seems to come to a standstill as the music begins—slow and tentative at first, before bursting into a burgeoning storm of feeling.

"That..." Yuyu frowns. "What did you say to her?" she asks, her eyes fixed on Noelle.

I don't reply as my attention is fully focused on *her*.

Her back is straight, her head slightly tipped in the air as she sways ever so slightly with every note she plays. Her eyes are closed, her lips slightly parted to accommodate the tip of her tongue to peek through.

She looks completely gone as she transfers magic from her fingertips into the keys of the piano, each stroke bold and confident but without coming across as contrived.

My own lips part in surprise as I become entranced by the vision of her. It's like she's a completely different person as she controls the music that emanates from the piano.

The melody starts out with her trademark gloom as she channels Bach's Little fugue, a glaring anger underscoring the execution as she glides her fingers aggressively over the keys. There's a twitch in her cheek as she gives herself to the sound.

Suddenly, her hands still, the sound abruptly stopping as she catches her breath. There's a deafening silence in the entire restaurant as people are gaping at her.

The pause is too brief, however, as she jumps straight into the next piece. A calmer yet unusual one, she's playing Clara Schumann's Mazurka in a way that both soothes and scintillates the senses. The tone is melancholic, exacerbated only by her rapt expression as she gives herself to the music, her brows slightly pinched together, the muscles in her neck corded with tension.

But it's a false calm that she lulls everyone into. And just when least expected, her fingers erupt in a cacophony of sound, the melody stilted and screeching of conflicting and unresolved emotions.

Everyone is frowning at the choice of music.

She's channeling Schoenberg's atonality to prove a point—a *fuck you* directed straight at me.

As she starts to blast that sound into the air, her eyes snap open, her gaze firmly placed on me as she gives into this emotive display of madness.

Look what you made me do.

This is all for you.

I recognize the fire in her eyes, the way her feelings are transferred on to the keys of the piano before resounding into room for the whole world to hear. The intimate and raw way she conveys her emotions, using her music as the head of an arrow meant straight for my heart.

Hit me it does, leaving me reeling as I can't seem to wrench my gaze away from her.

Haunting.

There's only one way to describe her at this moment. Haunting.

As if she could imprint herself on one's very soul, leaving behind a searing trail never to be healed again.

The anger is palpable—and fuck if it doesn't awaken something inside of me, the sound so intoxicating it makes my insides seethe with unreleased tension.

I feel her melody on my tongue, the taste tangy and metallic, not unlike tears of sorrow mixed with the hopelessness of life. But beneath it all there's a sweetness that is, paradoxically, imbuing her anger.

The taste of her song is exhilarating, her emotions so vivid it's like I'm getting drunk on them. But to give in would mean the start of a *new* addiction. One that once it sinks its claws into me, it might *never* let me go.

Closing my eyes, I swallow, marveling at the pure taste of agony that assaults me as she launches into Schubert's Winterreise.

In a spectacular move, she overlays the two songs, emphasizing both her precarious mental state and her anger at the world, using one hand to play Schubert in a lower octave, while the other is adding hints of Schoenberg in a higher octave.

The result is truly spectacular in its monstrosity. To the untrained ear, it sounds as if an amateur is playing the piano haphazardly, hitting random keys to create the semblance of a sound.

Beneath all that cacophonous dissonance lay the seed of genius —one that's been hurt and battered and now bleeds from the piano keys.

I don't realize when she stops playing. So enraptured I am by the vision in front of me that I can't react even as people start clapping at her.

She rises from her seat, slowly wading her way back to the table. And as I raise my gaze towards hers, meeting those stormy brown eyes peppered with flecks of green, it's to find myself rooted to the spot.

I've seen her before, yet now I *see* her.

She puts one step in front of the other, walking stiffly towards us, almost as if she's self-conscious about her display. For a second I have to wonder if she regrets giving away too much of what she's feeling, because her melody is still fresh on my senses, that pure anguish wrapped in resentment that lives inside of her leaving its mark on me.

But just as I'm about to take a step towards her, meet her in the middle where there are no other ears to intrude on what I want to ask of her, a loud noise permeates the air.

Everything happens at once.

The shouts. The commotion. The screams of pain.

I'm vaguely aware of Cisco swiftly maneuvering the dinner table as a shield to protect his wife, barking an order and charging me with Noelle's safety while he takes care of Yuyu. Knowing Cisco and his extreme obsession with his wife, nothing will stand in his way in making sure both her and their unborn child are safe.

Which leaves *her* to…me.

Chapter Twenty-Six

Rafaelo

Her eyes wide, she looks around the room petrified, the shouts only getting louder as people jostle her on their way out, their terror unmistakable.

Shots are fired, round after round discharged in the restaurant as some meet bare air while some meet flesh.

She's stopped moving, wildly looking about the room in an attempt to make sense of what's happening around.

But there's nothing to make sense.

Not when there are at least five people waving guns around and aiming for the kill.

It all happens in slow motion as I turn slightly, making eye contact with one of the gunmen and seeing an arrogant smirk spread across his face before he lifts his gun, aiming it straight at Noelle.

Conscious thought leaves me as my body acts on its own, my feet moving before I realize.

It's a flurry of movement as I charge her to the ground, my body covering hers and serving as a shield for the incoming bullets. Adrenaline runs through my veins, masking the pain as a bullet hits my shoulder. The only evidence of the shot the blood that pours from the wound.

My body is flush against hers on the ground, and I feel her stiff with fear against me. Her mouth opens on a silent scream, her eyes wild as she terror engulfs her.

"Shh," I whisper softly, bringing the back of my hand to her face. "It will be over soon," I tell her before I use all my strength to roll us over from the ground and the incoming path of more bullets.

Holding on to her midriff, I keep her tugged to my side as I push us towards one table, kicking at its feet and turning it sideways to find some cover from the other shots.

She's trembling in my arms, her breathing punctured. But she's not yelling, or screaming in fear, and for that I'm thankful. Especially as the situation demands my entire focus.

The shots continue amid the crowd's screams, and I sneak a peek to see Cisco and Yuyu nestled behind their table. Cisco is assembling a gun while Yuyu is helping him with the parts.

Our eyes meet and he gives me a sharp nod that I return.

"Why are they shooting at us?" she asks in a small voice, coming even closer to me, her hand on my arm as she squeezes it for comfort.

"Who knows," I reply grimly. "That remains to be ascertained. For now," I pause as I remove my own small arsenal from the back of my pants. "We need to make sure they're taken out."

I take out two handguns and a couple of knives, placing them in front of us.

"Do you know how to shoot?" I turn to her.

She shakes her head ever so slowly and my lips stretch into a thin line.

"Here," I hand her one of the guns, quickly explaining how the safety works and what she should do if anyone comes near her.

"But you..."

"Someone needs to take them out," I add, knowing that Cisco would not dare to leave Yuyu's side for a second.

"Don't go," Noelle's hands grasp on to the material of my jacket, trying to keep me by her side. "Please," she pleads.

But it's in vain as I disentangle her fingers from me, shaking my head at her.

"You know what to do." I nod to the gun in her hand before raising my head over the table.

There are three men inside, all shooting randomly at the many people hysterically running around, and two men at the front door, ensuring *no one* gets out alive.

Propping the barrel of the gun on the edge of the table, I aim at the closest man, hitting him right in the chest. As soon as he drops to the floor, though, the others' attention is fixed on us. So without lingering, I roll on to the floor, visibly moving away from the table and distracting them from Noelle's location.

Bullets fly past me as I barely make it to cover, taking just one breath before looking back and firing at the other men.

The two by the door, noticing that the others have difficulty in managing the situation, leave their posts and come inside too, swinging their guns around.

They don't make it much further than the middle of the restaurant though. Not as both Cisco and Yuyu move in sync, their fingers on the trigger of their guns as they fire at the incoming men.

The effect is immediate as both drop dead, holes forming in their foreheads and blood pouring out of them.

With three down, it's only a matter of getting to the other two.

Seeing that they might be outnumbered, the men are quick to pick some people off the floor and use them as shields, all the while shooting at both our locations.

"Noelle," Cisco yells at me, motioning to the direction of his sister.

But just as my attention is drawn to her hiding place, so is the shooters'.

A brief moment of eye contact and the race to Noelle begins, one of the shooters staying behind and trying to take out Cisco and his wife, while the other dashes to where Noelle is.

My feet move—faster than they've ever moved—and I only manage to reach her side a few seconds before the other man. Tugging her to her feet, I waste no time in twirling her around, keeping her nestled to my side as I extend my arm to shoot at the man.

Guns drawn out, we're both at a standstill as we stare into each other's eyes. Just like a gunfight in the wild west, it's all about speed as both of us have our fingers on the trigger, ready to fire.

The seconds stretch, and time becomes null and void as I hear my heart thumping in my ears.

Noelle's small body is draped across my chest as she nestles even closer. She's holding tightly onto me, her hands wrapped around the material of my shirt, a small sob escaping her lips.

But I can't worry about her now. Not when my full attention needs to be engaged in the matter at hand.

Slimy hair and dirty clothes, the shooter looks like a completely regular person. In fact, all the others had been rather nondescript too—all of it compounding my confusion as to why they would attack the restaurant in the first place.

My intuition, though, is telling me that the attack isn't random. That they'd had a target all along.

And as my mind remaps the trajectory of the bullets, from the first one fired, I have to admit to myself that there is only one probable answer.

They're here for the bounty.

Fuck! I should have realized that sooner or later this was going to happen—that someone was going to try to get the bounty regardless of the dangers involved. And I probably would have been more prepared if my entire attention hadn't been distracted by a certain someone.

Grounding myself in the present, I force myself to focus on the target at hand.

Sweat trickles down the man's temple, his eyes blinking rapidly as he looks at me, ready to pull the trigger.

But as soon as my mind's ascertained that, I realize that I'm likely dealing with amateurs—especially considering the haphazard way in which they'd tried to burst into the restaurant.

My eyes narrow on his trembling hand, noting the way he's

trying very hard to keep it extended in front of him in order to aim at me.

A slow smile pulls at my lips at his actions, and I give him a false sense of security as I emulate his movements.

But just as he gains a little more confidence, his pointer finger making contact with the trigger, I quickly pull on mine, not giving him any chance of actually firing.

My bullet hits him square between his eyes. Still staring at me with wide eyes, he drops to the floor, the noise a thundering bang that makes Noelle jump in my arms.

Cisco helps his wife up, getting out from their hiding place.

Yuyu is completely unfazed as she takes in the bloodbath on the floor.

In their bout of madness, the shooters had managed to kill quite a few innocent people, their blood currently staining the floor.

Cisco dusts his suit, looking unbothered as he studies the dead shooters.

"Now, that was unfortunate," he mentions as he stoops down to search one of the men, coming up rather empty handed.

Yuyu, too, does the same with another, eliciting a look of surprise from me.

Certainly, you don't see every day a seven-month pregnant woman rummage so clinically through pure carnage. It's even more striking when comparing her reaction with that of Noelle, who is still holding on to me for dear life.

"Noelle," I softly call out her name, but she doesn't answer.

Her teeth are clattering, her eyes unfocused.

My hands on her shoulders, I move her off me, stooping down on one knee so I'm closer to her eye level.

"Noelle," I repeat, waving my palm in front of her.

"Is she alright?" Yuyu asks, coming from behind me.

"I don't think so," I answer grimly when I note that she's entirely unresponsive, her features a tad too pale. Her eyes are fixed on the blood on the floor, and she doesn't seem to acknowledge our presence.

"Damn, we better hurry," Cisco mentions as he comes to our side. "The police should be here any moment."

"Any survivors?"

He shakes his head.

"There were around thirty people in the restaurant to begin with. Everyone who tried to leave was killed by one of those," he points to the two men he and Yuyu had dispatched. "The others were simply killed in the chaos," he pauses, his gaze on my shoulder. "You should get that looked at," he nods at the blood slowly trickling down my arm.

"Not now," I shrug, the pain minimal considering the things I'd been accustomed to. "Let's go through the back," I say, turning my focus back to Noelle.

Swaying a little on her feet, her eyes roll in the back of her head before she loses her balance. Catching her, I simply swing her over my non injured shoulder and follow Cisco and Yuyu out.

"At least there were no witnesses," Cisco jokes once we are in the car and heading back home.

"I'm surprised that the first people to come after me were *those*," I chuckle, gently cradling Noelle's head to my chest.

"*That* is rather interesting. Everyone knows you're under my protection now, so theoretically speaking, only fools would dare pull a move like that."

"I think you're right on that account. They didn't seem to have any experience. The last man was practically shitting himself when he was trying to shoot me."

"They probably jumped at the opportunity to make some money. Certainly, if they had known who they were up against they wouldn't have come so unprepared," Yuyu comments, her brows pinched together as she stares at Noelle with a worried expression.

"On that note," Cisco smiles. "I must give it to you," he winks at me. "You didn't disappoint."

"I wasn't aware it was a test," I raise an eyebrow.

"It wasn't," he replies, though his words don't seem very convincing. Especially as he shares an amused look with his wife. "So to speak."

"Meaning?" I shoot back. Of course nothing is ever black and white with Cisco. There's always some kind of test, even deep in the middle of a bloodshed.

"He's joking," Yuyu waves her hand. "A little?" She pauses before laughing, and her reaction makes me even more confused. "We just wanted to see how you handle yourself," she shrugs.

I look at them flabbergasted. Now that the adrenaline is starting to wear off, I can assess the events more rationally. More than anything, I get their meaning as it dawns on me that they had delayed their involvement on purpose.

"So it *was* a test," I state in a deadpan voice, unable to believe they would play like that with Noelle's life. Because while I could get myself out of a difficult situation, they couldn't have known I would be able to defend her too.

"Now, don't look like that," Cisco says dismissively. "We wouldn't have let anything happen to either of you."

His words make me even more confused. Especially as he continues with an odd question.

"Have you heard of the Black Monarch?"

"Yes. I don't think there's anyone in New York who hasn't," I frown.

The stories have been around since I was a kid, the Black Monarch almost legendary in the underground world. One wrong step, and you'd fall prey to his merciless swords—two butterfly blades that would separate your head from your body.

One season in particular, the hunt for the Black Monarch had been in full swing after a succession of headless bodies had been found all around the city. After years, it became an urban legend, no one knowing his identity, or his affiliation.

"Should we tell him?" Cisco asks with a knowing smile.

"He's going to be part of the family," Yuyu answers, eyeing the sleeping Noelle in my arms.

"Very well. The Black Monarch," Cisco nods. "You're staring at it."

"You?" I blurt out, taken aback by the confession.

"Not me," he makes a funny face. "The lady next to me."

"You? You're the Black Monarch?" My voice must betray my awe, especially as Yuyu winks at me conspiratorially.

"Not many people know, since we've tried to keep it under wraps. But she was my right hand before she was my wife," he chuckles. "She's the skilled one in the family when it comes to killing," he murmurs, looking at her adoringly.

"Oh come on," she swats him on the shoulder. "You forget you were the one who taught me everything I know."

"Maybe. You're still the best."

"That's very surprising," I interrupt their saccharine exchange. "I don't think *anyone* would have ever imagined that the Black Monarch is a woman."

"Was," Yuyu corrects. "I retired some time ago."

"That still doesn't explain why you'd risk your sister's life like that," I jibe, a little put off by their behavior.

"You're a wanted man, Raf. Can you fault me for being curious to see how you'd handle yourself?" Cisco shrugs.

I grunt, his reasoning solid. Yet why does it still make me uncomfortable?

As the car wades through the streets of Manhattan, Cisco changes the topic, giving me a short rundown of his history with the Black Monarch.

I listen to him talk, my fingers move absentmindedly over the smooth skin of Noelle's cheek, *this* proximity not affecting me as adversely as before.

And as we pull in front of the house, I say goodbye to Cisco and his wife as I take two steps at a time, hurrying to the third floor to tuck Noelle in her bed.

Her reaction to the shooting, while not unwarranted, had been a little blown out of proportions. She'd been white as a sheet of paper as she'd looked at the dead men on the floor. And to my everlasting chagrin, that worries me.

Kicking her door open, I head straight for her bed, gently lowering her to the mattress. Instead of leaving, though, I find myself taking a seat by her side, my eyes on her face as I study her features.

Her expression as she'd played the piano flashes in my mind, the animated way in which she'd given herself to the music showing me a different side of her—an *appealing* side of her.

And *that* is a problem. Add to that the lingering realization that her music had been my mental escape while in captivity, and I'm faced with a dilemma.

Brushing my hand across her forehead, I can't help but think back to those times, and to the power of her melody as it had helped me cope with the shitshow that had been my life.

Thank you.

The words are on my tongue, ready to be released into the air. Yet as much as I want to, I find that I can't utter them.

Not when she'd also been the architect of my suffering—and that of Lucero's ultimate demise.

Can one right make up for all the wrongs?

I sigh, the night's events taking a toll on me, especially as pain shoots up my shoulder, more blood pooling down my arm.

But just as I'm about to rise from my seat, her eyes snap open, her irises swirling into a hypnotizing mix of brown and green. She's staring at me, those gorgeous eyes of hers big and full of curiosity.

Maybe I would have expected fear, or apprehension. But there's none as she quietly looks at me, her small hand coming up to tug at the sleeve of my blazer.

She doesn't speak as she pulls herself to a sitting position. She doesn't say a word as she swings her legs over the bed, coming in front of me and pushing the blazer off my shoulders.

There's a certain calm in the silence of the night as she softly unbuttons my bloodstained shirt, slipping it off my shoulders to reveal the nasty wound.

I can only look reverently at her as she dabs at the blood, going to her bathroom to wet a towel before coming back and tenderly cleaning my wound.

Thankfully, the bullet hadn't entered my body. Rather, it had only grazed my skin, causing a big enough gash to bleed a bucket, but unlikely to be life threatening in any way.

Raising my eyes to her face, I watch her movements—brisk and efficient and wholly unlike someone who just fainted at the sight of a dead body.

She's so focused on thoroughly cleaning the blood that she doesn't realize the sight she strikes, especially as she pulls her lower lip between her teeth in concentration.

Once again, I find myself entranced by the vivid play of emotions on her face, and it's like time stands still as I lose myself in *her*.

When she's done, she gets a small first aid kit, taking out a medium bandage and applying it over my wound.

She releases a satisfied sigh as she surveys her handwork, stepping back to assess me.

For once, I note no animosity. No fear. *Nothing*.

There's a certain vulnerability to her expression that's laid in the open for me to see, and my heart constricts painfully in my chest at the sight.

We stay like that for what feels like forever, our eyes affixed to one another.

It's her who speaks first, breaking the spell.

"Thank you," she utters softly, the hint of a smile on her face.

"For what?" I frown at her.

"For this," she lifts her hand, the ghost of a touch as she trails it over my bandaged wound. "You saved me," she murmurs, almost reverently.

I nod at her, not wanting to dwell on the particularities. Because truth to be told, I hadn't been fully conscious of my actions as I'd pushed her to the ground, putting my body between her and the bullet. Even now, as the events replay in my mind, I can't say for sure why I'd done that—and why the action had come to me so naturally.

Annoyance spears through me at the thought as I realize that would have been my chance to get Noelle to pay without having *any* fingers pointed at me. I could have used that opportunity to hurt her—maybe even kill her.

All I should have done was to stay put.

Abruptly, I stand up, grabbing my soiled clothes and heading for the door.

It's by chance that I hear her whispered words—and oh, how I wish I didn't. Because they have the power to haunt me…

"No one's ever saved me before."

Chapter Twenty-Seven

Noelle

"Sign here," the officiant points towards the sheet of paper.

The last step.

Once the tip of my pen hits the parchment, I'll be forever tied to him. I'll become his property. His to do as he sees fit.

For days I've been fretting about this moment, thinking of countless ways to escape my fate. After all, I know exactly what happens when I'm not my own self anymore.

Yet no matter how much I plotted and schemed, I reached a point where I had to admit to myself that there was nothing I could do. The outcome had been decided long ago.

Just like before, I'm powerless to do anything but to let others dictate my fate.

My fingers grip the shaft of the pen, my hand shaky in one last bout of flimsy rebellion.

Looking back, my family is on one side, their watchful eyes on me since God forbid I make a scene. Raf's friends are on the other side of the room, all sporting bored looks on their faces—probably aware of the sham that is this marriage.

And then there's *him*.

The heat of his body seems to permeate every atom of my being—though we are not touching.

His steely eyes meet mine, their coldness suffocating and antithetic to everything else he makes me feel. But the disdain that greets me as I look at him is sobering enough to remind me of my place. I'm merely a pawn in his game—in everyone's game.

My mouth opens on a sound that won't come out—all my grievances suddenly muted by the inevitability of fate.

He narrows his eyes at me, and taking a step closer, he stoops low, his mouth brushing against my ear.

"Don't you dare," he whispers, his tone stern and unyielding.

Leaning back, there's just the hint of a smile as the corner of his mouth pulls in a sick representation of what my life has become.

The smugness on his face does nothing to alleviate the emptiness forming inside of me as I turn my attention back to the paper, pressing the tip of the pen against the white surface and watching a leaky substance flow out of it.

A brisk move and my fate is sealed.

"Congratulations," someone speaks, but it's hard to make out whose voice that is.

Not when there's a numbness inside of me that drowns everything out. My ears stop working, my mind foggy as I'm passed around from person to person for useless platitudes.

For a moment, I have to wonder if this is the reality I find myself in. If it's not a nightmare—a vision of horror produced by my sick mind.

Minutes trickle by. Then hours.

A screeching noise pounds in my ears—a sound that I belatedly recognize as my errant heart.

"A little smile won't hurt," a snide voice comments, that one sentence bringing me back to the present.

My sight clears, my eyes focusing on the moving items outside of the window of the car, the atmosphere stifling on the inside as I feel his presence more than ever in the small, enclosed space.

"Don't want to," I mumble, shrugging.

"Now, that's an issue, little liar," he says, and suddenly his fingers are on my jaw, tightly gripping my flesh and forcing me to look at him. "Your family believes in our *great* love story. It wouldn't do well to disappoint them," he flashes me a mocking smile.

"You might be able to win actor of the year with your golden boy looks, but I won't help you. You got what you wanted already, so leave me alone," I grit my teeth as I shove his hand away.

"That's where you're wrong. I didn't get what I wanted. Far from it, Noelle," he smirks. "This is just the beginning. And by the time I'm through with you..." his smile widens.

"Do your worst," I shrug, already resigned to my fate.

At the end of the day, what can be worse than being married to Sergio? With all the threats hanging over my head, Raf hasn't been violent towards me.

A manipulative bastard? Maybe. But he's never lifted a hand against me, and that is my *only* solace at the moment.

He seems surprised by my easy acquiescence, a twitch in his jaw signaling his annoyance as he turns his focus back to the road.

It's a very short while later that I realize we're not going towards the house. My eyes widen as I watch the city skyscrapers quickly become small dots in the distance.

"Where are we going?" I demand, my head whipping back and forth as I try to make sense of our location.

Suddenly, images of him taking me in the middle of nowhere to kill me and get rid of my body flash before my eyes. And no matter how much I try to put on a strong front, slowly, the fear is getting to me.

He's going to kill me.

That was what he wanted to do from the beginning, wasn't it? But why now? Why marry me first?

A barrage of questions make their way into my mind, and while I do my best to rationalize my situation—that it wouldn't be in his best interest to get rid of me *now*—somehow I can't help but feel that I'm heading straight for the guillotine.

"Our honeymoon, where else," he chuckles, but the mirth doesn't reach his eyes.

In fact, there's a chilliness coming from him that makes me

shiver, my hands going around my arms in an attempt to warm myself up.

"What are you talking about?"

"Your brother thought we should have a weekend to ourselves," he answers in a curt tone, "since we won't have too much intimacy at the house. He also told me he was remodeling the third floor to give us some privacy."

"Wh—what?" I blink repeatedly, unable to believe what I'm hearing. "Honeymoon?"

"It's nothing fancy," he shrugs. "Just a couple of days at one of your family's properties upstate. I can't be away from New York for too long anyway," he mutters under his breath before promptly ignoring me.

Soon, silence descends over as he continues to drive. One look behind us, though, and I see an entourage of cars—our guards no doubt.

The knowledge that these are my brother's people should make me more at ease, since Raf couldn't possibly do anything to me under their watch.

Right?

There's an echo in my brain as the question remains unanswered.

Because not all things that hurt are physical.

The journey doesn't take long as we reach the house, and my spirits plummet even more as I realize *which* property he'd been talking about.

This particular house has a vast field surrounding it, with no neighbor in sight for what feels like miles.

My fear mounts again as I realize how trapped I am—how I'll be unable to ask for help should I need it.

Raf doesn't notice my change of mood. He barely spares me a glance as he parks the car, opening the trunk and getting a couple of bags out of it.

"Yuyu packed you some clothes," he says as he throws a bag at me.

I don't get to reply as he turns his back to me, heading straight to the house.

Trudging my way after him, I mumble a few curses under my breath.

It's a couple of days, how bad can it be?

A FEW HOURS later I realize just *how* bad it can be.

"You're not going anywhere." He raises an eyebrow at me as he places himself in front of the door, blocking my way.

"I didn't realize I was a prisoner here," I retort, trying to bypass him.

As soon as we'd arrived at the house, we'd each laid claim to a room and then proceeded to ignore each other. Not that I'm not thankful for *this* version of a honeymoon. But the invisible chains around my wrists started to jiggle, and I found that I couldn't stand still—especially since I *knew* he's bound to make a move at some point.

"You know just as well as I do that it's dangerous to go outside alone," he grabs my arm, swinging me around to face him. "No matter how safe and secluded the location is, there's still the possibility that someone could launch an attack," he continues, looking entirely put out with me.

"Right. Let me get this straight. I can't go out because I might get killed. But I *should* stay inside in case *you* decide to kill me. After all, wasn't that your goal from the beginning?" I throw at him, trying to wrench myself from his grasp.

"That's right," a smile erupts on his face. "If anyone's going to kill you, it's going to be me," he declares proudly, leaning in so close I can feel his breath on my lips. "Even more so now, little liar. Your life is in my hands," he chuckles. "Figuratively, and..." his hold tightens. "Literally."

"Can you just get it over with then?" I release a weary sigh. "Just do whatever it is you want to do," I say flippantly, already tired of having the threat hanging over my head.

"Where's the fun in that? Keeping you on your toes is much more appealing," he drawls, pulling back and looking at me expectantly—as if he's waiting for me to break out into hysterics any moment.

I purse my lips, gazing at him in frustration.

He has a smug expression on his face as he regards me, and for the first time I realize what he's wearing. No longer the black suit I've come to associate with him, he's now dressed in a white shirt and baggy sweatpants.

I tilt my head, my brows furrowing in surprise as I take in this new side of him.

With everything I've learned of him so far—particularly his unyielding intensity—I hadn't thought there was a more...leisurely side to him.

His sculpted chest is emphasized by the tight fit of the shirt, his pebbled abdominals almost peeking through.

"What are you looking at?" he barks, folding his hands over his chest and narrowing his eyes at me.

A smile pulls at my lips because for all his domineering attitude, there's also something soft about him. Something...rather innocent.

"Am I not allowed to look?" I shrug, taking a step forward.

"Not like that," he grumbles under his breath.

"Like what? You're a handsome man, Raf. And you're my husband..." I trail off, amused at his scandalized expression. Especially as I bring my hand up, brushing my fingers lightly over his forearm.

He doesn't move, although his entire body is wound tightly as he keeps himself rooted to the spot.

Just when I think I have the upper hand, though, ready to play with him a little, he turns the cards on me.

My back connects with the hard wood of the door, the breath knocked out of me as I blink, staring up into his chilly eyes as he looks down at me with that mocking disdain I've come to associate with him.

His body is crowding mine, and I can feel all those hard planes pressed against me. That strength in his arms that makes me yearn for a place to nestle between them...

"Done playing the meek victim?" he asks spitefully, his face twisted in a scowl. "Let's see," he laughs drily. "Is this when you beg me to fuck you again?"

"I never begged," I grit out.

"Right. Why don't we remedy that?" His voice drops to a dangerous notch. "Get on your knees and *beg* me, and I might indulge you," he smirks.

"I'm not going to *ever* beg," I state confidently, meeting his stare head on.

He might intimidate me, and he might inspire uncomfortable feelings in me, but that doesn't mean that I'm simply going to sing to his tune.

"We'll see about that, little liar," he smiles at me, but he doesn't make to move.

We are at a standstill, our eyes locked in a vicious battle that neither wants to abandon.

I don't blink.

He doesn't blink.

It's a battle of the wills as our breaths become labored, the air growing hotter with the intensity of our perseverance.

The heat emanating from his body seeps into mine, every spot he's touching inflamed by the impossibility of the situation.

His pupils grow larger, his nostrils flaring as his upper lip twitches. Yet he doesn't abandon his position. He keeps me locked in this arctic embrace—the ice in his eyes staying strong even in the face of infernal fires.

My mouth feels dry, my limbs heavy as I feel the press of his body to my core. My tongue slips out to wet my lips, and a shiver goes down my spine as his gaze dips to my mouth.

There's a striking intensity to the way he stares at me—as if he can't decide whether to kill me or fuck me. Alas, it's a conundrum I'm very familiar with and one that often keeps me up at night.

As he realizes the direction of his thoughts, and the fact that his desire is written all over his face, his gaze snaps back to mine. The corner of his mouth curls up in something akin to disgust as he continues to look at me—conflicted emotions visible in every micro-expression.

But as the stare down continues, a low sound erupts in the air, building up until it vibrates in the room.

My mouth pulls into an amused smile as I realize the source.

"Why don't *you* beg me?" I ask cheekily. "I *might* take pity on you and feed you." I barely keep myself from laughing out loud. Especially as his cheeks redden in a mix of embarrassment and anger, his hold on me tightening as he brings me even closer to his body.

"Beg me," I murmur, pushing my chin up in a defiant move as I close the distance between our faces.

On the tips of my toes, my lips are barely an inch away from his. Inhaling, his breath transfers to me, the air filling my lungs and filling *me*.

The tension in his body doesn't abate. If anything the proximity is making his muscles coil, his strength palpable and enveloping me like a fine glove.

"As if anything coming from you could ever sate me," he jibes, arrogance dripping from his words, the double entendre an obvious taunt.

"It could," I whisper, my voice husky in an attempt to sound seductive. "It might be just what you need."

His jaw clenched, he breathes hard as if he's one step away from actually strangling me. Somehow I know I'm treading on thin ice, but I can't help myself when it comes to him. He brings out a side of me I long thought buried—a daring side that makes me want to push his buttons. Make him feel what he makes me feel.

There's a pause where neither of us speaks, the wind howling through an open window and inviting a forlorn sound into the empty house.

Yet just as he opens his mouth to say something—chastise me for my *wanton* behavior, no doubt—another sound penetrates the air.

We both still, our gazes swinging back and forth as we try to identify the source of the noise.

"You..." I start, but he shakes his head, the hint of a smile on his face.

"You," he states confidently, just in time for another growly noise to resound in the air.

My eyes widen, my arms immediately dropping to my stomach as I hold on to my midriff. And with a startling realization, I jump back, out of his grasp and out of his reach.

He's silently laughing at me, his eyes crinkling with amusement.

"Don't," I grit out, annoyed.

"Maybe *I* should feed you." He leans back, the tension all but leaving his body.

We stand like that for a moment—me clutching at my stomach in embarrassment, while he is smugly gloating at my mortification.

Then, just like the previous confrontation never happened—as if we weren't on the verge of tearing at each other's throats and clothes—we both burst out laughing.

"Half an hour truce?" I propose.

"You have a deal," he replies jokingly. "Until we replenish the fuel."

"Fine," I wave my hand in the air, though the smile on my lips doesn't want to dissipate. One look at him, though, and he's in the same situation as he follows me to the kitchen.

"Your brother said it was fully stocked," he mumbles as he checks the cabinet while I open the fridge.

"It seems he thought about everything," I mutter drily. Of course, with my brother being a control freak, he wouldn't stop micro-managing *every* aspect of my life—even though I'm theoretically off his hands now.

We do a quick inventory of what Cisco had gotten for us, and it seems he *did* think of everything—to my great chagrin.

"So what now?" Raf asks, hands in his pockets, as he looks at me like a lost puppy.

"Now we make food," I almost roll my eyes at him.

"Yeah, but..." he trails off, confused.

"You don't know how to cook, do you?" I ask point-blankly.

A sheepish smile and he shakes his head at me.

With a punctured huff, I turn to the lined up items.

"Any preferences? Allergies? Anything?" I raise an eyebrow at him.

"Nope," he simply answers, walking to the table in the middle of the kitchen and plopping himself in the chair.

Turning sharply, I place my hands on my hips, glowering at him.

"And what do you think you're doing?"

"Waiting?"

"No, no," I raise my pointer finger, swinging it back and forth. "You don't get to sit around while I work," I state, not leaving room for argument, especially as I dump a sack of potatoes in front of him. "You peel the potatoes, I cook the meat."

A moment passes as he looks at the potatoes, then back to me, then back to the potatoes. Swallowing hard, I can see he's weighing his options. More than anything, I can see he doesn't know how to peel potatoes, yet he doesn't want to embarrass himself further by admitting that.

I almost smile at the display of foolish male pride, but I let him figure it out on his own.

Turning my attention to the meat, I cut it into smaller pieces, adding spices on top of it and placing it on a tray to put in the oven. And while I'm waiting for Raf to finish with the potatoes, I also whip up a sauce for the meat.

"Done!" His words take me by surprise since it can't have been more than ten minutes since he started.

Coming to my side, he presents me with a plate full of peeled potatoes—or what's left of them. He appears extremely proud of his work as he more or less thrusts them in my face.

"Great," I mumble, taking the tray from him and noting the small frown that appears on his face. Ah, golden boy wants to be praised for his abysmal peeling skills?

"I'm impressed," I add in a fake tone, and his face lights up immediately.

"I used my hunting knife," he proudly states, lifting a monstrosity of a knife in the air.

My eyes widen.

"And why would you do that?" The words tumble out of my mouth. "Why do you even have that?"

"To hunt, of course." He frowns.

I blink, taken aback.

"To hunt?" I repeat, shock written all over my features. He nods effusively.

"You can't cook, but you have a hunting knife...to hunt?"

"It's not the same," he mumbles. "When you hunt," he pauses, scrunching up his nose. "You just peel off the meat from the carcass and cook it on a fire," he shrugs.

"Why would you have to do that?" I frown. I wouldn't imagine him engaging in that type of behavior in the heart of the city. Somehow that one image is enough to elicit a low laugh out of me.

A dark look crosses his face, the amusement from before all but leaving his features.

"Because not everything in life is sunshine and rainbows, Noelle," he replies in a harsh tone. "And because," he takes a step forward, making me lose my balance as I bump into the kitchen counter. "Sometimes you do whatever it takes to survive."

The fire in his eyes could burn a hole in me. But just as he's about to speak further, he's off me and back at the table.

I let out a big breath, my heart beating like crazy from his proximity. But instead of dwelling on that, I simply adorn the meat tray with potatoes before placing it in the oven.

While we wait for the food to cook, I tentatively take the seat opposite to him at the table.

He has a grave expression on his face, and for a moment I feel guilty for dispelling the carefree mood we'd shared minutes ago.

But he's right. Life is not sunshine and rainbows. And until we lay all our cards on the table, we won't be able to reach *any* understanding.

"How did you end up at the *hacienda*?" I find the courage to ask.

His gaze pins me with its intensity, and for a moment I don't think he's going to answer.

"My brother sold me," he shrugs. "He wanted to be the sole heir to the family, so he shipped me off to be sold as a slave, killed my parents, and proclaimed himself the new boss." The words roll easily off his tongue, but the pain is evident in the way he makes a conscious effort to seem blasé.

"Why... He's your brother. Why would he do something like that?"

"Some people don't need a reason to do evil things, do they? My brother isn't well. He's never been particularly sane, but I can't say I expected him to go off the rails like this."

I nod sympathetically. Family drama is something I can more than understand.

"Do you miss your parents?"

I wish I could ask him more about his time at the *hacienda*, but I know that is equal to opening a can of worms I'm not ready to face. Most of all, I don't want to see the disdain in his eyes as he blames me for his misfortunes, and even less do I want to hear the love in his voice as he utters Lucero's name.

I want to know more about him, yet some things are outside my comfort zone—for now.

"You know," he starts, waving the hunting knife in the air in a playful gesture, "I haven't even visited their graves. I heard that Michele had them buried somewhere in the city to save face, but I haven't been able to go there yet..." he stops himself abruptly, his head whipping up as his gaze meets mine. "I don't know why I'm telling you this," he smiles ruefully to himself.

"I can't say that I know what you're going through. My father died when I was too young to really miss him, and my mother is... Well, my mother is healthy enough, I suppose. She just doesn't really care about me—about us."

He frowns.

"What do you mean?"

"She had me pretty late in life. An accident from what I'm told," I shrug. "By that time she was done being a mother, and by all accounts, I was an unwelcome surprise."

"Who raised you then?"

"Whoever was there at the moment, I guess," I reply, trying to keep the hurt from my voice. "Between my brothers and extended family, I had enough people to baby me—at one time or another," I force a smile.

"That doesn't sound very reassuring," he raises a brow.

"What about you then? How was your relationship with your parents?" I deflect, changing the topic.

He grimaces.

"My relationship with my father wasn't always the best, but that doesn't mean that we didn't get along. He always had my best interest at heart," he gives a stiff smile. "My mother... For all her faults, and I don't say that lightly since I am well aware she wasn't a good person, she was a good mother."

"I'm sorry."

He grunts, the knife still in his hand as he twirls it around his fingers.

"What's done is done," he shrugs. "She may have been a good mother to me, and I will undoubtedly miss her, but to everyone else she was a shrew. I know for sure she didn't make my sister's life—or my brother's for that matter—easy."

"Sister?" I frown. "I didn't realize you have a sister too."

A slow smile appears on his face.

"She's not affiliated with the family anymore," he doesn't say more, and I take it as my cue not to inquire further.

"I see," I nod awkwardly.

There's a brief pause as neither of us speaks, our breathing the only sound in the air. Yet as I gaze at him, is to find a ravenous look in his eyes—something beyond mere hunger.

Unconsciously, I bite my lip, the reaction immediate.

There's something primal about the way he looks at me, and it makes my skin tingle in an uncomfortable way.

"What about your brother?" I cough, clearing my throat as I attempt to steer my thoughts into a different direction—one that's less likely to end with *me* as dinner. But damn if I wouldn't gladly offer myself on a platter...

Stupid brain!

I mentally chastise myself for the direction of my thoughts. It's not something new, since Raf's presence usually elicits some type of visceral response from me.

"What about him?" His brow arches, the topic clearly an unwelcome one.

"What do you plan to do about him?"

He regards me intently for a moment before shrugging.

"I haven't yet thought of the particularities. I'll have time to think up plenty of punishments after I catch him," he pauses. "When," he corrects himself.

"You're going to kill him?"

"That's the plan," he nods tensely. "The *how* is still undecided," he adds mysteriously.

"Why haven't you caught him until now, then?" I ask curiously since I know he and my brother have been working together to find Michele.

I'm sure I'm not supposed to know this, but over time, I've developed an unparalleled ability to eavesdrop. One that's served me well until now.

He purses his lips, clearly unhappy about that outcome.

"He's been eluding us on purpose. He's scared," he smirks. "Which he should be. But that means he's been very good about covering his tracks," he explains, and I nod along.

Especially as he continues talking, detailing some of the missions he and his team had completed in an attempt to get Michele out of his hiding place. So animatedly he's recounting those events, that I think he's forgetting whom he's talking to.

I listen attentively to his words, swallowing each syllable and getting drunk on his voice—the normal, non-growly one that isn't insulting or taunting me.

The more he talks, the more he relaxes around me, and a warmth unfurls low in my belly as I realize *this* is the real Raf—the funny, laid-back one.

The beeping of the oven wakes me from my reverie, interrupting our discussion. Begrudgingly, I have to admit that I would have preferred to starve than have him stop talking to me like this—like a normal person instead of the object of his disdain.

But as I get ready to take out the tray, I'm surprised to see him quietly set the table. I bring the food and we each help ourselves to a serving.

"This is very good, thank you," he says, his genuine tone startling me.

"You're welcome," I murmur, a blush creeping up my cheeks. Lowering my head, I focus on my food, afraid my expression would give away what I'm feeling.

There's a familiar coziness as we sit in silence, enjoying the meal without the usual jibes and mean comments. And for a moment, I forget he hates me. I forget that he married me for revenge. I forget that I'm not supposed to...like him.

For how long this pretense lasts, I feel a heat traveling down my body, my entire being burning from this small comfort that is his presence. And for the first time in so long—too long, really—my mind feels at peace.

"Raf?" I ask a while later, wanting to take advantage of the temporary lack of animosity.

My voice startles him as he turns his attention towards me.

"What do you plan to do with me?"

My eyes meet his as his hand stills on his fork.

"That's not for you to know," he answers flippantly, his deep voice sending a shiver down my body. Setting his utensils down, he rises from the table. He takes his plate to the sink, quickly rinsing it before leaving the room.

And leaving me...

I guess there's a limit to our civility.

Chapter Twenty-Eight
Noelle

There is one thing about this house that I'm not mad at.

The bathroom.

The master bathroom is the size of an entire room, a huge tub in the middle as big as a jacuzzi. From the first moment I'd seen it, I'd claimed the bedroom for my own, planning to take advantage of the luxuriant atmosphere and relax.

After all, it's not every day that I get a weekend away from my family and their watchful eyes.

Checking the temperature of the water, I smile in satisfaction. Turning to the big vanity by the side, I open a drawer and I choose a cherry flavored bath bomb, dropping it in the water and watching the bubbles as they start to erupt to the surface, the color of the water slowly turning a pinkish red.

The smell is already wafting through the air, and I release a sigh of contentment.

"Exactly what I needed after this day," I whisper to myself, the corners of my mouth curling up in a smile.

Slipping my robe off my shoulders, I carefully fold it on a chair. The icy air of the night hits my naked skin, and a chill travels down my back. Without any preliminaries, I dip my toes in the water before slowly submerging my entire body.

"Damn," a sigh escapes my lips as the hot water envelopes me.

And for the first time since the wedding bells had sounded, I let myself relax.

Married... Again.

I still remember the joy I'd felt at hearing Sergio had died in the fire and that I'd been widowed. At that moment, I'd vowed never to submit to another man again—never to let myself be used and abused.

Yet here I am. Once more at the mercy of someone else.

The moment my name changed, so did my fate.

Forever.

Or until one of us dies first. Strangely enough, though, I don't want him to die.

I should. God, but I should, if only to rid myself of the danger that looms over my head—the danger he poses to both my body *and* my heart.

I take a deep breath, leaning back and letting my head rest against the frame of the tub.

Raf—Rafaelo. The name rolls easily on my tongue, images of his baby blue eyes flooding my vision.

I could hate him—and maybe I should. But he's not my enemy, just like I am not his. Yet he cannot see past the curtain of hate that shields his eyes. He cannot see past the preconceived notions he has of me. And I can't help him either, since I don't have the information to confirm or deny his accusations.

He's been living with us for enough time that I've managed to learn more about him—and maybe that's the issue. Because the more I get to know him, the more my regret deepens, my hope soaring when it knows it will get shot down.

I've seen his bad side, but I've also seen the good.

He's harsh and domineering, his words often biting and bruising. But he's also a fighter—and his perseverance is truly awe inspiring. Not many can say they have survived Sergio's trials and lived to talk about them—much less thrive in spite of the toll those drugs would take on the body.

I remember how he'd managed his prisoners, and how ruthlessly he would use them, the drugs more or less stripping humanity from them. Yet Raf hadn't let that stop him. If anything, it had spurred him on.

The muscles he hides under his clothes must have been the result of hours upon hours of hard work—going against himself and what his body had been accustomed to. Everything in his presentation, from his body language to his countenance, speaks of both inner and outer strength.

And *that* makes him all the more admirable in my eyes.

The breadth of his shoulders invites protection and inspires reliability—something I've never had in my life.

Maybe that's why I feel so heavily drawn to him. He is everything I've never had but always wanted.

Most of all, even in his worst moments, he's never once tried to lift a hand against me.

He hates me, that much is sure, yet he hasn't tried to hurt me until now.

Maybe my standards for what makes a good man *good* are too low, but my experience has taught me enough about the world to recognize how rare those qualities are.

And that's my dilemma.

I know what he feels for me—hatred, animosity, disdain. He can barely stand the sight of me, and most likely detests himself for desiring me. I know that, and yet all I see when I look at him is safety.

There's a warmth that spreads all over my body in his presence. It's in the way his big body engulfs mine, his velvety voice caressing my senses and lulling me into a sweet sense of comfort and security.

It's completely antithetic to the nature of our relationship. And for someone with my history, it's completely illogical that I should feel that way in the presence of someone, who by all intents and purposes, wishes me harm. Someone who *did* harm me. What he threatened to do in that dark room...he probably has no idea that it's still messing with my head.

And so I feel guilty.

I feel guilty for still feeling this way about him, my insides tingling at his nearness, my heart bursting in my chest of happiness. It's not conscious, though. If anything, it's instinctual —primal.

I've tried to stop myself. Talk myself out of this fanciful notion I have about him. Because the truth is that at night, in the confines of my room, I let myself dream. I let my mind draw up scenarios of what ifs.

What if he didn't hate me? What if he could feel more for me...? What if he could love me?

Dipping myself under the water, I open my eyes, staring at the distorted gilded ceiling.

It would be infinitely easier to nurture my own dislike of him if he didn't act so contrary all the time.

Why did he save me?

For days after the restaurant incident I couldn't remove his actions from my mind. If he wanted me to *pay* for everything I supposedly did to him and Lucero, then why had he not taken the opportunity to get rid of me?

Because he'd had it.

I'd seen the barrel of the gun as it had been aimed in my direction. If Raf hadn't jumped in front of me, knocking me to the ground, that bullet would have made its home in my head.

Yet it hadn't.

Instead, it had grazed his shoulder.

He says he wants to destroy me. But why does he keep on saving me?

He proclaimed himself as my villain, but why did he have to end up as my hero?

Coming out for air, I take a deep breath, water clinging to my lashes as I stare into empty space.

Why did he save me? Why?

Now I'm plagued by maddening thoughts that don't seem to leave me be. The what ifs are getting louder in my head, my hope slowly climbing its way towards the sky.

Maybe if he'd been truly evil to me, I would have hated him.

And *that* is the true danger. For a moment I have to wonder if he isn't engaging in emotional warfare. Giving me an inch before retreating, just to start it all over again. Get me addicted to his brand of cruelty mixed with kindness until he's all I'm craving.

The idea does have merit, especially since so far he's succeeded.

All my life I've been in the shadows—the little kid no one wanted to take care of. Then I grew up and became a bargaining chip to the family, only to be traded to a man who saw me as his personal whipping post.

Until him.

Until he strode in and saw *me*.

I bring my hand to my neck, trailing it down my breasts. Goosebumps are already forming on the bits of skin not touched by the warmth of the water, and the sensation only makes me clench my thighs together, heat traveling to my lower belly at the thought of him.

Beyond my admiration for his character, there's the undeniable attraction that simmers between us—and the fact that I know it's not one sided.

He makes me feel hot and bothered, his proximity awakening things inside of me I'd never thought possible—things I'd never dared to hope for.

I've read books and watched movies, all of them talking about the suffocating need for someone's touch and how the body comes alive under a lover's attentive gaze, becoming wet and needy and thoroughly out of control.

Before, I'd known the theoretical side of lust.

Now…I know it intimately.

My hand trails even lower, my fingers brushing against that place that tingles with awareness.

My eyes snap shut as I feel a spear of pleasure burst through me. It only takes imagining him—those big, capable hands that have the power to bring me to unmeasurable heights but also push me to unimaginable lows.

In my mind, I see the way his muscles cord and ripple, images of his naked torso making me gasp as I circle my clit, my mouth opening on a small o, yet no sound coming out.

But soon, my thoughts turn more outrageous. Suddenly, it's not just images of *him* that spur me further. It's of *us*.

I see him doing things to me—dirty, dirty things I'd never have the courage to utter out loud.

His hand on my ass, painting it red again, but this time, the sharp pain is followed by sweet pleasure and…

I gasp, my eyes flying open as I feel something mount inside of me. But just as I'm about to reach that place, the spell is broken and I scramble back in the tub, my eyes wide at realizing there's another person with me in the room.

"Don't stop on my account," he smirks at me, his arms crossed over his chest as he leans against the tiled bathroom wall.

It's then that I realize I'd never closed the door.

"What…" the words slip from my mouth. "What are you doing here?"

How long have you been sitting there?

"Enjoying the show, it seems." His mouth pulls into an even wider smile as his eyes rove over my naked flesh.

Immediately, I have the urge to cross my arms over my chest in an attempt to cover myself. But that would be exactly what he wants—to see me squirm.,

"I didn't realize you were a pervert, Raf," I arch a brow, settling back in the tub and relaxing.

His eyes dip to the peaks of my breasts currently visible above the water before he catches himself, bringing his gaze back to my face.

"A pervert?" He intones, taking another step inside the bathroom as he looks around disinterestedly. "No, I'm not a pervert." He smiles wolfishly, stopping at the end of my tub.

Flexing his arms, he places his hands on either side of the tub as he leans down, bringing his face closer to me—close enough that I can see every play of emotion on it.

"I guess you forgot about the wedding night?" He inquires mockingly.

I grit my teeth at his question. Especially as I know he's doing it to get a rise out of me.

"Don't tell me you came here to do your husbandly duty," I reply, moving towards him.

Still in the tub, I switch my position so I can meet his gaze head on, my hands gripping the sides of the tub right where his are. Our fingers are close to touching, but not quite.

"What if I did?" he drawls, his breath fanning over my cheek.

His eyes hold a dangerous intensity as he forces himself to look at my face and not lower, and a smile pulls at my lips as I realize that he's having a hard time controlling himself.

Seconds trickle by as we engage in a silent battle of wills, neither willing to look away first.

"Ours isn't a real marriage, Raf," I tell him sternly. "Or is a little pussy all it takes for you to forget your hate for me?" I ask suggestively, the corner of my mouth lifting in a derisive smile.

A twitch in his jaw lets me know my words have hit their mark. Still, he doesn't move.

So with a huff, I turn, making myself comfortable in the tub and promptly ignoring him.

"The door is over there. You can see yourself out," I say dismissively.

He's looming over me, rooted to the same spot. There's an inscrutable expression on his face as he looks at me—a deadly tension accompanied by unwanted lust. Because he probably desires me as much as he hates me.

And to my everlasting displeasure, it's a sentiment I return. I'm even more ashamed to admit that it wouldn't take too much coaxing to go to bed with him. If only he didn't hate me...

Annoyance spears through me at the direction of my thoughts. And seeing that he's not planning to move, I raise an eyebrow at him.

One second I see him turn, presumably to head towards the door. The next, I feel hands wrapped around my neck, the hold tight but not deadly.

His eyes gleam dangerously—dangerously numb. There's something scary about this side of him, and all amusement flies out of the window as a chill goes down my back.

"What..." the words are barely out of my mouth before I feel the water enveloping me. My eyes wide open, I watch in shock as he pushes me down, holding me pinned to the bottom of the tub.

It's pure instinct that reminds me to hold my breath so that the water doesn't force its way inside my nose and mouth.

I simply sit there, watching his blank expression as he holds me down—the intent to drown me clear.

For a moment, panic takes hold of me. Especially as his hands feel like an unbreakable chain around my neck—both literally and figuratively.

The thought of struggling crosses my mind, but I soon realize it would be in vain.

So I let him.

I sit there, calmly staring at him as I wait for my time to run out.

"Fuck," he curses out, taking a step back and bringing his fingers to his temples, massaging them.

The moment I'm able to draw breath again. I cough lightly, wiping at my mouth and nose as I try to regulate my breathing.

"Couldn't kill me, eh?" I taunt.

If I'm completely honest, there was a part of me that knew he would not kill me. That he wouldn't be able to go through with it.

"You..." His voice snaps as he turns around suddenly, one hand around my neck as he raises me up in the air, the force of his hold stunning me still.

My mouth opens in shock.

"One day, Noelle. One day," he mutters, as if trying to convince himself.

"One day what? You're going to *actually* kill me?" I smirk at him. "Well, guess what," I say as I grab on to his sleeve, tugging him closer to me. "I'll be waiting. So do your worst."

He scowls, his face contorted in a mix of annoyance and *want*—to kill me or do something else, unclear.

His hold loosens enough that I fall back on my ass, the water making a splashing sound as droplets end up on the floor and on his shirt. Still, he doesn't release me.

His hand is still on my neck, his eyes glazed as he stares at me. Slowly, he moves it, reaching my jaw. His thumb on my lips, he brushes it lightly over them before parting them.

"One day, Noelle," he repeats, his features stern, his lips unsmiling, "I *will* fuck the brat out of you. I'll make it so that you won't *ever* talk back," he sneers, pushing his thumb into my mouth.

I can only look at him in awe, outrage and lust mixing low in my belly at his words.

"Is that so?" I ask on a breathless tone.

I reach out, grabbing his hand with my own, keeping him locked in place as my tongue peeks out to lick his thumb before sucking it deep into my mouth.

There's a brief flash in his eyes as he zeroes in on my lips, his pupils growing larger under my very gaze. His attention momentarily distracted, it's all it takes for me to bring my teeth down on his thumb.

But he doesn't react. He merely tilts his head in amusement, watching me as one would watch a child throwing a tantrum—indulging me in my little display.

Irritated, I feel the need to get a rise out of him, so I casually inquire. "Who are you trying to fool, Raf? Shall I remind you of your words?" I raise a daring eyebrow. "I am the last woman you'd *ever* fuck," I lean forward, whispering his vehement statement from before.

There's a pause as he doesn't react, his eyes narrowed at me.

"You're playing with fire, Noelle," he grunts low in his throat.

"Me?" I bat my lashes at him. "I'm not the one spying on my unsuspecting spouse while they are bathing. Or wait," I chuckle. "Don't tell me that's one of your kinks. Besides choking, since we've ascertained you have a thing for that," I mock, satisfied when my jibe hits its mark as I watch his hands ball into fists, his lip twitching in annoyance.

But just as it appears, it's gone.

He leans back, wholly relaxed, as he gives me a bored look.

"Maybe it is," he shrugs. "Can you blame me for wanting to sample the goods? After all, I did pay a small fortune for you."

"You..." I take a deep breath, knowing his game is to rile me up. Instead, I try to calm myself down as I continue my brave act. "What do you say then? Do I pass?" I ask in a saccharine tone, peering at him from beneath my lashes.

"Hmm," he takes a step back. "Undecided. I think I need to see more," he drawls, this time letting his eyes greedily roam over my flesh.

In a gesture of unprecedented courage, I simply rise from the bath. The water clings to my skin as I get up, droplets gliding over the planes of my body and emphasizing the curve of my breasts, my waist, and lower.

Placing my feet on the floor, I stand up to my full height, my entire body naked and bare for his assessing gaze.

His eyes widen briefly, before his features darken as he takes me in.

"What about now?" I take a step towards him. "Do you regret your purchase yet?" I ask sarcastically.

Because I know exactly what he's seeing—and it's not pretty.

Scars run down the front and back of my body, concentrated heavily around my stomach and lower back area.

He gulps down as he looks at me, his expression indecipherable.

My courage, though, extends only for so long, so I turn on my heel, intent on putting my robe on and getting the hell out of here.

The heat of his presence and the deep burn of my mortification are enough to send me flying out of the bathroom. But I can't do that. I can't show him how affected I am by his nearness, or how self-conscious I feel about my appearance.

So I straighten my back and put on a confident look as I move to exit the room.

I don't get to take one step though, as he wraps his fingers around my elbow, pulling me backwards and making me stumble as I crash into his hard chest.

"What's this?" he asks in a harsh voice, his eyes narrowed at me, his muscles spasming with unreleased tension.

"What's what?" I feign ignorance, though I know exactly what he's referring to.

"This," he says just as his other hand makes contact with my skin, his fingers brushing against the area right under my rib cage and going lower, leaving in their wake a scorching trail of fire.

My breath hitches at the first contact, but I mask my reaction as I try to put on a strong front. Especially as he spreads his palm over my stomach—over that place that's been hideously scarred.

"Nothing," I shrug.

"Noelle," his voice vibrates in the air, the threat unmistakable.

"It's nothing," I reiterate confidently. "Because it can't be anything if I've never been a victim, right?" I throw his words in his face, satisfaction blooming inside of me when he visibly flinches.

"Tell me," he barks the order as if I were one of his minions, ready to comply with his every command.

"No," I simply reply, looking him in the eye. "You don't get to make demands of me. Not with this. And certainly not *now*, after you've repeatedly thrown my past in my face."

"These are cigarette burns, Noelle. Who did this to you?" His tone turns softer, just as his features start to lose some of the previous tension.

"It doesn't matter now, does it?" I whisper, blinking back tears. "You can still get an annulment, you know. It's not too late," I give him a sad smile.

"Who did this to you?" He grits out, his hold tightening over my arm.

A low chuckle erupts from my throat.

"Are you asking because you don't know?" I raise my eyes to his, letting him see the pain and humiliation that resides there. But most of all, I want him to see the hopelessness—of the past, present, and future.

He blinks, as if he wasn't expecting such honesty in my expression.

"Sergio," he states, the name hitting me in the chest like a bullet. Yet, now the pain is just a dull ache—numbed by the passage of time and the knowledge that he can't harm me from the grave.

"Congratulations," I retort mockingly. "Do you want a prize for your correct guess?"

"Why? Why would he do something like this to you? You were his wife."

There's a certain confidence in his voice, as if he's told himself this version of events so many times that he is infinitely sure of it.

"Wife," I give a dry laugh. "Sure. I was his wife. But that didn't get me any special treatment. In fact..." I trail off as I wrench myself from his grasp, turning around so my back is fully visible to him. "This is the *only* special treatment I got," I say as I present him with the worst of my scars.

On my lower back, lines upon lines of red bumps cover my skin —all caused by belts, canes and anything *he* would find that would inflict most damage.

"What... how..." the words are barely above a whisper, but I hear them, nonetheless.

"I feel sorry for you, Raf," I tell him with a sigh, turning to see his ashen face. He's gazing at me as if he's never seen me before, and I don't know why that sight has the ability to break my heart. "You have such a warped version of the truth, that you simply can't see beyond your resentment and your hate." I pause, and I note a flicker of emotion in his eyes. "I admit there were times when I behaved like the worst version of myself at the *hacienda*. But none were of my own volition," I tell him, taking his hand and bringing it to my thigh.

"Do you feel this?" I ask, brushing his fingers against a faded mark. He gives a brisk nod.

"One time, I said something wrong in public. We were at a dinner party, and I made a mistake," I take a deep breath as the memories slowly trickle in, the pain almost fresh in my mind. "He stabbed me under the table with a fork, and he told me that if I dared make a sound, he would pass me around to his ranch hands.

I felt the pain to my soul, but I didn't make a sound. The blood was flowing out of me, but my smile didn't falter."

His brows furrow, and there's a hint of emotion on his face as he gazes at me. Yet I don't want his pity. That is the *last* thing I'd ever want.

"So you see, the truth isn't yours, or mine, Raf. It's somewhere in the middle. You have your trauma and I have mine. But just because you have limited knowledge of mine doesn't mean you can deny it exists."

"Noelle..." he starts, but I place a finger on his lips, shushing him.

"My entire family thinks I'm crazy, and that I'm exaggerating for attention," I laugh sardonically. "Everyone thinks I'm crazy, so frankly," I shake my head at him. "I don't care what you think of me anymore. I just ask that you leave me alone," my voice breaks as I utter a last "please."

Before he can reply, before he can say something and irrevocably break my heart, I dash out of the room. I don't even stop to don my robe as I run out of the master suite and lock myself inside an empty room.

My breath ragged, my heart in my throat, I can't help it when sobs overtake me—the courage from before all but gone.

I start trembling uncontrollably, coldness seeping in my pores and seemingly never leaving my body.

And as I huddle between clean sheets, searching for some semblance of warmth, my mind can only wander back to him.

Does he believe me? Does he hate the look of me?

A myriad of questions go through my head, one worse than the other in their outcome.

But worst of all is that... I care. I care about his opinion, just as I care about him knowing the truth.

Out of everyone in my life I wish at least *he* didn't think me mad.

If only...

I bring my knees to my chest as I feel a burst of pain erupt in my lower abdomen, the ferocity of it making me moan in response.

So it begins…

I thought I'd have some reprieve from it, but I guess when it wants to come, it comes.

Huddled into a ball, I hum a melody as I lull myself to sleep, trying to ignore the growing pain inside of me.

Instead, I focus on my little dream world—that marvelous world of what ifs.

Because there…the opportunities are endless.

Chapter Twenty-Nine

Noelle

There's heat. Scorching, blistering heat. A sheen of sweat envelops my entire body and I feel each and every droplet as it makes its way down my skin.

My breathing feels heavy, my throat numb with pain as everything inside of me boils to an infernal crescendo.

"Noelle!" I think I hear my name in the distance, but I don't feel capable of moving.

In fact, I don't feel capable of anything *but* lying down, seeking some solace from the pain that threatens to overtake me.

"Noelle, open the door!"

More noise. There's so much noise. Loud knocks, and deafening bangs. They all seek to make me even more uncomfortable as a sharp pain erupts in my head.

"No," a moan is wrenched from my lips as I feel foreign hands touching my body.

"Noelle, can you hear me?"

It's that voice. The same voice as before.

Such a pretty voice…unlike mine.

"Shit, you're burning up," the owner of the voice curses, and then his hands are once more on my skin.

Somehow, his cool touch makes it better—it makes everything better.

He brushes the back of his hand across my forehead, swiping my damp hair aside as he tries to assess me.

My strength is almost nonexistent as I push myself to open my eyes, finding unusually blue ones gazing back at me.

"Noelle," my name on his lips feels like a decadent treat, and I can't help the whimper that escapes me as I burrow closer into his arms, feeling his body snug against mine.

"Please," my voice is ragged as I utter the word, though what I'm asking him, I don't know.

"What's wrong with you?" He demands sharply, before catching himself and softening his tone as he gently inquires where I'm hurting.

I shake my head at him, not quite understanding his meaning.

My entire brain is foggy, and it is with great effort that I remember who he is.

Raf—my husband.

"Raf," I call out his name at the height of my delirium.

"I'm here," he coos, bringing me closer to his chest.

"Raf, my Raf, forgive me please," I continue to utter nonsense after nonsense, feeling myself slip.

My hold on reality is feeble at best, and as I feel him lift me in his arms, and then taking me out of the house and to the car, I realize how hard it is to hold on.

"Raf..."

My eyes snap closed.

One.

Two.

Three.

The world shifts.

Chapter Thirty

Rafaelo

"Is there not one goddamn doctor who can tell me what's going on?" I pace around, my anger getting the best of me.

A few nurses scurry out of my way, while another tells me to wait patiently.

"We've been here for an hour already. What if she's dying? What if there's something wrong with her and she's dying?" I demand, my voice harsh.

She just purses her lips at me, shaking her head and moving out of my warpath.

I know I'm not making any sense. But since they admitted her to the emergency room, they only gave her something for the pain. They didn't fucking try to find the cause.

Something could be seriously wrong with her. She could be having an internal hemorrhage and no one would be wiser—until it's too late.

"Fuck," I curse out loud, bringing my hands to my face and rubbing at my eyes.

When I'd noted her absence at breakfast, I thought she was doing it to spite me. Especially after our conversation last night when I'd had the cards turned on me—literally.

I don't think I've felt greater shame than when I'd looked at her naked body, and the many marks that mar it. I was ashamed because the truth was staring me right in the face. And I was ashamed for desiring her anyway.

I'd seen hints of her naked flesh before, but that was the first time I had an unobstructed view of *everything*—of every blemish and every scar. All staring me in the face and making me feel like the worst type of bounder.

I've always prided myself on being a fair man. But with her? I've been anything *but* fair. From the beginning I let my distorted yet limited view of her shape my entire perception of her.

But that's not all, is it?

As much as it pains me to admit, it hadn't only been my preconceived notions of her that had shaped my behavior towards her. It had also been the way I reacted to her—the primal feelings she awoke in me, unlike anything I'd ever felt before.

Unlike her…

Lucero's memory and her stories had spurred me forward, the very idea of being attracted to her tormentor screwing with my head and making me more likely to see her in a negative light. Admitting she made me *feel* would have been akin to betraying Lucero—a betrayal to everything I'd promised and held dear.

Subconsciously, I knew how forbidden she was to me. That acting soft towards her would mean dishonoring both Lucero and myself—because I'd be disrespecting *her* memory and the hardships I went through to get to where I am.

Yet how am I to reconcile everything I thought I knew of her with the marks on her flesh?

Because those hadn't been simple scars. No, they had been deliberate wounds to hurt and to humiliate. Her entire stomach had been covered in scars—scratches, cuts, and cigarette burns—all forming a mosaic that spoke of her history.

A history I'd mocked.

The differently formed scars spoke of continued abuse—of healed wounds that were open again and again.

I'd been so struck by the sight of her that I'd felt my entire reality shift.

What could be worse than being so convinced about one thing, shaping your entire reality around it, only to find out it was an illusion?

I let my biases shape my opinion of her and I refused to see what was right in front of me.

She *was* a victim.

And it had only taken for her to turn around and show me her lower back for me to feel even sicker to my stomach. Those marks hadn't been from the fire. No, I'd seen those before, the badly healed pink skin I'd made fun of.

My lip twitches in disgust as I recall that particular moment, how I'd ridiculed her and called her scars ugly when they were anything but—they are her marks of courage.

The wounds on her lower back, though...

Those had been horrible and gnarly, and I can only imagine the pain she must have gone through to get them—repeated, agonizing pain.

A pained sigh escapes me as I realize the extent of the abuse—of the invisible abuse. Because had anyone known?

To everyone's knowledge, she was the untouchable mistress, the spoiled, apple of Sergio's eye doña. Even daring to look her in the eye could warrant death.

She was special. Everyone knew that.

But it wasn't quite like that, was it?

In public, she'd looked like a mighty *doña*. In private, however...

My hands ball into fists at the thought, and I can't help but be mad at myself for not looking closer into her claims—for branding her a liar before I knew the full story.

I'd had the entire night to ponder over that realization, and I'd begun to feel increasingly like a bastard as it dawned on me I was no better than anyone else in her life.

Under a magnifying glass, suddenly her behavior started to make sense.

Everything started to make sense.

I'd just been too fucking blind to consider the possibility that she might be telling the truth. So hell bent I'd been on my so-called revenge, that I'd ignored *every* little sign.

I'm a fucking idiot.

I'd stayed up until dawn going over every single interaction and cataloging her responses, coming up with a rather dire conclusion.

I was wrong. I've been wrong all along.

And like every other fucking person in her life, I continued to abuse her, mocking her claims and making a liar out of her when she was anything but.

What had she said? That I had no right to deny her trauma?

She was fucking right.

How could I have been so obtuse when I experienced similar things on my own skin? When I still bear both the physical and mental wounds from my time with Armand though I always do my best to bury them beneath the surface? How the hell could I have been so judgmental as to discount her trauma just because of my narrow view of it?

With a new clarity, I can finally question everything, including the box of matches I'd found in her hand. How could someone as small as her—as dainty as her—set fire to the entire hacienda with just a few matches? The smell of gasoline had been strong that night and coming from all directions. Anyone could have set that fire. But not anyone could have doused the entire place in gasoline.

She's just a collateral victim.

For the first time, I have to admit that my ego got the best of me. It had been infinitely easier to vilify her in my mind, because then, I didn't have to look deeper into the things she made me feel.

And *that* is on me.

I've been so disgusted with myself for desiring her that I preferred to believe the worst of her in order to feel better about myself.

To justify this intense yearning I feel for her.

And for that alone, I feel like the worst fucking scum.

When the morning had come, I'd outlined a plan on how to approach her and mend the fences—or at least some.

But as the hours had trickled by with no sign of her, I'd gotten worried.

Worried enough that I'd broken down the door to her room.

And when I'd seen her...

She'd looked so small and helpless huddled in her sheets, her face contorted in pain as she released soft whimpers. Her skin had been so hot to the touch, I'd immediately gotten concerned. Even more so when I'd realized she was unresponsive.

Mad with worry, I'd acted on the spur of the moment. I'd swooped her into my arms, and I'd taken the car to the nearest hospital.

Not that they've helped much.

Certainly, they administered her an IV to help with the pain and gave her something to bring down her fever. But other than that? They can't even fucking tell me what's wrong with her.

"Sir, please calm down," a nurse tries to pacify me, but I'm already out of control.

"Not until someone can tell me what the hell is wrong with her," I point towards her salon, aggression rolling off me at the thought that something could happen to her.

"She's in good hands. Please..."

I don't get to tell her off again as a doctor finally decides to come to my side.

"I'm sorry for the delay, but we had to pull her medical records before we did anything," he explains, giving me a stiff smile as he goes over the protocol.

"Fine. Now can you look at her?" I bring down my voice a notch, realizing I'm acting out and taking out my frustration on people who have no fault in this.

"That's what I wanted to talk to you first," he starts, looking a little apprehensive.

"What is it?" I bark out.

"Since she was admitted she's been complaining about lower stomach pain. We want to do an ultrasound to check the state of her uterus..." the words drown out as I frown at the doctor.

"Her uterus?" I repeat, dumbfounded.

"In someone with her history it's not unlikely to see extensive scarring. And that can lead to a whole slew of issues."

"Wait," I put my hand up. "Someone with her history?" I ask, confused.

The doctor's brows furrow, and for a moment he seems reluctant to go on. But as I reassure him I am Noelle's husband *and* her legal guardian, he finally deigns to tell me.

"I'm sorry. I was under the impression you knew," he mutters. "A few years back she was brought in with a uterine infection caused by a retained placenta. She had to be operated on as soon as possible to remove the placenta, but the infection resulted in a lot of internal scarring and likely caused the onset of endometriosis," he continues to talk, but my focus is already shaken.

"Retained placenta?" I repeat bleakly, my mind going a thousand places at once. "You mean she was pregnant?"

He gives me a grim look.

"I wasn't her attending physician, so I can only tell you what's in her medical file. She was brought with severe burns and bruises and she was almost septic. It was a miracle she survived considering the extent of her injuries. If I were to make an educated guess..." he trails off, looking in the direction of her salon.

"I'd say she gave birth without any medical assistance. Her file indicated she exhibited untreated second degree vaginal tearing, as well as the retained placenta. To be perfectly honest, I don't know how she survived."

TO BE CONTINUED